BEYO

Theresa hadn't come _____ _____ _____ __ _____
to abandon her search ___ _____ ___ _____ ____ ___
hadn't travelled on her own across an ocean to face
defeat at this first obstacle. She'd never pounded on a
desk before or called attention to herself, but she was
doing it now. She hit the desk again.

'I thought newspapers wanted stories about people.
I'm offering you one.' She found herself imitating the
way the editor spoke. 'Girl Comes from England to
Look for Long-lost Father. Doesn't that make you want
to know more? Why do you just sit there, looking
blank?' She raised her voice. 'Why?'

Edouard's reaction surprised her. She had almost
expected him to shout back, and had braced herself for
it. Instead, he smiled. 'There's no question that the
readers of the _Clarion_ will be interested. But I wonder if
you know what you're doing, Theresa Russell? I warn
you, once started, I won't let go. I'm a newspaper man,
and I'm building a newspaper empire.'

Barbara Cooper was born in Montreal, Canada, the second of five children. She was educated there and earned an Arts Degree from the University of Montreal. She met her first husband working at the Canadian Atomic Energy Project at Chalk River. They made their home in Oxfordshire and later in Lancashire. When he died she turned her hand to part time work to have time to bring up her three children. Now married again, she writes romantic fiction.

BEYOND PARADISE

BY

BARBARA COOPER

WORLDWIDE ROMANCE

London ● Sydney ● Toronto

*First published in Great Britain in 1986
by Worldwide Romance,
15–16 Brook's Mews, London W1A 1DR*

*This Paperback edition published in 1986
by Worldwide Romance*

*Australian copyright 1986
Philippine copyright 1986*

© Barbara Cooper 1986

ISBN 0 373 50298 2

Set in 10 on 10½pt Linotron Times
09–0386–121,900

*Photoset by Rowland Phototypesetting Limited
Bury St Edmunds, Suffolk
Printed and bound in Great Britain by
Cox & Wyman Ltd, Reading*

CHAPTER ONE

'I'D LIKE to speak to the editor.' Theresa's voice sounded nervous in her own ears as she looked at the young man sitting on the desk facing her and the door. She was just a little breathless from climbing all those stairs.

'I am the editor.'

Theresa's eyes were fastened on him. He must be very tall when he stood up—but he didn't stand up, just remained there, his long legs dangling. He was in his shirtsleeves and examining a long sheet of paper. He ran one hand through his dark brown hair so that it stood on end like a boy's, and he smiled at her.

So infectious was that smile that Theresa smiled back without meaning to.

'Edouard Hippolyte Moreau, at your service.' He touched his hand to his forehead in a mock salute.

'Is that really your name?' The question slipped past the girl's lips without conscious volition, and she put her hand to her mouth in surprise.

'Stopped you in your tracks, has it? Not many Hippolytes around where you come from?' His eyes were very blue, and laughing at her.

'None,' Theresa admitted in some confusion. She adjusted her large black hat, knowing it went well with her outfit. She smoothed her black skirt with its white broderie trim and wondered why he was still looking at her so strangely. It must be her skirt . . . It was the new shorter mid-calf length. She had felt it was exactly right for June 1922 and bearding an editor in his lair. Now she wasn't so sure. The few women she had seen in the streets of Creswal, Ontario, this morning had been wearing ankle-length skirts.

She touched the black and white scarf at her throat and wished this Edouard Hippolyte Moreau, editor of the *Clarion*, would remove his eyes from her legs.

He did, asking lazily, 'Is that the latest thing in England—sandal shoes with high heels and short skirts?'

Her cheeks were colouring under that interested gaze. 'Yes . . . Yes, it is. How did you know I was from England?' she added, a little resentfully.

'Your voice gives you away. You don't sound Canadian, and you certainly don't look it. Take that scarf, for instance . . .'

The girl's hand went to her scarf again. It was a present from the twins, and she wasn't going to let him say anything about it.

'Who but an English girl would wear a scarf at ten o'clock in the morning with the temperature already in the eighties?'

Theresa opened her mouth to protest, but he went on, 'What's your name?'

'Theresa.'

'Thank heaven for a mother with no pretensions to grandeur. Around here they call their daughters by the most romantic-sounding names they can find—Desirée, Magdalena, Henrietta. Even Rosie over there'—he pointed to the only other desk at the rear of the room, and Theresa realised for the first time that there was someone else here—'even Rosie was christened Rosalinda. I ask you: does it suit her?'

Theresa looked from the girl to Edouard. 'I—I don't know.' She felt sorry for the other occupant.

But Rosie just shrugged and gave a cheerful smile. 'Have a heart, Eddie! She's a stranger.' She didn't get up.

Edouard Hippolyte Moreau scribbled something on the paper he held. 'Have I been hard on her, Rosie?' He didn't wait for an answer, but shot another question at Theresa instead. 'What are you doing here, then? What's your name?'

Theresa hesitated. Which name to give him?

'Don't you know who you are?'

'I'm called Theresa Mellor,' she faltered. 'But it should be Theresa Russell. That's what I've come to see you about.'

'Changing your name?' She had his attention for a moment.

'No,' she replied. 'Finding my father.'

Edouard Moreau looked down at her legs. 'You're a big girl to need a father.'

She wished he wouldn't do that. Unnerved, she began to flick the two ends of her scarf. She looked at the girl at the other desk, who was watching them, a languid hand patting the shining black hair which she wore in a neat braid, like a crown, on the top of her head.

To her, Theresa said, 'This was the last place my father lived.' She amended that by adding, 'That I know of.'

'Perhaps you should hire an agent, or go to the police,' suggested Rosie.

'Disappeared, has he?' Edouard's tone had no trace of sympathy. He leaned back. 'This country spawns men like that.'

'What's that supposed to mean?' Theresa looked from one to the other.

It was Edouard who replied, 'You couldn't know, being from England.' He frowned at her, as though this was somehow a fault. 'Heaven deliver me from your kind. I'll tell you what we have here in the northern part of Ontario—in the whole north of Canada—a shifting population.' He waved a finger at her. 'This is an area for transients. In a simple sentence: Men don't stay in one place. They come and go when opportunity beckons. Creswal's merely a town that some of us live in. It's fairly stable for us, but the area around is full of floaters. Don't ask me what they're looking for. I don't know. My guess is they probably don't know either. A taste of the wild, the freedom of the open spaces, the opportunity to hunt and fish'—He paused for breath—'whatever they dream about. Creswal is a timber town where the logs are collected after their rush down the river from the log camps. Was your father a logger?'

'No.' Theresa had no chance to say more.

'Maybe you don't know it,' Edouard went inexorably on, 'but this country developed along its rivers. They were and still are the highways here. Mining equipment goes up river, and so do disappearing dads. Think of it this way: Nothing ties a man down more than a family —God help him! And if God won't, the river will.'

Theresa felt herself drowning in his rhetoric. She opened her mouth tentatively, and gave her scarf another twitch.

Edouard wasn't finished. 'Are you going to take off that scarf which seems in danger of strangling you, and that enormous hat? I can't talk to a woman whose face I can't see.'

'Can't you? It didn't seem to stop you,' she observed coldly.

'Now, now,' he admonished. 'I was just putting you at your ease.'

Rosie laughed. Theresa gave an unwilling smile.

Edouard continued, 'Have you lost him permanently, or just misplaced him?'

For the first time he sounded interested, and in spite of her reservations, Theresa took a step forward and removed her hat as he had requested. She laid it on the desk, well away from the editor, and automatically tried to fluff up her brown hair where the hat had flattened it. Her shaking fingers caught at one of the pins holding her long thick mane in position and curls tumbled to her shoulder, a few escaping completely at forehead and cheeks. Flushed, and feeling decidedly foolish, she tried to rearrange it.

'Leave it alone,' suggested the smiling editor. 'It suits you better that way. You look younger; so young that I must ask you what you are doing here on your own? Come, sit down, and tell me where you lost this errant father.' He pushed a chair forward with one foot.

Theresa sat down to find herself looking at this upsetting man's legs, as the chair was very low. She raised her gaze to his face. He wasn't handsome. His features were too sharp for that, but the corners of his mouth turned up, and his thick dark eyebrows over those very blue eyes added a look of humour and inquisitiveness to his face, which gave it interest and presence. He waited for her to speak from his elevated position on the desk.

'My father went to Peru after I was born,' Theresa began. 'I haven't seen him since I was two. I don't really remember him at all.'

'You've waited a long time to chase him.' Edouard threw the copy paper carelessly on to the desk beside him and folded his long legs so that they brushed against the girl. 'Was your mother not interested in finding him?'

'She thought he was dead,' she tried to explain. 'He was an engineer, and he went to South America to work. The company he went to wrote to her and said he had been killed in a mining disaster with twelve others. They stopped sending her his allowance.'

'Pretty conclusive,' Edouard observed with a shrug. 'Married again, did she?' His expression was bland, as though he'd heard stories like this before.

'Yes,' Theresa agreed, 'after the Coroner's Court had declared he must be presumed dead. There wasn't a certificate.' She didn't add that this was all information which she had only found out recently, from her stepfather's last letter to her.

'Um-hum.' Edouard had lost interest. 'If he's gone to his Maker, he's gone. I can't call him back.'

Theresa felt a childish impulse to stick out her tongue at him. Why did he automatically suppose she was asking the impossible? 'Your paper ran an article on him six years ago, and he was alive then.'

The editor laughed, those expressive eyebrows of his rising. 'Before my time. Do you have anything to back that up?' He held out his hand in a gesture that the girl thought somehow foreign. 'I was playing soldiers then in the war, and you—I suppose—you were still playing with toys.'

'I was not.' Theresa reached into the black and white cloth bag which she had been clutching in her lap and pulled out a faded newspaper clipping. She thrust it at him and their hands met as he leaned forward to take it from her. A tremor of excitement shook her—not because of touching him, of course, she told herself.

If Edouard had felt any like sensation, it did not show. He studied the cutting, reading aloud: 'Charles Russell, Engineer, takes up new appointment at big dam project.'

'I have my parents' marriage certificate and my birth certificate.' Theresa produced these next, making no mention of the fact that her stepfather had provided those with his letter.

Edouard gave them a cursory glance, then went back to the picture that had been featured above the article. 'You're sure this is your father?'

'Oh yes,' the girl assured him. 'Everything fits—date of birth and occupation. Besides, my stepfather gave it to me, although I didn't know he was my stepfather. It seems strange to think of him as that.'

Edouard made no comment on this revelation, perhaps because Rosie abandoned her desk and came forward to take the documents from Edouard.

'Good-looking chap, your father!' she exclaimed, smiling.

Theresa noted that she was wearing a mustard-coloured crêpe-de-Chine dress whose bodice was bloused loosely over a low waistline and whose skirt reached almost to the ankles. She might have reflected that it seemed a little dressy for the office, but she was too interested in its length to give that a passing thought. The Canadians hadn't adopted the modern shorter skirt, then, she decided; Rosie was an attractive girl who would want to wear the latest fashion. She looked at her closely. On a less vivid person, the mustard shade would have been deadening. It suited Rosie, and the black halo of her braided hair gave her a sleek dignity, and a poise which she herself had not achieved in this encounter with the editor. She supposed that Rosie must work here.

Edouard picked up the sheet he had been studying when Theresa had entered, and rose from the desk. 'Phone the dam,' he suggested.

Theresa wasn't sure whether this directive was meant for her or for Rosie. 'I wrote to them.' She found herself speaking to his back, as he went to the far desk to deposit his paper there. 'They don't know where he is. He left five years ago, and they don't have a forwarding address.'

Edouard turned round at that. 'So much the better, I would have thought.' He came towards her and put his hand on the back of her chair. 'Leave well enough alone. How do your mother and stepfather feel about you raking up the past?'

'They're both dead.' Theresa got to her feet, biting her lip, but facing him. 'My stepfather left me some money in his Will to come to Canada and search for my real father. He gave me those things.' She waved her hand at the documents Rosie held.

'Guilty conscience?' asked Edouard softly, standing very close to her. 'I suppose there are other children from your mother's second marriage?'

Theresa faced him, green eyes blazing, her temper beginning to rise. 'I don't know why you're saying and thinking ill of him. My stepfather was a good man. He loved me like his own. And yes, I have twin half-sisters, Melody and Felicity. They're eighteen. Poppa left them the house, but they don't need it. They both have husbands.' Her hand flew to her mouth. That sounded as though she resented Poppa's action. She didn't know why she had added that about the house; it was none of this man's business.

It had caught Edouard's attention. 'You're the oldest sister, so you might have supposed it was yours. What are you—twenty . . .?'

'Twenty-two, nearly twenty-three.' Theresa's lips were stiff.

'And no husband in sight,' he nodded. 'You might have expected to have the house.'

She felt as though she had betrayed her stepfather; she didn't want to discuss it. 'No husband,' she agreed. 'When my mother died some years ago, I stayed at home to look after the girls.' She surely didn't have to explain how it was, but there was about this man a quality that invited confidences.

'Of course,' Edouard patted her arm and she wanted to step back—or did she? 'What else would you have done? But now . . .' He left the words hanging in the air so that she thought it was a question, until he continued, 'He left you the money to leave the country, and to cause no embarrassment to his true daughters. I suppose they know nothing of the reasons?'

'No, they don't. I haven't told them.' Theresa's cheeks were flushed, but she was in control of herself —almost. 'I could have told them. They offered to let me stay on in the house, but I wouldn't. I said Poppa had always known that I wanted to travel, and he had left me money to do so.'

'How much?' Edouard shot at her. 'How much money?'

'Two hundred pounds.' Theresa's tongue was more willing than her mind to divulge this information.

'That won't last you long,' was the crisp comment. 'What then?'

'Why, I shall get a job,' she declared to those blue eyes meeting hers so searchingly. 'Women do, these days.'

'Of course they do!' Rosie gave Theresa back her papers. 'I work for you, Eddie.'

'Yes, and it's time you were at that wedding you're reporting on this morning. They'll all want to know about the bride's finery.' Edouard's glance swung from Rosie to Theresa's legs and feet. 'They won't be wearing the latest style from England. I suppose it's meant to drive the men wild. It won't catch on here.' He went towards his desk.

'Don't mind him,' Rosie advised, galvanised into

action. 'That only means he likes it.' She snatched up a pad and pencil from the editor's desk and jammed her own hat on her head as she raced for the door, slamming it behind her.

'I'm sorry I can't be more use to you.' Edouard turned round the chair Theresa had used and pulled it to the side. Then he sat down at his desk.

Theresa was dismissed, and knew it—just like a child, she fumed, and refused to allow herself to be sent away without a struggle. She wanted this man's help, and meant to have it. She took the few steps to face him. She'd make him think of something else besides her legs.

When she struck her hand against the flat surface of the desk, the sound was louder than she had expected. It surprised her, but she hadn't come all the way from Liverpool to this Canadian backwoods town to abandon her search before it had properly begun. She hadn't travelled on her own across an ocean to face defeat at this first obstacle. She'd never pounded on a desk before or called attention to herself, but she was doing it now. She hit the desk again.

'I thought newspapers wanted stories about people. I'm offering you one.' She found herself imitating the way the editor spoke. 'Girl Comes from England to Look for Long-lost Father. Doesn't that make you want to know more? Why do you just sit there, looking blank?' She raised her voice. 'Why?'

His reaction surprised her. She had almost expected him to shout back, and had braced herself for it. Instead, he smiled. 'Suppose he's one of my big advertisers, and a long-lost daughter would be a definite embarrassment to him? Suppose he married again, after he was declared dead? How's he going to feel about the human interest story—and my paper?' His eyes were sharp.

'Why should he be embarrassed?' Theresa felt cross and upset. 'He was married to my mother. She's been dead for some time—the newspaper doesn't need to say how long. I'm not asking him for anything. I just want to see him and talk to him, to find out what kind of a man he is. Poppa said it was my right and his that we should know each other.' Her eyes had filled with tears, and she turned away so that Edouard should not see them.

The editor sighed. 'I'll tell you what I'll do. I'll give them a call out at the dam. Stanislaus Margold is an old hand there. You might get something out of his memory which isn't in the records. He's manager now, and he's been there since it all began.' He rose to his feet.

'Thank you.' Theresa put out her hand in a spontaneous gesture of gratitude across the desk, and Edouard took it in his. He hadn't really promised her anything except an introduction to someone she had already contacted, but she began to feel confident, sure even of his involvement. He was not a man to commit himself lightly, or to withdraw, once committed.

He held her hand for a long moment, and Theresa found herself enjoying the sensation of mattering to him, however fleetingly. Since Poppa's death a few short months ago, she hadn't mattered to any man. She caught her breath, as memory swept over her. Perhaps with her real father she would know again this feeling of belonging, of kinship.

Edouard freed her hand and reached up to the wall phone beside his desk, cranking it into action. Theresa wondered why it was attached to the wall instead of sitting on the desk where it would be more convenient, but dismissed the thought as unimportant as he got through to Stanislaus Margold.

She listened to the conversation. The man on the other end of the phone seemed to be protesting, but Edouard smoothed him down with explanations and a little flattery about the man with the longest memory in Creswal. At one point, something that Mr Margold said appeared to surprise the editor, for he drawled, 'You don't say! Fancy that! You must tell her yourself. I knew you'd come up with something.' When he put the receiver back on the hook, he turned to her and said, 'That's all set, and I'll take you now. It's on my way. I'm going to see the army. They have a new tank they're testing near there. I'll leave you with Stan, and pick you up on my way back.'

Theresa longed to ask him what Stanislaus Margold had said, but she suspected he wouldn't divulge it. 'That's putting you to a lot of trouble,' she protested. 'Couldn't I get a taxi or a bus?'

He laughed. 'This isn't an English city, you know! Buses, if they ran at all, would run once a week—or once a month. You'll have to make do with me, unless you're afraid?'

'Afraid?' Theresa considered the idea. 'Why should I be? Do you mean afraid of what people would think? I don't know the people, and I've come this far on my own. I'll just have to brave their opinion.'

Edouard's eyes were dancing. 'I see you're a properly brought up young lady, but that wasn't quite what I meant.'

'You mean going alone with you—Should I be afraid of you?' She frowned at him. 'You must be respectable; you're the editor of the newspaper. But, perhaps, you have a wife. Would she be upset? Your wife, I mean.' Theresa hesitated. Why didn't she want to hear of any such woman?

'I have no wife or family,' he replied curtly. 'I'm even more alone than you. You have sisters.'

There was such a bleak look to his face that she wanted to change the subject. 'I don't think I'm afraid of you,' she said slowly. 'I don't know much about men and how they act, but I don't think you mean me any harm.'

'Quite right. I don't. The young and innocent are perfectly safe with Edouard Moreau, but don't be so trusting with all men.'

He took her arm, and Theresa wasn't altogether flattered by the reference to the young and innocent. He led her down the stairs and then outside, to a car. 'I suppose you're used to motoring?' he commented, as he helped her up to the seat. 'But you may not have driven in one of these. It's Henry Ford's latest. He's the man who says you can have any colour you want so long as it's black.'

Theresa wasn't sure if this was a joke, but she smiled politely. The car was black. It had a canvas roof like a canopy so that it was open to the air. She didn't like to tell Edouard that this was the first time she had ever been in an automobile. Of course she'd seen them before, and in different colours. She sank into the leather seat, or as far into it as she could, for it was rather hard and unyielding. What should she do next? She had rammed her hat upon her head, stuffing the curls into it and hoping it would hold them. Now she tied her scarf round it. That was what she had seen other women do when they were in motor cars.

Edouard didn't seem to expect any more, for he cranked up the engine and clambered into the driver's seat, and with a great clatter and shaking they were off.

'Newspaper men need to get about quickly. The editor before me had a horse and buggy, and nothing wrong with that, as he travelled the whole area. I'm a firm believer in the automobile and its future. One of these days, everybody will use them. Families will own them.'

Though it was noisy enough to limit conversation to a minimum in Theresa's opinion, Edouard directed her attention to passing buildings and points of interest as if it didn't matter in the least if the passers-by heard him. 'Timber mill over there on the left, quarry on the right, railway station down the road,' he announced cheerfully, taking his hand from the wheel.

Theresa forbore to tell him that she had come in on the train the day before. It had been a hot, dirty journey, with smoke and steam staining her travelling frock, and there had been a cinder in her eye which the stationmaster had helped her to remove. Once out of the town, the road surface was only well packed dirt, and she was bumped up and down on the seat, sometimes thrown towards the door, sometimes towards Edouard.

'Exhilarating, isn't it?' He was smiling, clearly

enjoying himself. 'I suppose you've done a lot of motoring? It won't have been on roads like this.' He answered his own question.

Theresa didn't want to tell him she hadn't done any, whatever the state of the road. Poppa hadn't believed in these new-fangled machines. He'd always kept a carriage and horses, but the twins talked of nothing else. She was sure that when the family home was sold and the money divided, both of the twins' husbands would have cars . . . A longing for Melody and Felicity swept over her, a longing for their company and for the ordered way of life she had left at home in England. It was a life she suddenly knew she could never return to or expect to share with them.

She clung to her hat and scarf and tried to think about the scene about her. Trees were everywhere, with the odd glimpse of a river and houses tucked away from the road. To her eyes, it wound before her and behind and around in ceaseless monotony, mile after mile of forest, with very little to break its endless green sameness.

'Beautiful, isn't it?' shouted Edouard as they climbed a winding hill, the car even noisier as it wheezed its protest. Suddenly he pulled in to the side, and stopped with a sharp bounce on the top of the rise. 'It's getting hot.'

Theresa took a deep breath, and her hand automatically went to her hat.

So did Edouard's. He snatched her scarf from it, and pulled off the hat. 'There, that's better,' he exclaimed. 'You're sitting there like a little old lady waiting for the car to cool, when the wind should be blowing through your hair and you should be drinking in great gulps of fresh air and laughing in pleasure to feel the sun on your face.'

Startled and indignant, she tried to get her hat back, but he held it out of reach, and she wasn't going to risk attacking him. Besides, she had been brought up to act in a ladylike fashion, whatever others might do.

'Would you please return it to me?' she asked primly,

curbing her temper. 'I don't wish to suffer sunstroke.'

He laughed at her. 'You won't. The car does have a roof. Now take that frown off your face; I want to show you something.'

'What?' Theresa's question was sharp, as she tried to make sure her hair was pinned in position. 'What is there to show me here?'

'A thousand things, if you have the eyes to see them. Look over there at that squirrel hanging from a branch and wondering what we're doing here. There's a robin over there, watching you. He's forgotten that worm he was pulling at for his breakfast.'

Theresa looked where he pointed. Sure enough, she was being watched.

'Smell the scent of the pines and the spruce and the cedar,' Edouard advised softly. 'Headier than the most exotic perfumes in the world.'

She did as she was bid, and breathed in the odour of the woodland. It was very quiet here, now that the motor was at rest. The sun felt warm on her hands and face.

'Mr Margold will be waiting.' She spoke more gently, almost forgetting that he had something to tell her. It didn't matter so much. Nor was she alarmed or alive to any danger in the odd situation in which she found herself.

'Let him wait.'

'What about the army tank?' Theresa questioned, but there was no urgency in her tone.

'It won't go away.' His voice said he had all the time in the world. 'I want to show you something,' he repeated. 'A magnificent view of the river I told you about.'

'You mean the river which is the highway to the north?'

'The very same.' He jumped down from the car and put her hat on the seat. He came round and held out his hand to the girl. 'Will you come with me?'

'Is it far?' Theresa forgot about her hat as she looked down into his eyes. She put her hand in his and let him help her to the ground.

As he swung her down, he looked at her sandals. 'Not quite the shoes for walking, but it's no more than five minutes, and an easy path,' he assured her, leading the way into the trees.

Theresa followed him along a narrow path. It was cooler in here and quite strange to her; she wasn't used to woods or wilderness, and shivered slightly. Almost she wanted to turn back, but couldn't bring herself to call out to him. When they came into a little clearing, she gasped in pleasure. Glinting in the sun, the river stretched before them, with ducks swimming on its surface and a big bird swooping down for fish. Further down the bank, a deer was drinking.

She stood in wonder. 'It's lovely!' she breathed.

Edouard nodded, watching her. 'I thought you'd like it. The Ottawa isn't one of the enormous rivers of the world, but it's pretty impressive in its own way.'

He said no more, but allowed her to stand in silence and imagine canoes and boats and fleeing men. She wondered if he was trying to show her how impossible it might be to trace a man who wanted to disappear here?

'What's that?' she asked, pointing to a good-sized hill in the distance.

'They call it Mount Martin, I believe.' Edouard was leaning against a tree. 'I don't know why.'

'Who does it all belong to?' Theresa was awed by the splendour she saw before her.

'No one.' Edouard shrugged. 'Everyone. I like to think it's mine.' He brushed a few leaves from a fallen tree-trunk, and indicated that they could sit down.

'Do you often come here?' she wanted to know, as she sat beside him.

'Now and again. Sometimes I fish; mostly I just look.' He had picked up a piece of grass and was chewing on it. 'There's good hunting here. The Indians think there'll be hunting in heaven, but I had enough of guns and hunting in the war.'

Theresa stole a quick glance at him, hearing the note of bitterness in his voice. He was older than she had at first thought: there were fine lines round his eyes, and a hint of grey in his dark hair. Probably he was in his thirties—well into them.

'You weren't always a newspaper man, then?'

'I've done a bit of everything . . . Grew up in city streets, and never knew anything like this till I came to Creswal. "Beyond Paradise", I call this place . . . Funny, but when I saw it first, I thought it was too quiet, too silent, for me. Now I come to listen to its noises. They never stop. Shut your eyes and you'll hear them.' His voice was mesmeric.

'Listen to the cries of the birds as they call to each other.' He whistled softly, and further away she heard the self-same song and the beating of a bird's wings. 'The insects cry and strum,' he went on, as a high-pitched humming began beside her. 'That's a cicada. It talks of heat and sunshine.'

Theresa's eyes were fast shut. Above the other noises that he described she could distinguish the wind in the top branches of the trees and the splash of a fish in the river. A feeling of great peace and timelessness descended on her. She didn't know how long they sat there, unmoving, listening.

'All griefs slip away here.' His voice was low.

'Yes,' she sighed. 'I can remember feeling like this in church when I was little.'

'There's a fox barking.' She opened her eyes. Edouard had risen to his feet and was looking at her.

'I thought you were plain when I first saw you, but I was wrong. You're pretty. I think it's the eyes. You have unexpected eyes, so green and wide, so trusting. They make promises to a man.'

'What sorts of promises?'

'Promises of sweetness, of understanding—They're your best feature.'

Theresa blushed under his scrutiny. She gazed up at him, unable to look away, aware of strange feelings and emotions. She couldn't explain to herself why she found him so interesting and so upsetting.

She licked her lips nervously with the tip of her tongue. There was nothing menacing in his face or his attitude, and yet she felt threatened . . . helpless, if he should come close to her.

'I was never considered outstanding in any way,' she protested.

He began to laugh. 'Fishing for more?'

Theresa was stung into adding, 'I've always been the plain one at home. The twins are lovely, blonde and blue-eyed, like Momma was. I must be like my father.'

'Probably.' He shrugged. 'Although his photo didn't look much like you.'

Theresa had to admit the truth of that, and searched her mind for a safer topic. 'Did you get to England,' she began, 'in the war, when . . .'

He cut her off in mid-sentence. 'I did.' Then he was silent. That surprised her.

'What part?' Her curiosity was aroused.

'We landed at Liverpool, your home town,' was all he said.

Still Theresa persisted. 'Didn't you like it?'

'We weren't there long. We were soon in France. Canadians were expendable.' His expression was so bleak that she knew she had been warned off, but she didn't want to let the subject go.

'A great many British men died, too,' she said softly. 'All the boys I knew. Every family lost one or two.'

'Yes,' he agreed. 'I didn't mean that the British hadn't suffered, but I saw the slaughter among the Canadians.' Then he held out his hand to her, and taking it, Theresa was raised to her feet. He made no move to leave the place.

'Your father might have joined up and gone to France, and been wounded—or died. Ever thought of that?'

Theresa hadn't even considered that. 'I suppose he could, but I don't think so. I think he's still alive and living in this country.'

'Woman's intuition?'

Although she had half thought he might laugh at her again, he did no such thing. 'You might be right. Life is full of the unexplainable. I used not to think so, but I've come round to that point of view.'

Theresa was conscious of his warm, firm hand holding hers, of the length of his fingers—and of her vulnerability. What was she thinking of to be here alone with him? A respectable girl would not have followed him into the bush as she had done. A tremor of alarm shot through her, and somehow must have communicated itself to him.

'There's nothing to be nervous of,' he assured her. 'You told me you weren't afraid of me before we set out. Changed your mind, have you?' His blue eyes looking down at her were challenging.

She found herself shaking her head. No, she wasn't frightened of him, but rather unsure and curious and interested. She had no way of knowing what he would do or say next. He wasn't like any man she had ever met before.

'Where are you staying?' he asked abruptly. 'At the hotel?'

'No, at a boarding-house—Pleasant View, it's called. The stationmaster recommended it when I got off the train. He was very kind.'

'Most men will be kind to you,' he said. 'I think it's something about your face . . . reminds them of their sisters, I suppose.'

Theresa didn't feel flattered by that observation, but she had no time to tell him so, for he announced that it was time to go back to the motor car. Releasing her hand, he led the way out of the clearing. She followed him as meekly on exit as she had on entry.

It was time to go with her search; she mustn't allow herself to be deflected from that. And yet there was something about this man, some dark depth of feeling in him that cried out for release. Let him find it here; Theresa chided herself. He had as good as said that was why he came to this spot. 'Beyond Paradise', he had called it. Had she spoiled it for him with talk of war? She hoped not, but he was singularly silent as he drove the rest of the way to the dam, not even commenting when she replaced her hat upon her head and tied the scarf round it.

CHAPTER TWO

EDOUARD LET Theresa out at the gatehouse of the dam, and she was shown from there to Stanislaus Margold's office.

She had expected him to be an older man, foreign and tall. There wasn't any reason why she should have assumed this would be so, other than his name, which had built up this picture in her mind. He was stockily built with ginger hair, spoke in a very Canadian accent and was no more than in his late forties. His eyes were pale blue and he had a neat little moustache, dark brown, in decided contrast to his hair.

With a quick 'Hullo', he waved her to a chair, saying, 'I understand you'd like to know where your father is. So would I, because Charles Russell disappeared five years ago and, to my knowledge, hasn't been seen since. I told Edouard Moreau that on the phone.'

'Disappeared?' Theresa was glad she was sitting down. This Canadian didn't waste any time in preliminaries. He was immediately direct. She swallowed hard. 'People don't disappear,' she protested.

He ignored this comment. 'Coffee?' he asked. 'And some biscuits?' At her nod, he pressed a button on the desk, and both appeared on a tray at the door, delivered by a young office-boy.

'It's hard for you to accept, I guess,' Mr Margold went on. 'By the way, you can call me Stan. Everyone does.' He helped himself to a biscuit. 'Disappear is exactly what Charles Russell did—it was in all the papers. I'm surprised you didn't read about it.'

Theresa shook her head. 'Tell me all you know about him. Did you work with him?'

'Not directly.' Stan sipped his coffee. 'But I knew him, of course. Well liked, a first-rate engineer, handled his men well, too—we were sorry to lose him. It came as a shock to everyone, I can tell you. True, he called himself a rolling stone and said he'd worked in South America, but I don't think he wanted to go back there. He had arranged to have a few days off, and there were more holidays due to him. When he didn't turn up for work after the few days, we supposed he'd decided to add them on.'

Theresa blinked. 'Didn't they miss him where he lived?'

'Yes. That's how we eventually found he was gone.' Stan offered another biscuit. 'Some woman rang up after a few days and wanted to know where he was.'

'Some woman? What woman? Did he have a wife?'

'Not that anyone knew of.' Stan frowned. 'It was a long time ago, you know. Ask Edouard to get out the back issues of the *Clarion* for you—it was the middle of October, I think, and it'd be 1917—there was war news. It was soon forgotten.'

'Yes.' Theresa pushed her coffee away, barely tasted. 'Wasn't there any sort of investigation? Did he leave clothes and things somewhere, or were they all gone, too?'

'I remember he left money in the bank in Creswal, a month's salary and bonus payment as well. We paid it into his account, thinking he'd turn up.' Stan was matter of fact. 'I don't know what happened to it. I can give you the name of the bank, and you can ask there.'

'Please, if you would.' She wasn't interested in the money itself, but it was a possible lead.

'No problem,' he assured her. 'It's a local bank, next door to the *Clarion*. They'll be pleased to talk to you, if you can prove you're his daughter.' He finished on a rising inflection, inviting an exchange of confidences.

'I can prove it.' Theresa wasn't prepared to discuss her circumstances. 'Where did my father live?'

'When he first came, he was in a boarding-house, one a lot of our men used. A foreign lady ran it—I expect she's given up long ago. He and the boy were quite comfortable there, but I think he had furnished rooms or a flat after that.' Stan drained his cup.

'What boy?' she interrupted.

'Charles's boy. His son, I suppose.' Stan's look was assessing. 'Don't you have a brother?'

'Not that I've ever heard of.' This was information she hadn't expected.

'Fancy!' Stan's blue eyes were sharp. 'A bit of a dark horse, Charles was, then.'

Theresa didn't want to go into that. 'Where is the boy? Did he disappear as well?'

'I don't think he did.' His smile was knowing, secretive even. 'That was part of the mystery.'

'But what happened to him?' she persisted. 'Did friends take him in?' She was as curious now about this unknown brother as she had been about her father.

Stan shrugged. 'I wouldn't know. Perhaps someone came forward to claim him.'

Theresa's heart went out to this brother or half-brother—claimed like a parcel. How had he felt when his father disappeared?

She asked more questions, but Stan either didn't know or couldn't remember. Yet she had the feeling that he could have added more to her knowledge if he had wanted to. She sensed that he had put a brake on his tongue, and wondered why. Was there some piece of gossip connected with her father that he would not mention to her?

Then Stan smiled, and said he couldn't help her further, but would be delighted to show her the dam project while she waited for Edouard to come back from the army camp. Theresa accepted, thinking she might somehow glean more from him, but he spoke only of the dam, and the work that had been completed and was still being done.

In spite of her own confusions and doubts, she was impressed with the size and grandeur of the site. She stood watching the roaring water cascading into the enormous pool, where it was then held captive, and thought about her father, the man who had helped to build it and had even planned some of it, who then walked off without a backward glance, leaving it and his boy behind him. How could a man whose work spoke of strength and endurance disappear willingly? Surely his character must have lent some of itself to the monument he had left in his wake.

It was more than possible that Charles Russell was dead and her search ended before it had properly begun. And the boy? Had Stanislaus Margold mentioned him to the editor of the *Clarion*, earlier on? Is that why he had brought her here? She supposed the old issues of the *Clarion* might reveal something about him, if she wanted to know. Where was Edouard, anyway? Although he was taking a very long time, it was ungrateful of her to consider that, as he was, after all, doing her a great favour.

Edouard Hippolyte Moreau, editor of the Creswal *Clarion*, drove back slowly from the army camp and the sight of the new tank. No doubt weapons were necessary to defend freedom and free people, but did their manufacturers ever consider the lives their weapons could destroy—and had destroyed in the past—as his had so nearly been.

Shivering, he felt cold dread in the base of his spine. He remembered that his mother had put her hand once to the centre of her chest and had told him that was where her heart was, and the heart was where emotion began. It had never been so with him, and that had puzzled him in his childhood. As far as he was concerned, pain started in the back, and he knew the exact centre where it began—in the small of his back. The first kick he had suffered in his life had been there, and it was the place the bullet had lodged—the piece of shell, he corrected himself. The doctors had agreed that it might be sensitive for years, perhaps for ever. Well, that was, after all, a small price to pay. He sighed. Usually the glimpse of that stretch of river which he called Beyond Paradise was enough to banish all thoughts of war and hurt, but not today.

It was all the fault of that English girl, Theresa Russell —no, Theresa Mellor she called herself—who had turned those wide green eyes upon him, and he hadn't sent her away as he should have done. Instead, he'd taken her on a sudden impulse to his most secret spot. She wasn't like any woman he had ever been involved with. He'd probably never see her again after what Stan would tell her. After all, a half-brother would present a new problem for her, and she'd surely have the sense to see that. Some things were better left alone, especially family skeletons. Why did this Theresa think it was so important to find a father she didn't know and hadn't ever known? Was there more to the story, that she hadn't told?

A picture of his own father flashed into his mind as he drove to the dam. He hadn't thought of him in years—he hadn't allowed himself to—but there he was, laughing, talking to him in French, taking him to Mass on Sunday and then walking home with him, hand in hand. They had been very close, whereas it had never been like that with his mother. And yet, a long time ago, before he was seven, his mother had been smiling, light-hearted, teasing and being teased by his father. Odd, he'd forgotten that.

Perhaps this Theresa sensed how it might have been between herself and her father, and was searching for that idyll. She'd never find it, of course, even if she located him. Dreams never matched up with reality.

What was it she had said—that it was her right to know her father. Which of us, Edouard asked himself sardonically, could ever claim to know a parent, even after a lifetime? Had he ever really known his mother? No, the answer came back; but he had known his father—and loved him. The suddenness and certainty of that sharp reply from the very depths he usually kept hidden from himself startled him.

Well, it had nothing to do with green-eyed Theresa.

The miles vanished under his wheels, and his thoughts turned to the girl. Poor girl, this Theresa—He found it in his heart to pity her. Her half-sisters, younger than she, were married. She might never achieve that state. So many men had been killed in the war that a whole generation of girls would never be brides or mothers. In realising that, she might have made a conscious choice to leave England and find a new life in Canada, and find her father. It might be all she would ever have. She might be searching for some meaning to her life.

Rosie had said he'd been hard on her. Perhaps he had. He must be gentle with her, now that her search was over, let her down a little lightly, advise her to find a job in one of the big cities—there was nothing for her in Creswal. He'd take her to the vantage-point above the dam, and she could see the country spread out before her for miles. After all, in a short visit as hers seemed destined to be, it would be neighbourly to let her see as much as possible, at least to let her feel the grandeur of the country she had come to. A little kindness never hurt anyone, neither the giver nor the receiver . . . He began to whistle to himself, his spirits lifting. It was a lovely day.

When Edouard picked Theresa up at the dam, he wasted no time in greetings or apologies but just held out his hand to help her into the automobile.

As Stan waved them good-bye and they drew away from the entrance, Edouard turned the car away from Creswal.

'That isn't the way we came,' Theresa protested.

'No,' he agreed. 'But you aren't in a hurry, are you?'

'No,' she admitted uncertainly, and he smiled.

'I thought you might like to see the whole landscape spread out before you,' he went on, as he directed the car along an even narrower road than the one they had used before.

'That would be nice, if you have the time.'

Her reply was polite, even accommodating, but

Edouard had the distinct impression that she wasn't too enthusiastic about the idea. Never mind, she'd come round. It might be better if he stopped the car a little way from the bridge, and they approached it on foot.

'Is it a sort of belvedere you're taking me to?' she asked, thudding against him as the car hit a hump in the road.

'Sorry about that!' Edouard slowed down as she straightened herself. 'It's an observation-point, a look-out. You'll be impressed with the view.'

'Yes,' Theresa agreed, holding now to the side of the car.

'It's not much further,' he encouraged, as they hit another bump and she bounced up. 'I think we'll walk the rest of the way.' He brought the car to a halt in a grove of trees. He could have sworn she alighted gratefully, her hat still firmly on her head, the scarf still in place. 'Just straight ahead,' he directed, wondering if this was such a good plan. 'There's a bridge to cross, and then the most marvellous panorama. People come for miles to see it.'

'Yes,' Theresa repeated. That was when she saw the bridge. 'What's that?' She walked towards it, and looked.

'Ah, it's a rope bridge, and you're being privileged to use it. That's what engineers like your father use all the time. It's perfectly safe,' he assured her, watching her face as she put her hand on the thick rope rail.

'You mean we have to cross that?' It was clear that she didn't want to.

Edouard put his hand on hers. 'Look, I'll show you.' He took a few steps across the plaited rope. 'It's been here for years.'

'No,' she cried, looking down into the gorge it spanned. 'I couldn't!'

'Of course you can. I'll help you. No one's ever been lost from this bridge. Your father probably crossed it a hundred times. What would he think of a daughter who wasn't willing to follow in his footsteps?' He saw her gulp and bite her lips. Perhaps he shouldn't have said that, but it had served to make up her mind.

'Very well.'

'Take off your shoes and your hat,' Edouard told her, 'and leave them there. You'll find it easier without them.'

Theresa obeyed, and he said that she must go first and he would walk behind her to make sure she was all right. She stepped on to the rope bridge, her curls tumbling about her face and down her back as she put the first uncertain foot on the supporting rope. As she half-turned towards him, he thought for a moment that she meant to refuse.

'Would you—could you—put your hands on my waist?' she asked breathlessly. 'Then I'd know you were there.'

Edouard complied. Her waist was small, and somehow more yielding than he would have expected. He liked the fact that she trusted him. He was now so close to her that he could smell the clean feel of her hair against his face as she began to move forward, and a wayward breeze blew a fat curl towards him.

'That's it, one foot after the other.' She must not stop as the bridge swayed with their movement across it. He felt her draw in her breath, and he held her a little tighter, drawing her body closer to his and letting her feel his strength. 'Don't look down.' She fixed her eyes on a tree at the other side, while Edouard looked down without a qualm. He rather liked the sensation of being part of space, of gliding through it.

When Theresa reached the other side, he felt her body relax, the tension go from her, and he held her for another moment, turning her round in his arms and lifting her across the rocky ground towards the lookout shelf. Then he set her on her feet.

She stood, barefooted, her hair by now cascading over her shoulders, looking without a word over the parapet down into the valley below. No, she wasn't a beautiful girl, Edouard reflected, but she filled the eye in

a very satisfactory manner. A pity she wouldn't be
staying; she had fitted so neatly into the curve of his arm.
Ah, Edouard Hippolyte, he chided himself, she's too
young for you anyway, and English girls are no longer
attractive. Not after Josie . . .

Theresa looked down at the vista of valley and dam and
tiny town in the distance. Edouard was right. It was a
magnificent view; it was like being at the seaside. Everything came into perspective, and troubles and perplex-
ities faded. The eye was meant to view the scope of
nature, the size of the world. Was that why he had
brought her here? She sighed and stole a look at him,
wondering why he was silent. She had almost refused to
cross the bridge, and shivered a little at the thought of
recrossing it. No, it would be better going back.
Edouard would not let any harm come to her.

'Well, was it worth the trouble?' He stirred, perhaps
feeling her gaze on him.

She nodded. 'Thank you for bringing me.'

'It seemed the least I could do. I don't suppose you'll
be staying, now.'

Theresa looked down at her feet. Was she going to
stay?

'I didn't know about the boy,' she said slowly. 'He told
you about him on the phone, didn't he? You might have
warned me.'

'It was better that you should hear it from him.'
Edouard went to the heart of the matter. 'It would
appear that your father married again, before his first
wife was dead.'

'We don't know that,' she protested. 'The boy might
not have been his.'

'No man takes a boy around with him,' he was quick to
point out, 'unless he has some responsibility for him.
Did your father have any relatives?'

'None. Poppa told me that.'

'Well, then,' Edouard seemed to think the subject was
finished. 'You'd best leave it alone—a closed chapter.

Turn your mind to other things. Travel a little, find a job in one of the cities. You'd like Toronto.'

Theresa didn't like the way the conversation was going. She didn't want to admit defeat, though she was perfectly aware that he was talking sense. 'Do you suppose,' she asked hesitantly, 'that there'd be a marriage certificate somewhere?' I think if I could find something as definite as that, I might think again.'

She noted that he looked a little surprised. Well, she had come a long way just to turn back now.

'I expect you could have enquiries made about certificates in the name of Russell. Disappearing dads, I've heard, often use their own names through habit or sheer bravado. Death certificates might bear looking into, as well as a birth certificate for your half-brother.'

Edouard's voice didn't offer much encouragement, but Theresa continued, 'Where would I start?'

'Why start at all?' he countered with another question. 'You may not like what you're likely to find.'

'I'd have to risk that.' Theresa took a step towards him. 'That's the risk I've run all along, ever since I started.' She stumbled over a small stone, and her hands waved in the air as she tried to right herself. Edouard caught her in his arms with one quick step.

Her heart was beating fast, and she tried to disentangle herself at once. Why did he have such an effect on her? And why was he pressing her to go away? If she went away, she'd leave this place, and never see him again. That didn't matter, of course, but this place held the answers—or some of them, she was sure of that. Edouard still held her.

'You were never meant to wander the world, searching for a father.' He spoke softly, his face close to hers. 'You were meant to be a wife to some lucky man.'

Even as she thought he meant to kiss her—and, of course, she wouldn't allow such a liberty, she told herself firmly—Edouard released her. 'Someone your own age, who'll take care of you.'

Theresa turned away from him, her eyes on the

dwarfed dam and winding valley. She sought for control over her errant emotions. 'Why are there two rivers?' She was pointing down.

'They diverted some of it into the old river-bed, but it's the same old river. The loggers use the diverted part, as do fishermen and canoes.' He turned to face her. 'What are you going to do?'

'I don't know,' she admitted. 'Is there some registrar of births and deaths and marriages I could write to about my father?'

Edouard frowned. 'I suppose you could try the cities first—Quebec or Halifax. Most emigrants come through the ports. But are you sure you want to?'

As she wasn't sure of anything, she didn't reply, but turned away from him.

'Tell me about your life before you came here,' he suggested gently. 'Did you stay at home all the time and take care of your sisters?'

Theresa swung round. She didn't want to be treated as a child—not by him! 'No, I didn't, and I wasn't at home playing with my toys when you were fighting the war!' It seemed important to set him right on that. 'I worked in a munitions factory.'

'Doing what?'

'Typing, office work. If you must know, I'm a trained typist.'

He smiled at her disarmingly. 'I'm an untrained one, self taught on Tom McGregor's machine.'

Theresa didn't ask who Tom McGregor was. 'I can see you don't take me seriously. My stepfather didn't either, when I found myself the job. "You won't last two weeks" was what he said . . . But I did.'

Edouard laughed.

Theresa's temper began to rise. 'You men are all the same. You don't mind how hard women work at home. You don't think that's work. But when there's a war on, women have to work because there aren't the men to do it. And working in a munitions factory can be pretty frightening. I didn't know that at first; not until one of the girls had her foot blown off as she packed the shells. Not that I was terrified all the time. After a while, you didn't think about it. I suppose if I crossed that bridge of yours often enough, I might do it easily.'

'Perhaps you might. I admired your courage in trying it. Some girls would have turned back.'

'Is that why you brought me here?' she demanded. 'To see what I'd do? Is it some sort of test for girls?'

'I've never brought any other girl here, but your father helped to build this dam. I thought you'd like to see it.'

'That's all right, then.' Theresa looked down at her dusty feet.

'Did you work all through the war?' Edouard's tone was friendlier.

'Yes, but afterwards we all had to go. I tried to get another job, as I liked having my own money and my independence. But all the men came back and wanted work. It didn't seem fair, somehow.'

'A suffragette, were you?'

'Not chained to the posts, if that's what you mean; but with them in spirit.'

'Well, they got the vote at the end of the war.'

'Oh yes,' Theresa agreed. 'Women over thirty did. I didn't, nor any of the girls I worked with. The age should be brought down to twenty-one. Woman are quite capable of deciding whom to elect by then.'

Edouard put his arm lightly round her shoulders. 'I can see I mustn't get into any political discussions with you, but I find I can't resist asking you more. What do you think of women police? I confess it shook me considerably when I saw them in London.'

Theresa wasn't sure if he was laughing at her or not. His face was serious, but there was something about his voice that made her wonder. She slipped from under his arm. She wasn't going to be patronised.

'They've been doing a splendid job since 1914,' she told him stiffly. 'I think that speaks for itself.'

'Yes,' he agreed gravely. 'And I mustn't tease you. I do think women did a wonderful job in the war, and, what's more, I think they'll go on doing it—They'll have to. The war killed off so many men. Your country won't be able to manage without them. Neither will Canada.'

Theresa was considerably mollified by this statement. She sighed, and went back to studying the view. It would be easy to forget all about the quest she had set herself.

Edouard brought her back to it. 'Did Stanislaus tell you anything else that might lead anywhere?'

She hesitated, and then said slowly, 'He mentioned something about money in the bank—Money my father left.'

'Worth following up,' he nodded. 'You didn't want to tell me about that. Why, I wonder?' He put a hand under her chin so that she was forced to look directly into his eyes. They were bright and assessing. 'If I'm going to help you, you're going to have to trust me.'

She was very uncertain with those blue eyes still holding hers. 'Are you going to help me? Back in your office, you didn't want to. What made you change your mind? If you have, that is.'

Edouard's eyebrows rose till they nearly met his hairline. 'Are you always so quick?'

She was unable to look away. 'It's your face that gives you away.'

'My face?' He seemed considerably taken back.

'It lights up somehow when you're interested.' She tried to explain it more fully. 'It's a bit like a monkey's face, it moves a lot.'

He began to laugh. 'Very flattering, I'm sure. Are you always so direct?'

'I—I didn't mean to hurt your feelings.' Theresa bit her lip. 'I've just never seen a face like it.'

'Apart from the monkey's?' Edouard took his hand from her chin.

She coloured hotly. 'If I say any more, I'll make it worse. Could you forget I said it?' She held out her hand to him in apology.

He took it in his own. 'I might.' He continued to hold her hand.

Although she didn't like to snatch it away, somehow she began to feel uncomfortable. 'You didn't answer my question,' she faltered.

'What question was that?' Edouard's fingers were long and supple around hers. 'Oh, yes. What made me change my mind?' He paused. 'A pair of green eyes, let's say.'

'I don't think it was that,' she replied gravely. 'I think there must be another reason.'

'Yes, perhaps there is. Your story has touched a nerve, a raw spot, in my life.' He stopped as though unprepared to go on.

'What spot?'

He looked down at their clasped hands. 'No harm in telling you, I suppose. I was seven when my father died, and I was told that I was the man of the family. I had to give up my bedroom—yes, even though I was the man of the family—and was moved to a couch in the dining-room. My sister moved in with my mother, and there were two rooms free for boarders.' Again he paused.

Theresa waited, making no move to free her hand. 'And then?'

'I hated the dining-room. The furniture made huge shadows. It loomed around me, and it was cold and lonely. I wanted someone there with me, so I invented cousins, French cousins; my father was French. Perhaps I do have French cousins somewhere—I was sure I had heard them mentioned once.'

'Couldn't you ask your mother about them?'

Edouard shook his head. 'She never talked about either family, his or hers. They'd both been cut off by them for marrying the wrong person, the wrong language, the wrong religion.'

'Oh!' was all she could say.

'There was no forgiveness in her. She prided herself on being alone in the world, and she didn't need any of them. She was a Shaw—whatever that meant.' His smile was bleak. 'But I was made of weaker stuff. I wanted relatives. Is that the way you are?'

'I suppose it must be.' She found she was still gripping his hand, wanting to comfort the boy he must have been, alone and frightened in the dark. In a way, that was how she felt about her father. She wanted his companionship, to belong to someone. 'It seems wrong never to have known him,' she murmured.

Edouard let go of her hand. 'We must see what we can do, then.' He seemed suddenly alert and alive. 'There's no question that the readers of the *Clarion* will be interested. But I wonder if you know what you're doing, Theresa Russell? I warn you, once started, I won't let go. I'm a newspaper man, and I'm building a newspaper empire.'

'An empire?' she repeated, surprised by this sudden change of subject.

'I own other papers,' he added, by way of explanation.

'Does that mean my story might be in other papers, in other places?' The thought was strange. But of course she wanted people to know, she told herself. How else would she find this father of hers?

'Yes.' He shrugged. 'It's up to you, of course. But the way I see it, you'll be taking part in an exercise in personalised journalism. I'll introduce you to my readers as a flesh-and-blood girl who'll be very real to them. Are you willing to face that kind of being known?'

Theresa swallowed. 'I'm not sure if I know quite what you mean. Will you want to put my picture in your paper?'

'Yes, and more than that. I shall introduce you to the people of Creswal, and tell them all about you.'

'But that isn't the way newspapers go on!'

'Perhaps not in England,' he replied. 'But on this side of the Atlantic we're a bit more venturesome. We try to involve our readers. Human interest, we call it.'

'Intrusion into people's lives might be a better name for it.' She didn't like the idea.

'Now's the time to draw back,' he suggested, 'if you feel those sorts of qualms. But I can tell you that it does work. The *Clarion* led the fight nationwide for veterans' rights, after we had begun telling the stories of individual ex-soldiers and the hardships they faced. Now we're fighting for better roads in the north, and lower taxes for farmers.'

'Yes, but those are big issues, and it wouldn't just be one story you'd tell.'

'True, but the technique's the same and the results are good.' Edouard smiled. 'Would it be so terrible to have people interested in you?'

'No,' Theresa admitted. 'I suppose it wouldn't. After all, I don't have anything to hide.'

'You may think you haven't,' he pointed out agreeably.

She thought at first that he meant to help her to a decision, but his next words surprised her. 'You might find the opposite. What if your father had committed some crime, and we uncovered it?'

After a minute, she replied slowly, 'That would be in his life, not mine.'

'You've made it yours, by going after him,' he stated. 'Be very sure you want to do this, Theresa, before we begin. Because once the public gets interested in a story, they want to hear how it ends.'

She realised that he meant exactly what he said. If she wanted his help, it would have to be on his terms. Well, what choice did she have? Refuse them and abandon her search, or accept them with a good grace? She could see he was watching her, waiting for her to make up her mind.

'What's it to be?' he asked quietly. 'Do we go ahead with it, or not? It's up to you.'

Theresa hesitated no longer. 'All right, I accept. I want to find my father. I've come this far, and I'm not going back empty-handed. Is it customary to shake hands in the newspaper world when people agree?'

'If you like.' Edouard smiled suddenly, and put out his hand.

Once again Theresa took it, this time in a businesslike

way. But her hand suddenly seemed to have a will of its own . . . It lingered in his.

'We'll go back to the office and have a search in the back issues. Rosie can give you a hand there. Then there's a picture to take. But first we'll have to cross that bridge again. Let's hope some wild creature hasn't disappeared with your hat and shoes.'

'You don't think that could happen?' she said in alarm.

He pressed her hand, and released it. 'I like teasing you—You react so well!'

Theresa looked at him. Why had he gone back to treating her as a child? She lifted her chin and allowed an expression of disdain to cross her face.

Edouard laughed. 'Let's make a start.' He offered to carry her over the rough ground again, but she refused his help and followed behind him to the bridge. Once there, she wasn't too proud to ask for his aid. The swaying rope still held terrors for her, as he must have known it would.

CHAPTER THREE

THERESA AND Rosie spent the afternoon poring over the back issues of the *Clarion*. When she had finished, Theresa wasn't much wiser. All sorts of theories had been advanced in those old pages, but the only real fact was the actual disappearance of Charles Russell. One day he had been in Creswal, the next no one knew where he had gone.

There was a picture of Antony Russell, referred to as his five-year-old son, looking sad and lost. She tried to find some resemblance between father and son, but she could see none from their photos. The boy looked much fairer, his features less clear cut, his jaw less aggressive. She couldn't detect even a fleeting look of herself in the lad's face. The paper called him Tony, and she thought the name suited him. There was no mention of any other relatives, or even of where he had gone.

Edouard had sent out for coffee and sandwiches, and they had gone on working while they lunched. He had also phoned about birth and death certificates, and had chosen Montreal to start his enquiries.

'Why Montreal?' asked Theresa.

'I could guess that it's the port where he entered the country, and stun you with my powers of deduction, but I happen to know from Stan that when he was hired to work at the dam, he was interviewed in Montreal.'

'How long will it take to look up the records?'

'A day or two, perhaps a week, before we hear,' he shrugged. 'Don't worry, I'll let you know.'

She looked at her watch, and discovered it was after three. That was when Edouard took her picture.

'There's nothing more to be done today,' he said. 'So why not go home and wait?'

Dismissed, she requested Rosie to draw her a map of

Creswal. The girl obliged, as Theresa gathered up her scarf and gloves and placed her hat back on her head.

Rosie was very quick. She even put lines for streets, and indicated where the river lay, and the timber mill, which was the main industry. She showed her where the paper factory was located, and named the residential streets and the best shops. So detailed was the presentation, that Edouard looked up from the copy he was writing to ask, 'How many people were lost in Creswal last year?'

'None, that I know of,' Rosie replied. 'But most of them have lived here for years. All right, perhaps I am overdoing it. I'll get on with the wedding write-up.' Smiling, she escorted Theresa to the door, handing her the map. She didn't appear at all put out.

'Go to the bank tomorrow morning,' Edouard called after her as she went down the stairs. 'Ask to see the manager.'

Of course she would go to the bank to find out about her father's account. Why did Edouard suppose she would forget?

Theresa didn't even bother to call back an assent, but went through the lower door and out into the sunny Main Street without bothering to tie her scarf about her neck. It was hot enough without it.

She was grateful that there was a little breeze blowing now, and the sun had lost some of its fierceness. Why not take a look at the town? She consulted her map and decided as she strolled along that it wouldn't take too long to reach Acacia Boulevard. She hadn't mentioned it to Rosie or Edouard, but she had a letter of introduction from her godmother to a Canadian friend here, a Miss Marguerite Falconer. It would be quite proper to take this note and her calling-card to leave at this lady's house, and it would give some point to her walk.

Main Street was busy, and Theresa passed a few pleasant moments gazing in shop windows. One of them displayed corsets and lacy camisoles very discreetly in the back of the window, and she smiled at that. She and her sisters didn't wear corsets any more. The free, fluid line was all the rage at home. Her mother had worn corsets and hadn't considered herself properly dressed without them, but Theresa had never needed or wanted them. She wore quite comfortably only an elastic girdle. No hard bones to cut into her waist, her figure was firm and supple.

Fabrics were displayed in another window: satins, organdies, silk, broderie anglaise, plain cottons, ging-hams. The basic materials were the same, but the dresses she saw (though she wouldn't have described them as dowdy) were a little behind the fashions she had known in England. They lacked the sharp edge of style, she thought, until her eye was caught by a furrier's window. There, displayed before her, was a black seal coat which had everything lacking in the frocks she had seen. Well cut and smooth, it was beautiful. And in the same window was a red fox fur meant to be worn as a scarf. One day, if she had money, she'd wear furs like those.

She walked on, not envious, but with her spirits lifted. The bigger shops began to give way to smaller ones and then to workshops. At the corner of one street was a horse-trough with a horse drinking from it. Then she was in Acacia Boulevard, which proved to be longer than she had expected.

The houses at first were tiny and mainly of wood, but as she progessed down, the dwellings became more impressive. Some were faced in stone and some in brick, and they sat further apart in big gardens.

Number 167 proved to be the largest of them all, with a white wood fence. The garden had several large trees and a sloping lawn. There was a big bed of red and white peonies in bloom, and as she opened the gate to enter, Theresa paused to look at them, drinking them in. A garden swing was suspended under one of the trees, but there was no one in it. She hesitated and almost turned away, more than a little awed by the sight of the house itself.

Set upon the highest ground, it was of wood and stone,

very large and sprawling, with an enormous veranda stretching its full length and down one side, painted white. The windows all along it were open, but completely screened with wire netting.

A uniformed maid took her card and note, and said she would see that Miss Marguerite received them on her return. Theresa saw that the maid placed them on a silver tray before she shut the door.

It was a long hot walk back up Acacia Boulevard and into Main Street and the other end of town where she was staying. She found herself thinking of the voyage from England, and the man she had met on board during the crossing. When she had mentioned to Simon Radcliffe, a fellow passenger to Montreal, that she was going to Creswal, Ontario, he had been astonished.

'Imagine that!' he had exclaimed, a smile lighting up his handsome face. 'That's the very place I'm going. I work there.' He told her he had been in England on a business trip, and was going back to set up a new process at Cliff's Paper Mill.

Theresa said she knew nothing of paper mills, and he smiled and assured her, 'There's no reason why you should. A pretty girl doesn't need to bother her head about mundane things like that.'

Simon was tall and fair and everything Theresa thought manly—and, yes, exciting. Their common destination had seemed to forge a link between them. They sat at the same table in the dining-room, and sunned together on the boat deck. He taught her to play quoits, and danced with her in the evenings. Theresa loved to dance; she considered it was the one thing she did really well. Sometimes one of the ship's officers danced with her, and when that happened, Simon was always waiting impatiently for her return. She had felt flattered by that, but she told herself it was because there weren't many young people on board rather than because he was eager for her company.

She had liked him, and had half thought that they might travel from Montreal to Creswal on the train together, for she knew it was a long journey. Unfortunately he had had family to visit, but he had advised her about train times and railway stations, and that had been a great help.

As she passed the bank and the *Clarion* office once again, Theresa wondered if she would see Simon in Creswal. It was no use day-dreaming about him, however attractive she thought him, she chided herself. She had come to search for her father, not romance. Still, if she should find that, too . . .

Arrived back in her room, she loosened her clothes and lay on the bed. It was certainly hot in Canada on a June day. Perhaps she should dispense with the twins' scarf till cooler weather.

She lay on a flock mattress, rather hard, but at least it wasn't lumpy. The sheets were clean and smelled of fresh air and good soap. Simon had given her good advice when he had suggested she would find a boarding-house quite comfortable, and more the thing for a girl on her own. Stretching her legs, she encountered several blankets at the foot of the bed. There were certainly more than she would need on the warm summer night. The cotton quilt that covered the bed was new and pretty, mainly reds and blues. The floor was bare wood, but there were two faded red and blue scatter rugs, one by the bed, the other by the washstand. Though the screen frame which held the window open looked well worn and a little rusty, it allowed the air in and kept the mosquitoes out. Theresa's eyes closed, and she drifted off to sleep . . .

When she woke, she poured water from the big jug into the bowl on the marble-topped stand, and washed. Then she changed her camisole for a clean one and put on a green cotton frock that emphasised the colour of her eyes. It was flounced and layered, but it was cool.

She had already met the other boarders—two teachers, a man and a woman both in their forties, neither of whom had much to say to the others; a gaunt woman of fifty who was a nurse at the hospital; and a white-haired man of about the same age, who was a salesman of some sort. He was the friendliest of this group, and referred to her as 'the little English Miss'. This had made Theresa laugh the first time, but after the third time she had wished he would stop.

She went down to supper—as they called the evening meal, though it was served at six o'clock. It was tasty and substantial, and she found it very filling. Afterwards, the others all disappeared, and she sat on the veranda at the front of the house with a book on her lap. It was still light and still warm.

Would she ever feel this country, this place, was home? she wondered. If she found her father—when she found her father, she amended to herself—would there be a sense of recognition between them, instant kinship or at least friendship?

She was startled out of her reverie by the sound of hoofbeats. Was there some sort of patrol around the town on horseback? Certainly she hadn't noticed that last night, but she had been very tired after the long journey. It was a solitary horseman, who stopped at the gate, tethering his horse there.

As he came up the path, she saw that it was Simon. He waved to her, and she got up to meet him, glad of the company. How delightful it was that he had come to see her, but how had he found her? He was wearing a plaid shirt and riding breeches. 'I keep a horse at the livery stable,' he told her, 'and Moonlight was as anxious for a gallop as I was. We've been through the woods.' He held Theresa's hand as he spoke. 'I've been to two other boarding-houses.'

Although Theresa had considered him handsome on the ship in conventional clothes, here in this northern town, dressed as he was now and with the late sun on his head and face, he was impressive. The firm clasp of his fingers, the grace of his lean figure, the masculine smell of wood and pipe and horse were all pleasing to her. Her heart beat faster as she smiled and looked up at him.

'Green eyes, green frock,' he exclaimed softly. 'It does suit you. I hope you don't mind being called on like this? I wanted to see how you were getting on.'

'I don't mind at all,' Theresa was quick to assure him. 'It's so good to see you. Come and sit on the veranda, and we can talk.'

'For a few minutes,' he agreed. 'Moonlight has cooled off. You're quite comfortable here?' he went on, as they both sat down on one of the wooden benches that lined the wall. 'Don't mind if I smoke, do you?' He took out his pipe and measured tobacco into its bowl. 'It will help to keep off the mosquitoes.'

She discovered she had been suffering a little from the insects' attentions. She scratched at a bite on her arm, glad to hear of was something that would keep them at bay.

'Probably a hole or two in the screening,' he said when she held out her arm for his inspection. 'You'll soon get used to them, anyway.' He lit his pipe. 'What have you been doing with yourself all day?'

Theresa was delighted to tell him. As Simon knew she had come to find her father, she poured it all out to him, including how Edouard Moreau had taken her to see Stan Margold. But she made no mention of how Edouard had stopped the car and taken her to see the river and the forest in that secret spot of his.

'A first-rate newspaperman, I've heard him called, this Eddie Moreau,' he observed, puffing at his pipe. 'I've always wondered about that girl he has working for him.' He stopped abruptly.

'What do you mean?'

'What exactly does she do there?'

'This morning she went to a wedding, and wrote it up. This afternoon she helped me with the back issues,' she explained.

'I suppose she must be useful to him in all sorts of ways.' There was an edge to Simon's voice.

'You're hinting at something between them, aren't you?' Theresa was curious, and somehow upset. 'Lots of girls work, these days,' she added, perhaps wanting to convince herself.

'Yes, in England,' he agreed, 'and in the cities here, maybe. But in Northern Ontario, girls stay at home till they marry.'

She considered this in silence. She didn't want to quarrel with Simon, but she might soon find herself wanting to work.

'Did you or your sisters go out to work in England?' Simon questioned.

'I did in the war,' she said, 'but not since then. I would have liked to go on, but after my mother died there were the girls to look after—and my stepfather. I told myself that in a way I was doing a job. I was looking after the others.'

'Of course, that's a woman's natural work: looking after her family.'

'Just because that's the way it's always been, it doesn't mean it has to go on like that,' Theresa protested, something in her rebelling at his calm sureness and superiority.

'You can't change the world,' Simon told her comfortably. 'Perhaps this office-girl of Eddie Moreau's needs the money. I understand her mother is a widow. But, just the same, you must guard against being too trusting.' He took her hand in his. 'The world is full of people who try to pretend they're better than they are. A girl on her own has to be careful. You don't want to get the reputation of being one of Eddie Moreau's girls. I wish you wouldn't drive about with him in his automobile. Promise me you'll be careful?'

He looked into her eyes with such concern for her that Theresa was moved. She let her hand rest in his.

'I'll be careful,' she assured him. 'But I can't promise that I won't go in his car again. It may be the only way to get somewhere in a hurry. Besides, he behaved very properly towards me. If he found out something about my father, I'd have to go with him,' she went on. 'You do see that, don't you?'

'Yes, but if that should happen, don't get carried away with feelings of gratitude. He'll be doing it for his paper and its circulation.' His fingers pressed hers.

Theresa liked the sensation of being cared for. She liked the feel of her hand in his, but she couldn't stop herself from defending Edouard. 'He'll be doing it for me, too.' She took her hand away from Simon. 'I'd be a poor sort of person if I didn't feel grateful.'

'Of course you'll be grateful. That isn't what I said. I said you mustn't be carried away with gratitude.'

'I'm not likely to be that!' Theresa was indignant.

'You're not very experienced.' He put his arm gently round her shoulders and drew her closer to him, explaining to her. 'A man like Moreau could turn your head. They say he's mixed with all sorts, worked as a porter in hotels, laboured on the roads, was a factory hand and an apprentice printer, waited on table . . .'

'And fought in the war,' Theresa interrupted, half wanting that arm that drew her near him to remain where it was. It would be easy to lean against him, to cling to him.

It was Simon who moved away. 'I can see he's impressed you,' he commented. 'He impresses all the women. I understand there was a girl in England too, but I think that's all over and done with. Of course, he's well fixed. He owns property here, and the newspaper. Inherited it from a relative, I believe. Just one thing, Theresa, if you'll let me advise you.' He paused as though awaiting her permission.

'What?' she asked, uncertain whether she wanted his advice or not.

'You mentioned your father leaving some money in the bank. If it should happen to be a large sum, don't let Eddie know about it. You won't want to spread it about. All sorts of people might come forward to claim it.'

Theresa thought about that, a little puzzled. 'Stan said it was only a month's salary. I suppose there could be interest on it, if it's still there. Anyway, I'll keep what you say in mind.' She didn't want to antagonise Simon, who was, after all, her only friend here. 'Tell me about your day,' she suggested. 'You must work for Cliff's Paper Mill. Rosie showed me where it is.'

Simon smiled at her. 'It's named for my father. Of course, it's only one of his mills. It's strange, really. I never thought I'd work for him—I wanted to be a dentist.'

'What happened to change your mind?' She was interested.

'Family pressures, I guess.'

There was a tone of finality in the way he said this, so although curious to know more, she only asked, 'Has it worked out well for you?'

'Oh, yes, very well.' Simon took a lazy puff at his pipe. 'I didn't think so when I went straight into the Montreal mill after university. I had to start at the bottom and learn about the whole business, and the same amount of work was expected of me as of anyone else—a little more, perhaps. But now, things are different. I've had this trip to England, to study factories and methods, and I'm going to make my mark with this new product and the new process that's going to be set up here in Creswal.'

'What is it, if it's not a secret?'

'I don't see any reason why I can't tell you. Half the town will know shortly. It's cardboard boxes.' Simon sat back, as though pleased with himself. 'Reinforced cardboard.'

'Cardboard boxes?' echoed Theresa. 'Reinforced? Do you mean so strong that they'll replace wooden boxes and tin ones?' She was trying her best to be impressed.

'Exactly.' He gestured with his pipe. 'Think of it. Every manufacturer in the world wants some cheap packaging for his product, something he can throw away if he wants after it's been used. Cardboard boxes are the answer.'

'Yes.' She was thinking of the shells and guns she had

seen in wooden crates in the war. 'What exactly is cardboard?'

'It's made from timber, of course, in something the same way as paper is.' Simon looked as though he was enjoying enlightening her. 'That's why we're trying it here. Falconer's are able to supply us with the right kind of wood.'

Theresa nodded. 'Do Falconer's supply a lot of your factories, then?'

'Quite a few. Why?'

'I just wondered. Rosie said Falconer's were the biggest employer in town. Are there many Falconers?'

'There's only old man Falconer—Big Bob they call him. He runs it all. He has a daughter, Sidney.' He hesitated, or perhaps he paused for breath.

'Sidney is a boy's name, isn't it?' she remarked.

'Yes! Big Bob expected a boy, and he'd picked the name. He used it anyway.'

'Didn't his wife object?'

Simon shrugged. 'It's plain you've never met Big Bob. His wife did like everyone else does. She gave way to him. In a way, perhaps, he was right. Sidney is his only child. His wife died some years ago, giving birth to a boy. The boy was born dead.'

Theresa sighed. The story had saddened her. 'He could marry again.'

'I suppose he could. He's been interested in one or two. I don't imagine Sidney would be too pleased, but that wouldn't stop him if he set his mind on it. Then there's Marguerite, of course.'

'Marguerite?' she asked quickly, afraid that Simon had stopped there.

'His sister. She took charge of the household when the wife died. She must be in her thirties; a good-looking woman, but determined on her own way.'

Theresa took a deep breath. Perhaps she shouldn't have let him say quite so much about the Falconers without declaring her interest.

'I have a letter of introduction to Marguerite

Falconer,' she announced hesitantly.

Simon looked put out. 'You might have told me, before I rattled on. That wasn't quite fair.'

'No, I suppose it wasn't,' she admitted, a little ashamed of herself. 'I was curious. The twins have always accused me of wanting to know everything.'

He thawed a little with this confession. 'No harm done; it's all common knowledge, anyway. People in small towns always gossip about each other. Where did you get the introduction from?'

'From my godmother. They met ages ago, when Marguerite Falconer had a year in England. They became friends. I think Marguerite stayed with her, and they've kept in touch ever since. I wonder . . .' She didn't finish the sentence out loud, but only inwardly did she wonder if that was the source of the clipping about her father. Perhaps Marguerite had known him, and she must certainly have heard of her mother.

Simon ignored her silence. 'What are you going to do with the introduction? Hold on to it for a few days, and see what happens?'

'Why would I do that?'

'I don't know.' He was uncomfortable; Theresa could see that. 'You might go away to follow your father's trail to some other town.'

'All the more reason to produce it promptly,' she pointed out. She had the distinct impression that Simon didn't want her to get in touch with the Falconers, and it puzzled her.

'What's this Sidney like?' she asked sharply.

'She's beautiful'—Simon's voice took on a hint of enthusiasm—'tall and blonde with blue eyes. I suppose she's used to getting her own way with a doting father and aunt, but when Sidney walks into a room, all the other women look pale and insipid. She knows how to talk to men; she makes them feel important to her. She's a charmer.'

'What about the other girls?' she prompted. 'Do they like her?'

Simon shrugged. 'They must feel disappointed that they aren't like her, but they all come round her. She's the centre of the wealthy young people of this town.'

She would be, Theresa reflected to herself. She could already picture this paragon.

'The Falconers give a lot of parties,' he went on. 'There's always a good crowd there. They usually have open house on a Saturday night, and all dance to the phonograph. There's plenty of food and drink. Big Bob and some of his cronies play cards. Your friend Moreau is a great pal of his.'

Theresa had a long moment to consider this aspect of social life in Creswal. She was a nobody, a girl from England who was looking for her father. It wasn't likely that she'd be included in any parties at the Falconers'. That was probably what Simon meant by not being in a hurry to leave her note of introduction. Perhaps he felt, knowing these people as he obviously did, that she wasn't likely to receive a call from Miss Marguerite Falconer at her boarding-house. He might wish to spare her embarrassment.

She began to wish she had waited, and not rushed in that afternoon without finding out more about the family. Now she didn't know whether she should tell Simon what she'd done. But that was foolish: she might as well admit it.

'I went to the Falconers' this afternoon,' she said baldly. 'I left my card.'

'Did you?' He gazed at her, dislike printed on his face. 'Why didn't you say so in the first place?'

'I didn't know you knew them,' Theresa tried to explain.

'I suppose you talked all this over with Eddie Moreau?' He was clearly angry. 'I wonder he didn't introduce you to Big Bob himself.'

'He doesn't know anything about it.' She was getting angry. 'Why should I tell him, or you, for that matter? My godmother gave me a letter of introduction to a local woman, a friend of hers. Why shouldn't I use it?'

'No reason at all,' Simon agreed smoothly. 'Have you thought how Moreau is going to feel when he finds out?'

Theresa was even more astonished at the turn the conversation had now taken. 'What's it to do with him?'

Simon laughed, but it wasn't a happy-sounding laugh, more a bark of derision. 'You have only to wait to find out.'

'What's that supposed to mean?' Her voice was sharp.

For the space of a minute, she thought that Simon didn't mean to answer, then he frowned. 'I've been away for five weeks, and I'm a relative newcomer, but I don't suppose things have changed since I was here. Unless I miss my guess, Eddie Moreau will be decidedly put out that you didn't tell him you were going to approach a woman whom some would say he's courting.'

Theresa's mouth opened and then closed without a word issuing from it. She felt as though she'd been hit when she wasn't looking.

'Of course,' Simon continued, 'others might say it's Sidney he's after, and he's only sweetening up the aunt. After all, Sidney is her father's daughter, and some girls prefer older men.'

This time Theresa's tongue wasn't stilled. 'He can't be courting two at once—in the same family. How would they act towards each other?' She couldn't believe it, wouldn't believe it, of Edouard. He was too sensitive a man for that.

'I'm only telling you what people say, and what I've observed for myself. On Saturday nights, if he has one dance with Sidney he has the next with Marguerite. He takes them both to the movies. That's easy enough—he owns the picture-house. Then he takes them both for sodas or ice-cream.'

Theresa began to giggle. The idea of Eddie taking two ladies out for ice-cream and dividing his attention absolutely equally between the two of them struck her as entertaining. She didn't know the ladies in question, but she could imagine the scene with Edouard's eyes dancing. Besides, if there were two of them, her common sense told her that there couldn't be anything to worry about. Not that she was worried about what Mr Moreau did, she added quickly to herself.

'What's so funny?' Simon demanded, aggrieved.

She didn't try to explain it. 'You weren't too pleased when I said I'd left my card at the Falconers'. Why was that, Simon?'

He stuffed more tobacco into his pipe and lit it up again. 'I suppose I wanted to keep you to myself. Everybody else has been here for years, and I'm tired of being the new boy. You've no idea how pleasant it would be to have a friend of my own. It was very selfish of me, I suppose.'

He smiled so disarmingly that Theresa was touched. She put her hand on his free one. 'That's very sweet of you, Simon. We can still be friends, can't we?'

'Of course. I mean, I hope so.' He gripped Theresa's hand. 'Forgive me?'

She nodded. What was there to forgive, after all? He had only wanted to keep her to himself, and the thought gave her a warm glow. It was very comforting to be valued for oneself.

Simon, even though he had just relit his pipe, now put it down on the small table beside him and put his arm round her. 'You're a sweetie, Theresa. A real pal. I'm glad you understand. But I guess I've left Moonlight standing long enough, and I'll have to take him home.'

Theresa, with his arm about her, wondered why he spoke of going home. 'Where is home?' she asked, leaning a little closer to him.

'I have rooms with a widow-woman, a Mrs Knight. She cooks for me and cleans, and generally makes me comfortable—a very kind old soul. Of course I have my own key. I was staying in the hotel at first, but I wanted some place of my own.'

Simon's arm was drawing Theresa closer to him— disturbingly closer, she found. She had to keep him talking. 'You didn't think of a little house?'

'I thought of it,' he admitted, his lips fanning her hair

around one ear as he replied. 'But there didn't seem much point until I had someone to share it with. Eddie Moreau has a house, of course—inherited it with the paper. But why do we keep talking about him?' Simon's lips found Theresa's.

It was a short kiss, but enjoyable. A friendly kiss, a gentlemanly kiss, Theresa described it to herself. Why then did she feel just a little disappointed that it wasn't longer, more intense, perhaps? It was the first time he had kissed her, and he probably wasn't sure of her reaction. Come to that, she wasn't too sure of it either. Certainly she liked Simon and wanted his friendship. Did she want more than that? She sighed.

Simon drew back. 'Have I frightened you? I've been waiting to do that for a long, long time. You have very kissable lips, Theresa.' His arm was still round her, and his other hand clasped hers.

'No, you haven't frightened me. I liked it! You can kiss me again if you want.' She raised her face to his.

He obliged with a kiss that was only slightly longer than the first, then put his finger against her lips. 'I'll say good night. Girls are meant to be wooed and courted, not rushed at. Till the next time, Theresa.' He rose to his feet and she rose with him, his arm still encircling her. He squeezed her waist, and then released her. 'Good night, Theresa.' Picking up his pipe, he left the veranda.

A brief wave, and he had mounted his horse. Moonlight neighed, and obedient to the command of Simon's knees and hands, trotted off into the gathering dusk of evening.

Theresa remained on the veranda, smiling dreamily, her chin cupped in her hand, her eyes watching the picture that man and horse made.

CHAPTER FOUR

THE NEXT morning after breakfast, dressed again in her black and white costume, Theresa set out at ten to call on the bank manager. She had wondered whether she would have to wait, but she was shown immediately into his office, which was a small side room. It was bright with the morning sunshine streaming in, and very clean. There was a desk facing the door as she entered, and a small dark man sat there.

He waved her to the only other chair, and introduced himself as Mark Johnson at her service if she wished to open an account.

'It's not quite that.' Theresa was unsure about how to begin. 'It's about my father that I've come. His name was Charles Russell, and he had an account here five or six years ago.'

'Just about the time I started as manager here.' Mr Johnson gave her a wintry smile. 'Charles Russell? I know that name. And you're his daughter? I suppose you have credentials to prove that?'

She hadn't expected such a direct reaction, but she still had her birth certificate and her parents' marriage certificate in her cloth bag. She pulled them out for his inspection, and he spent some time studying them.

'He did bank here?' She ventured a question at last.

'Yes, he banked here.' A short reply, as he laid the documents on his desk.

'Did he ever close his account?' she sensed that the bank manager wasn't going to volunteer any information.

'Why should you want to know that?' He countered with another question. 'Has your father died, or given you power of attorney?'

Theresa was forced to admit that neither of these

applied, but that she was looking for some lead to her father's whereabouts, and for the first time she got a human reaction from him.

'Never turned up, then? I've always thought that one day he'd come walking in here to ask for his money.'

'Did you know him personally?'

'Not to say personally, but of course I knew him. Very proud of that boy of his. He'll be what?—ten, now. Has he grown into a fine lad?'

When she said she didn't know, Mr Johnson's face was surprised into an expression of puzzlement. He picked up his pen. 'He is your brother, isn't he?'

'Half-brother,' Theresa corrected. 'I didn't know Antony existed until yesterday.'

He tapped his pen against his teeth. 'Far be it from me to question anything about my clients' private lives, but how can that be?'

She hesitated, and then found herself explaining the circumstances of her father's supposed death in South America, and the subsequent Coroner's Court in England which had declared that death a fact.

'So your father disappeared before,' the manager observed, hitting his pen against the desk as though to emphasise his words. 'That throws an interesting light perhaps on his second disappearance.'

'In what way?'

'It shows a pattern of conduct. He abandoned his wife and baby daughter in England, started a new life in Canada, acquired a son, and then in turn abandoned him. My dear, it may be that you'll never find him if he's gone to yet another country.'

This took Theresa's breath away. 'But,' she protested, recognising that Mr Johnson might be right, and considerably shaken by the thought, 'there might be some explanation.'

'What explanation?' he asked baldly. 'It seems to be the character of the man to shrug off his responsibilities. No, my dear,' he went on, as Theresa opened her mouth to speak. 'We must face facts, mustn't we?'

She nodded dumbly. She didn't want to face that kind of fact about her father—if indeed it was fact.

Mr Johnson took her nod as confirmation of her agreement. 'It's seven years to presumption of death from the time of disappearance without any evidence,' he continued. 'But you are of age, and there is the boy . . .' He left that thought dangling.

Strangely, she didn't consider the boy at that moment. She wondered instead how the manager seemed to know all about her father without consulting any records. Perhaps Edouard had mentioned to him that she would be calling.

She didn't have time to ask, because he continued, 'You could perhaps make some sort of claim in the courts.'

'Claim?' Theresa seized on that. 'Is there something to claim, then? Did my father leave money here?'

Mr Johnson gave her a shrewd glance. 'Yes, I think I can be frank with you on that. There were two or three hundred dollars in his account when he disappeared. There'd be interest on that. The branch kept it for six months.' He paused, perhaps waiting for some reaction from her. 'In English money, it might come to a hundred pounds.'

Theresa was too stunned for coherent speech. She sat in silence.

'After that, we moved it to Head Office in Ottawa. It was, you understand, a *cause célèbre*—written up in the newspaper—and it appeared he had some securities there,' the dry voice went on.

Theresa found her voice at last. 'You say he had money, and yet he left it all safely in your banking system and abandoned his boy. That doesn't make sense to me.'

He shrugged. 'Sense or not, he did it. There's no way round that.'

'Are you sure the money's still there?' she pressed on. 'You can't know that without checking, can you?' She felt she was clutching at straws, but she wanted to believe the best of her father, not the worst.

The man across the desk gave her a small smile. 'Your loyalty does you credit, but I'm reasonably sure the money is still there. It was, six months ago, when I raised the matter with them.'

'May I ask a question? Why did you raise the matter six months ago?'

Mr Johnson blinked at her. 'Because I was interested, of course. It was one of the first cases I dealt with as manager, and I've always thought of it as unfinished business. Banking people don't like unfinished business. It's untidy.'

She had to be content with that. This fussy little man would want things neatly put away.

'Naturally, I'll check again,' he assured her, 'since you've raised the matter. Do you have no knowledge of where the boy is?'

'I was going to ask you that. There was no mention at all of him, or where he went, in the *Clarion* records; just his picture. You don't have any ideas?'

'I'm afraid I can't help you there.' The reply was bland.

Excessively bland, was Theresa's immediate reaction, but she chided herself for being hopeful that he might help. This Mr Johnson was too correct for her liking; too impressed with his own position. But that was his nature, she told herself. Why did she feel he was holding something back?

As he handed her back her documents, signalling that the interview was over, he added, 'You'd do well to take legal advice about inheritance. I know the sum isn't large, and you would seem to be the eldest child and to have a possible prior claim. There might be others, of course, that you know nothing about.'

Theresa didn't want prior claim on her father's money: she wanted to find him. She thanked the manager and promised to come back again in a few days, after he had contacted Ottawa.

As she left the bank, her first thought was to see Edouard Moreau and tell him about it, in spite of

Simon's warnings of last night. She paused, undecided, by the printing office of the paper, which fronted on the street. Edouard was there, bending over the press. That decided her. No one else was there, so she went in.

He straightened up, wiping inky hands on a well-used rag. 'Been to the bank, have you?' he greeted her. 'What's the latest, then?' His sleeves were rolled to the elbow, his tie discarded, his shirt open at the neck.

'Not much. There might be a couple of hundred dollars, but it's been moved to Ottawa, and there's no touching it while no one knows where my father is. Mr Johnson is going to get in touch with his Head Office.'

Her disappointment must have been plain in her voice, because Edouard directed a searching glance at her. 'Thought you'd do it all in one day, did you? The bank was going to tell you where he went to?'

'Not exactly that.' Theresa ran her finger along the edge of the machine Edouard had been examining, and it came away black. She looked down at it in dismay.

He flicked the rag to her. 'I'm glad to see you've dispensed with your gloves.'

She rubbed at the ink. 'I haven't. They're in my pocket. I just hadn't had time to put them on when I saw you through the window.'

Edouard nodded. 'I might have expected that. Well, now that you're here and you've already got the feel of ink on your hands, perhaps you could give me a hand?'

'Doing what?'

'Just handing me things: holding a wrench or anything else I need. That is, if you're not afraid of a working man.'

Theresa shrugged. 'I've nothing else to do, and you don't look very frightening. In any case, we're in full view of the street.'

'You are downhearted, aren't you?' He smiled at her. 'I can see you need to do something worth while. Put the rag down and hand me that screwdriver over there.'

She did as she was told, and watched as Edouard attacked the machine.

'I suppose you know what you're doing?' she hazarded. 'I thought Rosie's brother was the printer.'

'Yes to both of those,' was the crisp reply. 'Now you can give me the wrench. Not that big one—the little one further over.' He pointed to the bench, where several tools were laid out.

Theresa gingerly picked up a rather greasy-looking tool and brought it to him. Their hands touched as he took it.

'Good,' was all he said, but her fingers tingled at the touch. Alarmed, she wiped them on the rag. Perhaps it had something to do with the oil.

'Rosie's brother is in Renfrew this afternoon, helping out on a sister paper, and we want this job done before the presses roll again. Let's have the big spanner, then.'

This time she made sure there was no contact between them as she gave it to him.

'You needn't be doubtful about my abilities,' Edouard grunted, as he struggled to exert enough pressure on the spanner. 'I began my newspaper career down in the print room, not upstairs in the office.'

'Indeed,' she said, suppressing a desire to giggle as sections of the machine came apart suddenly at Edouard's efforts. 'Was that your first job?'

He looked up briefly from the part he was examining. 'No, first I was kitchen-boy in a hotel. Just as I thought. This is what's causing the trouble—Lucky we have another one.' He pointed to the bench, and she fetched it.

As he waited for it, Edouard continued, 'My mother meant me for a banker.'

'Oh no!' exclaimed Theresa. 'That wouldn't have suited you.'

'Why not?' He put the faulty part on the floor. 'Not pompous enough?'

'It's not that.' She hugged the new part to her, considering. 'You don't act important. You don't look it.'

He began to laugh. 'You have the knack of putting me in my place, don't you? Well, my mother didn't agree with your assessment. I was allowed to stay on in school till I was fourteen, because the bank was going to have me.' His face suddenly looked grim.

'But you escaped?' Theresa prompted.

'I suppose you could call it that. I was told I was mulish, pig-headed, stubborn—in short, just like my father.' He held out his hand for the piece of machinery clutched in Theresa's arms.

'Didn't she like your father?' she asked hesitantly.

'I don't think she ever forgave him for dying and leaving her with two children to bring up.' Edouard turned back to his work.

'Who was the other child? A brother?'

'No, a sister, Ellen.'

'Where does she live? Here in Creswal?'

He straightened up and wiped his forehead. His eyes met Theresa's briefly. 'She doesn't. She died of the flu after the war. Two of her little girls died too, Maud and Clara. Only Thelma is left, and she's with her father, Tom McGregor.'

'I'm sorry. I had no idea . . .'

Edouard said nothing as he fitted the new part in place.

Theresa would have liked to ask after his mother, but in face of the last answer she didn't dare. Her fingers played with the oily rag.

It was Edouard who broke the silence. 'Spanner.' 'What's the matter?' he asked, as she gave it to him. 'Cat got your tongue?'

'No.' Her reply was indignant, and too emphatic in her own ears. She rushed into speech. 'My mother always said that if a man was doing a job, a woman had to wait on him hand and foot.'

He smiled at her. 'She sounds like a sensible woman. Tell me, when you started to work in the munitions, did you find the job for yourself?'

'Yes, in a way. Bessie, a girl who lived down the street, told me there were jobs going, and I applied at once. Why? Didn't you find your own jobs?'

'I certainly did. I had to. Since I wouldn't go to the bank, I got no help from my mother. I was a stable-boy first, and then a garage hand when my boss turned to motor cars. He went broke, and I found labouring jobs on the roads and on the docks. Then I had a spell in a telephone factory. I hated it, but that job saved my life.' He held out his hand. 'Wrench.'

'How could it save your life?' Theresa felt the conversation was on safer grounds now.

'In the war, the army considered I was an expert with telephones just because I'd had six months in that factory. It was in my records, you see. How were they to know that all I'd done there was roll cable? The ways of officialdom are passing strange.'

She didn't know whether to believe him or not. 'You mean that you worked in a factory somewhere in the war?'

'Not quite that, but they took me out of the trenches in France and sent me back to Britain, seconded to the British army. I worked with a special team on improving field telephones. We must have done a good job, as they gave me a medal afterwards. I still have it.' Edouard straightened up. 'Let's have the rag.'

'I thought men got medals only for being wounded in action or doing something very heroic?'

'Why should that be?' he asked reasonably. 'The bullet or the shell might just as easily have gone into the next man. Why should medals be handed out to targets?' He was smiling broadly.

'You're making fun of me,' she protested. 'I didn't mean that you didn't deserve a medal.'

He nodded. 'Just surprised that I got one? In my opinion, the ones who should have got them were the girls loading the shells. You must have known the ones I mean, the ones who turned yellow from the cordite. They went on working and suffering.'

'They looked so strange that their mates shunned them,' Theresa exclaimed, surprised that he would know about them.

'That's enough about doleful subjects.' He dismissed the subject of medals. 'I'm just about finished here. Did you know you have a big black streak on your cheek?'

Theresa's hand flew to her face.

'You're making it worse!' He was laughing. 'Trot upstairs to the editorial office and Rosie will fix you up. There's a sink up there, and a mirror. Tell her I sent you, and that I'll be back some time this afternoon. She can try her hand at editing till then.'

She rushed out of the print room and upstairs without another word.

Rosie was gazing at a large mirror on a stand on her desk at the rear of the room, and she gestured towards the sink, behind a screen. 'Have you been helping Edouard? Pete's gone to Renfrew. He tried to talk me into it, but I've been caught that way before. Besides, someone had to be here, to answer the phone or take down a story.'

Theresa washed her hands, and then came back to the mirror with a towel dampened at one corner.

'Help yourself,' said Rosie, good-naturedly offering her the whole mirror. 'I was just looking at my hair.'

Theresa glanced at her. 'What's wrong with it? You've got lovely hair.' She admired its sleek perfection, black and gleaming, and coiled in a thick braid like a halo round her face.

'It's all right, I suppose,' the girl said, grudgingly. 'But it's straight—Not like yours, all curly and wavy. I was visiting my cousin in Toronto last week. She got married three months ago and lives in the city. She had beautiful clothes—all the women have—and some of them have short straight hair. It looks ever so smart. Jess wants to get hers cut, but her husband won't hear of it. I don't have a husband to consider. What do you think? Would it suit me?' Rosie undid the braid and tried to show the effect of short hair. 'A little bang over the forehead, perhaps?'

Theresa tried to visualise it. 'It might suit you. Some girls look very smart, with it short. I almost had mine done when I worked at the munitions factory, but my stepfather wouldn't let me. He went on about hair being a woman's crowning glory, but he didn't have to comb mine and get the snarls out and brush it every night. I was sorry I hadn't just had it done without saying a word about it.'

'Men,' sighed Rosie, but she didn't enlarge on which of those men she had in mind.

'I suppose you have a boy friend,' Theresa said tentatively. 'A girl as striking as you must have.'

'Um-m, several,' she admitted. 'But nobody special. I don't want to spend my life in this little town. I want to go to Toronto. There are women on newspapers there.'

'Have you mentioned it to Edouard?' Theresa made no attempt to curb her curiosity.

'He wasn't much help. He should know what I mean about small towns. He's from Toronto. Sometimes I'm sure he wants to go back there. If I went with him . . .' Rosie left that sentence unfinished. 'There's no sense in planning ahead, is there?'

Theresa shook her head, but she wasn't quite sure what she was denying.

'Eddie said I needed a change from weddings and club meetings. He let me do a real interview!' Rosie was smiling. 'Do you know, I felt quite nervous about interviewing a man, but I enjoyed it. He was ever so nice and came into the office earlier on this morning, so I wouldn't have to go to the plant.'

'That was very considerate.'

'Wasn't it?' Rosie put the mirror back on the shelf over the sink. 'He's young and rich, and handsome as well. He answered all the questions I asked. I've been typing the story out—Have a look.' She ruffled through the papers on her desk till she found the right one.

Theresa took it from her, half-guessing already who the subject was. There it was in black and white—Simon Radcliffe—and the story, of course, dealt with cardboard boxes.

Rosie had evidently asked intelligent questions,

because the answers were there in some detail. Certainly the plant and process were described in more detail than Theresa had been given last night.

She read it through, and was very much impressed with what Rosie had achieved. She might have said then that she knew Simon and that he had come to see her, but it might seem as though she were stealing the other girl's thunder, so she only congratulated her on a fine write-up.

That pleased Rosie, but she tried to make light of it. 'It must be lovely to be born with a silver spoon,' she said wistfully, 'like this Simon Radcliffe. I know it says he's worked his way up the company like anybody else, but how can it be like anybody else if you're the boss's son? Still, he's here, the same as you and I, all of us in Creswal. He was there for a few months before, but I didn't know him then—to speak to, that is. If I meet him in the street, he's bound to recognise me—not that it'll make any difference, of course. He's well in with the Falconer crowd. I'm not, and am never likely to be.'

'Are they so exclusive?' Theresa probed. 'I thought Canada wasn't like Britain, and everybody was the same. Aren't they?'

'The rich are the rich and the poor are the poor.' Rosie's smile was bitter. 'You should hear Eddie on the subject. It's funny, really, because he was born poor and has managed to join the rich. But he never talks down to anyone or seems to make any difference show. The old farmers love him, and even the lumberjacks respect him. I suppose they know that he, too, has worked with his hands.'

Theresa could well understand that, having seen Edouard downstairs with the spanner. There was a kind of strength and reality about the man, and that must be why she thought about him so much. She respected him, because he had no pretensions about him.

'Did you know he was wounded in the war?' Rosie went on. 'He was shot in the back, and was in a wheel-chair, paralysed, for nearly a year.'

Theresa shook her head, unbelieving. 'But he said he worked on field telephones. I thought . . .' She didn't finish what she had thought—that Edouard had somehow cleverly escaped the fighting and the killing. He knew that was what she had thought, and he'd let her go on believing it, and joked about medals being given for targets. How could he?

'He doesn't tell anybody. He hardly ever talks about the war.' Rosie appeared to have no pressing work to do. 'It was written up in the papers, him being a newspaper man, and fighting afterwards for veterans' rights. He might never have been cured, never have had the chance to walk again, let alone work, except for his cousin who owned the *Clarion* then. This man went to see him, and put up the money so that he could go to some American doctors somewhere in the States—I've forgotten the name of the place. Anyway, they did something called neurosurgery, which nobody had heard of before, and Eddie got up and walked, just like the man in the Bible.'

'How wonderful,' Theresa breathed. 'How he must have hated being in a wheelchair—all that energy, and nowhere to direct it!'

'I never thought of it that way,' Rosie said. 'I just thought about him getting up and walking. He said once it was like falling in love—every day was exciting, something to be cherished. But he's full of fancy words —I expect that's the French in him. Funny how everything went right after that. His cousin caught the flu and died, and left him the paper—hard on the cousin, I guess—and his mother did, too, and left him the house. He sold it and spent the money. He called it his inheritance dedicated to making people happy. I suppose his mother must have been a happy sort of person. She took care of him when he was paralysed. He put the money into movie houses. The one in Creswal belongs to him, and so do three or four others in towns on the way to Ottawa. They've made a lot of money. He laughs about that, and says the joke's on him. I don't quite know what he means.'

'Perhaps his mother wasn't quite such a happy person as you imagine,' suggested Theresa, 'but a grim sort of woman.' She remembered suddenly the bleak expression on Edouard's face when he had told her that his mother had intended him for banking.

Rosie shrugged. 'I wish he'd start a dance-hall here. There are only church socials, and it's mostly barn dances there. Jess taught me all sorts of new steps, and we went dancing almost every night when I was in Toronto.'

'Why doesn't he?'

'He says they aren't ready for it yet. They've just got used to the movies.' Rosie sighed. 'I'm ready for my lunch. I suppose I'll have to wait till Eddie gets back, and I don't think that will be much before two. I wish I'd brought something today, but I was sure I could slip home.'

'Why don't we both have something here, like we did yesterday? If you tell me where to go, I'll get it, if you like.'

'What a good idea,' Rosie gave her a big smile. 'I know what the best thing to do would be. If you'll stay and mind the office, I'll go and fetch it.'

'Very well, but let me treat you. Here's a dollar—Will that cover it?'

'I should think so.' Rosie tucked the money into her pocket. 'There's nothing to it, really. Just answer the phone if it rings, and take down the message. The phone on my desk is just an extension Eddie's rigged up. You can't call out on it, but you don't need to.'

Theresa sat down at the desk as Rosie clattered down the stairs to the street. It was strange to be alone in the empty office. She hoped Edouard wouldn't come in, as the minutes ticked by and she waited for Rosie to return. The ringing of the phone startled her considerably.

'*Clarion* office,' she breathed into the mouthpiece.

'Speak up, speak up,' said the caller, a man with a deep voice. 'I can't hear you.'

'*Clarion* office.' Theresa repeated it very loudly.

'Is Monsieur Moreau there?' the man went on. 'I've got the information he wanted.'

Reluctantly, it seemed to Theresa, he agreed to give it to her if she promised to write it down and deliver the message.

'Of course I will.'

'It's Montreal calling, Henri Deslauriers—got that? I've found the marriage certificate he was after in the name of Russell—Charles John Russell and Violetta Ortenzi married in the Parish of St Raymond on June 9th, 1911.'

Theresa gasped. Her father had married!

The caller enquired if she was all right, and offered to spell the names. She let him do so.

'There was a baby the following May, on the 19th —Antony Dominic Russell. But there were no more entries after that. Only a death certificate for Violetta Russell, in 1916; she died in childbirth, and the little one died, too.' The voice came to an abrupt halt.

'Too many women die in childbirth,' Theresa exclaimed. Whatever happiness her father had had with Violetta had been short lived. Antony was without a mother as well as a father. Poor little lad! Theresa couldn't help thinking about him as she sat there, the pencil still in her hand, staring down at the words long after the Montreal man had stopped talking.

Rosie's return awakened her from her thoughts. 'I've got hot dogs and french fries and coffee and peanut butter cookies.' She spread the feast on the desk. 'Any messages, then?'

Theresa held the slip of paper out to her.

'That's splendid. Eddie was right. That's the first step. You know he's your brother? Half-brother, I suppose. Come on, eat up before it all goes cold. I bet you've never had a hot dog before. It's got relish and mustard on it. I hope you like both.'

Theresa bit into her hot dog. She found, though it was strange, that she liked it. Perhaps it might be the same with this little brother of hers. She might like him—if she knew him.

She helped herself to french fries, and decided they were just like chips—only thinner.

'It's beginning to happen.' Rosie spoke through a mouthful of hot dog. 'Isn't it exciting?'

'Yes!' Theresa nodded enthusiastically, but she wasn't quite sure what was beginning to happen, and whether she wanted it to happen. It was too late now to turn back.

CHAPTER FIVE

When Theresa returned to the boarding-house that afternoon she made arrangements for hot water for a bath. She put all thoughts of Tony and her missing father out of her head. She'd always found that when you had problems, it was better to forget them for a while—if you could . . .

The bath was enormous, and stood on four claw feet well away from the walls of the bathroom on all four sides. It was white, but there were yellowish scald-marks near the tap end. She filled it, undressed, and lay back in complete enjoyment. She had time, as the others were all out at work. She washed her hair, too.

When she went back to her room, she chose to put on her green and white gingham with its large white collar; it was the coolest frock she had. Now she could relax, sitting on the veranda in the warm sunshine, and dry her hair and maybe write a letter to the twins.

The warmth of the sun made the soft shorter hair round her face spring into immediate curls, but the thick back hair had to be lifted and divided so that it, too, could dry. As she brushed it, Theresa wondered what it would be like to have short hair like a man's. If she had it cut, it would be so much easier to manage than waist length. She tried the effect of a fringe, such as Rosie had been considering, and decided it wouldn't do for her. She'd just have a short bob—it would curl anyway, and never have to be held in place. It wouldn't tumble about her ears when she took off her hat. She'd be able to run her fingers through it.

She propped a tiny mirror against the screen window and tried to bring some sort of order to her unruly tresses. It just didn't want to lie straight and neat. Finally she decided to let it fall into its natural waves, and tied it in a loose bunch at the back with a piece of green ribbon. It made her look sixteen instead of twenty-two, but it would have to do for now. Tomorrow she would pin it up.

The letter-writing came easily, so that she finished a letter to Felicity and Melody, and was reasonably well pleased with her efforts.

The evening meal was steak and kidney pie, followed by stewed plums with thick cream. Conversation at the table was no more enlivening than it had been on the previous evenings, and afterwards Theresa retreated again to the veranda. She was beginning to think of this stretch of porch as her own. The others didn't appear to use it, and she thought wistfully that she would welcome some company.

For the first time since her interview of the morning she allowed herself to think of what the bank manager had said, and to wonder about her small half-brother. What would he be now? Ten? How lonely and alone he must have felt when his father had disappeared. Her own loneliness in this strange place paled by comparison to his.

She might have been sitting there for thirty or forty minutes before she realised that someone was standing on the other side of the screen door to the outside. Because it was facing into the sun, she couldn't distinguish who it was, but could see a long shadow. It must be a man. Startled, she jumped up.

'The very person I'm after!' It was Edouard's voice as he opened the door. 'I've come to take you to the fair.'

'What fair?' stammered Theresa. 'I didn't know there was a fair.' She was surprised that he made no mention of the phone call from Montreal.

'It comes every year at this time,' Edouard smiled at her. 'Tonight is opening night. Wagons have been coming into town all afternoon. I don't suppose they even mentioned it to you in this mausoleum. They're past the excitement of merry-go-rounds here.'

Theresa was forced to smile at that.'

'I know you're still young enough to relish mingling with your fellow men,' he went on.

Theresa's hand flew to her head as she nodded. 'I'll have to go and tidy up and put up my hair,' she began.

He seized her hand. 'Don't touch it. It suits you that way. I only take young pretty girls to fairs.'

She coloured up in pleasure at the implied compliment. 'I'll just get a key, and tell them I'm going out.'

'A key? A key to what?' Edouard asked.

'To the door.' Her hand was still tingling where he had held it.

'No one locks doors here, and I had a word with your landlady. Mrs Brown knows you'll be with me. Just come as you are.' He wouldn't let her fetch her hat or her gloves, but took hold of her arm and led her down the path. 'Have you never wanted to be whisked away, to leave without looking back?'

Theresa giggled, and said she'd always dreamed of it. 'Are we going far?'

'Far or near, what does it matter? The paper has been put to bed for the day; the magic motor car awaits us.' He opened the gate and helped her up into the waiting auto.

As he cranked the engine into life and leaped into the driver's seat, she was filled with pleasure. It was splendid to be carried off to the fair, to be taken out of herself and her sad imaginings. Forgotten were Simon's words of warning about the man beside her. What did she care if there were other women in his life? She was the one he'd called for tonight.

Down the main street they went at a good pace and then along a long winding road that led to the river. There they had to go more slowly, because there were horses and carts, horses and open carriages which Edouard called buggies, even people on foot, all hurrying. He waved to several of the family parties, and they called greetings to him. Theresa knew they must be greetings, but she couldn't hear them above the noise of the car. In any case, she smiled.

The fairground was an open field beyond the boundary of the town, and in the slanting rays of the late evening sun the whole site was golden. They left the car to one side of the stationary buggies, and Theresa jumped down onto the rough grass.

Edouard took her hand. 'I don't mean to lose you, so stay close.'

She was quite happy to follow that order. All she wanted was to stay close to this man. Any girl would stay close, she told herself, when there were so many people about. Children were tugging at parents, begging them to go faster, pointing out the prizes to be won, the rides to be enjoyed. Edouard stopped at the hoop-la stall and took three hoops for her and three for himself. He won a ferocious-looking little china dog and presented it to her as a consolation for not winning when she tried.

At shove-ha'penny, which was of course played with Canadian coins, Theresa won ten cents and was inordinately pleased. She darted away to buy some popcorn, and when she gave it to Edouard, he was surprised, saying that girls never gave him presents. She could see he was pleased as he shared it with her. She had never tried any before. So they went all around the field, stopping at stalls where their interest was caught, watching the men showing their strength by hitting the hammer, or shying at crockery. Sometimes they tried their skill, sometimes they didn't. But they laughed a good deal, and Edouard kept her hand in his in a very light, easy possession. Theresa felt happy and delighted with life.

On the merry-go-round, they rode high horses side by side, and she was glad to sit after all the walking. Refusing to ride side-saddle, she swung her leg over to straddle the horse, as she had done when she was a child. Edouard laughed at that, and said he was glad she was no lady. When he caught the ring that entitled him to a second free ride, he gave it to a grubby-faced little lad whose dark eyes shone with sudden delight.

It was then, as the merry-go-round slowed, that

Theresa looked out at the crowd around and found
Simon Radcliffe's eyes upon her. They were surprised
and unfriendly as she swung her leg over with a whish of
petticoat. There was a girl beside him—blonde, very tall
and very beautiful in a cream linen dress trimmed with
navy, a dress for afternoon tea, not a fair. Mid-calf
length, and with a string of large navy beads setting off
the long bodice, it set its wearer apart from the other
girls who wore cotton or gingham. This could only be
Sidney Falconer, and she was holding on to Simon's
arm.

'Seen a ghost?' asked Edouard, as the platform came
to a halt and Theresa was thrown against him.

'Just someone I know,' she mumbled.

'Do you know anyone here?' His arms were round
her, steadying her.

Theresa nodded, and he followed the direction of her
eyes. 'Simon Radcliffe and Sidney Falconer! How do
you know them?'

'I met Simon on the ship coming over. I don't know
the girl at all.'

'We'll soon remedy that.' Edouard helped her from
the steps, as the machine started up again. He strode
after the other couple, pulling the now reluctant Theresa
along with him.

Simon acknowledged Edouard stiffly; Sidney smiled
at him warmly, and then swung her gaze on Theresa as
the introductions were made.

'Theresa Russell from England,' she repeated. 'Are
you staying long?'

When she replied that she wasn't sure, Sidney
appeared to lose what little interest she had had. She
linked her arms through Simon's and Edouard's and
exclaimed, 'Take me to the shooting-gallery. I feel lucky
tonight! I'm going to win something.'

For a moment Theresa was left standing alone, with
only the little china dog for company. Her hand closed
about it in her pocket as Edouard disentangled himself
and brought her along with him behind the others.

Sidney was already sighting along a rifle towards the target, a line of moving tin ducks. She hit six of them out of ten, and then handed the weapon to Edouard. He hit seven, and would have given the gun to Theresa, but she shook her head, saying that she couldn't shoot. Simon took it from him and scored five.

The stall was lined with all sorts of prizes—small boxes of sweets and chocolates, large sticks of peppermint rock, a row of small celluloid dolls in the same green and white gingham that Theresa wore, necklaces of all sorts, tumblers, penknives, stuffed animals and, sitting on its own on a little shelf in the place of honour, an enormous black kewpie doll with a knowing expression on her painted face and wearing only a grass skirt and a string of amber beads. Theresa thought it even uglier than her little china dog, but she could see that Sidney was eyeing this trophy.

The three contestants fired another round and another, and Sidney and Edouard both hit ten of the running ducks, but Simon only seven. The stall-owner wanted them to have prizes from the row of chocolates or sweets. He even held out one of the small dolls to Sidney, but she scorned that. 'I've never liked green and white gingham,' she declared.

Theresa could have hit her for that!

'It's the big black doll or nothing,' Sidney stated. 'What do I have to score for that?'

The man took out a marked target-board. 'Just hit the centre of this so that the bell rings,' he told her. 'Three shots for twenty-five cents.' He hung up the target in the back of his booth.

'That's robbery!' exclaimed Simon. 'It's only ten cents for a row of ducks.'

'Does the bell really work?' growled Edouard.

'Of course it works, if you hit it right.' The man put his hand to the target, and the bell rang to prove his words. 'What do you say, Ladies and Gents. Are you going to pit your skill against the gong? Any one of you could win—any two of you, if you like.' He addressed Simon now, and pointed to Theresa. 'Show your girl how to shoot. You hold the gun, she presses the trigger. She'll bring you luck.'

At that, Sidney snatched up the rifle and fired three shots as Edouard and Simon paid up. By now a crowd had gathered and they applauded her; but there was no sound of the bell although the three shots had seemed to centre. Edouard was next, and the same thing happened.

Simon then took up the weapon and looked at Theresa. 'I'll show you,' he offered. 'Stand here in front of me, Theresa, and hold the gun.'

She picked it up, and held it to her shoulder as the others had done. Simon's arms came round her. 'Sight along there.' His voice was a whisper stirring the air above her ear. 'Now press the trigger.' He guided her hand.

Theresa pressed—once, twice—and the third time the bullet rang the bell. Someone in the crowd cheered. Simon laughed in triumph and kissed Theresa's cheek. The stall-keeper reached up for the kewpie doll and handed it to Simon.

Sidney's hand reached out to take it from him, but he handed it to Theresa. 'You won it!' he exclaimed. 'You brought me luck.'

As she clutched the doll in her arms, Theresa saw the look of hatred in Sidney's eyes, and glanced at Edouard. He was watching her closely, but she couldn't even guess at what his feelings were.

Sidney broke the scene. She examined the doll. 'Now that I'm close to it, I can see it's hideous, and cheap as well. I don't know why anyone would want it.' Her mocking glance encompassed Theresa as well as the celluloid toy, and she turned to Simon. 'Take me home, Si. I've had enough of fairs.' She twirled her navy beads and waved to Edouard. Then she walked off through the crowd so that Simon had to follow her.

Theresa's hand had clenched on the doll's legs at Sidney's words. Now Edouard loosened her grip. 'No need to hold your prize so firmly; you'll only dent her leg.'

Biting her lip, she looked at the doll. Already the celluloid leg had curved in slightly. She thrust it at Edouard. 'I don't want it.'

'She's upset you,' he said. 'Don't let her. You should feel flattered. She recognises you as a rival.' He took her by his free hand and led her away from the staring crowd.

'A rival?'

'A rival,' Edouard repeated firmly. 'You took her young man from her.'

'Is he her young man?' The words came from Theresa's dry lips involunatrily.

'I think she means to have him,' was the instant response.

Theresa shivered slightly. It wasn't that she was cold, although it was cooler now with the setting sun colouring the sky deep red and purple and grey. A few naked electric bulbs had come on along the path where they walked.

'You're cold; it will soon be dark,' Edouard observed. 'I think perhaps we've had enough of fairs, too. I'll race you to the car.'

Once in the automobile, he put the doll on the back seat and reached under it for a blanket. 'Wrap this round you. You'll need it.' He started the engine and they drove back on the same road they had come. But instead of steering towards the town, he turned along the river.

'That's the wrong way!' exclaimed Theresa, burrowing in her blanket in the sharp breeze of dusk.

'Don't worry. We'll watch the stars come out, and find ourselves at peace with the world again.'

She might have demurred at the idea of watching the stars alone with Edouard, but the thought of her peace being restored was appealing. She had been upset by the encounter with Sidney, and was unsure of her feelings for Simon. Edouard seemed to understand a great deal.

Within a few minutes the road was very bumpy, and

the car halted almost of its own accord. The river lay before them, and a thin sickle of moon lay half in the sky and half reflected in the water. It was very still and quiet.

'You'll see fish jumping. You might even hear the thump of a beaver. I know there's a fine old granddaddy building a dam along here.' Edouard made no move to leave the car, or to touch her.

Theresa put her head back against the seat, and heard the soft plop of the river and the hoot of an owl from the trees behind them. After a little, the first faint stars appeared in the sky.

Then she stirred. 'I didn't like some of the things the bank manager said this morning.' Sitting up a little straighter, she loosened the blanket.

'What things?' Edouard prompted gently.

'He said that my father had twice followed the same sort of pattern. He had left my mother and me, and then when he disappeared from here, he left Antony. He meant he lacked responsibility—though he didn't come right out and say it, like you would have.'

'Um-m,' he grunted, more to show he was listening, Theresa felt, than to express an opinion.

'Do you think he's right?'

Edouard grunted again.

'I kept feeling he was holding something back.' She might have been talking to herself, sighing in this silvery landscape. 'He could have said more. Why have I the best claim to the money? Why not his son?'

'Think about it,' suggested Edouard. 'A man, even though he's declared legally dead, is still legally married. Charles Russell couldn't have been married to Tony's mother while your mother was alive. What does that make Tony?'

Theresa drew in her breath. Was this true?

'His bastard son,' Edouard supplied. 'And your half-sisters?'

The question hung between them, as she began to understand all its implications.

'But that makes him a bigamist, and my mother as

well,' she finished on a whisper. 'My mother was married to my stepfather. They didn't know Charles was still alive.'

'Didn't they? The clipping was six years old. One of them—perhaps both of them—must have known. When did your mother die, Theresa?'

'Four years ago,' she sighed. 'But she wouldn't have . . . couldn't have . . . No, I can't believe it.'

'You don't want to believe it,' he pointed out. 'Remember, I warned you, you were going to find out things you might rather not know.'

'Yes,' Theresa agreed. 'But my mother was sweet and good, not shocking. She wasn't that sort of woman.' In her agitation she had drawn closer to Edouard, and the blanket had slipped, forgotten, to the floor.

'What do you know about motives, about raw human emotions?' His voice had taken on a new intensity. 'Don't think badly of your mother. She probably genuinely believed your father was dead, and then somewhere along the line she found he wasn't—maybe even before the clipping came.' He paused for breath.

'She would have gone to him.' Theresa spoke with authority, as much to convince herself as Edouard.

'Would she?' he probed deeper. 'What do you suppose marriage is? A game played by strict rules? What would you know of it? A young innocent like you . . .'

She felt something shrivel inside her. Why was he speaking to her like this, in this tone of contempt? She couldn't help being young and inexperienced.

His next words stung her even more. 'Sidney Falconer, for all her faults, knows more than you. She knows by instinct how it is between men and women.'

Theresa was very angry. 'If you think so much of her, why isn't she here with you now? I can learn, can't I? Even if I'm young? Tell me how it is between men and women. I'll try to understand.' There was a break in her voice, the hint of tears in her throat, but she desperately wanted to comprehend.

Edouard groaned and spread his arms as though in

supplication. 'How can I tell you? You have to feel it.'
He stared into her eyes grimly. 'Has a man ever kissed
you, Theresa? Really kissed you, so that you'd do
anything for him and give him anything he wanted?'

She shook her head slowly, unable to look away from
him. She was caught up in what he was saying. No one
had talked to her like this before. She could feel the beat
of her own heart, unsteady, throbbing. When she raised
her hand as though to ward him off, he took hold of it.

His lips were on hers, his arms round her as he slid
from under the wheel and drew her to his lap. Cradled
there, held prisoner there, his body hard and taut, his
mouth fastened on hers, demanding, giving. Her lips
opened to him and she was forced to wild, sweet surrender. Half-protesting, heady excitement threatened to
engulf her, and it was frightening, impossible to resist.
Her body wanted to go on, to acknowledge his mastery.
Her arms stole around his neck and she pressed herself
against him.

Abruptly he released her. 'Thus endeth the first lesson,' he drawled. 'You might develop a taste for it. Most
British girls did during the war, but perhaps there's
something about Canadian men . . .'

There was something so mocking in his tone that
Theresa tried to draw away, and only succeeded in
getting closer. She wasn't sure whether he misinter-
preted her action, because his arms tightened around
her. 'Shall we continue?'

'No,' she exclaimed, though she longed to say Yes, to
beg him to kiss her again. Whatever the cost, she wanted
that hot fire within her to meet the need she felt in him.
He had awakened in her a sensation she hadn't known
before, hadn't even dreamed she was capable of feeling.
She yearned for him to brush her objections aside.

'A British girl capable of saying No!' His arms were
still round her, keeping her prisoner. 'I find it hard to
believe.'

Theresa's body stiffened. She stuck an elbow into his
ribs and won her freedom, sliding along the seat as far

from him as she could in the confined space. 'I don't know why you say that. Are Canadian girls full of refusals?'

Edouard laughed. 'I wouldn't say that—It's relative, after all. Perhaps it's just that British girls are easier.'

'Well, if that's what you think about them—and me'—Theresa's temper was rising—'all I can say is that you've met some peculiar English girls, and I don't want to stay here alone with you. Take me home, please.'

He made no move to start the car, nor did he move back to the driving seat. 'Let's talk for a minute.'

'What about?'

'Life, I suppose. You're the one who wanted to know what it was all about. Now that I've supplied you with a taste of it, you want to turn back. The way you kissed me, I could have sworn you wanted to go on. Are you the kind of girl who loves to tease? To press herself against a man and then draw back?'

'I don't know what you mean.'

'I think perhaps you do.'

Theresa was very conscious of his body beside her. If he touched her again . . . Of course she'd wanted more, wanted it still. Yet there was something about his waiting and his silence that made her think it was important for him to understand how she felt.

'I've never been alone with a man before, like this,' she tried to explain.

'Never?'

'Never. And I never thought men were so demanding . . . or so exciting,' she added honestly. 'I thought marriage was comfortable and quiet, somehow . . .'

Edouard chuckled—there was no other way to describe it—he chuckled. 'Spoilt your rosy view of life, have I? Well, it's time you woke up to reality.'

Theresa bridled at that. 'Everyone doesn't have your way of thinking about life—and love. Your rough way.'

'Who mentioned love?' he asked sharply. 'It was sex you wanted to know about.'

Theresa put her hands over her ears. She wasn't going to listen.

Edouard pulled them away. 'No, you shall listen. Sex is what keeps men and women together, not that wishy-washy thing you call love. Save that for your sisters.'

'But love is important, and it's not the way you think it! You talk about it as though it's nothing—a hot bath . . .'

This time he gave a shout of laughter. 'You have a nice turn of phrase; an original way of putting things! Well, I suppose that's what you'd expect from a girl who tells a man he has a face like a monkey.'

Theresa frowned. She knew she was right about love. There must be something more than sex, or what would keep people together? She asked him that, and risked more merriment.

But he considered it gravely. 'What does keep men and women together? I don't know. Self-interest, perhaps, like minds, bodies that match well. Whatever this love you talk about is, I've never found it—and don't expect to.'

'I pity you,' she exclaimed, 'if you've never loved anyone.'

'What makes you suppose I haven't?' Edouard's eyes flashed in the pale light from the moon. 'I loved my father and my sister, but that's different.'

Theresa noted that he didn't say he'd loved his mother. That was a strange exclusion, but she made no comment on it.

'Besides,' he went on, 'what makes you an expert on love? Only a few moments ago you were asking me to explain how your mother could have known about a husband she had thought dead, and not gone to him. Perhaps she trusted the new one more than the old.'

'Perhaps she did.'

'Perhaps she had reason to,' Edouard added. 'One can only wonder why Charles Russell didn't return to claim her—and you. Why do you suppose that was?'

'I—I don't know.' Her voice trembled. 'I've asked myself that . . .'

'And can't find the answer,' he supplied. 'Perhaps he didn't know about your kind of love, either.'

'You're horrid! You twist everything I say. I don't know why you want me to believe men and women don't love—what do you feel when you kiss a girl? Don't you think about her as someone—special? Someone you like?' Her voice almost broke on that.

For a moment she thought Edouard wouldn't answer, or would laugh again. Instead, he took her hand. 'Present company excepted, of course, since you asked me to show you and I obliged! When I kiss a girl, I feel good. I'd like her to feel the same—and some girls are honest enough to admit their feelings, not cover them up in flowery language.'

Theresa drew in her breath sharply. 'All right,' she exclaimed, 'I liked it when you kissed me. I wanted you to kiss me again. But I don't any more, because you don't even like me.' she disentangled his hand and pushed it away from her.

'What makes you think that?'

'Any girl would do just as well, wouldn't she?' she asked stiffly. 'Next time, kiss some other girl—some Canadian girl, since you seem to think more of them.' Even as she spoke, Theresa knew she didn't want him kissing anyone else, and certainly not a Canadian girl.

'I certainly shall.' Edouard sounded cold and cross. 'I'd prefer one that doesn't analyse the whole performance, but just enjoys it.'

'Good!' But Theresa wondered why his words had wounded her. She'd been a fool, she told herself; a fool to melt in this man's arms, to welcome his kisses. Now she was paying for it. Why had she admitted she'd liked him kissing her? She burned with shame.

Edouard got out and cranked the engine. Theresa bundled the blanket round herself and huddled into the far corner of the seat against the door. The trip back to the boarding-house was accomplished in silence, and she jumped out of the car before he had time to come round to open the door.

'Good night.' She hovered uncertainly on one foot. What did one say to a man one had quarrelled with?

He sprang down beside her, and smiled. '*Au revoir*, young Tess. Some day, when you're a woman ready for life, you may remember tonight with kindness and say to yourself that a real man kissed you and you didn't know how to respond. You were still a child, but he woke you up a little.' He patted her bottom gently. 'Now, off to bed.'

That pat infuriated Theresa. She wasn't a child to be treated like this. 'Good night,' she snapped, and because she had been brought up to be polite, added, 'Thank you for taking me to the fair.'

Edouard laughed out loud at that. 'Always the lady! It's a nice quality. Just a minute.' He put out a hand to stop her flight. 'Don't you want your brown doll, your hula girl?' He half reached towards the back of the car.

'No, I don't. I don't need any reminders of this night.' Theresa almost shouted the words as she flew up the path as though a demon pursued her. He had no right to laugh at her!

'The paper comes out the day after tomorrow,' he called after her. 'Remember to get a copy.'

Her hand in her pocket clenched round the china dog he had given her, and she longed to throw it at him. That would show him how much of a lady she was! No, better to keep it—to remind herself of what he was like, what kind of man he was. She opened the screen door and let herself in without looking back.

Edouard started up the car and drove through the silent streets towards home.

Home? An empty house, a life without a woman waiting for him, without—as Theresa had said—love. He admitted the word to his mind. When had he dispensed with that emotion? In his childhood? When his father died? No, not then, for he could remember the rush of love and gratitude that had nearly overwhelmed him when Ellen his sister had rescued him from his first fight with Tom McGregor. Tom had been kicking him in the back and calling him names, telling him he wasn't wanted here, that he could go back to his papist school.

He would have gone willingly, but his mother wouldn't let him. Now that his father was dead, she was the boss, and she had decided that Edouard would go to the same school as Ellen, speak English, and worship the god of her fathers. Only Ellen had seemed to understand the tug on his loyalties that leaving the school of his father's choice and religion had imposed on him. Being bigger than he, she had helped him to fight his battles at her school. Ellen had grown up, married Tom McGregor, and been carried off by influenza. It hardly seemed fair that he should have survived her.

Edouard told himself that he was free of all family ties. Independent. He had only himself to consider—and his readers, and his plans for the future. When he felt it was time, he could marry. But his mind shied away from that, He was all right as he was. Perhaps what he really longed for was this love Theresa talked about.

Why did she keep intruding herself into his thoughts? She wasn't the sort of girl he'd settle for. She was far too young and naïve for him. Still, she made him laugh—at himself as much as at her. A face like a monkey, indeed! She had somehow crept inside his defences like a favourite child. Imagine it, she had felt she must thank him for taking her to the fair, when she had quarrelled with him. She had a kind of dignity that he liked, and had somehow made him feel guilty about kissing her. The whole scene had got out of hand. He hadn't expected the immediate reaction she'd given him, and it had caught him off balance. Yes, he'd wanted to go on kissing her. He was a man, wasn't he? And she had pressed herself against him.

Moonlight makes fools of us all, he chided himself. Watch it, Hippolyte, he cautioned, you have this streak in your character. You can be carried away by your emotions—the ones Edouard Moreau denies we share.

Edouard will deal with her. Next time she appears, he'll be bland, and pretend it never happened. She won't want to be reminded, any more than he will.

As he parked the car before his house, he began to whistle. He reached into the back and pulled out the black kewpie doll. 'I have the perfect place for this, Hippolyte,' he announced, and walked up the path to the front door.

CHAPTER SIX

ON THURSDAY Theresa did not need to go out to buy the *Clarion*. It was waiting for her at her place at the breakfast table, spread open to page 3 which carried the article about her search for her father. The others let her finish reading before they began questioning her. They were so kind and so interested that she began to wonder why she had ever thought them unfriendly. They had just needed a starting-point, and Edouard's article, so simple and clear and readable, had provided that.

When there was a knock on the dining-room door and the little maid brought in an envelope addressed to Theresa, they all waited expectantly, forks poised half-way to their mouths, for her to open it.

It was from the *Clarion*, and said: 'Come to the office at 9.15. There is someone who wants to talk to you.' Edouard Moreau had signed it. She read it aloud.

'A lead,' said the old gentleman on her right.

'Good luck, my dear!' exclaimed the teachers in unison.

'*Drat!* It's time to get to work,' cried the nurse.

All of them looked at the time, and rose to their feet.

Theresa was too excited to do justice to her breakfast. Even the little maid was stammering as she cleared the table. 'Mrs Brown was sure you'd want to see it right away.'

Theresa had to go to the kitchen to thank the good lady for her thoughtfulness. 'I knew something was up when Mr Moreau took you out last night,' she was told. 'Such a nice man.'

That wasn't the adjective she would have applied to him after her experience of the night before, and she would certainly have preferred not to meet him again so soon, but smiling at Mrs Brown, she agreed with her politely and went to get ready.

It was five past nine when she arrived at the *Clarion* office, unable to keep her impatience in check. Only Rosie was in, and she assured her she didn't mind at all that she was early. Eddie had stepped out for a few minutes. Theresa's eyes were drawn to a shelf near Edouard's desk, as they spoke. On it stood the black kewpie doll she had won last night.

'Like it?' asked Rosie, noticing the direction of her gaze. 'Eddie calls it his trophy. He won't say for what. He says all girls should wear grass skirts.'

'For shooting,' Theresa exclaimed faintly, and wondered why he had kept it and displayed it so prominently. She sat down in Edouard's chair. 'Do you know anything about this person who wants to see me?'

'Only her name; Eddie took the call. She's a Mrs Malinsky. He told me to put both of you in the little office off this one, as she was most insistent that she speak to you on your own. Why don't you wait in there, and I'll show her in when she comes?'

Theresa fell in readily with that suggestion, and very soon Mrs Malinsky arrived, punctual to the minute. She was a small, foreign-looking woman in a raincoat, despite the heat of the day, with dark button eyes and a pale complexion. She introduced herself in a strange accent, half Canadian, half middle-European.

'So, you're the boy's sister.' She looked Theresa up and down as she seated herself. 'Have you seen him?'

Theresa shook her head. 'How could I? I don't know where he is. Do you?'

Mrs Malinsky made a noise between a grunt and a laugh. 'I sent a Christmas card to him last year, and something for his birthday in May. Where were you when he needed you?'

Nonplussed by this direct attack, Theresa explained that she hadn't known of Antony's existence until two days ago.

Somewhat mollified, Mrs Malinsky informed her that

she had been her father's landlady and had taken a great liking to the lad.

'My daughter thought I was foolish when I kept Anton after his father left, but I was sure he'd come back for him. They were very close, you understand.' The woman's dark eyes took on a brooding expression. 'So Milcha was right'—her head went forward in a darting movement—'and I was wrong. He left without a trace. Perhaps he's dead.' She paused, and Theresa felt a stab of pain in her heart.

'Anton grieved for him,' Mrs Malinsky went on. 'It was easier for him to think his father was dead than to believe he would have left him. But I—I know he is alive. No, I have no proof.' She silenced Theresa's interruption almost before it had time to begin, and pointed to her chest. 'I feel it here. Charles Russell is alive. I kept his son till they took him away from me. I know he wouldn't have wanted his son in one of those children's homes—children's prisons.' She sighed deeply. 'I have a mother's heart.'

'I'm sure you did all you could for him.' Theresa was apologetic in the face of such fierceness.

'And more besides,' Mrs Malinsky was quick to tell her. 'If I could have, I would have kept him as my own—I would have him still. But Milcha told the authorities, and they took him from me. They said I wasn't suitable.' She crossed her arms on her breast and rocked herself. 'They took Anton to a children's home, and he cried to come to me, so they let me visit him at first.'

'At first?' Theresa moved her chair closer to Mrs Malinsky. 'Is he in a home near here?'

'Not any more.' The woman raised her arms to the ceiling, as though words weren't enough to express her feelings. 'They moved him to a home in Ottawa. I can't visit there—it's too far. Oh, he's happy enough, they say.'

'Ottawa?' Theresa was puzzled. 'Why should they move him there? Do you have the address?'

'Yes, I have it.' Mrs Malinsky folded her arms. 'I won't give it to you if you only want to upset him and ask him questions and put it in the paper.' She looked hard at the girl, and put out her hand to her. 'Anton would be glad of a sister. He didn't have a mother.'

'Didn't have a mother?' Theresa seized on that.

'Of course, you know nothing—I forget that.' Mrs Malinsky's hand was still grasping Theresa's. 'The mother died when he was a baby—the flu epidemic, I think.' She shrugged. 'What does it matter where or how? Why should he tell his landlady about his past?' She turned Theresa's hand over in her own and traced the lifeline. 'You've come from the other side of the world, as I did. No, don't say to yourself I saw that in the paper.' Her eyes were sharp. 'I see it here. You'll stay and you'll help Anton. I haven't read that anywhere but in your hand. I'll tell you where he is.' She dropped the hand and pulled a scrap of paper out of her pocket and thrust it at her. 'Milcha wrote it out for me. I think she's always been a little sorry about the boy, especially now that she has two of her own.'

Theresa took it and scanned it. 'Is Ottawa far?'

'One hundred, two hundred miles.' The woman was vague. 'No matter to one as young as you. You can take the train. You'll find a way.' It was a statement, not a question.

The astonished Theresa felt as though a storm had buffeted her, despite Mrs Malinsky being only a small woman. She marvelled that she had thought her insignificant on first sight. 'Will I find my father? Does my hand tell you that?'

'If he can be found, you'll find him,' she quickly answered. 'It is Anton who needs you, not his father. Besides, she may not want to let him go.'

'Who may not?' Theresa questioned sharply.

'How should I know?' was the only reply she received, as Mrs Malinsky rose to go. 'He is a man who attracts women. I've told you all I can. See Anton.'

She would add nothing to that, and would not even

give Theresa her address. Neither had she anything to say to Rosie, but only left both girls staring at her retreating back.

'What a queer old soul,' the girl exclaimed. 'I was listening—I couldn't help it—the wall is very thin. I heard everything she said. Are you going to see the boy?'

'I don't know,' Theresa shivered suddenly. 'She was sure I would. What would I say to him? I came to find my father.'

'If you do go to the boy,' Rosie pointed out, 'Eddie will want pictures and an interview.'

Pictures, an interview—with a boy she didn't know. It was too much for Theresa. If Eddie had been there, she would have told him so, particularly after what Mrs Malinsky had said about upsetting Antony.

'You don't have to do anything now.' Rosie gave her a quick pat on the arm. 'I tell you what, think about it. I'm going out on a story, a women's club meeting. Come with me, and forget about it for a while. You'll want to talk to Eddie.'

Theresa felt the last thing she wanted to do was talk to Edouard, but she was pleased to go with Rosie. The meeting was a much larger one than she had expected, and was held in the local hotel. When they arrived, coffee was being served, and a cup was pressed on each of them.

Rosie began to circulate among the ladies present and talked to some of them. Since they all wore labels with their names and official duty, interviewing was made easy.

'What is the other name on the badges they're wearing?' Theresa whispered to her guide.

'The village or the town they come from. It's a meeting of the women of the whole district of the Daughters of the United Empire Loyalists. They hold a summer project to raise money for charity.'

Theresa had no idea who the United Empire Loyalists were, but followed in Rosie's wake and was introduced to several of them. When Rosie went to organise a group for a picture, one of these ladies plucked her sleeve and enquired, 'Are you the girl who's looking for her father?'

When she said that she was, she was surrounded by a little crowd of them, all eager to hear about her search. They asked if she had had any results from the write-up, and she found herself telling them about Antony and the home in Ottawa.

'I envy you,' cried a lady whose badge proclaimed she was a Mrs Appledore. 'My brother and I were left orphans when I was six and he was three. We were separated, and I've never seen him since. I miss him still after all these years.' There was a hint of tears in her faded blue eyes. 'I always feel I failed him.'

'Did you every try to find him?' Theresa asked gently.

'Yes, I did, but I could never find out anything more than that the family who had taken him had moved out west. I didn't even know their name.'

She was very moved by this story, so moved that she didn't at first take it in when Mrs Appledore asked her if she'd like to say a few words to all the ladies. It was only when she added that she would be pleased to introduce her to the whole gathering that the girl realised what she meant. She was petrified at the very idea, and said No, she couldn't. But the Loyalist lady was quick to assure her that she would help, and memories might well be jogged. As soon as she saw that Theresa was wavering, Mrs Appledore lost no time. She led her to the front of the room and demanded quiet. Then she made it very easy, because she began to ask questions. So pleasant and so helpful was she that Theresa forgot the sea of faces before her and just talked to her interviewer. The ladies clapped and thanked her when it was over, and promised to do anything they could to help.

'That was splendid,' Rosie said. 'They liked you, and you may be surprised by the results. When they go back to their towns and villages they'll talk about you, and about Charles Russell and the boy Antony. Ask the women, if you want something done around here, is what I always say.'

Theresa laughed. 'Is that why you brought me along to the meeting?'

Rosie laughed, too. 'Don't tell Eddie, but I think the personal approach is worth a column of print. Are you coming back to tell him all about your morning?'

Theresa still was not sure that she wanted to see Edouard, but there was no resisting Rosie. How could she face him?

When they arrived at the *Clarion* office, he was on the phone, and waved to them both and motioned Theresa to a seat near his desk. 'I'll let you know, Sal,' he promised, as he hung up.

'Can you drive a car?' He shot the question at Theresa.

She shook her head and began to breathe more easily. He wasn't going to say anything about the other night.

'Ride a horse?'

'Yes,' she admitted in some astonishment.

'Ever driven a horse and cart?' he kept on.

'Sometimes my father let me take the reins when we were in the trap.'

'Not afraid of horses, then?' Edouard's eyes were sharp. 'Ever done any books or accounts?'

'I always kept the household accounts, and I write a neat hand.' She didn't know where this was leading.

'Um-m. You might do,' he commented.

'Do for what?'

'To make a start in the world of business.'

'The world of business?' Theresa repeated after him. 'Ride a horse? It sounds like a travelling salesman.'

Edouard grinned at her. 'Not far wrong.' He changed the subject. 'Did Mrs Malinsky have anything interesting to tell you?'

'She gave me Antony's address at a children's home in Ottawa, but she didn't know anything about my father,' Theresa replied.

'And what do you mean to do about it?'

'I shall go and see him, I suppose.'

'You don't sound very sure.' Edouard pushed his chair back from the desk.

'No.' She hesitated. 'Mrs Malinsky made me think. Will it do Antony any good to find he had a sister he didn't know about, if he's in Ottawa and I'm here?'

'Cold feet?' Edouard asked, her going to the heart of the problem. 'Or are you thinking of doing something for the lad?'

'A bit of both.'

'Want to talk about it?' His tone was kind.

'I don't have anything to offer him—no home, no income, no news of his father.' She twisted her hands in her lap. 'He might not even like me, or I him.'

'You don't have to decide today.' He picked up a pencil from his desk and put it behind his ear as he spoke. 'The pictures would look nice in the paper, though.'

She looked at him enquiringly. 'The pictures?'

'Long-lost sister and brother meet,' he suggested, putting his hand up and miming a camera shot.

Theresa couldn't help smiling. 'Yes, the Daughters of the United Empire Loyalists would love it. Where did they get that name?' She was diverted, in spite of herself.

'That's not the proper tone of reverence,' he admonished her. 'You're striking at the roots of Canadian history. The United Empire Loyalists were the loyal British who refused to join the Boston Tea Party. They left the American States to their own devices, and came to Canada. They gave up a great deal—their homes, their money, in some cases their family—but the rest of us have never been allowed to forget it,' he finished drily.

Rosie sniffed. 'There speaks a French-Canadian!'

'Mostly they settled in Ontario, and their women clung together, hence the Daughters of the United Empire Loyalists.' Edouard wasn't put out by the observation.

'They do a lot of good,' Rosie declared.

'Of course they do.' He smiled at her. 'I'm always surprised by the extent of their good works—and by their absolute insistence on pure membership.'

'Pure membership?' Theresa looked from one to the other.

'There is a lady here in town,' he explained, 'who would dearly like to be one of them, but is disbarred from membership because her ancestors were Scandinavian.'

'I think it's funny.' Rosie hid a grin. 'It's the only organisation in Creswal that she can't join—and run.'

He looked at Theresa. 'You see, wherever you live, there are currents and cross-currents.'

'Norwegian,' Theresa thought to herself. She knew that the Falconers were originally Norwegian. She remembered being told that. So it must be Marguerite Falconer they were talking about. She didn't say anything, but she felt it was strange that such a wealthy woman would be excluded from any club.

'Why don't you write to the children's home and ask if your brother's still there?' asked Edouard.

Theresa was only a little surprised when she realised that he had returned to the previous subject.

'You don't actually know he's in that home,' he went on. 'He might have been moved again. They will have records.'

'That's just putting off any decision.'

'Isn't that what you want, now?' he questioned. 'Time for the newspaper to circulate, for people to talk and perhaps remember? Time for you to get used to the idea of a brother?'

She felt a lightening of her spirit. It was true that she wasn't ready to make any decision about this lad she didn't know. Edouard had skirted round several topics, and made her realise that. He had made her realise something else, too.

'If I could get a job,' she began. 'You were sounding me out before, weren't you? I'm sure Creswal is the right place to be. Tell me what you had in mind when you asked those questions. I had a good look through your paper, and there didn't seem to be anything I might do.'

'I was talking to Sal when you came in.' He took the pencil from behind his ear. 'She runs O'Reilly's Realty, lets flats and houses, sells property, I think you might suit her.'

'Sal's kind of hard on staff,' protested Rosie.

Edouard waved aside this interruption. 'She's been unlucky.'

'Unlucky, or hard to get along with?' Rosie refused to be silenced.

'Theresa's tougher than she looks.' This opinion came out easily, as the two girls looked at each other. 'Sal wants someone who can soothe the customers, set things right, avoid double bookings . . .'

'Someone who can do everything,' Rosie supplied smoothly. 'And drive that big brute of a car as well.'

'I can't!' Theresa exclaimed.

'Of course you can,' he assured her. 'I'll teach you to drive, and the whole thing will fall into place.'

'Will you?' asked an astonished Theresa. 'There's no reason why you should help me.'

'I'm a philanthropist!' he announced. 'Let's just say that I've taken a liking to you. Besides, I like to attempt the impossible.'

Perhaps that should have made her angry, but it amused her instead. She laughed out loud, which made Rosie shrug her shoulders and tell her she must be mad.

'Sal's always taken on a young man,' Edouard said. 'Young men drive too fast, and they don't like being bossed by a woman. But you're a sensible girl, Theresa. You won't mind that. Now then, when shall we have the first driving-lesson?'

Theresa, bemused, agreed to that very evening, and left the office, thanking both its occupants for their kindness. She had promised herself she wouldn't be alone with Edouard in his car again, and here she was, planning to do just that, and being grateful for his interest.

*   *   *

Edouard called for her after supper, and he had driven out of town before he declared that it was her turn. She was nervous about taking the wheel, but she did so.

'Take a firm grip,' he instructed. 'You're not pouring tea.'

Theresa clutched the wheel so tightly that he loosened her hands slightly.

'Right. It's in gear, so just release the brake slowly and step on the gas gently.' His voice was low and easy.

She did as he directed, and the car rolled slowly forward. This was exhilarating! She turned a smiling face towards him.

'Keep your eyes on the road,' he commanded.

She obeyed. 'What do I do to go faster?'

'You don't,' was the crisp reply. 'You're wavering over the road as it is. Keep in a straight line.' He put his hand on hers on the wheel to show her.

'But there's no one else in sight,' she protested, negotiating a bend at five miles an hour. Edouard kept his hand on hers, and she found its presence unsettling. When he removed it, she breathed more easily. A rabbit ran across the road, and she took her hands from the wheel.

Edouard pulled on the hand-brake and the car came to an abrupt halt, half-way across the road. 'Never do that,' he said sternly. 'You're the driver. You can't give up.'

'I'm sorry!' she exclaimed. 'I didn't know what to do.'

'Now you do. Try again.'

For forty minutes, Theresa tried over and over again. She began to master the art of steering, and then was made to use the clutch to get into gear.

'Remember,' instructed Edouard. 'You must press the clutch twice to change gear, and as smoothly as you can. You don't want the car leaping forward or stalling.'

'I'll never master it!' she exclaimed, despairing, after several attempts.

'Of course you will.' He allowed her to rest for a

moment. 'I'm going to make a passable driver of you by Monday.'

'Why are you doing this for me?' she asked mutinously. 'There must be jobs other than this one. Are you just showing me how stupid I am?'

'You're not stupid at all. If there were other jobs, I wouldn't waste my time on you. I thought you were different from most women—and not lazy about learning. It comes from always having a man to do things for you. Now that you have a chance to make your own way, to get a job, are you going to take it or not? If you are, put a little stiffening in your spine and get on with it.'

She bit her lip. She had felt like breaking down and crying when he began, but now she wouldn't admit defeat. His words had stung her.

'Very well,' she vowed to herself. 'I'll show you.' She shot him a look of loathing. 'If you can do it, I can,' she said, and put the car in gear. A minute later she drove over a small boulder in the road. They wavered wildly once again, and his hand reached out to steady hers.

'Keep it to yourself,' she commanded. 'I'm the driver here.'

Edouard pulled back his hand. 'Then watch out for hazards!'

After this, he lapsed into silence, and things proceeded more smoothly. She began to feel she might master driving after all. But there was more to learn. When she stopped the next time, to show she had control of the brakes, he told her that if she wanted to be truly in command of the car, she must crank the engine into life.

'Now?' she sighed.

'Now.' They both got out of the car.

'The most important thing is holding the crank properly. You don't want a broken wrist or a broken hand, and you may very well need to start the car on your own. There may not be a man in sight.'

Theresa almost stuck her tongue out at him at this quip, but gave him a look of what she hoped was haughty dignity instead.

'If you're going to bend a man to your will,' he advised her, 'and prevail upon him to crank for you, I suggest you practise a weaker, more appealing, expression than the one you're wearing now. Try it before a mirror, but you can spare me from it!'

She would have liked to hit him. Why did he always laugh at her and keep his temper, while she lost hers?

'I'll stand behind you and guide your hand.' He suited his actions to his words, and she found his body hard against hers, his arm on hers, his hand holding her thumb firmly to one side of her hand so that she couldn't grip the handle as she wanted.

'That's the knack of it.' He kept firm hold of her thumb. 'I know it feels unnatural, but it will save you injury.'

Theresa only nodded. She couldn't look at him because they were pressed so close. A memory of his kiss of last night swept into her mind, and she wanted to wriggle free. She didn't like the effect he had on her. She didn't want him so close.

'Stay still! Surely I don't frighten you?' His voice made the hair around her right ear flutter as wildly as her heart was pounding.

'Yes—No,' she stammered, scarcely knowing what she meant. 'What if someone came along?'

Edouard laughed. 'Here? The road is empty, as you pointed out before.'

Theresa felt the rumble of that laugh along her spine. It heightened the tension between them, and she moved in his grasp and twisted her head round so that she spoke to him over her shoulder. 'Please, shall we try the crank?'

'We'll do it together.' He guided the handle with her towards its hole. 'That's right, pull down, keep that thumb still. Now up sharply—that's where you feel the pull.'

The engine sparked into life, and Edouard looked at his watch. 'An hour and a half. Have you had enough for today?'

When she admitted that she had, he climbed into the driving seat and they went back to town. She found she was tired, more tired than she would have thought possible, but she watched all his actions very carefully —his hands on the wheel, his easy confidence in changing gears—and she promised herself she'd soon be doing the same.

'Same time tomorrow?' he enquired, as he bid her goodbye at the boarding-house.

'Same time tomorrow,' she agreed. She felt she should thank him; she wanted to thank him, but the words stuck in her throat and he had gone before she could utter them. He had teased her and goaded her into learning, and she couldn't be grateful for that. What kind of a man was he? One minute she hated him, the next she liked him.

She went into the house, her legs unsteady. She was hot and dusty and exhausted. On the hall table was an envelope addressed to her, and she looked at it without much interest. Who could be writing to her? It must have been delivered by hand.

She ripped it open and pulled out a note. As she did so a card fell out and she bent to pick it up. 'Miss Marguerite Falconer' was printed on it in gold. Then she unfolded the note. It said simply in upright script: 'I shall be pleased to see you on Saturday evening. The car will call for you at 7.15.' There was no signature. It sounded more of a command than an invitation, but Theresa knew that she would be ready and waiting two days hence at 7.15.

All thoughts of Edouard Moreau and his strange effect on her were swept from Theresa's head.

It was always the same nightmare. The agony in his back had returned. Edouard groaned, and tried to move.

A doctor, smock covered in blood, was bending over him, giving him an injection, mouthing the words, 'It's Blighty for you.'

Then there was confusion and movement and endless

journeying by stretcher, and train and boat and train again. More doctors were leaning over him, and more injections, and soothing voices trying to explain the unexplainable.

'Oh yes, we can ease the pain, but you'll never regain movement in your legs.'

Doomed to lie like this for ever, a silent scream rising from deep inside—all part of the nightmare.

The comforting voices went on. 'In time, you'll probably be able to manage a wheelchair.'

A wheelchair—God, he'd rather be dead! Why hadn't they killed him in this bloody war?

He tried to turn his face to the wall, but they wouldn't let him. They all used that quiet tone. The nurses joined it to a simpering smile. 'Some chicken to tempt you. A little custard?' As though food would give him back the will to live.

'You're at Cliveden,' they told him. 'Lady Astor's hospital. You don't know how lucky you are.'

They brought Lady Astor to him. 'Lady Bountiful' he called her to himself in derision.

'I suppose it's because you're a Canadian, and a French one at that, that you've lost the will to live. They always were a weak sort of people. No stamina, no strength to fight or win.'

She always said the same thing, the words that hurt. He always looked back with hatred. There was no pity in her eyes, only contempt. Who was she to despise him and all his race?

Edouard woke, cold sweat on his brow. It was only a dream, after all.

No, not a dream. Reliving the past. He sat up, feeling his legs and arms. He could move. He was whole again, nursed back to health. But it wasn't the English doctors who had cured him, or the Canadian ones in the veterans' hospitals, or even his mother's careful nursing. Two American doctors and his cousin's money had effected the cure. Jim Shaw had rescued him and brought him north to work on the *Clarion*.

'Jim Shaw.' He said the name aloud. The cousin he hadn't known existed. What a grand man he'd been: it was his bed he slept in, his house he lived in, his paper he had inherited. Dead men's shoes were tight sometimes, but comfortable for all that.

Still, perhaps now was the time to strike out on his own, to find the future which he was sure awaited him in bigger fields. He mustn't let himself get bogged down in parochial stories of missing fathers. Out there, bigger issues were waiting: roads and schools and hospitals to build—people to be wakened to prosperity.

It was time to get up and face them. Life was full—and busy. He had the use of his legs. A man couldn't ask for more.

CHAPTER SEVEN

THE NEXT morning, Theresa decided she must buy some new stocking and perhaps some beads to wear with the frock she had decided on for Saturday night. Also one of the teachers had given her directions for the library, and she wanted a book on cars, and a novel. Shopping should come first. It was at the haberdashery counter at the largest store in town that she saw Sidney Falconer. Theresa was more than a little surprised when she turned and smiled at her.

Sidney was in pink and white dimity, with a white sash and neat white strap shoes. She looked young and fresh and pretty, and the colour lent softness to her face. 'Shopping is such a bore!' she exclaimed, after ordering several yards of écru lace and some pearl buttons. 'I'm always glad when I finish.'

She didn't ask Theresa's opinion on shopping, or even whether she had completed hers, but suggested that they have coffee and cakes in Delarue's across the road. Theresa agreed, wondering at the other's seeming friendliness after the set-downs of the shooting-match.

Once inside Delarue's, Sidney led the way to a table in the window and a waitress appeared immediately. It was only a small place, but very clean and comfortable with white wood tables and chairs, chintz curtains and cushions. So early in the morning, there were only two other shoppers at the far end of the room.

'They do the most divine gâteaux,' Sidney declared. 'We'll have a plate, so that we can help ourselves.'

The cakes soon arrived, with the hot, steaming coffee. Theresa was beginning to enjoy the experience, since it was the nearest she had come to feminine companionship in the town. It reminded her of shopping with the twins at home. Sidney chose a strawberry confection with whipped cream piled on top and Theresa contented herself with a piece of delicious-looking chocolate cake.

'You're searching for your father.' Sidney had polished off the strawberries and the cream and was now wiping their last traces from her lips with a pink-tipped tongue. 'Is it true that all you've found so far is the kiddywink? I suppose you aren't too overjoyed at that.' She didn't wait for Theresa to comment. 'I knew your father. I was only a child, then—fourteen, and not very much interested in older men—but he used to come to the house to see my father, and my aunt.' Sidney's gaze was fixed on Theresa's face.

'Oh!' exclaimed Theresa, somehow surprised by this revelation. 'What was he like?'

Sidney shrugged. 'Like his picture, of course. You'll have to ask Aunt Maddie if you want to know more than that. She liked him—at first anyway.'

'At first?' Theresa said, abandoning interest in her gâteau.

'I don't think she took to the boy, Tony, very much, and he was always around your father.' Sidney frowned.

'Why was that? Wasn't he a likeable lad?'

'I wouldn't know.' Sidney pushed that aside as of no importance. 'Maybe a little girl would have been more to her taste. In any case, it didn't really matter. Your father disappeared quite unexpectedly—and quite finally. Why don't you leave well enough alone?'

This last was delivered innocently, with a fluttering of eyelashes.

Theresa felt as though she had been kicked. She played with her fork and the dark cake on her plate.

'When people disappear, it's because they want to.' Sidney hammered the point home. 'Wouldn't you agree?'

'Perhaps.' Theresa's voice was cool; cooler than her thoughts.

'I'm sure you'll soon see it that way.' Sidney took a last sip of her coffee. 'It's not as though there's anything to keep you in Creswal. It would be different if you were a man; my father might give you a job.'

'Doesn't he hire any girls?' Theresa was driven to ask.

'Of course not.' Sidney's smile was smug. 'Big Bob hasn't a single woman working for him; he doesn't hold with it. None of the men around here do.'

'There are girls working in the shops and the houses,' Theresa pointed out, knowing it was really as Edouard had said.

'Well, naturally,' Sidney didn't bother to smile at this. 'That's different, isn't it? So menial. You couldn't think of it.'

Theresa bit her tongue. Sidney had manoeuvred the conversation so that she knew she wanted a job. At least she wouldn't tell her about the driving-lessons, or Sal.

'Well!' Sidney was triumphant. 'That's settled, then. So you probably won't be staying long in the neighbourhood. I really must run now. So much to do, and I do want to swim this afternoon. I'll leave something for the girl, shall I?' She put some small change by Theresa's plate, and waved to the waitress as she left.

Theresa was on her own, her cake unfinished, her coffee cold, and the account to settle. She sat for a moment, angry and indignant, and then began to ask herself why Sidney was so eager to be rid of her. Was it jealousy over Simon, or was there something else? Theresa had no answers, but one thing was sure. She didn't mean to leave. She meant to stay and find work.

In thoughtful mood, she completed her shopping and borrowed two novels from the library. The young man there was very helpful and chose a splendid car book for her. In the afternoon, she was studying it in the shade of the veranda, where Simon Radcliffe found her soon after four.

'How nice to see you!' she exclaimed, putting the book to one side. 'But how is it you aren't at work at this time of day?'

He sat down beside her. 'I had toothache this morning, and the dentist managed to fit me in. I've given myself the rest of the afternoon off. What have you been doing with yourself all day?'

'I had coffee with Sidney this morning. I don't know why it should matter to her, but she doesn't think I'm going to find my father. She as good as told me to go home.'

'She's a practical girl, is Sidney.' Simon picked up the book Theresa had discarded. 'I wouldn't have expected a girl to be reading this.'

'What do you mean about Sidney being practical?' she asked. 'Do you think, as she does, that I should leave things alone? I haven't come all this distance to go home.'

Simon looked at her, his dark eyes full of concern, and put the book down on the bench. 'You might get hurt, you know. This father of yours might not—I don't like to say this, Theresa—but he might not want you. You're banking on there being instant rapport between you, and it may not happen.' He reached out his hand to her. 'You do think there's going to be some sort of instant recognition, don't you?'

Theresa let her hand stay in his. It was comforting, somehow. 'I suppose I do. There must be something between a father and daughter.'

'You're building up a romantic picture of a man who will understand and love you.' Simon patted her hand. 'It's natural, but it's like a fairy-tale. You may be in for a terrible disappointment.'

'Why are you so pessimistic?' She snatched her hand away. 'Isn't there a kind of recognition between parent and child, a reaching out towards each other?' It was the first time she had talked to Simon like this.

'Maybe.' He frowned. 'But it's one thing for a parent to confront a pretty little baby, and another to face a grown-up daughter with a mind of her own and a whole unknown life. Believe me, I know.'

'How can you know?' Theresa demanded. 'Has it happened to you?' She was tired of people telling her they knew best.

Simon hesitated. 'If you promise to keep it to yourself, I'll tell you something I've never told another living soul. But you must promise.' He took hold of her hand again.

Theresa realised that he was very serious. 'Cross my heart'—with her free hand she made an X across her chest—'I do promise.'

'My mother gave me up for adoption when I was born.' He spoke softly. 'My adoptive parents were wonderful, and they made no secret of the fact that they had chosen me, but somehow that wasn't enough for me. I wanted to know my real mother, to find out what she was like; even to let her know I was all right. Well, I found her.' Then he paused.

Theresa didn't know how to break the silence that had fallen. It lengthened between them, as he turned her hand over and traced the lines on the palm.

'I think it was the worst moment of my life—so far, at any rate.' He smiled briefly. 'She was a beautiful woman, fair-haired like me, dark-eyed, and she looked so tired. Perhaps I should have written to her first, but I thought I'd surprise her. I walked up to her door and rang the bell.'

Theresa held her breath. She could imagine the scene.

'"I'm your son, Simon," I announced. I don't suppose there is any easy way to say it,' he went on. 'I was seventeen, and not very smooth with it.' His hand tightened on Theresa's.

'She said, "Oh my God!", and her hand flew to her mouth. We just stood there staring at each other. I didn't know what to say, what to do. "Go away," she whispered. "Go away. My husband's out in the back yard cutting the grass. He doesn't know anything about you, and he's a violent man."'

Simon took a deep breath, and his mouth twisted. 'Clearly, she didn't want to know anything about me.'

'Didn't she say anything else, or do anything? Touch you?'

'She said good-bye, and that I'd turned out a fine big boy.' Simon half choked on the words. 'She put out her hand as though she might touch me; then she thought better of it.' There was bitterness in his voice.

'Poor soul!' exclaimed Theresa. 'Poor tortured woman.'

'Why poor woman?' He dropped the girl's hand.

'Because it was harder for her than for you.' She thought it was obvious. 'She was still ashamed and guilty—that's how it is for a woman.'

'She still didn't have room for me in her life. That's what came across to me.' Simon spoke quietly.

Theresa met his gaze. 'Why was that so important to you? She'd done her best for you. She'd given you up to be placed in a good home. She had to make the best of her life, then.'

'Exactly,' he agreed. 'She'd given me up when I was born. This time she gave me up for ever—She rejected me completely. That was the end, as far as I was concerned. I went back home and told my adoptive mother that she was my real mother. I thanked her for wanting me. I think that was probably when I decided against dentistry.'

Theresa had a sudden picture of the seventeen-year-old boy, hurt and bewildered, but generous enough to thank the woman who had brought him up and loved him. 'Did you never tell her about seeing the real one?'

'No, I couldn't. She was so pleased, so relieved, that I'd given up the idea. She hadn't wanted to share me with that other woman, my physical mother.' He shrugged. 'I never told anyone. I've only told you to warn you, really, because I think you're building too much on finding your father.'

'Perhaps I am,' Theresa admitted. 'But my stepfather thought I should find him, and he was a wise man. I'm not really asking anything of Charles Russell. If he wants to walk away from me, he can.'

'First you'll have to find him, and you may never do that. What, then? It might be better to give up the search now, before you get hurt.'

'I don't think I can do that.' She sat back. 'It's like a

puzzle, and I want to find out the answer. He didn't have any reason to disappear. He had a job and a son and a home, and no money problems. Why should he go? Where would he go? I want to know.'

'Curiosity, you mean? Well, if that isn't just like a woman!' He began to laugh. 'After a while you'll get tired of it, and some man will come along and sweep you off your feet. Then you'll be living in the real world again. Come to the pictures tonight with me, Theresa, and forget all about it. *The Perils of Pauline* is playing. You'll like it.' He touched her arm. 'I'll pick you up around seven, shall I?'

'I'd love to,' Theresa sighed. 'But I can't. Edouard is teaching me to drive.'

'Teaching you to drive? Whatever for? Girls don't drive motor cars. That's what that book is all about.' He picked up the offending volume and leafed through it. 'You don't want to know about brakes and clutches and gears and spare tyres. Besides, I thought you weren't going to go out with him in his car again,' he finished angrily.

'That's what you advised me to do, I know, but . . .'

She wasn't allowed to go on, as Simon interrupted her. 'But you don't take my advice. I only gave it for your own good. You don't want to be thought of as fast. Really, Theresa, I thought you had more sense than to fall for a man like Moreau.'

'I haven't fallen for him! He offered to teach me.'

'And you're enjoying it, I suppose?' He snapped out the words.

'Not exactly enjoying it, but I'm going to be able to do it.'

'I don't know what girls are trying to be, these days!' Simon threw the book down on the bench. 'They want to do everything a man can do. Big Bob says they're losing their femininity, and I'm inclined to agree with him. He won't hear of Sidney learning to drive.'

'Perhaps she wouldn't be very quick about learning, anyway.' Theresa felt goaded beyond endurance.

'What do you mean by that? If you can drive, there's no reason why she can't. You needn't sound so superior about it. She's quite a gifted girl, a real artist. She wants to go to Toronto to study, but Big Bob won't agree.'

Theresa gave him a withering look. She might have told him there was no need to be so pompous. She might have told him then that she had an invitation to see Miss Marguerite Falconer on the following evening. But she did neither of these, and managed to smile at him. 'Let's not quarrel, Simon. I'm sorry I can't go to the pictures with you tonight. Can't we leave it at that?'

Somewhat mollified, Simon took his leave.

By the time Edouard called for Theresa after supper, she was in a calmer mood.

The lesson went much better this time, and he was more patient. He insisted that she crank the car without any help from him, and then allowed her to drive out of town.

It was as they were proceeding along the road after the last straggle of houses and sheds that another car came up behind them. Theresa kept well over to her side to allow the other to pass, but after passing, the driver stopped his automobile a little distance ahead, blocking the way. She braked to a halt, looking at Edouard anxiously as the other driver got out of his car and walked towards them.

'Robert Falconer.' Edouard introduced them with a smile. 'Miss Theresa Russell.'

Theresa's hand was seized in a crushing grip. This was the man who wouldn't allow Sidney to drive.

Big Bob was well named. Over six foot tall and broad of shoulder, he was an impressive figure. Thick blond hair fell in an easy wave over a wide forehead. His eyes were a deep, deep blue, his chin square, his teeth white in a face that had been burned by the sun to a becoming bronze.

'So this is Charles Russell's daughter!' His expression was interested. 'Yes, I can believe it. You have your father's green eyes. But Edouard didn't say what a pretty girl you are.' He shot him a quizzical look. 'No wonder you're keeping her to yourself; but you won't be able to do that after tomorrow night.'

'What's happening tomorrow night?' Edouard looked from Big Bob to the girl.

It was Big Bob who answered. 'Hasn't she told you? Marguerite has invited her to our open house. I think she means to get her to one side and have a real gossip with her—you know the way women are.'

Theresa had the feeling he would have thumped Edouard's chest, if he had been on that side of the car.

'Save a waltz for me,' Big Bob instructed her. 'I usually come in at the end of the evening to see everything's going well. I like young people about the place.' He turned to Edouard again. 'I'm off to dinner at the army camp. I thought you might have been there, too.'

'Not this time.'

Big Bob hardly waited for his comment; his attention was on Theresa. 'Your father was a great fisherman. That's how we met. I often think I'll see him again on his own in that red canoe of his some early morning. Funny thing, no one's ever found his canoe—or his body.'

Theresa tightened her lips at this bald statement, but he went on. 'I didn't think so at first, but now I'm sure he must have disappeared on purpose. Some woman after him, probably—it's the same old story after all, as Eddie'll tell you. Creswal has been the starting-off place for many a runaway man heading for the north. Never mind, Theresa, you'll have had the adventure of trying to find him. You'll be able to tell your grandchildren about that.' He gave her a smile and a nod, and went back to his car.

'Is he always like that?'

'Like a cold wind on a sunny day?' Edouard knew what she meant. 'Yes. How did you get an invitation from Marguerite? I wouldn't have thought Sidney would have done you that sort of favour.'

She ignored the remark. 'I had a letter of introduction

to Miss Marguerite Falconer, and I left my card there the other day. When I left you last night, there was a note from her.'

Edouard laughed. 'I might have known it! How very English that sounds. You are a prim little thing sometimes.'

Theresa resented that. 'I know how to act correctly.' When he laughed again, she asked crossly, 'What would a Canadian have done?'

'Picked up the phone and said her friend So-and-So had said she must get in touch. It would have been done with a chat,' Edouard replied. 'But I like your way. It has style, and that would appeal to Marguerite. What did you do to get this letter of introduction? I believe Maddie has friends in England. Did you canvass all your acquaintances, or just come up lucky?'

'I came up lucky, as you put it,' she said stiffly. 'The introduction was given to me.'

He laughed again. 'You continue to surprise and enchant me with your predictability. You're sure you're going to find your father, aren't you?'

'Yes!' Theresa was emphatic. 'I know I am, in spite of everyone telling me I'm not. I'm beginning to wonder if they're hiding something. That's three of them today advising me to give up: Sidney, Simon, and now Mr Falconer. Don't you think that's strange?'

'Not really. I might tell you so myself. I tried to, that first day.' Edouard had become serious.

'But you put it in the paper.'

'It's news. I couldn't resist it.' He put his hand on her knee. 'You think it's important to find your father in order to discover who you are.'

Theresa wanted to deny that; but his hand, touching her, robbed her of speech.

'I think you will find yourself,' he said softly. 'But I'm not so sure you'll find him.' He lifted his hand. 'No, don't say anything.' He put a finger to her lips. 'Promise me you'll think about *not* finding him?'

Confused as much by that gentle pressure against her

mouth—that gesture that was almost a kiss—as by his words, Theresa was silent.

'Let's get on with the lesson,' he suggested. 'It's cranking time.'

She obediently climbed down and started the motor, then concentrated on her driving, putting all other considerations out of her mind. After a few miles, she headed back for town when he directed it, and halted in front of the boarding-house.

'Well done!' was his verdict. 'Sal will see you at ten on Monday. I'll show you tomorrow where her office is. By the way, Saturday is a half-day for me. Rosie and I will pick you up, and you can drive us to the beach. Bring your swimming costume. You do have one?' At Theresa's nod, he continued, 'If you ask Mrs Brown tonight, she'll do you a packed lunch, and we can have a picnic.'

He stilled Theresa's protests by, 'Nonsense, you won't be in the way. Rosie will be pleased to have your company.'

At one on Saturday, Edouard and Rosie called for Theresa and she ran out to join them. He relinquished the driver's seat to her, and she steered her way through the streets, carefully avoiding the cars and horses and carts and walkers. Rosie was impressed.

'Swim first, or lunch first?' He asked, as they arrived at the beach.

'Swim,' cried the girls in unison, and went to change. Theresa's costume was dark brown with a cream trim, and reached, as did Rosie's almost to her knees. Rosie was in navy and white.

Theresa was suddenly shy about parading herself in front of Edouard so scantily dressed, but she needn't have worried. He seemed to take no notice, but just grabbed both girls by a hand and marched them to the river's edge. The water was very cold, and they would have held back, except for him. He wouldn't release them till they had ducked. Rosie struck out immediately in a strong breast-stroke, Edouard floated after her on his back, and Theresa swam on her side.

'The water's very deep,' he shouted to Theresa, and raced after Rosie. 'Don't come out too far!'

Theresa stayed where she was, not because she wasn't a good enough swimmer but because she felt somehow excluded. Rosie and Edouard swam and splashed and played in the water like a pair of children. Finally he chased Rosie and caught her, as Theresa watched them.

'A forfeit to let you go!' she heard him cry. 'What shall I claim? An apple from your lunch? A bite of your ear?'

Theresa could hear Rosie's laughing 'No!' She looked away, and swam slowly inshore. There was no reason why she should feel left out. He had known Rosie a lot longer than he'd known her, and there was no cause for her to feel downhearted. Edouard had been kind to her, but when the lively Rosie was there he was drawn to her, of course. That was understandable, and she was just being childish in wanting his attention. It didn't really matter to her. How could it? She'd only known him a few days. She couldn't be jealous. Anyway, she was cold. It was time for lunch.

Rosie and Edouard must have thought so too, because they followed her in, and wrapping towels about themselves, began opening lunch-boxes.

'My mum's given me sausage rolls and egg sandwiches,' announced Rosie.

'I have cold meat and fresh bread,' said Edouard.

'Here's a chicken leg and tomatoes, cheese sandwiches, six plums and three cup-cakes.' Theresa named them as she pulled them out. 'That's one for each of us.'

They shared out the food, feasting on it in the open air, the sun warming them. Rosie had brought a flask of tea, and she poured it for them.

'Why did you never get married, Eddie?' she asked, as she gave him a small tin cup. 'You're not bad looking; better in your clothes than in that yellow and blue thing you're wearing!'

'I thought it was rather dashing,' he protested.

speak of her in the third person as though she weren't there. He addressed himself to Rosie to escape looking at her; her eyes made him uneasy.

'What's that supposed to mean?' They were both ignoring Theresa.

'She gets a satisfaction out of being in charge of people—she equates that with love.'

Edouard didn't quite know why he wanted Theresa on the defensive, why he still wanted to prove her wrong about love. But he enjoyed seeing the light of battle in her eyes.

'How do you know what I do? How I feel?' she demanded.

He shrugged. 'I observe. I listen. You took charge of your stepfather and your sisters. That made you feel good, didn't it?'

'I loved them. I did what I could for them.'

'Why?' Now it was between the two of them. Rosie was silent. 'You saw it as your duty?'

'Yes, I suppose so. There wasn't anyone else. But I did it freely, not grudgingly.'

Her eyes were flashing. She looked almost pretty. Edouard couldn't resist teasing her further, yet in a way it wasn't teasing. He wondered what had driven her.

'Now they're married,' he went on, 'you'll be looking for a replacement. This half-brother will just fill the bill.'

Theresa glared at him. 'You're horrible.'

Edouard regarded her thoughtfully. 'How will you stop yourself from being jealous of him?'

'Why should I be jealous?'

He sat upright, his eyes fastened on hers. 'Unless you're an absolute saint, you're bound to be a little jealous. He is the proof that your father had another life, another child. It changes things, doesn't it? Destroys your picture of a dad waiting for you?'

'What if it does? I can share, can't I? I shared a stepfather,' Theresa looked puzzled.

'This half-brother, abandoned at five, may be a rough wild boy, just as hungry as you are for that lost father.'

Once started, he felt he must point out the pitfalls. This girl was too vulnerable. She had her eyes fastened on a dream. 'Remember he's been in an orphanage.'

'Why do you make it sound as though we'd hate each other? Perhaps we'd take to each other very quickly.'

'There speaks a soft heart. It's going to lead her into trouble.' Edouard turned to Rosie. 'You talk to her, Rosie. She doesn't want to listen to me.'

'But, Eddie,' Rosie protested. 'She must do what she really wants to do, whatever that is. I don't know what to make of you sometimes. I thought you wanted her to look up her brother—after all it sells papers—a hundred extra copies this week.'

'Yes, we sold a hundred extra copies this week,' he agreed.

'A hundred extra copies this week!' Theresa exclaimed. 'There's profit in my story. Is *that* what it means to you?' She looked at Edouard.

He shrugged. 'I'm a newspaperman. I warned you about that. Why should you be surprised now? And why should you round on me? If you go to your brother, I'll sell more copies. But I was just pointing out the disadvantages to you. Give me credit for that, at least.'

'I'm sorry, Edouard.'

Rosie didn't say anything. To Edouard's surprise, she was waving—waving to someone approaching along the beach.

It was Simon Radcliffe, striding towards them in a black and gold costume. He was a well-set-up specimen, Edouard noted, with fair hair on arms and legs and none at all on his partly exposed chest. That should appeal to the girls who'd objected to his dark mat. Simon was smiling as he reached them. He looked sure of a welcome.

They all greeted him, asked him if he wanted anything to eat, and discussed the weather.

'Won't you take pity on a lonesome man?' Simon appealed to Edouard, whom he knew from meeting him at the Falconers'. 'Lend me one of these lovely girls for an hour or two. I've borrowed a canoe for the afternoon. Unfortunately it won't hold three, or I'd invite you all.'

The request was so charmingly made that Edouard could not refuse to consider it. 'Where's Sidney, then?' he asked innocently.

'Out sailing.'

Both girls were looking at Edouard. Which one of them was Simon after? he asked himself. 'The girls will have to settle it between them,' he suggested. He noted that Rosie glanced at Theresa, who shook her head ever so slightly.

'I'll come, Simon,' offered Rosie. 'I'll show you a sandy beach further up the river where my brother sometimes takes me, and we'll have a swim.'

If Simon was disappointed, Edouard reflected, he gave no indication of it, but gave Rosie only a minute to collect her things and go with him. The two of them set off for the river and the beached canoe.

He was left with Theresa. 'Why didn't you go?' he asked her. 'It was you he meant.'

'I came with you.'

'So did Rosie.'

Theresa didn't meet his eyes, but wrapped her towel round her shoulders.

'Still, I suppose, waiting will only make him keener. That's the way girls think, isn't it?'

Theresa's gaze met his. He could see anger there.

'That's an unkind thing to say!'

'The truth is often unkind.'

'How do you know what the truth is? I happen to know Rosie likes him. She wanted to go with him.'

'And you didn't? You seemed to like him well enough the other night.'

'I do like him, but I came with you.'

'Don't keep repeating that! It doesn't mean anything, except that you've been brought up to have good manners.'

Edouard saw that her lip quivered at that gibe, and he

asked himself why he was taking out his bad temper on her. She hadn't done anything to deserve it, except to hear that he'd been thrown over by a girl.

'What do you want me to say?' she demanded. 'You've been kind to me. It would be a poor way to show gratitude if I went off with someone else.'

For some reason that incensed him. 'I don't need your gratitude. I'm using your story to sell papers—as Rosie told you.'

To his surprise, Theresa smiled at that, a smile that lit up her face. 'You say some hard things, Edouard. You seem to think the worst of people. You don't want anyone to know about your soft centre. There's a goodness in you which you don't want anyone to see.'

Edouard was astonished. He opened his mouth to speak, and closed it without a word. This girl was like a puppy. You pushed her away and she came back for more. He shook his head. She was determined to like him.

'Shall we go for another swim?' she asked. 'It's still very warm, and I'd like to cool off.'

'Very well.' Edouard rose to his feet, and the two of them approached the river.

Theresa stood with her toes in the water, hesitating as she felt the cold.

'I know you have other friends here, Edouard,' she said. 'I didn't mean to take up all your time, and I didn't know whether you wanted Rosie to stay or not. I didn't think about your feelings, only hers.'

'What's that supposed to mean? Rosie works for me. We have a friendly relationship, but she's free to go out with whom she pleases. I invited both of you today because I thought you might become chums, as you would put it. I didn't expect Simon to happen along to spoil the party.'

'Is that what he did—spoil the party?' Theresa took a step into the river, not meeting his eyes. 'Do you like having two girls around you rather than one?'

Edouard guessed that her feeling were hurt by his

unguarded remark about Simon, but he wasn't going to apologise. If he wasn't careful, this girl might adopt him instead of her half-brother.

'There's safety in numbers,' he laughed, and taking Theresa's hand, he pulled her into the river as he rushed in himself.

Whatever comment she might have made in return was swallowed in a great splash as they lost their footing and were submerged in the shock of cold water.

CHAPTER EIGHT

WHEN THE CAR called for Theresa on Saturday evening at
7.15, she was ready. In a rust-coloured jersey frock,
low-waisted and just below the knee, she felt she looked
smart enough for the occasion. The dress, though loose
fitting, clung to her slender waist and rounded hips and
enhanced the glowing sheen of her hair. She had found
beads of a slightly deeper hue on her shopping expedition. Her white stockings, set off against her black
patent-leather sandals, completed the outfit. A simple
black band encircled her forehead, holding back but not
quite containing the errant curls round her face. She
carried a small black velvet bag and a black lace shawl.
Settling back comfortably for the short ride in the back
of the big car, she noticed the smoothness with which the
uniformed chauffeur, a man in his early thirties, handled
the driving.

On her arrival at the Falconers' house, a maid ushered
her into a small sitting-room, and said that Miss
Marguerite would be with her directly. Theresa had time
to take in the pleasant book-lined room with its rose
curtains and cushions and its well-upholstered maroon
chairs. There was a round light wood table, and the walls
were cream. The carpet was grey, patterned with deep
red and paler pinkish roses. The window was open but
well screened, so that the room was cool and pleasant in
the late evening sun.

When Marguerite Falconer entered, Theresa was surprised. She had expected an older version of Sidney. But
this woman was much younger and shorter than the
picture she had built up for her. Her eyes were greyish-
blue and her strawberry blonde hair was wound around
her head in a thick braid, giving her a little height and
a good deal of presence. Sidney was pretty—but

pretty would have been too insipid a word to apply to Marguerite. She was arresting and lively. Her features were even, her teeth small and pearly white. Her frock, pink chiffon over taffeta, was beautifully cut, and fitted at waist and bust. Soft pleats fell from the hips and swirled about her slender legs as she came forward to take Theresa's hands.

'My dear, so glad you could come.' She stood back a little from the English girl. 'How you've grown!'

'Grown?' Theresa echoed the word stupidly.

'Don't look so surprised.' Marguerite's laugh was a silvery tinkle. 'I saw you when you were five years old. You won't remember me, but I was staying with your godmother when you came to visit with your mother. A solemn little thing you were, too! And how is Alice?'

'She's fine,' replied Theresa, calculating that Marguerite couldn't be more than thirty-five. That a woman as attractive-looking as Sidney's aunt had never married was a mystery. 'She sends her love,' she added.

'I owe her a letter.' Marguerite gave a rueful smile. 'But never mind that. I saw the article in the *Clarion* about your search for your father. How enterprising of you to come all this way. Do sit down and tell me about him.'

Theresa sat in one of the big chairs, and her hostess in another. 'There isn't anything to tell.' She sighed. 'I never met him. I believe you did, so perhaps you can tell me what he's like.'

'I?' Marguerite's face had a closed, wary look for a moment. So fleeting was the moment, that Theresa wondered if she had imagined it. 'It was five years ago, but I shall try. Charles was almost as tall as my brother Bob, but not so solid-looking. He was often serious, but he loved a good joke, especially a practical joke, and he could keep a straight face while he told you some nonsensical story you didn't know whether to believe or not. But when those green eyes of his began to sparkle, you knew he was fooling. When he disappeared, we all thought it was another of his jokes—but he never came back.' There was a puzzled note to her voice. 'If he were alive, he couldn't have resisted returning to see the effect.'

This was a side of her father that Theresa could never have guessed at. Somehow it made him more of a person to her. She smiled, in spite of the feeling of uncertainty that Marguerite's words, 'if he were alive', had roused in her.

'Was there anyone he was particularly friendly with?' Theresa asked. 'Some man he worked with—or some woman? Mrs Malinsky seemed to think he was a man who liked women.'

Marguerite didn't ask any questions about Mrs Malinksy; perhaps she knew who she was. She only shrugged. 'Most men like women. I don't think there was any gossip about him, if that's what you mean.'

It wasn't what Theresa had meant. She had the odd sensation that Marguerite could have said more, that she was holding back. But that might have been her imagination playing tricks with her because she wanted to hear more.

'I met your brother last night,' Theresa said, hoping to introduce the topic of the red canoe.

Marguerite broke in, 'Yes, he told me, and of course you must stay and meet the young people. Sidney will be delighted to introduce you to them.'

Theresa wondered, if she hadn't met Big Bob last night, whether she would be staying to meet the young people. She was sure that Sidney's feelings wouldn't be ones of delight at the prospect. She smiled at her hostess, and agreed it would be very pleasant.

Marguerite half rose and than sat back. 'You won't be upset if I speak frankly to you, will you?'

Theresa shook her head.

'I've had a marvellous idea—if you're interested, of course.' Marguerite leaned forward. 'I don't want to depress you, but there's nothing to hold you in Creswal, is there? If you're thinking of staying in Canada and finding employment, you want to head for one of the big cities. You'd like Toronto, and I have a friend there who'd be happy to help you. She has a very good job herself, and she'd be willing to put you up for a week or two till you found your way.'

'That's very kind of you,' Theresa managed to say, in spite of a feeling of considerable surprise. Her knowledge of the geography of Canada wasn't very extensive but she had a good idea that Toronto was some two or three hundred miles away. If this was a genuine friendly gesture, it was something she should think seriously about—and yet, why was everyone so eager to see her leave Creswal? It made her feel that there was something here they didn't want her to find out. She made no mention of the fact that she was to have an interview with Sal for a job on Monday. 'I'll certainly think about it, Miss Falconer.'

'I knew you were a sensible girl!' Marguerite beamed at her. 'Do call me Maddie. Everyone does. Now let's go and meet these other guests.'

Theresa followed her out of the sitting-room and down a short corridor into a larger room with a polished floor, in which all the furniture had been pushed to the sides.

Simon Radcliffe was there, supervising the rolling up of some large scatter rugs. 'Just leave her with me,' he told Maddie. 'I'll see she has a good time.'

'Lovely,' Maddie smiled at him. 'I knew I could rely on you. I'll just check with the kitchen to make sure that there are enough sandwiches.' She slipped away with a flutter of chiffon.

Simon put a record on the gramophone. 'I'll have the first dance. Can you do the Charleston? I was disappointed you didn't come with me this afternoon.'

'It's my favourite!' Theresa was in Simon's outstretched arms for a brief moment, and she ignored the remark about the afternoon. Then out of them, as she began to dance energetically. Simon was as enthusiastic as she was and they laughed in pleasure. When the first record stopped, he put on another—a foxtrot, this time.

She was held this time in a firm embrace, as their steps matched themselves to this more graceful dance. She found it very pleasant.

It was in the middle of this second record that Sidney arrived and stood pouting by the player. They both greeted her, but did not stop.

'I hate that tune,' she said plaintively. 'You know I do, Simon. I'll change it.'

'Let it finish,' he exclaimed, his tone sharp, but Sidney's hand reached out to the gramophone arm.

It was stopped in mid-air as Edouard Moreau entered the room. 'Dance with me,' he suggested, and Sidney glided into his arms, her dislike of the music forgotten.

Edouard was a very smooth dancer, who led Sidney into all sorts of intricate steps, and Theresa couldn't help being impressed. For the first time, her feet missed the beat, and Simon stepped on her toe.

'Sorry,' he apologised.

'It was my fault,' Theresa admitted, as the music stopped.

The four of them gathered round the gramophone, and Simon wound it again.

Sidney picked a record. Tonight she was in pale blue silk, with a blue feather in her hair and a gold locket on a fine chain around her neck. Her dancing shoes were gold, thin strapped and very expensive-looking.

Edouard greeted Theresa, taking her hand in his. 'Did you enjoy the ride?' he asked. 'It's a lot smoother than the Ford.' He made no reference to the afternoon.

Whether he would have added anything to that, Theresa didn't know, because Marguerite returned to the room just then with two young men in tow, and said she must meet them. Introductions accomplished, Maddie put her hand on Edouard's arm. 'Come with me, Eddie dear. We'll leave these youngsters to their own devices. Theresa will want to get to know boys and girls of her own age. We'll retire gracefully to the card-room.' She swept him away.

Theresa noticed that he made no protest, but he

wouldn't if he and Maddie were friends, and the pos-
sessive way she had claimed him surely proclaimed that.
It was none of her business, she told herself firmly.
Perhaps he had found the right girl at last—only
Marguerite was no girl. She was a woman, and a very
direct and managing one, if the Daughters of the
United Empire Loyalists were correct about her. How
old would Edouard be? It was something she hadn't
really thought about before, but she supposed he must
be about the same age as Maddie.

She put the thought away from her. She was here to
meet people and enjoy herself. She gave the young men
to whom Maddie had introduced her a dazzling smile as
the music started up again, and both of them asked her
to dance. She chose one, and promised the other the
next record. Everyone was so friendly and welcoming
that she was having a pleasant time. She had always been
fond of dancing, and the twins and their friends at home
had always included her, so she knew all the steps. When
Simon asked her what they were doing in Liverpool
these days, she showed him the Cakewalk. As soon as
the others saw them doing this, they clamoured to
learn.

Big Bob, Maddie and Edouard and an army officer
came in to join the party for coffee and sandwiches.
They mingled with the young people, working their way
singly to different groups. Edouard came over to the one
where Theresa was last of all. The music started up again
then, and she thought he might have asked her to dance,
but Big Bob was there, too, claiming his waltz, and after
him the army officer, Colonel Jackson. By that time
Edouard had disappeared, and so had Marguerite.

At twelve the party broke up, and Maddie appeared
on her own to organise the departures. 'The car is
waiting for you,' she said to Theresa. 'Two of the girls
live in your direction, and I believe Simon is going along
with the three of you.'

Theresa thanked her hostess and said her good-byes.
The others went with her to the automobile, and the two

girls were dropped off very shortly along the way. She and Simon had the back of the car to themselves.

'A lovely party!' she said. 'I did enjoy it.' There was no need to feel something was missing just because Edouard hadn't danced with her. He'd made his feelings clear enough on the beach—and here with Marguerite.

'You're a great dancer.' Simon took her hand in his.

'Doesn't Sidney's aunt dance?' she asked him, hardly noticing the pressure of his fingers.

'Yes, very well indeed. She and Edouard were dancing in the side room—didn't you see them? I suppose you wouldn't. It was when you were teaching everybody the new steps. I expect they wanted to be on their own. It was very dark in there. I couldn't really see whether they were dancing or not, but it doesn't matter, does it? That's their affair.'

'Are they . . .' Theresa's voice faltered. 'Are they good friends?'

Simon squeezed her hand. 'They see a lot of each other. I know they're going sailing in the morning. Big Bob has a sailboat. That Colonel Jackson has a boat, too. I think there's a race of some kind. Edouard might be crewing for the Colonel.'

'I've never been sailing.' She wasn't going to let Simon know that it mattered a jot what Edouard did in his free time. 'Have you?'

'I've been out with Big Bob and Sidney now and then. I'm not much of a sailor, I'm afraid. I much prefer a canoe. Your friend Rosalinda is quite at home in one, too. We had a lovely paddle this afternoon.'

'Good!'

Simon dropped her hand abruptly. 'Is that all you have to say? Most girls would be jealous if a fellow mentioned another girl.'

Considerably taken back by this remark, Theresa asked sharply, 'Is that what you do with girls? Play them off against each other?'

'No, it isn't,' he snapped. 'But I have quite a few people working for me, and I can't help but notice how they react to each other. I thought perhaps I was beginning to mean something to you, but if you aren't the least little bit piqued when I mention another girl, I can't mean very much.'

She had to smile. 'I'm sorry, Simon, but I think that's a poor way of deciding if you're liked.'

'Is it? Whenever Edouard's name is mentioned, you're all attention. You didn't like it when I said just now that he was dancing in the dark with Maddie. What does he mean to you?'

'Nothing.' Theresa tried to keep the hurt out of her voice. Edouard had made it very plain to her that she meant only extra papers to him . . . He meant nothing to her. 'How could he mean anything to me?' she added. 'I only met him a few days ago.'

'And have spent quite a bit of time with him since,' Simon suggested in a quieter tone. 'Including this afternoon . . .'

'He's been kind enough to give me some help.' She put out her hand to Simon. It might have been better if she had gone with him. 'Let's not quarrel? He's not worth quarrelling over.' She repeated that firmly to herself.

'Just the same'—Simon appeared somewhat mollified, but not willing to leave the subject—'he's made an impression on you.'

'Suppose he has.' Theresa wasn't admitting it. 'A lot of people make an impression on me, as you put it.'

'Like who?' he persisted.

She searched her mind for an example. 'Like Big Bob or Colonel Jackson—or—or Marie Lloyd or Douglas Fairbanks.'

'That's not the same thing, and you know it, but we won't talk about it any more. You think it over, and you'll see I'm right. You're allowing yourself to dwell too much on Edouard Moreau. There's no sense in wasting your time that way—and perhaps getting hurt. He's not the kind of man for you. I'm only saying this for your own good, Theresa. He won't allow you to mean anything to him.'

She drew in her breath sharply. She knew to her cost that he was right. Edouard Moreau had stated the same thing to her, only that afternoon, in a different way. Was she so transparent, she asked herself bitterly, that everyone could see through her? Was that why Marguerite had suggested she should go to Toronto? In her innocence, she had thought it had to do with her father.

'I wish I could take you out in the canoe tomorrow,' Simon went on, 'but I'm going to be working all day. Not at the mill, but at home. I have to have the whole project outlined to present on Monday morning. Tell you what, though. We'll go to the pictures on Wednesday evening. Will that suit you?'

Theresa agreed that it would suit her very well, and returned Simon's good-night kiss with more affection than she had previously shown him.

Sunday was a long day, and Theresa had ample time to reflect on her life so far in Creswal. Marguerite wanted her to go, but Edouard had found her a job. She'd show him just how independent she could be! He might have dismissed her from his life, but she wasn't going to be frightened away from the town or from her search for her father. She had a brother she had never seen, and perhaps he held the answer to her father's disappearance. She would get in touch with him.

By afternoon she had written a letter to the children's home in Ottawa. She borrowed a stamp from her landlady, and walked to the Post Office to send it off.

On Monday morning. Theresa dressed carefully for her interview. She wore a green dress which reflected the green of her eyes, and a little white hat and white gloves. Her reflection assured her that she looked quite businesslike. With a last smoothing down of her hair and rubbing a little powder on her nose, she set off for O'Reilly's Realty and the redoubtable Sal.

When she arrived at the shop which bore the legend

O'Reilly's Realty, its only occupant was a small woman with large glasses perched on her nose and a quantity of soft brown hair gathered into an enormous bun at the back of her neck. She wore a neat blue and white dress in a light cotton, and it was fitted at the waist, unlike Theresa's own frock which was tunic-line. Was this Sal? This tiny, pretty little creature with eyes of soft blue? Theresa had imagined someone older, and harder. This woman couldn't own a business and run it efficiently. Surely she wasn't more than thirty.

'Edouard Moreau sent me about the job,' Theresa began. 'Are you Mrs O'Reilly?'

'Sal,' replied the other, and the blue eyes which had seemed so soft suddenly acquired sharpness, shrewdness. 'So you're the girl from England. You seem to have impressed Eddie. Tell me what you've done before.'

That was soon told, and she ended the short recital by saying that she could drive.

'They all say that, and then they drive too fast. Fifteen miles an hour is fast enough for anyone.' One small hand was waved in the air. 'As long as you don't try more than that, you just might do. You sound sensible. Sometimes you might have to work evenings or Saturday afternoon. How do you feel about that?' The question was asked softly, and Sal looked small and defenceless.

'All right.' Theresa had worked in a factory, and knew the importance of bargaining. 'As long as I can have time off in lieu.'

'In lieu.' Sal raised one eyebrow. 'You know some fancy words! Of course you'll have time off. I'm not a slave-driver, no matter what they told you at the *Clarion*. Can you start now?'

That was it. Theresa had the job. She didn't have much idea what she would be doing, but she was hired to do it anyway, and at a reasonable salary, seven dollars a week.

'Let's see what your driving is like.' Sal rose from her desk. She led the way to a big green Oldsmobile parked at the back of the shop. 'Beautiful, isn't it?' She put her hand on the front of the car. 'I like big cars—and big men.'

'Is Mr O'Reilly a big man?' Theresa asked, eyeing the 'green brute', as Rosie had described it to her. She only hoped she would be able to manage it.

'Mr O'Reilly?' Sal echoed. 'You mean Captain O'Reilly? He was killed in the war. I don't suppose anyone's told you.'

Theresa murmured that she was sorry, and from the bleak expression in Sal's eyes, she realised she shouldn't have mentioned him. She was surprised when Sal went on, 'He was six foot three, and handsome with it.' Sal climbed into the passenger seat, and Theresa was left to crank the engine into life.

She was in luck. The big car started easily, and she manoeuvred it out on to the road without too much difficulty, allowing for the difference in size of Edouard's Ford.

'We'll have a look at the summer cottages,' Sal announced, as Theresa looked to her for instructions. Her directions were clear and easy to follow.

The cottages were on the outskirts of town, facing on to the river with a small beach of their own. On a wooded site, ten of them stood a little apart from each other. Theresa was impressed with them. They were built of wood, and painted in different soft colours, with wide screened-in verandas, and flowers growing in small tubs by the doors.

Sal tested a front doorstep and a rail. 'That'll need strengthening. Make a note of it. I have a man who does repairs for me. He'll come along some time this week, and you can check he really does what he charges for.'

'Are these your houses? Do you own them?'

'Some are.' Sal stopped to examine a torn screen. 'Add that to the list. I handle some for other people —for a fee, of course. There are enquiries in already for most of these, and some bookings. I'll put them in your hands when the holiday people start using them. You can deal with most complaints by that time.'

'What kind of people rent them?'

'City people mostly,' Sal said. 'They like to get the family away from the heat. Some come every year, sometimes for a month. The air's good for the children. They love it here. Have a look inside this one.' She opened the door, and Theresa stepped into the kitchen.

'All the conveniences, you see.' Sal was pointing them out. 'Running water.' She indicated the sink and the pump. 'You don't get taps out in the wilds,' she added, noticing the expression on Theresa's face. 'That kerosene stove needs cleaning, and the coal-oil lamps on the counter there need polishing. You'll have to see that's done. Ruby needs watching.'

She had no idea who Ruby was, but she added another note to her page. Working for Sal was going to be full of surprises. She might be small and helpless-looking, but she knew what she was doing—and what everyone else should be doing. Theresa went through the house at Sal's heels, scribbling things down. They went into the large sitting-room with a big open fireplace, round dining-table and six straight chairs, a settee and several comfortable chairs. Leading off it were three bedrooms, one large with a double bed, a smaller one with two singles, and a tiny one with two built-in bunk beds.

'Harry Smith made those,' Sal informed her. 'Ruby's husband. He's my handyman. It all needs airing and sweeping and cleaning. The curtains had better be done, too.' She was enumerating it all.

Theresa looked up from her notebook. 'Where's the bathroom?'

Sal looked at her sharply. 'Next year I'm hoping to make a start on indoor lavatories, if that's what you mean. For the present, there are outdoor privies. You needn't worry about them. They're all on new sites. Harry moved them last fall.' She led the way along to the next cottage. 'Once I put bathrooms in the cottages I own, the others are going to have to do the same.'

Theresa held her tongue, and added to her notes. She

couldn't understand how these cottages would be rented when they lacked so many amenities. Who were the other owners? When they went back to the office, she found she had made a considerable number of notes.

'Before you start writing those up,' Sal said, 'you can go for lunch. Be back at two sharp.'

Theresa decided to call in at the newspaper on her way, to tell them she had the job. When she arrived, only Rosie was in, and she was pleased to hear the news. Theresa was glad, she told herself, that she didn't have to face Edouard.

'Eddie's gone to Renfrew,' Rosie told her. 'There's an exhibition of agricultural machinery today, and he's off to Ottawa tomorrow for the Highway Commission meeting. About country roads,' she added, for Theresa's benefit. 'He'll be back on Wednesday to get the paper out. I'll pass on the message about the job. How did you get on with the "green brute"—and Sal? I don't suppose you know she's a war widow?'

'I do now. What was he like, this Captain O'Reilly?'

Rosie laughed. 'You won't have had much information from her. She's very loyal. He was a lad from the wrong side of the tracks, and she married him in spite of her family. They came round, though, and set him up in business. He had no head for it at all, and went through most of her money. When he went off to fight the war it must have been an enormous relief for the family, though they say the shock of finding out he'd lost all his money killed Sal's father. Captain O'Reilly never came back, and Sal took charge of the realty company. It's very prosperous. She lives above the shop. People who've seen it say that the flat's a picture. She has a real knack for prettying things up and for selling property.'

'Does she live there on her own?'

'Yes, her married sister lives in Renfrew, and the mother went with her. I suppose if Sal had gone back to live in the family house when Captain O'Reilly left, her mother might be with her. But the family home had to be sold, along with everything else.'

'It's no wonder you work on a newspaper,' Theresa exclaimed at the end of this history of her employer.

Rosie didn't take offence at this, but only smiled and said, 'Eddie says I'm a natural, but it's really that Creswal's a small place and people know each other. They haven't much else to talk about.'

In the next few days, Sal initiated Theresa into the intricacies of the realty business. She had rented property on her books, and also property for sale, both houses and farms. She seemed to sense what clients wanted and the exact price a house would fetch. Theresa wasn't yet allowed to collect rents or handle requests for repairs. Instead, she was set to putting the files in order and entering the ledgers. She dealt, too, with the enquiries for the summer cottages. Although Sal was an exacting employer, she was very entertaining, with a lovely manner when dealing with the clients, and a dry shrewd humour which made them laugh.

After three days of the ordinary running of the office, Theresa still had no idea who the other owners of the cottages were, and any questions she asked Sal about them were deftly turned aside. She had not yet had an answer from the children's home, and no word from the bank about her father's money. In fact she had put both things out of her mind, and was settling to her work quite happily.

On Wednesday evening Simon called for her as arranged to take her to the pictures. The cinema, which she remembered Rosie had told her Edouard owned, was quite small and not as well appointed or decorated as picture palaces she had attended in Liverpool, but the seats were comfortable. The pianist was good—better than Theresa would have expected—and the audience very appreciative of her talents. When the feature film started, she lost herself in it. Mary Pickford and Douglas Fairbanks exerted their magic on her, and she was swept away into ancient Baghdad.

Afterwards, Simon took her for an ice-cream soda to

an Italian café that stayed open late. Some of the people there she recognised. She spotted Marguerite Falconer and Colonel Jackson, Rosie and a man friend, and Sidney and one of the party-goers of Saturday night. Sidney ignored them completely, but her aunt halted at their table and exchanged greetings.

'Such a pity,' said Marguerite, 'that Edouard didn't manage to stay for the whole film. He had to get back to the paper.'

'A pity,' Theresa repeated politely, wondering why she was being given this piece of information. Marguerite smiled at Colonel Jackson. Wasn't one man enough for her?

'Theresa's got a job,' Simon was quick to tell the others. 'She's at O'Reilly's Realty.'

'How lucky for Theresa,' the Colonel murmured, and smiled in her direction. 'You'll be all right with Sal—a charming woman.'

'I shouldn't think you'd like working for another woman,' Marguerite commented. 'Still, I suppose it's pin-money. Not that you really need it, of course. You are an heiress—or so I've heard.'

She swept herself and the Colonel away before the thunderstruck Theresa could reply to this.

'An heiress?' she exclaimed to Simon. 'What makes her think I'm an heiress?'

'Aren't you? You said that your stepfather left you some money, and you did travel first class on the *Morning Star*.'

'Only because he worked for the shipping company all his life, and when the manager heard I was going to Canada, he insisted that I go first class at his expense. He said it was the least he could do. Why does Marguerite think I'm rich?'

Simon fiddled with the straws in his soda. 'Perhaps she got that impression from me. She asked me all sorts of questions about you last night, when I was invited there for a meal.'

'Simon, how could you?' Theresa was indignant.

'Rose was right when she said that all people in a small town did was gossip about each other.'

'There's no need to get worked up about it!' Simon was very much on his dignity. 'Where's the harm in people thinking you're wealthy? Everyone loves an heiress.'

It was useless for Theresa to protest that it wasn't honest or sensible to pretend to be what she wasn't. Simon assured her that people would take her at her own valuation.

'What's it like, working for Sal?' Simon asked as they walked back to the boarding-house. He seemed to have forgotten that only last week he had disapproved of girls working for a living.

'It's good that you're working for a woman.' He squeezed her hand as they came to a dark spot on the road under a tree. 'It sounds almost like keeping household accounts and running a home. I'm glad you've found something so congenial. It means you'll be staying a while, too.'

Theresa just prevented herself from commenting. Congenial it might be, but it wasn't much like running a home—not with Sal in charge. Still, if Simon wanted to think of it like that, she had no objections. Men were funny creatures, and it was best to humour them. The twins had always said that. She could see that in some odd way she'd gone up in Simon's estimation. It was pleasant to be well thought of.

It was pleasant, too, to be escorted to one's front door and kissed good night.

Theresa went to bed, reflecting that it was welcome to have a friend like Simon who treated her so nicely, with such consideration, and who made no demands.

The next morning, Theresa came down to breakfast smiling, and greeted the others. Once again the local paper was at her plate, and she picked it up as she began eating. There was a feature article about roads planned for the area on page 1 and another about the agricultural machinery show on page 2. She turned another page, as she attacked her egg and toast. On the middle of page 4 was a story headed, 'English Girl Discovers Delights of Creswal'.

Theresa's spoon dropped to her plate. It was about her and everything she'd done in the last few days. It was all there: winning the black kewpie doll at the fair, picnicking on the beach, learning to drive and getting a job—even teaching the Cakewalk at the party and going to see Douglas Fairbanks. Edouard must have written it. How could he have done this to her? No wonder Maddie had told her about him being at the pictures. She must have known what he meant to do.

'Isn't it grand to be written up in the papers?' asked the little maid, bringing in more milk for the tea. The others were all in accord with this.

She herself seemed to be the only one dissenting. If this was personalised journalism, she didn't want any part of it. She finished her breakfast somehow, trying to calm down. The first thing she was going to do was to see Edouard. If she left at once, she would have time to do it on her way to work. She jammed on her hat and left the house, paper under her arm.

Edouard was alone in the editorial office when she arrived. She put the paper down on his desk and pointed to the article. 'Did you write this?'

'Yes,' he replied, smiling pleasantly. 'Good, isn't it?'

That did it. Her anger exploded into words. 'How could you?' she demanded. 'I thought you were being kind and friendly, and all the time you were just watching me and storing it up so that you could tell your readers all about me, and what a simple girl I really am.' Her voice broke on that, and a tear ran down her cheek.

He rose to his feet and pushed a chair forward. 'Sit down and stop that snivelling.' He gave her a handkerchief from his pocket. 'I haven't said anything there to be ashamed of. I've given the readers a very fair picture of you—heart-warming, in fact. What's upsetting about that?'

'That's just it.' Theresa had her emotions under control now, and the handkerchief was a ball in her fist. 'I didn't want a picture of myself for everyone to see. You didn't ask me about it. I wonder you didn't say I was an heiress—everyone else seems to think so.'

'Violated your privacy, is that it?' He didn't raise his voice. 'How very English and proper you are.' He stood over her. 'When you came to this newspaper for help, you gave up your right to privacy. Did that thought never occur to you?'

'Never,' she snapped. Her anger was mounting. 'I suppose you're going to stand there and tell me you did it for my own good, not to sell papers, of course?' She remembered his words on the beach.

'Of course I sell papers.' The taunt stung. 'I'm a newspaper man, and I know what the public wants and how to get their sympathy and interest, too. How do you imagine you're going to find anything out about your father, if that isn't done? This is a tight, provincial community. You're not going to get anything out of them unless you give them something of yourself. That's what I've done for you. How did the people at Brown's take it?' he asked softly.

'They loved it.' Theresa spoke through stiff lips, not yet convinced.

Edouard grinned. 'You're honest, at least.' He sat on the edge of the desk, and she almost smiled back at him.

'It's not what I expected from a newspaper,' Theresa protested. She might have added, 'or from you', but she couldn't bring herself to let him see that she had regarded him as a friend.

'Thinking of turning back? It's too late for that. I warned you in the beginning that I wouldn't let go.'

'Yes, you did,' she replied with some bitterness. 'I didn't know what you were like, then.'

'What am I like?'

'Like no one I've ever met before. You tease me and laugh at me and call me too polite and well brought up!'

She was full of indignation. 'And you tell people about me.'

'I see.' Edouard nodded. 'I think you're trying to tell me that you don't like me. It would be easier for you if you could consider me as a friend; someone older who has your interests at heart.'

'A friend?' Theresa was incredulous. Did he seriously expect to be numbered as a friend, when he kept hurting her?

'Yes, a friend,' he repeated. 'I'm the best friend you have here. I'm trying to help you to find your father. I wrote this article on Saturday night—late—because I knew I had a very busy week ahead of me, and I didn't see any other time to get it done.'

'Saturday night!' she interrupted. 'You couldn't have known then that I was going to get the job.'

'Oh yes, I could! I own most of those summer cottages.' He stopped abruptly, as though he'd said more than he had intended. 'I saw you at the pictures last night—with Simon. How is it you travelled first class on the ship coming over, if you're not an heiress? You told me you had only two hundred pounds.'

'That's the truth.' She wasn't going to let him think otherwise. She had forgotten all about the money which might be in her father's bank account. 'My stepfather worked for the shipping company, and they paid my passage.' She dismissed the subject as of no importance. 'Is it true, what you said about owning the cottages?'

'Yes.'

'I suppose Sal had to hire me. Well, I don't have to stay.' She wasn't going to allow Edouard to put her any further in his debt.

'Don't be childish, Theresa.' He looked down at her. 'I didn't mean to tell you. I know what it's like to come as a stranger to a place like Creswal—you need all the help you can get. Sal's the perfect employer for you. She knows everything and everybody here. Her family owned a good part of the town. Creswal is a strait-laced, conservative place, and girls like you don't get

'Maidens all over the world have gasped at the sight of it. Don't you like it, Theresa?'

Theresa was mortified to find herself blushing. She had been gazing at the long black hair plainly visible in the V-neck of Eddie's one-piece costume—she couldn't help it. There was something compelling, something very masculine, about it. Now, to cover her embarrassment and to hide the fact that she had been affected by it, she exclaimed, 'You do have hairy legs!'

Rosie saved the situation by giggling, 'A real admirer.'

'I've always had them.' He nodded solemnly. 'But if they disturb you, they shall go.' He sat cross-legged, so that they were hidden.

Theresa was still very conscious of the hair exposed on his chest.

'But why haven't you married?' Rosie asked again.

Edouard didn't like the way the conversation was going, but he smiled at her. Once she got hold of a subject, she hung on to it, and with Theresa here she'd play to the audience. The only way was to deal with her was to return with a question.

'Never found the right girl. You must know how that is. I'm just like you, Rosie, I flit from flower to flower. Who was it last winter with you? Paul, the under-manager at the General Store, and more recently that lumberjack, Daniel.'

'Oh, him! I've finished with him. Growing pains, my mother called him.'

'Growing pains! He was six foot tall. I shook in my shoes when he came to see who you were working for.'

'You did nothing of the kind. Don't think you can change the subject.' Rosie wasn't going to be deflected. 'Didn't you ever have a special girl?'

Oh yes, I had a special girl. Josie was her name. It was in the war, and she was a Londoner.

He bit into a plum. 'It was a long time ago, and she preferred someone else. Just as well, I suppose.'

'But you liked her?' Rosie smiled at him, inviting confidences.

'I liked her.'

'Did she know how much you liked her? Did you ever tell her?'

No, he'd never told her. There had been no declaration of love on either side. But she had known; only she'd always said the present was enough, she didn't want to be tied down.

Both girls were waiting for his answer.

'She knew.' He gave Rosie a short answer.

'You're very unsatisfactory, Eddie,' she commented. 'I've worked for you for nearly two years, and you never tell anything about yourself. Why don't you?'

'You know all about me,' he was stung into replying.

'I don't know anything,' she protested.

'All right, what do you want to know?'

That was all the opening Rosie needed. 'What was she like? What did you do? How did you meet her?'

'I met her in air-raid—a Zeppelin raid. We were all terrified. She had black shingled hair and was as slender as a boy. She had big dark eyes, and she was the only one who seemed cool.'

Cool—She was never cool. Nor had he been. That Zeppelin raid had shaken both of them to life's briefness. They came together as though they had been meant for each other. They had gone to her flat and made love. That first time had set the pattern.

'You dated her after that?'

'Every time I had a pass, I went to London. We went dancing. We went to shows. The new musical *Chu Chin Chow* was playing—I think we went three times. She taught me the veleta and the waltz. I introduced her to jazz.'

We found love. Oh yes, Theresa Russell, sitting there with your big green eyes on me, we found love . . . and lost it.

'And then?' Rosie prompted. 'Did you go back to the front?'

'The field telephone was ready for its big trial—under battle conditions. I went back to France and the war.'

'You were separated,' Rosie sighed. 'How sad.'

The war was only a temporary separation. It was the shrapnel in my back that separated us for ever.

'We said good-bye when I left, and promised we'd meet again. When we did, I was flat on my back in hospital. She came to see me. I don't suppose I was very welcoming.'

It wouldn't have mattered how welcoming I'd been. Tom McGregor came to see me at the same time as she did. She walked out on his arm, and I never saw her again. Tom McGregor was married to my sister. Josie didn't let that make any difference to her.

'Did she—Did she come to see you again?' It was Theresa who asked the question.

'No, she walked off with my other visitor, and that was the last I saw of her.'

'Didn't you try to find out about her—where she'd gone? She herself might have been injured in another raid,' Rosie suggested.

'She might have been, but she wasn't.'

She had sent a message—a message through Tom McGregor—that she couldn't bear to see Edouard so ill and weak and motionless. That was the cruellest thing of all. That Tom McGregor should bring such a message when Edouard had seen the way she looked at him on leaving. He'd known then what was going to happen.

'How can you know, if you never bothered to find out?' she continued, frowning.

Rosie was always the reporter, Edouard thought briefly. 'Someone always brings the news.' His voice was flat. 'It was over. Probably it was just as well. I can't imagine she would ever have settled happily in Creswal.' He'd never considered that before, but he wasn't going to have Rosie and Theresa feeling sorry for him. 'It was all a long time ago.'

A long time ago, but he'd never forgotten it, never been able to. Oh, Josie, how I loved you. I guess that was when love died. Now I've stopped expecting it. I won't let myself expect it.

'Fair's fair!' Edouard managed a laugh. 'Now I've bared my soul, you girls can confide in me.' He looked towards Theresa.

'There isn't anything to tell.' She looked uneasy.

'Nothing?' probed Rosie. 'No handsome young soldier in the war?'

'There was a boy in the navy,' she admitted slowly, her eyes on the ground. 'But I was only sixteen. He was eighteen, and so proud to be going to sea. He never came back.'

She looked so upset that Edouard nearly reached out to her.

Rosie spoilt it by exclaiming, 'Never mind, you'll just do for Eddie! Both of you disappointed in love.'

He saw the blush that mantled Theresa's cheeks. He'd better scotch that thought right away. 'Theresa's looking for a father. I suppose I'm nearly old enough for that!' he laughed.

Rosie smiled. 'I know when you're warning me off. Does this mean you're looking in another direction?'

'If I am, I won't tell you about it.'

Rosie took that like a good sport, and threw a plum at him. 'One of these days, you'll fall in love . . .'

He caught it deftly, and took a bite.

'Edouard doesn't believe in love,' said Theresa. 'He said so.'

'Did he?' Rosie looked from one to the other. 'When was that?'

'The other night.' She rummaged in the picnic bag and drew out the last cake.

'You mustn't believe everything he says,' Rosie advised. 'But some things he's right about. He thinks you're going to take on your brother. Are you?'

Edouard wished she hadn't said that. She was determined to put her foot in it today.

'Why do you think that?' Theresa turned to him.

'Theresa believes in love.' He found it was easier to

jobs and keep their reputations if they work for men. It's different for Rosie—her brother does my printing.' He forestalled any comment. 'Everyone accepts Sal, and they'll accept you. And that's important—for both of us.' He finished on a quieter note, putting his hand briefly on her shoulder.

Theresa's thoughts and emotions were in a turmoil. She wanted to think of Edouard as her friend—and it was very easy to do that with the touch of his hand. But she wasn't going to have him thinking she could be so easily won over.

'That's another thing,' she said. 'Since you own the cottages, why don't they have proper sanitation?'

He laughed uproariously. 'Indoor plumbing, you mean? No, they don't have it. They have outdoor privies, and some of them are three-seaters. Go ahead—say it!'

She blushed scarlet. How could she mention such things, and what had possessed her to bring up the subject in front of this man?

He could see she was embarrassed. 'It was you who brought up the subject. We don't have to talk about it, if it upsets you so much that you're speechless.'

Theresa said nothing. She couldn't.

Edouard shrugged, but continued, 'I don't know about you, but I've never seen three-seaters before. It was Harry's idea—Sal's handyman. Nobody's objected. Perhaps Canadians aren't quite so squeamish as you, or they like company more. Which do you suppose it is?'

'I don't know,' Theresa admitted, angry not to be taken seriously. 'I would have thought that people wouldn't come if they knew the arrangements. They smell.'

'Dear me!' he remarked, unperturbed. 'And the season hasn't begun yet. Hasn't Harry moved them to new sites?'

'Yes, he has,' Theresa snapped. 'Sal said he had.'

'Well, then, I can see we'll never make a Canadian of

you, but I'll try to make you understand why the privies are acceptable to my countrymen.' He assumed an air of solemnity. 'Every Canadian sees himself as pioneer stock. He loves to return to his roots, or what he considers might have been his roots—but only in the summer when the weather's hot and most of the living is outdoors. To rough it, with kerosene stoves and oil lamps and a pile of logs outside the back door for the fire on the hearth, fulfils a deep need in him for the meaning of life—for the history of the land, if you like—and outdoor privies are part of that mystique. After all, it's a natural odour, part of nature's great plan.' He held up his hand as though he feared an interruption from Theresa.

'One of these days, vacationing women will demand more in the way of comfort, and you and I and Sal will provide it.' He smiled kindly at her. 'Now be a good girl and get off to work. Sal doesn't like late-comers.'

The anger had gone out of Theresa during this long discourse. She rose to her feet, knowing she was being dismissed. She felt she'd made a fool of herself, but Edouard wasn't going to hold it against her. Whatever else he was, he wasn't her enemy, but she wasn't sure he was the friend he claimed to be. It would be better to keep him at arm's length—if she could. He had the irritating ability to win her round and manage her.

She wasn't going to give him any more information about herself. She had told him she wasn't an heiress —Let him pass that around, if he wanted. She didn't tell him she'd written to the children's home about Tony. She didn't tell him she was going to see the bank manager later that day; he'd find out soon enough.

She said good-bye, and turned her back.

'You've forgotten your paper.' He came after her on her way to the door and handed it to her. 'Mrs Brown will want it back.'

Theresa took it from him without a word of thanks. He even knew she hadn't bought a paper of her own.

The man was insufferable! She went down the stairs with her head in the air, assuming a dignity which had slipped away from her.

CHAPTER NINE

HER FIRST glimpse of the orphanage on Friday morning was enough to dampen Theresa's spirits. A squat and ugly building of uncompromising red brick, it was set in a square of black asphalt and enclosed in an iron-barred fence. The gate stood ajar, hanging on one dilapidated hinge. There was no trace of comfort or of beauty in the facade of small windows and heavy front door which faced her. How had Tony endured this for five years?

Perhaps it was better inside. She hesitated at the gate where the taxi had left her. She would walk round the building. She needed the fresh air after travelling all night by sleeper from Creswal. She still couldn't quite believe she was in Ottawa—It had all happened so quickly.

At lunchtime the day before, when she had gone into her father's bank, the manager had said his Head Office wanted to see her as soon as possible, and they had suggested Saturday morning. Theresa had replied that it was impossible, as she'd be working then. He had asked if she couldn't have Saturday off. That was when she first thought of approaching Sal. Then, when she reached her boarding-house, there was a letter from the orphanage telling her she might come and see Antony at any time. Why not combine the two? She began to think seriously about it over lunch.

'Why not indeed?' had been Sal's reaction. And she suggested that Theresa take the train that very night. 'You can make up the time next week, when we'll all be working all the hours God sends getting the summer places ready.'

'That's very good of you.'

'Call it some of that time in lieu you insisted on,' Sal commented drily.

Theresa still hesitated. 'I suppose I should tell Edouard.'

'Why do women always have to tell some man before they set out by themselves?' Sal demanded. 'I used to be just like you,' she added. 'Now I decide things for myself. A working woman has to. Ask yourself why you think you need to tell him. Won't he complicate things for you? He'll distract you, when you should be thinking of the boy. It's only between the two of you, after all.'

'Yes,' Theresa agreed.

'You like him, don't you?' Sal asked sharply. 'Our Mr Moreau has a way with the ladies. I don't know why.'

'Don't you like him?' Theresa asked in reply, curious, because it was what Simon had said of Edouard.

'I can take him or leave him. He's a fair man to work for, but very sure of himself. He's made a lot of money since he was lucky enough to inherit the paper. There was that court case, of course.' She paused. 'I think that's what makes me hold back and ask myself if he's quite as nice as everyone thinks him.'

'What court case?'

Sal put her pen down and sat back. 'You wouldn't know about it. It was a few months after Eddie came here. He worked for his cousin, and both he and Eddie's mother died of the flu within a week of each other.'

'That must have been a shock.' Theresa's sympathy was roused. No wonder Edouard had said he knew what it was like to be a stranger in Creswal.

'I expect so.' Sal continued with the story. 'His cousin left him the paper. Fair enough—War hero inherits. His mother left him the house in Toronto.'

'What was wrong with that?'

'Nothing, but there was his sister's little girl—Thelma I think she was called. She was left nothing, and her father objected. Her father is Tom McGregor, owner of a big newspaper in Toronto and several others in the province—ones Eddie Moreau hasn't managed to buy up . . .'

'Her father's rich, then?' Theresa was puzzled. 'Why should he want more?'

Sal smiled. 'That was what the judge said. He found in favour of Edouard. But I felt sorry for the little girl—not mentioned in her grandmother's will. Eddie might have settled something on her.'

'But she didn't need it,' Theresa pointed out.

'He never sees her, and never sends her a gift.'

'How can you know that?'

'You'd be surprised at the things I know.'

Theresa shook her head in disbelief. There was a ring of truth about Sal's words, but it had nothing to do with her how Edouard acted towards his family. Didn't it? She jeered at herself. He had pushed her aside very quickly, not wanting to be personally involved, although he had later declared himself her friend.

Sal had picked up the phone then, and arranged about a train ticket and a sleeper for Theresa, and even called a small hotel in Ottawa to book a room for Friday and Saturday evenings. She made it seem easy for Theresa in turn to get on the phone and tell the Ottawa Head Office of the bank that she would accept the appointment for Saturday morning.

Theresa hadn't expected to sleep very much on the train, and privately thought the expense of a sleeper wasn't warranted, but she'd been so tired that she had dozed off almost immediately and arrived in Ottawa comparatively fresh, though she supposed the train must have been travelling at some speed. This morning she had gone first to Sal's hotel and left her case in her room and enjoyed a splendid breakfast. There would perhaps be time later for sight-seeing. Up to now she had managed to take in only a general impression of Ottawa as a pleasant little city, much smaller than her native Liverpool, and much less hurried and busy.

Now she was going to meet Antony, her half-brother, her link with her unknown father.

As she walked round the perimeter set by the wall, she barely noticed the small houses on the other side of the road. Her eyes were fastened on the orphanage. The back was even more depressing than the front had been; the bricks were of a poorer quality, and the paintwork peeling; there were several overflowing dustbins by the back door, guarded by a mangy cat, and bits of paper scattered by them. It was no use hovering about outside. Theresa retraced her steps, and went through the front gate and up the path.

The front door was opened by a small girl of about eleven or twelve in a long grey smock. Her face was shining clean, her lank light hair pulled into two thin braids. Her pale blue eyes were sharp and wary.

'If you've come about the teaching job,' she announced, 'you might as well go away. It's been filled.' She almost shut the door, but Theresa put her foot out to prevent that.

'I haven't come about the job,' she said. 'I've come to see my brother.'

'You can't see him in school hours,' the child said firmly. 'That's the rules.'

'Who can I see, then?' Theresa wasn't going to be sent away by this miniature dragon, who still held the door to a narrow aperture.

'Maybe Mr Ablitt will see you. But he doesn't like to be disturbed.'

'Whether he likes it or not, I'm going to see him.' Theresa's patience was wearing thin. She pushed the door open, and entered. 'I have a letter from him, and I've come all the way from Creswal on the train.'

'On the train?' The pale eyes lit up. 'I used to live near the trains. It was grand! We don't see the trains here.' The little girl shut the door.

Theresa had a sudden glimpse of the deprivation of life for this waif before her. 'What's your name? Why aren't you in class like the others?'

This provoked a giggle. 'Maisie. I'm too old for lessons. Mostly we go out to work at eleven or twelve, but they kept me on here. I'm glad of that. My sister's

here, and I can see her sometimes. I'll go and see if Mr
Ablitt will talk to you.'

Maisie scurried away down the passage, and Theresa
had the opportunity of studying the hall where she
stood. On the floor was dark brown lino; the walls were
panelled in the same colour to shoulder level, and
painted an indeterminate sandy shade above that. The
only furniture was a single table with scuffed legs, and a
tin umbrella-stand. Stairs rose in the centre well, and the
rail and curved banisters were well polished. The stairs
themselves were covered in the same brown lino.

'Mr Ablitt is waiting for you.' Maisie reappeared in
a great hurry. 'I'll show you where he is.' Theresa
followed her to an open door, where she was suddenly
abandoned.

'Come in,' said a high-pitched male voice, and she
entered. This was a comfortable room with pale cream
walls, and chintz curtains in a big flowered pattern. Mr
Ablitt, a small dark-haired man, was sitting at the desk,
and he waved Theresa into a hard chair in front of it.
'What can I do for you?'

'I'm Theresa Russell, and I've come to see my brother
Antony.'

'Ah-h!' Mr Ablitt rubbed his hands together. 'Quite
so. You wrote to me. I didn't expect to see you so
soon.'

'No?' Theresa didn't feel welcome. 'I had other business in Ottawa,' she offered by way of explanation.

'It's very strange we've never heard of you or from you
before.' Mr Ablitt smoothed his thin hair.

'I explained that in my letter.'

'So you did. You can prove you are who you say you
are?'

'Naturally.' Theresa took out her birth certificate and
her parents' marriage certificate, and handed them
across the desk.

Mr Ablitt took so long examining them that she began
to wonder if he intended to return them to her. She held
out her hand, and reluctantly he gave them back.

'I suppose it's the same Charles Russell. What did your father do?'

'He was an engineer who built bridges and dams.' Theresa hadn't expected this kind of inquisition.

'That fits in.' He nodded slowly. 'When the boy came, he had some sort of album with pictures in it of bridges that his father had built. We took it away from him, of course—for safe keeping. It'll be here somewhere.'

He didn't sound too sure of that, Theresa reflected, and wondered why safe keeping entailed removing the child's property from him.

'Can I see him?'

'It's lesson time.' His tone was shocked. 'I tell you what I'll do, since you've come so far. We'll go up to the classroom and I'll point him out to you. It's not as though he'll know you, is it?'

Theresa was forced to admit the truth of that.

'Then this afternoon you can come back and talk to him,' the man went on. 'Friday afternoon is handicraft time. The boys do basketry, and the girls sewing and knitting. The boys and girls are separate for the rest of the week, but this gives brothers and sisters a chance to see each other. That's an innovation, I can tell you.' He sat back in his chair, well pleased with himself. 'I introduced it, in spite of some of my staff, and it's going well.'

She was appalled at the thought of brothers and sisters so segregated that they could talk to each other only once a week, but she supposed it was better than nothing. 'Very well,' she agreed, falling in with this plan because she realised that she had to.

Mr Ablitt bared his teeth in a smile of approval, and rose to his feet. 'Good. Come this way.' He marched out of the office and up the stairs, Theresa behind him.

When she had stood in the entrance hall she had noticed a faint smell of carbolic and bleach mixed with the odour of cabbage, but now the cooking smell was fainter and the carbolic stronger.

'The boys' classrooms.' Mr Ablitt gestured towards closed doors from which there came no sound. 'There are three. Your brother is in the top class.' He knocked on one of the doors, and it was opened to him immediately.

Theresa was overwhelmed by the sight and odour of thirty or forty boys sitting at low forms in absolute silence and stillness. They were all dressed in short grey pants and grey shirts. An arithmetic lesson was in progress, and a red-haired lad stood at the blackboard, looking frightened, while the teacher sat at his desk.

Mr Ablitt strode towards him, Theresa in his wake.

'Let that boy sit down,' he instructed the teacher in a low voice, 'and call Antony Russell out.'

Antony Russell was duly called out to take his place at the blackboard, and the red-haired boy returned to his form, looking relieved.

As Antony rose from his seat and came forward, Theresa had her first glimpse of her brother. He was a smallish boy, fine boned and sallow complexioned. Indeed the grey shirt, which she could see now was of a thick material hardly suitable for the heat of the day, took all colour from his face. There was perspiration on his forehead, and he wiped it away with one hand. His eyes were dark brown, as was his hair, and his legs —which she could see plainly, as he wore short boots and no socks—were thin. There was a thick scab on one knee.

He stared at Theresa, as indeed the whole class was doing, and she stared at him, with no eyes for any of the others now. She had no feeling of kinship. This was her half-brother, her father's son, and there was no recognition between them. She started to hold out her hand, wanting to say something to him, to hear him speak.

'Don't just stand there, Russell!' exclaimed the teacher. 'We haven't all morning. Finish that sum off —if you can.'

Without a word, Tony turned towards the board and picked up the chalk. He began to write in a clear, well-formed hand.

'I'll leave you to it,' said Mr Ablitt, and led the way out

of the room, ushering Theresa before him this time.

'I believe he's good at his sums and his writing,' he told her as they retraced their steps. 'Not a very keen reader, though. Still, that'll all be behind him next year.'

'Next year?' repeated Theresa, not sure of her feelings.

'Next year we'll find him a place somewhere—perhaps in the livery stable or in one of these new garages. They're always looking for boys there. Motor cars are the thing of the future.'

Everything in Theresa rose up at that prospect. Sent out to work at eleven! No, that wasn't going to happen to her brother! She'd find some way round it. 'That's too young!'

'We can't keep them idle any longer than that. We put them in a good trade and let them stay on for a year here, paying board. That gives them a start in life. After all, we have two hundred orphans here, and there are always more coming.'

In the entrance hall, he said good-bye and escorted her to the front door. 'Come back at half-past two,' were his parting words, 'and you shall speak to your brother.'

With that, she had to be content. She came out of the front gate and asked a passer-by for directions to the centre of town. She found the big shops, but she had no heart for shopping, and just wandered round. After a solitary lunch, she returned to the orphanage.

This time Maisie greeted her like an old friend, and Mr Ablitt took her to a very large room on the ground floor, which was sectioned off by partitions. There were groups of children everywhere, and he directed her to a fairly quiet corner where Antony and the red-haired boy from the blackboard were standing side by side in front of a table spread with cane in long loops and short lengths. Tony was soaking some in a large tin basin, and the other lad was dealing with boys demanding a share.

'Charlie will take care of you.' Mr Ablitt introduced her to the red-haired boy. 'He'll tell you anything you want to know.'

Theresa found herself left facing both boys, and Mr Ablitt had gone. She stood there feeling helpless while two pairs of eyes surveyed her.

'Are you a teacher, miss?' asked Charlie with a cheerful grin, as he dispensed cane.

Theresa shook her head.

Tony put out a damp hand in her direction, and said, 'You can sit here if you want.' He indicated a rickety stool beside the table and in close proximity to the basin of water. 'Are you looking us over?' His look was assessing. 'You remind me of someone.' He took some of the cane from the table and added it to the basin. 'Who are you?'

Theresa hesitated. It seemed too bald to say that she was his sister.

Charlie broke in before she could answer. 'Tony, you've got it all wrong. You don't rush in and ask them questions. That frightens them off.' He shooed the last boy in the queue away with a large loop of material. 'I don't know why Mr Ablitt has left you here with us. You're not French, are you?'

Theresa couldn't make any sense of this conversation. 'I'm not French. Why do you ask?'

'Everybody knows it's only French people who are willing to adopt boys like us,' Charlie explained slowly, coming to lean on the table beside her. 'The English only want pretty little girls like Elsie over there.' He pointed to a small girl playing with a doll at the end of the table, and she looked up and smiled.

Antony nudged Charlie. 'You could tell her that a boy would do more for her—carry things, chop wood, run messages, make baskets.'

Now that she was close to Tony, Theresa could see a slight resemblance to that old photo of Charles Russell. There was a brightness to his dark eyes and a tilt of the head that conjured up their father.

She smiled at him. 'I'll keep it in mind.'

Tony returned the smile. 'Who are you really?'

'My name is Theresa, Theresa Russell.'

'That's funny.' Tony was more relaxed now. 'My name is Russell, Antony Russell.' He paused. 'Where do you come from?'

'I've come from England, but I'm living in a place called Creswal.'

At the word 'Creswal', Tony caught his breath, and then a shuttered look came across his face. 'I've heard of it.'

'I should think you have!' Charlie broke in. 'That's where you come from. You used to talk about it a lot. What's the matter with you?' He turned a look of enquiry at his friend. 'Maybe she's a relation.'

'I don't have any relations,' declared Tony. 'Why are you here?' He looked straight at Theresa. 'She's probably come to see you, Charlie. Old Ablitt said you'd take care of her.'

Charlie's eyes lit up with excitement. 'Is it him or me you want, Theresa? Nobody's ever wanted either of us before. I'm the best baseball player, but he's the best at sums.' The boy was hopping up and down on one foot.

Theresa put her hand on Charlie's arm. How had they got to this state where she would have to disappoint this lad—and she could see it was going to be a disappointment for him. Mr Ablitt should never have left her with two boys.

'I'm sorry, Charlie,' she exclaimed. 'I'm Tony's sister.'

Hope died quickly in his eyes. 'I didn't know Tony had a sister.'

For his part, Tony looked stunned. 'I never had a sister before. It's not true!' He pulled a length of cane from the tub, and hit the table with it.

'Yes, it is. We had different mothers, but the same father.'

Tony was speechless, but Charlie had no such inhibitions. 'Why didn't you come before? He's been here a long time.' His tone was accusing.

'I couldn't,' Theresa explained. 'I didn't know about

him, and I had to take care of my twin sisters. Their father was different from mine.'

'Is that what you do?' Charlie was curious. 'Take care of children? Have you brought the twins?'

'No,' Theresa laughed. 'They're grown up and married.'

'Good.' He smiled. 'That means you can take care of Tony now. Golly, Moses, he's struck it lucky at last!'

Tony began to smile and then to laugh. He came up to her. 'Will you really? Really, Theresa?'

She reached out to the boy and held him close to her. In that instant, she knew that was exactly what she was going to do. And it wasn't because that made her lovable. It just needed doing. What did it matter that she would have to give up several years of her life to looking after this brother she didn't even know yet? She wasn't sure that she could afford to support him. But, with that hug, she accepted him as her own in much the same way as she had accepted Felicity and Melody when her mother had died.

'We'll have to get used to each other.'

Tony gave her a smile of pure joy. 'Can we go home soon? Home to Creswal?'

He was nothing if not direct, Theresa reflected. She hardly hesitated in replying. 'I have someone to see here in Ottawa tomorrow, and I'll have to talk to Mr Ablitt . . .'

She barely had time to get the name out. 'He'll be glad to let him go, you'll see.' Charlie was certain of that.

Tony looked at his friend and back at Theresa. 'I won't see Charlie again, will I?'

'Never mind that,' his friend said. 'You hafta go with her. You can find me a Frenchman.'

Theresa's heart went out to him. Such generosity of spirit called for acknowledgment on her part. She put her hand on his arm, 'Perhaps, later on, Charlie, you can come and visit us.'

'That's what they always say when they leave,' exclaimed Tony. 'But nobody ever visits.' He was clearly unsure as he looked at Charlie.

'I'll be the first one, then.' There was something so adult in the look Charlie gave Theresa that she felt he was older than she was—older in the ways of the world, at least.

'I've made you a promise,' she said. 'I'll keep it.'

He managed a smile, but the expression of his eyes remained the same.

After that, Theresa and Antony went to see Mr Ablitt in his office, and she told him she meant to take her brother home with her on the following day.

'There'll be papers to sign,' he told her. 'But they and the boy will be ready for you after lunch.' He seemed to take it as a matter of course that she would want her brother.

Theresa went back to her hotel and a meal, buoyed up. By the time she had finished her soup, she had begun to wonder if she was acting wisely. She knew in her heart that it was the step she must take. No child should have to stay in an orphanage if he had any family at all—and Tony had her, whether he had a father or not. For the first time she acknowledged that that father might never be found. Well, she would do her best for the son. She had a job and some money. They'd manage.

Afterwards, she sat in the lounge with pen and paper, trying to calculate how much it would take to feed and clothe a boy for a year. Tomorrow she would buy him something to wear, light clothes for the summer. He was not going to appear in Creswal in that dreary grey. Edouard would want his picture for the paper, she supposed, and Tony should be dressed like any other small boy. She had had no experience of dressing boys, but it couldn't be very different from girls. Tony would need everything, she was sure—underwear, socks, sandals. If she set aside ten dollars, surely that would make a respectable start. 'It's more than a week's wages,' she told herself. 'It must be enough.'

While she was deep in this financial wrestling, the

proprietor of the hotel, Mrs Harris, came over to her. She asked if everything was satisfactory and if Theresa was enjoying her stay. She went on to say that they had come to look on Mrs O'Reilly as almost one of the family over the years, and trusted that she was well.

'Such a pity she never had any children after the little boy she lost. She couldn't, of course; and then her husband dying in the war—such a tragic life Sal has had.'

Theresa agreed it was a sad waste, though she hadn't known anything before about a lost child.

'Remember my son Ian to her,' Mrs Harris continued. 'He always asks after her.'

'If you have a son, perhaps you can help me?' Theresa told Mrs Harris about her brother Tony whom she would be taking home with her the next day.

'How marvellous!' Mrs Harris clapped her hands. 'We'll set up a bed for him in your room. It will be no trouble, and no expense to you, either. I'll be glad to do it. And both of you must come to our little party tomorrow evening. It's for Lily, my daughter. She'll be twelve.'

Theresa accepted gracefully. After shopping with Tony, they'd be glad of some company. A party would be lovely.

'Delaney's is the place for boys' clothes,' Mrs Harris told her. 'You'll both really enjoy the experience.' She proceeded to give her directions to the shop from the orphanage.

By the time she went up to her room to bed, Theresa felt she knew the proprietor, and that she and Tony would both have a good time tomorrow. She fell asleep, certain it was all going to work out well.

In the morning she dressed carefully in her black and white costume, breakfasted, and set off for the Head Office of the bank. She had enough time to indulge in a little sight-seeing today. She saw the Parliament Buildings, the Prime Minister's Residence and two Royal

Canadian Mounted Policemen on their horses. These were the famous Mounties.

She had no difficulty finding the bank. She was shown without delay to Mr Roscoe's very nicely furnished and carpeted office on the third floor. He was a red-haired man in his thirties, not unlike Charlie at the home. He smiled at her in a friendly way and pulled forward a big black leather chair for her.

'Have you had any word at all of your father? I understand you've been trying to find him.'

Theresa said that she had no news yet, but she had discovered a brother of ten in a local orphanage, whom she was taking back to Creswal with her.

'That makes two heirs, then.' Mr Roscoe was matter of fact. 'The boy, of course, is too young to inherit.'

'Inherit? But there isn't any proof that my father is dead, is there, or that there's anything much to inherit?'

'As to proof, well, no,' he agreed. 'But with the passage of time, we must begin to accept the strong possibility that he has passed away. Our Legal Department feels that now is the time to begin some sort of action. Since you're prepared to undertake your half-brother's care, the case is naturally stronger. You should be able to petition the courts on your brother's behalf as well as your own. There is a sizeable estate—I think we can call it that.'

'A sizeable estate?' Theresa repeated his words, not sure that she'd understood correctly. 'How sizeable?'

'In the region of two hundred thousand dollars, I believe.' The man spoke reverently.

'Two hundred thousand dollars! Why, only last night, I was asking myself myself if I could afford ten dollars for new clothes for Tony.' Two hundred thousand dollars was a fortune.

He ignored this completely. 'Your father wasn't a rich man, but he had some mining stock—gold mines—which was of no great value when he left it with us. But mining stock has shot up recently, and this mine in particular is doing very well, I'm happy to say. It may not stay up, of course. That's another reason for taking some steps to realise it, if the courts allow.'

It was perhaps as well that she was speechless, as he seemed eager to continue.

'There was originally two hundred and eighty dollars in cash in his account.' Here, Mr Roscoe consulted a ledger. 'Some of that went on standing orders for insurance and the like; the balance is left, and has earned interest. We can't presume a client is deceased without a death certificate or an order from the courts. I assure you that our conduct has been quite correct.'

Theresa had not doubted that for a moment.

'You may want to take legal advice, or you may prefer to empower the bank to act as Trustees on your behalf. But I, for one, would like to see some at least of this mining stock realised. It's very volatile.'

'What if my father turns up—and we've spent some of his money?' Theresa's brain had begun to function again, although she still felt it was some other person discussing this fortune.

'If the courts have allowed it, I shouldn't think he'd be able to do much about it.' Mr Roscoe was very calming. 'In any case, I don't suppose they'd allow you to have more than the interest on it until the statutory seven years is up. With what you could earn, and 5 per cent on the capital, you and the boy could continue to manage very nicely. Courts are slow, of course, and mining stock is unpredictable, but you might come out of this very nicely indeed.'

'I'd like the bank to act for me.' Theresa was still half dazed, half disbelieving. Thank goodness she'd decided to take Tony the day before, prior to hearing about this money!

'Splendid!' He favoured her with a smile. 'There'll be papers to sign, of course. It will take a few days to prepare them, and they'll want all your documents. I understand you have a birth certificate and your parents' marriage certificate—we'll need those, and your brother's birth certificate. You'll have to locate that and send it to us.'

As Theresa had her papers with her, she handed them over and was given a receipt for them.

'If you should need them for any reason, you can just refer the enquiry to me,' Mr Roscoe told her.

'How long will all this take?'

'It's hard to say.' Having raised her expectations, he now proceeded to dampen them. 'It might take a year, or two years; perhaps never, should someone else come in with a prior claim. Perhaps, after your mother died, Charles Russell contracted a marriage that we know nothing of—his widow would have first claim. Perhaps the stock will be valueless before the due process of law. You mustn't count on this money—it may never be yours.'

Theresa could see that this might well be true. She didn't analyse her feelings—she was too worked up for that—but she had a strange certainty that the money would not come to her, and it was better to accept that now. Of course she would go forward with the bank's advice, but she wouldn't think about a fortune that was not going to come to her. She would forget about it, and act as though nothing had happened this morning. It was not something that she wanted to tell people—particularly not Edouard and, through him, his newspaper readers. It didn't concern him or them.

Mr Roscoe called in his secretary and she brought two cups of tea. 'I thought you'd prefer tea, being English. I like tea myself.' He asked her how she liked Canada and the Canadians, and what it was like to live in Creswal.

She drank her tea, and told him. He seemed genuinely interested, and she was feeling quite comfortable with him.

'I don't suppose you'll want to stay on at that boarding-house—not with a young lad. You'll need a place that is a bit bigger, with a garden, perhaps. Have you thought of anything?'

This took Theresa by surprise. She hadn't thought at

all—It was all happening so quickly. 'At least I'm in the right job for that! O'Reilly's Realty is bound to have something on its books. I'll ask Sal.'

'Very wise.' Mr Roscoe was in complete agreement. 'You'll need time to win his confidence, but Tony may be able to throw some light on his father's disappearance. He may hold the missing key, as you might say.'

'Yes,' she agreed hesitantly. 'But when I mentioned his father yesterday, he closed up completely.'

'Only natural,' he assured her. 'Don't push him. Let it come from him. Children remember a lot that they don't seem to know they knew about—if you follow me.'

Theresa did follow him, and she thanked him for his advice and his time.

'I'll be in touch,' he said when she left. 'I'll do everything I can to hurry the legal boys. It's been a pleasure meeting you, Miss Russell.' He opened the door with a flourish.

Theresa went out into the sun-filled Ottawa street. It could never happen, of course, but life was full of surprises after all. Still, she must put it out of her mind—not think about it, not tell anyone. There would then be no chance of believing it. She began to smile. She had a plan for the next hour or two, one she meant to put into immediate operation.

Besides getting the directions for shopping from Mrs Harris the night before, she also had the name of a good hairdresser, and earlier in the morning had made an appointment. Now she headed for the place.

'I want it cut short,' she told the girl, Angela, who came forward to attend to her. 'Like yours.' She knew a moment's indecision. 'Will it suit me?'

'Of course it will.' Angela smiled. 'You'll find it much cooler and easier, too.' She led her to a seat. 'I suppose you're thinking of the ones at home—have you told them what you're doing?' She put an apron around Theresa.

She shook her head, a little frightened now that the moment had come. It was useless to tell herself that she'd meant to have it done years ago, and only her stepfather's pleading had stopped her.

'Much the best way is to tell no one. They soon get used to it after the first look.' Angela picked up her scissors in one hand and a swath of Theresa's hair in the other. 'Seems a pity, almost. It's so curly. How would it be if I made it up into a thick switch for you after it's off? That's what a lot of the girls do, if they have nice hair. You can use it as a braid across the top or a fat bun at the back.'

At Theresa's nod, the girl began to cut. As the scissors began to do their work, she held her breath. Suddenly it seemed a terribly big step to take, all on her own, without consulting anyone. What if she hated it? It was too late now. Half her head was shorn of waist-length hair, and there could be no turning back. She closed her eyes, determined not to look until it had all been done.

'A lot of them close their eyes,' said Angela. Theresa could hear the laughter in her voice. 'They're pleased afterwards. So will you be.'

Theresa felt the long last piece of hair part company from her, and even before she opened her eyes, she experienced a lovely feeling of lightheadedness, of weightlessness about her neck and shoulders. She took a deep breath, and looked. A different girl faced her: a girl who looked smarter, more aware of herself, a girl who'd made a decision about how she wanted to look.

'I'll shape it to your head,' said Angela. You'll be surprised at what you can do with it. How lucky you are to have hair that curls and waves. When I've shampooed it, it will just fall into the way it wants to go. What about a little kiss-curl on the forehead?'

By the time Angela had finished with her, Theresa was well pleased with the result. They had compromised on gentle waves around the forehead and two kiss-curls just in front of the ears. At the back, she had not shingled it, but allowed it to fall naturally to the top of Theresa's neck.

Theresa looked at herself again in the mirror, and

shook her head in astonishment at the sense of freedom she felt. It did suit her!

'You don't really need a hat with it,' said Angela. 'But if you do buy one, have one of those new cloches. They come in all colours, and hug your face delightfully. I'm sure he'll like you even better now.' She patted her customer's shoulder.

'Who will?' Theresa was lost in the reflection of this new creature.

'Your boy friend, of course,' Angela smiled. 'What's his name?'

'Edouard.' Theresa had replied without even thinking, and blushed. 'Eddie, most people call him.'

Why had she answered with Edouard's name, she asked herself, as Angela wrapped her discarded mane in tissue-paper and handed it to her. He was not her boy friend; he had made that abundantly clear. But he had wanted to be her friend, Theresa argued, as she paid Angela. He'd said so.

Would he like it? It didn't matter whether he did. It was her hair, and she could do with it what she liked. She thanked Angela and stuffed the tissue-wrapped switch into her bag. There should be time to buy a cloche and have some lunch before she picked up Tony.

CHAPTER TEN

On Saturday morning when Rosie returned to the *Clarion* office, Edouard asked her if she had seen Theresa. It was absurd of him to keep thinking of the girl, he knew.

'No,' she shrugged. 'Should I have done? I thought she might drop in after she'd seen the bank manager, but she didn't. Simon says she's away for the weekend.'

Putting his pen behind his ear, Edouard frowned. 'Where's she gone?' His eyebrows shot up. 'And where did you see Simon?' Why did Simon know, when he didn't?

She smiled. 'He took me canoeing last night. I just happened to be down on the beach, and he saw me.'

He began to laugh. 'Don't tell me you're adding him to your list of scalps. You're amazing, Rosie.'

'I like him.' Her dimples showed in a wide smile.

'You like them all. How are the cardboard boxes doing?'

'Very well indeed. I wouldn't be surprised if Simon isn't on to something really good.' She stroked her hair. 'I've decided not to get it cut. I think most men prefer girls with long hair. Simon does. What about you, Eddie? Long hair or short?'

'Depends on the girl, I think.' He looked at her consideringly. 'Short hair would quite suit you, but not Theresa. Those long curls of hers are quite delightful, and she keeps losing the pins. When it falls all over her face and shoulders she gets so impatient with it. It's fun to watch her.' There he was, thinking of her again.

'You notice everything about Theresa, don't you?' Rosie sat down at her desk and spread her notes on it. 'The bride had long hair today. Beautiful, she was.'

Edouard took the pen from behind his ear, but he

made no move to go back to work. 'I suppose I do.' He spoke absently, almost to himself. 'She's not beautiful, not really pretty, but there's something about her eyes and the sweetness of her expression.'

'I've never heard you go on like that about a girl before,' Rosie uncovered her typewriter. 'Don't tell me you might be serious about her.'

'She's too young for me, in the way you mean,' Edouard snapped. 'But she's an appealing child.' Of course he wasn't serious about her, but where was she? Away where?

She laughed. 'It's funny that she didn't tell you where she was going.'

He tapped his pen reflectively against his teeth. 'Did Simon not know?'

'He seemed to think that Sal sent her somewhere on business.'

'What sort of business?'

'He didn't say. He seemed put out, too.'

'What's that supposed to mean? I'm not put out—just surprised. Where would she go?' She was a stranger, and he felt uneasy.

'If it's bothering you, why don't you ask Sal?'

'I never seem to get very far asking Sal anything. I don't know why. She seems to close up, somehow.' He used to wonder about that.

'She's very sharp—and short.' Rosie began to type. 'Perhaps it comes from growing up rich, and having everything her own way when she was young.' She paused after a few sentences. 'How do you go on with her with the summer places then?'

'She's perfectly straightforward about them.' He put the pen down on his desk. 'It's only on a personal level.'

She laughed at that. 'I thought you charmed all the women. That's what people say.'

'Do they, indeed?' Edouard's smile was rueful. He stared into space.

Rosie typed a few more sentences. 'Penny for them,

Eddie? I don't know what's got in to you today. You're not usually moody.'

He sighed. 'I have my moments. Odd—when I first came to Creswal, I was like a man reborn. The days weren't long enough to do all the things I wanted to do. It was a joy just to be alive—and walking. I didn't always see eye to eye with Cousin Jim on policy, but he was a splendid man to work for and he gave me my head on the veterans' campaign. That was before you came to the *Clarion*—before the flu claimed Jim.'

'You need a new campaign—that's what it is— something to make your voice heard all over Canada.' Rosie hesitated. 'I think . . .' She sat with one elbow on her machine. 'I think you're not very happy with this Theresa story and the way you're handling it—It upset you, didn't it, when she was so worked up about it?'

'Yes.' Edouard's reply was curt. 'You know me pretty well. But it's not entirely that. I have a feeling about this story. I had it from the moment she walked in here.' It was good, he found, to talk to Rosie.

'What sort of feeling?'

'I think in some strange way she's going to turn the town upside-down, unearth skeletons, change lives, probably get hurt herself in the process. That's fanciful, isn't it, when she's so open and single-minded about this missing father?'

'Maybe she's not as open as you think,' Rosie suggested quietly. 'She's gone away without a word to any of us.'

Edouard shook his head. 'It comes back to the same thing again—Where has she gone? Perhaps I shall ask Sal, after all.' He reached for the phone. 'Sometimes I wish they'd put this lower down on the wall. I might even move it myself.' He jiggled the receiver up and down, perched on the side of the desk. 'They wouldn't know. Operator, get me Sal at O'Reilly's Realty . . . You know she's not in? People have been trying all morning? Right, let it go for now. Call me if you get any reply later.' He hung up, sighing. Of course the girl was all right. What was he fussing for? . . .

After lunch, Theresa hurried to the orphanage. Collecting Antony proved to be simplicity itself. He was waiting in the entrance hall as Maisie opened the front door.

Tony put his hand in his sister's, and said, 'I'm ready.'

He was dressed in the same grey serge pants and heavy shirt he had worn the day before. His face shone; his boots were polished; and his hair had been cowed into submission by the heavy application of water, and where it had dried quickly, a tuft was sticking up at the crown. He had a brown paper carrier-bag, presumably containing his few possessions. It didn't look very well filled.

'Mr Ablitt wants to see both of you in his office,' announced Maisie. 'Isn't it grand, miss,' she added in a hoarse whisper, 'that Tony's going home?' She put her hand out to Theresa. 'Can I touch you, miss, just for luck? The kids always say good fortune rubs off if only you can touch. I don't believe everything they say—but just the same, can I touch?'

Theresa drew the girl towards her and hugged her. 'I brought you a present—and one for Charlie. Will you see that he gets it?' She produced two bags of sweets.

Maisie smiled in pure delight and put the sweets into her capacious pockets. 'Thank you, miss! You can trust me. I'll see Charlie gets his all right.' With great dignity she preceded them to Mr Ablitt's office. 'You have a new hat today,' she said over her shoulder. 'It looks nice. I like pink.'

The first paper Mr Ablitt presented released Antony into Theresa's care, and she signed it swiftly. Then he took a book and a paper from a shelf behind his desk, and said, 'Antony's birth certificate, and the book I mentioned that he brought with him. You can sign for these, too, if you will.'

Obediently Theresa picked up the pen again.

'I'll put the book with my things,' offered Tony, and

found a place for it in his carrier-bag. The certificate he handed to her.

That was all there was to it. Mr Ablitt extended his good wishes and told the boy to behave himself, and they were out of the room and by the front door. Maisie had disappeared, but Charlie stood there.

He punched Antony on the arm. 'Going, then? Bye-bye, kiddo, don't take any wooden nickels!' He held open the door. 'Better go quick, in case old Ablitt changes his mind!'

Before Theresa could say anything, Antony grabbed her by the hand and pulled her out. They ran down the front path and up the street. Only she turned back to wave to Charlie standing by himself at the gate.

Tony didn't speak till the orphanage was out of sight. 'Where are we going, Theresa? To the train?' He was rubbing his eyes.

'We're going shopping first. You're going to have some new clothes.'

'Oh!' was his reaction to that. 'Do you have a uniform for your children?' He had come to a halt.

Theresa began to laugh. 'No! Proper clothes, I mean —like ordinary people wear.'

He looked at her warily. 'They won't be grey, will they?'

'No grey at all,' she assured him. 'We think alike on that.'

'Yes.' Tony smiled now. 'We don't look much alike, do we? Our eyes aren't the same colour, or our hair. You're sure you are my sister? I wouldn't want you to find out afterwards that you aren't.' He left the words hanging.

'I'm certain,' she assured him, and they reached Delaney's in a companionable silence.

A fussy small middle-aged man came forward to serve them, and he and Theresa began to talk.

'Something for the young man?' he asked. 'We have some very nice grey flannel.' He looked at her enquiringly.

Tony was standing entranced before the wax model of a much older boy in a navy-blue suit with long trousers. 'My dad wore clothes like that,' he whispered to her. 'I'd like one like that.'

Theresa looked for guidance to the shop assistant.

'I believe we have a few small sizes,' he said. 'Mostly they don't go into long pants till they're thirteen or so, but I think he'll look smart in them.'

A willing Tony tried on two navy suits, one in serge and the other in more expensive flannel.

'Perfect for the summer,' said the assistant, and Tony's hand lingered on the flannel. 'Of course he'll need something for play. This will only be for good.'

She agreed that they'd have the suit and a white cotton shirt to go with it, and a little navy knitted tie. Then there was underwear and socks to choose, black cotton shorts for play, a bathing costume, two short-sleeved light shirts, one blue, one green, and brown and white striped pyjamas. The clerk escorted them to the shoe department, and sandals and soft kid boots were chosen to complement the rest.

When the bill was added up, it came to over seventeen dollars—nearly double what Theresa had planned to spend. She suddenly thought he'd better have a raincoat, and then the total was nineteen dollars and fifty cents. She paid it, reflecting that boys were much the same as girls, when it came to clothes. She had often taken the twins out, and found she'd overspent. It just meant economising in some other way. But they'd have to buy Lily a present, too. Luckily she had enough money, having been to the bank earlier, and in the shop next door she bought some beads and a parasol. Loaded down with parcels, they took a taxi back to the hotel.

At the reception desk, a beaming Mrs Harris met them and welcomed Tony. 'A parcel's come for each of you,' she announced.

'Who'd send anything to us, Theresa?' asked a wide-eyed Tony as the woman went into the little room behind the desk to fetch them.

'I don't know.' She was as perplexed as her brother.

'The card's signed by a Mr Roscoe,' trilled Mrs Harris, bringing two large boxes to them. 'A gentleman friend —isn't that nice?'

'I only met him this morning.' Theresa studied her parcel gravely.

Tony tore the wrapper off his. 'A box of Meccano . . . How did he know I'd rather have that than anything? Is it really mine, Theresa, just mine?' He turned a shining face on her. 'Mr Roscoe must like you, Theresa!'

She didn't know how to reply to that. 'Wasn't it —Wasn't it kind of him?' she managed at last.

'Aren't you going to open yours?' asked Mrs Harris.

'Yes, of course.' She undid the wrapping. Inside was the biggest box of chocolates she'd ever seen, with a little bouquet of red silk roses tied with a white ribbon. Attached to this was a note, 'To mark the occasion of your new life', signed, 'Andrew Roscoe'.

'You've made a conquest there!' exclaimed Mrs Harris, as she and Tony accepted a chocolate. 'These are delicious—and from the most expensive shop in town.'

Theresa bit into one, a lovely cream centre, that melted in her mouth. It was very pleasant to have a man send her chocolates and a dear little nosegay. It had never happened to her before. And to send a present for Antony as well—that was a thoughtful gesture.

'Will you marry him, Theresa?' Tony looked up from the floor where he had begun to spread Meccano parts.

'I shouldn't think so. I may never see him again.' She stopped him from embarking on an immediate construction, and gathered the parcels together. The two of them went up to their room. Mrs Harris had been as good as her word, and an extra bed had been set up for Tony.

Tony had the first bath and put on his new shorts. 'The man said they were for "play for the young man"', he told her, in such an imitation of the clerk in the shop that Theresa giggled. 'I'm going to play till you're ready, and then I'll change to the suit. That's right for a party, isn't it?'

Theresa nodded. Tony was certainly doing his best to please her. This might be a good time to go through his carrier-bag with him, and see what could be dispensed with. She asked him if she might do so.

He sprang to his feet. 'My book's in there. I want it!' He snatched it out and hid it behind his back. 'You won't want that—it's mine.'

Theresa was startled, and more than a little hurt, by this. 'Can't I see it?'

'No,' was the firm reply. Then he weakened a little. 'Maybe later, when I know you better. You can do what you like with the rest.'

'Why?' Theresa pressed him. 'Why can't I see it? What's in it?'

'Pictures. You wouldn't want to see them, anyway. You've never been to any of the places.' The book was still clasped behind his back.

She remembered Mr Roscoe's advice, and shrugged. She knew it was a photograph album. It must be very precious to the boy, and she must wait until he showed it to her of his own accord.

'Everyone has something that's very private, very personal,' she said. 'I wouldn't want you to go through my bag.' She held it up from where it lay on the bed. Then she dumped the clothes out of the old carrier-bag and handed it to him. 'This will be your bag, and you can keep your private things there. Is there anything among this lot that you want?'

Tony shook his head, and shoved the book into the old bag, shielding it with his body. He put it under his pillow, and went back to playing on the floor.

Theresa sorted through the tattered garments that the carrier had contained. 'I don't think we'll keep any of these.' She made a little pile to put in the waste-paper basket.

'You can throw out the grey pants, too. They're scratchy; not like my new ones. That is, if you want to,' he added, watching her.

'All right.' Theresa was in instant accord. They were

rough and ugly, and she could sense there was something symbolic in throwing them away. For good measure she added the grey shirt to the discard pile, and the orphanage boots which were very thin in the soles. She was rewarded with a wide smile, and Tony went back to playing with his Meccano.

After a moment he looked up at her. 'Yesterday, when you came to the orphanage, you had long hair. I couldn't see before, because you had your hat on, but today it's short. What's happened to it?'

'I had it cut off.'

'Why?'

'To be cooler for the summer.' She remembered she had the long switch in her bag and took it out. 'Look, this is what they took off.'

The boy rose from the floor and came to stand beside her at the bed. He put out his hand to the hair. 'May I touch it?'

Theresa gave it to him.

Tony ran his hand along it. 'It curls all by itself.' A tendril clung to his finger and wound itself round it. 'I have straight hair.' He lifted the swath of hair to his head, and tried the effect against his face. 'Even if I had long curls, I wouldn't look like you.' He said it sadly, and handed the hair back to her. 'You haven't made a mistake, have you, Theresa? Brothers and sisters should look a bit alike, shouldn't they?' His voice quivered to a stop.

She put her arm round him and gave him a quick hug. 'We had different mothers. I expect you look like yours, and I look like mine.' She knew it wasn't true that she resembled hers, but she wanted to help him.

'You have green eyes—like him . . .' he whispered.

'Like him?'

'Like my dad.' His reply was the merest sigh.

'So people say, but I've never seen him.'

'Never seen him?' Tony took a step back. 'Then how do you know about me? I thought maybe he'd sent you.'

Theresa told him the story, then, of her journey from England and her search for Charles Russell.

'Will the *Clarion* find him for you?' Tony sat beside her on the bed.

'I hope so. They're trying to.'

'Perhaps he won't like you, either.'

'Either?' she questioned gently. 'What do you mean?'

'Nothing.'

'He liked you,' Theresa stated firmly. 'Everyone says so. Stan Margold at the dam, Mrs Malinsky—do you remember her? She told me where you were.'

'I remember.' Tony nodded. 'She cried when they took me away.'

'We'll find out what happened to our father.'

'I called him Dad,' Tony offered. 'You can, too, if you like.'

'Very well,' Theresa smiled. 'We'll find out what happened to Dad.'

'But I'll be your boy now, won't I?' Tony's gaze was clear. 'We'll live together and go to parties.'

She nodded. 'Yes.'

The boy returned to his building, as though everything of importance had been settled between them to his complete satisfaction.

A very different boy from the orphanage waif she had collected earlier on went down to the party with Theresa, when it was time. In putting on his new navy suit, though he had struggled with the tie and had to be helped, he had assumed an air of pleasure and confidence that made him seem more grown up, more like a boy with a family.

He gave Lily her present of beads with a gruff, 'That's for you. I picked them out.'

That made her laugh, and they took to each other right away. She sat him on her left hand at the meal, and talked to him like an old friend.

'He has charm,' Mrs Harris whispered to Theresa. 'You'll have such enjoyment from him.' Then she intro-

duced her to the others. Her son Ian was a pleasant boy
with a tall frame that made him look older than his years,
with easy manners. His grandfather sat beside him.
There were several family friends as well, and Theresa
couldn't remember all their names, but they were all
welcoming and spoke to her.

Theresa sat at table between Tony and a dark-haired
girl of her own age. She said her name was Patti Bronski,
and she worked as a switchboard operator. She wasn't
exactly pretty. Her nose was long, her mouth very wide,
her cheekbones high, and her hair even shorter than
Theresa's. She looked foreign. Her eyes were her best
feature—a little slanted, brown in colour, full of life and
expression. She wore a chiffon dress in shades of mustard toning to dull orange and soft beige, rather like
Rosie's. Theresa wouldn't have chosen such colours
herself, but on Pattie it was admirable. Her dress was the
rust jersey she had worn on Saturday to the Falconers'.
She had packed it only on a last-minute whim, sure that
she wouldn't have any occasion to need a party frock.

Since Tony and Lily were getting on so well together,
Theresa chatted with Patti and found her splendid
company. She wanted to know all about the new brother
and how she'd come to find him, how she felt when she
first saw him and why she'd taken him on. For Theresa it
was wonderful to have a girl friend to talk to. She told
her all about her life and her impressions of Canada and
Creswal. In fact so sympathetic did she find Patti, and so
absorbed in her story, that she described not only
Edouard and her new job but also Maisie and Charlie at
the orphanage. The only thing she didn't mention was
her father's bank account. It didn't seem important.

There was melon, cold chicken, ham, beef, and salads
of all sorts, vol-au-vents, tiny sandwiches, jellies, petit
fours—and through all these Theresa and Patti ate and
talked. By the time the birthday cake was brought in, the
two girls had exchanged addresses and decided to keep
in touch. Patti produced a camera and took pictures of
Lily cutting her cake, and of Lily and her brother and

mother. It seemed quite natural, when she asked if she might take one of Antony and Theresa, to agree.

After that, they all adjourned to the lounge for coffee and the talk became general. It was an evening that Theresa really enjoyed, and by the time she and Tony eventually went upstairs it was eleven o'clock, and he was rubbing his eyes and hardly able to keep awake.

In the morning, there wasn't much time. Theresa packed; they went to church with Lily and her mother; had an early lunch and boarded the train, carrying all sorts of parcels. It was a long trip, but Tony settled happily to it. When he wasn't playing with his Meccano, he was pressed against the window, and Theresa heard him chanting to himself in time with the clanking of the wheels of the steam train, 'Going home, going home, Tony's going home.' It was dark when they arrived in Creswal, and at the boarding-house Mrs Brown was surprised to see Tony, but as the small room next door to Theresa's was empty, it was soon made ready.

On Monday morning, Theresa took Tony in his black play-shorts and blue shirt with her to O'Reilly's Realty, and Sal greeted her.

'Oh-ho, I thought you might! So this is Tony? Shake hands, young man, you'll be working for me today. Are you a good steady worker?'

Tony looked at her and nodded. 'What will I be doing?'

'Helping at the summer places. Harry'll find you something to do, if Theresa doesn't. We'll all be slaving.'

'I don't mind hard work. Look at that muscle, then!' Tony showed Sal his arm.

Sal felt it, and exclaimed, 'You'll do, my lad.'

The three of them went to the car and got in. Tony was very impressed when Theresa drove it.

'What a clever girl you are,' he said. 'Will you teach me?'

Theresa said she would.

'When you're old enough,' added Sal. 'And careful enough.'

When they arrived at the houses, the Smiths were waiting. Sal had spoken of Harry Smith, who did the maintenance work, but it was a whole family of Smiths and relatives. Ruby was there; she was Harry's wife. Maybella was her sister, and not a Smith but a Jones. They would do the cleaning. In addition there was a boy of seventeen or so, called Frank. He was a nephew, his name was Ashworth, and he was Harry's helper. Seemingly they had all worked on the cabins before, and knew exactly where to start, with the aid of the list Theresa had made earlier.

The men tackled veranda rails, screen doors, rickety steps and sagging shelves. Tony, numbered among the men, followed them round fetching pieces of wood, choosing nails and handing hammers to the other two as though he had been with them for years.

Maybella and Ruby began sweeping and washing. Theresa was detailed to take down curtains. Sal oversaw it all from a rocking-chair on one of the verandas. She had a pile of letters, and made charts of families who were coming and when, and to which house.

Before Theresa knew it, it was eleven-thirty, and Sal summoned her. 'I have a message for you. I want you to go into town, to the Italian café—they're making a stew for us. You can bring it back in the car. They'll pack it properly, and we'll all enjoy a hot meal. Oh, and before you pick it up, it might be a good idea to drop in at the *Clarion* and tell Edouard about your trip to Ottawa. You wouldn't want him to hear about it from anyone else. I haven't spoken to him.'

Theresa had been worried about that very thing. All morning, as she had worked, it had been nagging at the back of her mind. She had intended to pop in to the *Clarion* on her way to O'Reilly's Realty, but there simply hadn't been time. Breakfast had taken longer than usual because all the boarders had to speak to Tony, and he had been maddeningly slow with his food.

Now she put on her hat, climbed into Sal's car and drove to town. As she parked in front of the building and mounted the stairs to the editorial office, she hoped Edouard would be in.

He was—and alone. He looked up from his desk with a cold expression.

The smile froze on Theresa's lips, the greeting on her mouth.

'So you've come!' he exclaimed. 'I wonder you bothered.'

She halted in the doorway. 'I've come. Of course I've come,' she faltered. 'I've come to tell you about Tony.'

'A little late, aren't you?' Edouard's voice was icy. He didn't invite her to sit down, or make any move to rise to his feet.

Theresa came forward slowly, the sound of her footsteps on the wooden floor loud in her ears. 'I don't know what you mean. I came as soon as I could. Sal has us all working at the cottages today.'

'Stop playing the innocent,' he snapped. 'You went to Ottawa without a word to me. You took your brother from the orphanage—well, you were entitled to do that—but you gave the story to another paper. You haven't played fair with me, Theresa.'

'Gave the story to another paper?' She was astonished. 'Don't be ridiculous! I wouldn't do such a thing.'

'Oh, wouldn't you?' Edouard stood up, a newspaper clutched in his hand. 'What's this, then?' He thrust it at her.

Theresa looked down at the paper. It was the *Ottawa Journal*, and facing her was a picture of herself and Tony, and an article headed, 'Girl from England Finds her Brother'.

'Patti took that picture,' she stammered, 'But I don't understand! She took Lily's picture with her mother.'

'Patti Bronski?'

'Yes, how did you know?' She was stunned. 'She said she was a switchboard operator.'

Edouard smiled grimly. 'Pull the other one! She's

written the article—her name's on it. What did she offer you for the story?'

'She didn't offer me anything,' Theresa exclaimed, her temper rising. 'She sat beside me at Lily's party and we talked.'

'You can do better than that,' he suggested. He put his hands on her shoulders and shook her. 'Let's hear the real story. I'd rather the truth—even if I don't like it! She offered you national coverage, I suppose. Well, don't worry!' He released her. 'All the papers will pick it up. It's a real heart-warmer. The girl can write.'

'But I am telling the truth!' she protested. 'She sat beside me at Lily's party, and we talked. Why won't you believe me?'

'You met her only at a party?' He was standing very close to her, so close that she felt her heart was hammering, her breathing was rapid. 'And you confided in her? All this stuff about your feelings? I've never heard anything about your feelings, and I've talked to you several times about your brother and your father. How is it you didn't confide in me?'

'She was easy to talk to.' Theresa didn't stop to think how this would sound. 'I liked her.'

'And I'm not easy to talk to.' Edouard turned away from her. 'You don't like me. That much is obvious. If you had found me easy to talk to, if you had liked me, you would have told me before you went. I might have come with you.' He shook his head. 'Why am I wasting my time talking to you? Patti Bronski will find your father for you. You don't need my help.' He sat down at his desk. 'I suppose you arranged with Sal not to answer the phone, otherwise I might have gone after you.'

There was silence between them. Theresa looked at his angry face, and down at the paper still in her hands. 'I didn't arrange any such thing with Sal,' she said at last.

'What are you waiting for? There's nothing more to be said.' He looked at her in distaste.

She almost turned and fled, but some feeling of pride came to her rescue. 'You may not have anything more to say, but I have. It seems that all you newspaper people are the same. You didn't tell me you were going to write that article about life in Creswal, as Patti didn't about this one.' She threw the paper on the desk. 'The only thing you think about is a story. You don't care about my feelings any more than Patti does. And, whatever you may think, I didn't know she was a reporter. I couldn't have gone to Ottawa with you, in any case—it wouldn't have been proper.'

'Still afraid for your virtue?' Edouard began to smile, a smile that didn't quite reach his eyes. 'Come here, Theresa.' He beckoned to her with one finger. 'I want to show you something.'

She hesitated. There was something she didn't like about this conversation and the way he was looking at her. She moved slowly towards him, as he rose to his feet again.

'Do you suppose a determined man needs a trip to Ottawa to seduce you?' he asked softly. 'If I had wanted that, I could have taken you any time when we were out driving.' His hands reached out for her, his arms encircled her, his lips came down hard on hers. It was a demanding, bruising kiss.

Theresa resisted, hurt and enraged, and then her lips parted under his and she returned it, her body straining against him. When he let her go suddenly, she was trembling and close to tears.

Her hand went to her mouth. 'You don't like me, or you wouldn't do that. You don't like me any better than I like you.'

'Don't you like me, Theresa?' His hand shot out to imprison hers. 'You're fooling yourself, if you believe that.' He drew her close again.

This time he kissed her gently. A feeling of sweetness and surrender swept over her, and swiftly of their own accord her eyes closed, her arms crept round his neck, her pink cloche hat was knocked to one side, and almost unnoticed by her, fell to the floor.

But, unremarked by her, it was not so by Edouard. He

released her, thrust her to one side and took a step back.

'Good God!' he exclaimed, 'What have you done to your hair?'

Taken completely by surprise, Theresa tried to steady herself against the edge of the desk. She looked at her hat on the floor, and was so shaken that she didn't have the strength or the inclination to pick it up.

'I had it cut,' she stammered. Her hand flew to her bare neck as though to ward off his accusing gaze.

'Why?' he asked. 'Your hair was lovely, springy to the touch—it suited you.'

Why should his words upset her? But they did. Anger began to rise in her. It was her hair—hers to do as she pleased with it.

'Don't you . . .' she stammered, anger held at bay by hurt. 'Don't you like it short?'

'No.'

She blinked back tears, determined not to let him know how much his opinion mattered to her.

'The thing I liked best about you was your hair,' he told her. 'The first day you came here, it fell about your shoulders when you took off your hat. You were charming, young and innocent. Now you just look like any ordinary girl . . . Any . . .'

'Any factory girl, you mean,' Theresa interrupted. Only anger rescued her from breaking down and crying for her lost image.

'I didn't say that,' Edouard retorted, his eyes on her head. 'But I suppose it was the factory girls in the war who started this nonsense. I wonder you didn't have it done then. There would have been some reason for it.'

'My stepfather didn't want me to,' she snapped.

'A man of sense.'

Theresa suddenly remembered the switch of hair put back carelessly in her bag and still reposing there. She opened the bag and pulled it out.

'There, take it.' She flung it at him, eyes blazing. 'It means more to you than it does to me.' She had the satisfaction of seeing that it was an astonished Edouard who caught the length of hair.

'I'm more than just a hank of hair,' she raged stormily. 'I'm a person, a girl who can choose for herself how she wants to look, what she wants to do, without consulting you—or any man. How would you feel if I told you your hair was too short or your tie was the wrong colour blue to go with your eyes?' She stopped abruptly, because she realised she could no longer control her voice.

'I should feel flattered that you noticed.' His hand caressed the switch in much the same way that Tony's had. In much the same way, a curl clung to a finger and wound itself round it. 'Is it the wrong shade of blue?'

'Yes,' Theresa replied stiffly. 'And you needn't feel flattered. Anyone might have noticed.'

Edouard laughed. 'I'm sorry, Theresa. You're quite right. It's none of my business what you do with your hair.' He took a step towards her. 'Will you forgive me?' He let the hair hang from one hand, and held the other out to her.

'I—I don't know.' She wasn't disposed to forgive as easily as that . . . She ignored his hand.

He bent to pick up the pink cloche, and as he put it on the desk, the hank of hair swung gently from the other hand. He looked at ruefully. 'I can almost understand why the North American Indian scalped his victim. There's something very personal in a length of hair. It speaks about its owner'—he paused—'or ex-owner.'

'In what way?' Theresa coldly watched the gentle swaying.

He ran his hand along the switch. 'This could only be feminine hair, from a healthy young head. Look at the sheen of it, and the thickness. It catches the light.' He held it up so that the sun through the window beside him caught the highlights in it. 'I'd swear your hair was glowing brown, but there are reddish glints in it.' He rubbed it against one cheek. 'Surprisingly soft for such curly hair.'

As he touched it, Theresa felt a shock of pleasure. It

was as though he fondled her. She sensed how his hands
would feel on her body, against her skin—and drew in
her breath sharply. What was she thinking of? She
blushed in shame. She longed to snatch the hair from
him to stop these imaginings, and this pleasure that was
half pain, half longing.

He held it firm, and she had given it to him—thrown it
at him, in fact. She couldn't claim it back.

She had to stop him some other way. 'Tony touched
it like that.' It wasn't strictly true . . . When Tony
had touched it, she hadn't had a reaction like this. 'He
tried it on,' she added, 'to see if it made him look like
me.'

'And did it?'

'No, not at all. He was disappointed, and thought I'd
made an error about being related.'

'Wanted to be reassured.' He nodded. 'Think he'll
settle down?'

'I think so.' Theresa was beginning to thaw. Perhaps
she owed him some sort of explanation. 'I went alone'
—she hesitated—'I went alone because I had to. Don't
you see? I was afraid.'

'Afraid?'

'Afraid I mightn't want to have anything to do with
Antony when I saw him, afraid he wouldn't want me. I
was afraid of walking away from him—and of your
knowing it.'

Edouard took a step towards her. His face was gent-
ler. 'I've seen all sorts of people duck out of their
responsibilities. Do you think I would have thought less
of you if you'd backed off? He's only your half-brother,
after all.'

'I would have thought less of myself.' Theresa only
breathed the words, but he heard them. 'But it wasn't
like that. When I talked to him, it was very simple. Here
was a boy who needed any help I could give him—so did
Maisie and Charlie, Charlie especially. I couldn't take
them all; only Tony, because he's my brother.'

He nodded, but said nothing.

'Sal was very good about my bringing Tony to work today.' Theresa rushed on, unnerved by his silence. 'We're out at the cottages.' She looked at her watch, pinned to the lapel of her dress. 'She sent me into town to get the lunch.'

'You had better hurry along and do it, then,' he suggested, handing her both her hat and her length of hair.

Another wave of hot colour swept over her face. He was dismissing her again. She picked up the pink cloche, and would have jammed it on her head, but for the grip of Edouard's hand on hers.

'Don't cover it up.' He spoke softly, and looked into her eyes. 'It's very fetching, really. It's just that it makes you look more like a boy than a girl. I didn't mean to hurt your feelings.'

His smile was so kind and understanding that Theresa melted completely. 'It will be so much easier for me,' she murmured. 'If you'd ever had to wash and brush long curly hair, you wouldn't have it long, either.'

Edouard kissed the tip of her nose, and surveyed her. 'I suppose I'll get used to it.' His good humour appeared to be restored. 'Tell Sal I'll be along later. I'll see you then, too.'

'What for?' There was still a particle of indignation to be roused in her. She didn't want to see him again—not so soon, at least. She stood with her hat in her hands.

His eyebrows rose. 'To see your young man, of course,' he replied blandly, and watched Theresa stuff the contentious switch into her bag.

'You're not going to carry that round with you for ever, are you? I would have thought a person in her own right, a girl with a mind of her own, would put it firmly away.' His tone was teasing.

'Yes,' she agreed, trying for dignity. 'We were late in getting back. I haven't had time.' She turned to go.

She wasn't sure what Edouard meant to do about the write-up in the Ottawa paper and further publicity in his own, but she knew he was no longer angry with her. She was convinced that it was handling her hair that had caused the change in him.

How strange some men were, she mused, as she went to the Italian café to pick up the lunch. It was ready for her, in an enormous pot packed in a big wooden box with straw to keep it warm.

'Like a dutch oven,' the proprietor explained. 'It will keep all day and go on cooking very slowly.' He stowed it in the car for her with two loaves of bread, milk and butter and jam.

In a very reflective mood, Theresa drove back to the summer cottages.

CHAPTER ELEVEN

THERESA HAD not been gone for very long when Edouard had another visitor. This time it was Sidney Falconer.

She rushed in breathlessly. 'Is it true?' she demanded, without any sort of greeting. 'Has she brought the boy back?'

'What are you talking about?' he asked, looking up from his work and motioning her to a chair. He could have made a shrewd guess, but decided to let her speak for herself. 'Who's this she—and what boy?'

Sidney glared at him, and then sat down. 'You know perfectly well who I mean—Theresa, of course. Has she brought her brother back? I heard they arrived from Ottawa last night. I was sure you'd know if that was right.'

It was a warm day, and she looked hot and a little dishevelled. There was a beading of perspiration on her upper lip, and her cheeks were flushed. Her pretty pink and white dress had lost some of its crispness.

Edouard reflected that it was the first time he'd ever seen this girl showing any sign of being affected by emotion or by the weather. He wondered which it was.

'I wonder who told you that?' He paused, but no further information was forthcoming.

'Is it true?' Sidney repeated.

'Yes. Is it somehow important to you?' He leaned forward with a smile.

She ignored it. 'No, of course it's not important to me what she does.' She tapped her foot on the floor. 'But I like to know what's happening round here.'

For a girl to whom it didn't matter, Edouard reflected, his interest aroused, she was looking distinctly put out. Why should that be? He watched as Sidney picked up a piece of paper from his desk and began to fan herself with it.

'My father says it's a splendid thing for her to do.'

'But,' he suggested, 'you don't think so.'

'No, I don't. Not really.'

'Why not?'

'It's not the thing to do—Not for a girl on her own. Don't you agree?' She appealed to him, with a soft sigh.

Edouard noted the flutter of her eyelashes, and wondered for the first time in their acquaintance what part of that gesture was natural to her and what part was practice and artifice. Theresa never used such affectations. She was direct and unstudied.

'Women on their own bring up children all the time,' he replied shortly, 'and succeed in doing it. My own mother did.'

'That's different,' Sidney protested. 'She was your mother. She had to take care of you.'

He began to smile. 'Do you suppose that made it easier for her?'

'How should I know? She was a widow, wasn't she? Everyone helps widows.' She fanned herself energetically.

'Do they?' He got to his feet, finding that this girl was annoying him with such a sweeping assumption. It would be ridiculous to lose his temper. After all, she was very young and had lived with wealth all her life. She could never have experienced any sort of privation. He walked to the back desk and picked up some work of Rosie's.

'You're not listening to me, Edouard,' Sidney pouted. 'It's not just I who think that Theresa is being foolish. Marguerite does, too.'

'Does she, indeed?' He returned to his desk.

'She says she's asking for trouble.'

'More than likely.' He sat down again—this time on the edge of the desk, facing her. 'Of course, you could help Theresa, if you had a mind to do so.'

'I?' He noted that Sidney bit her lip. 'How?'

'I imagine she'd find a friend of her own age very

desirable.' Edouard was beginning to enjoy himself.

'Yes, I suppose she would, but she's not really my age. She's older than me.'

'Not that much.'

'Just enough to make her attractive to men,' was the swift rejoinder.

'Which men are those?'

'Well—you, and Simon, and my father. I don't know why. Really I don't. She's not what you'd call divine-looking, is she?'

Edouard smiled at Sidney's disgruntled expression. 'All the girls can't be as pretty as you.'

She fluttered her eyelashes again. 'I'm not sure whether you mean that. You're not being very nice to me, Eddie,' she complained. 'I came to see you especially.'

'Did you? I still haven't figured out why.'

'I thought you'd help me.' She suddenly seemed ill at ease. 'There's something I want to show you.'

Edouard sat back a little, waiting. 'What might that be?'

'Some sketches.' Sidney was in a rush to get the words out. 'You know I want to go to Art School, and Big Bob won't hear of it. I thought if I showed my drawings to you, and you thought they were any good, you might tell him. He'll listen to you.'

This was so unlike Sidney's usual self-assured delivery that he was intrigued. 'Let's have a look.'

She had a large white bag hooked over her arm. Now she undid the clasp, drew out a leather folder and gave it to him.

Edouard opened it. The top one was a watercolour portrait of Marguerite, pretty, but rather insipid. The second was a river scene in the same medium. That, too, he passed over quickly. The third was a pen-and-ink sketch of himself which made him chuckle. It wasn't flattering, but it was certainly recognisable. A portrait of Big Bob followed, scowling.

'That must have been the day he turned you down,' he

observed, his interest now awakened. There was nothing kind in the drawing, but it certainly caught the
strength and force of the man. He turned it face down on
top of the other discards, and looked at the next one.

It was Theresa who looked up at him, her hair tumbling over her shoulders, the black kewpie doll she had
won at the fair clasped in her arms. The mouth was too
large, the chin too pointed, but the eyes were wonderful.

'I'll buy this one from you,' he offered. 'I like it, and
you'll never see her hair like that again. She's had it cut.'

'Really short? You mean like a boy's? How could
she?'

'Not quite as short as that, and it still curls.' He held
the picture up.

'Do you really want it? Do you think it's . . . good?'
Sidney was unnaturally humble.

'The best thing you've shown me.' Edouard smiled at
her. 'It would be a pity not to develop such a talent.'

'Do you mean that? Really?'

'Of course I mean it. How much do you want for it?'

'I don't know. I've never sold any. What do artists
usually charge?'

'Name a price.'

'Five dollars?'

He paused for a moment. Five dollars, he supposed,
was a fair price. He would have paid more, he reflected,
but there was no need to let Sidney know that, neither
did he ask himself why he wanted the sketch so much.

'You drive a hard bargain,' he told the girl. 'But
—done. I'll take it.'

Sidney smiled and fluttered again. 'And you'll speak
to Big Bob?'

He nodded and extracted a five-dollar bill from his
wallet. 'I'll try my best to convince him, even if I have to
show him this. I don't suppose he's seen it?'

She shook her head and took the bill. 'You don't want
to buy the one of yourself as well?'

Edouard laughed. 'You can keep that one. You'll
need it to show what you can do.'

She took her folder back. 'Why, Eddie? Why do you want Theresa's and not your own?'

'She's handsomer than I am.'

'No, she's not,' Sidney contradicted. Her eyes went to the kewpie doll on the shelf over Edouard's head. 'You've kept her doll.'

'So I have,' Edouard admitted. 'She gave it to me.'

She didn't say anything to that, but her expression was knowing. 'Are you going to put the sketch up there, too?'

'No, I don't think so.' He propped the drawing up on his desk behind a wooden tray, and regarded it. 'I think I'll take it home.'

'I suppose,' said Sidney, as she stowed the folder away. 'I suppose I could ask her and the boy to do something—go on a picnic, maybe. No, what about roller-skating? We could all go, couldn't we, Simon as well . . .'

'What a good idea!' he agreed. 'I'll come too, and Rosie.'

Her face fell just a little, but she made no protest. 'Yes, I'll arrange it, shall I? Just leave it all to me.'

That suited Edouard admirably, and he smiled at Sidney. 'I'll speak to Big Bob. We'll see what we can do.'

It was the middle of the afternoon when Edouard arrived at the cottage site. The whole working group had gathered for a cup of tea on the veranda. He greeted them all by name, as Sal poured a cup for him. Last of all he shook hands with Tony.

'So you've come home, Mr Russell.'

Antony giggled, but it was plain he liked to be addressed as Mr Russell. 'Everyone calls me Tony,' he declared. 'You can, too, if you like.'

'Right, Tony, I shall. How would you like to have your picture taken with your sister?' Edouard began to set up his camera.

'For the paper?' Tony looked delighted. 'But not here. I'd like it taken by the canoe, since you want to know. By Frank's canoe, please. We've been fishing in it,' he added with a smile.

He hadn't expected such a direct reply or such a literal translation of his words, but there wasn't any harm in humouring him.

'By the canoe it shall be.' Edouard refolded the tripod and finished his tea. 'If Theresa will come with us, we'll do it now.'

The canoe was down by the shore, turned upside-down in the usual manner of beaching such craft. Tony led the way to it, rushing ahead and then waiting, patting it as the other two followed at a slower pace.

'Look, I never noticed before, Mr Moreau,' he called out. 'Underneath the black paint—it's red.' He fingered a scratch along the side.

'Yes.' Edouard gave it a cursory glance. 'People often paint canoes. Now, if you'll just stand there, Tony, and you too, Theresa, we'll get all three of you in the snap.'

Tony did as he was bid, cheerfully posing with an arm round Theresa, and talking all the time.

'You don't sound French,' he remarked. 'But your name is Moreau—that's French, isn't it?'

Edouard nodded, and clicked the shutter. The boy was certainly a chatterer, but he'd been just such a lad. He nodded. 'That's right.'

'You'd do for Charlie,' Tony went on.

Theresa, Edouard noticed, tried to shush her brother, but Tony was unstoppable. He took Theresa's hand. 'He'd be just dandy for Charlie! Don't you see? He could teach Charlie to help him on the paper, hold the camera and all that.' He turned to Edouard in some delight. 'Are you looking for a boy?'

'No,' he replied, now thoroughly convinced that Tony was Theresa's brother, though he could see no facial resemblance. He had the same sort of trusting expectancy about him. Why did both of them think he was the answer to their problems? He was well aware from the write-up in the Ottawa paper that Charlie was Tony's friend and hoping for a home with someone.

Tony was clearly disappointed by the curt answer. 'Well, if you should change your mind,' he suggested, 'Charlie wants a Frenchman.'

'I'll let you know,' Edouard said, with a dark look at Theresa, as Tony moved forward to fold the tripod for him.

'I'm sorry,' she apologised. 'He's quite above himself, and he's taken a liking to you.'

Tony appeared oblivious of this exchange. 'My father had a canoe just like this one,' he told Edouard, 'only it was red, of course. He carved my initial on the little front seat. I'll show you where.' He dragged him to the canoe, dropping down to his knees beside it, and reaching under the seat. 'It's there!' he squeaked in excitement. 'Theresa, come and see! The T is there.'

Edouard put his hand on the spot the boy was holding. True enough, the initial was there, and the canoe, now that he looked closely, was red under its black topcoat.

'It's my father's canoe!' Tony was jumping up and down, holding on to Theresa. 'Why has Frank got Dad's canoe?'

'Not so fast,' Theresa begged. 'Calm down! Even if it is the same one, Frank might have bought it from him.'

'He never sold it,' Tony asserted wildly. 'I know that. He loved that canoe.'

Theresa examined the carved letter, tracing it with one finger. 'It really is there. Do you think we could ask Frank?' She appealed to Edouard.

'I'll talk to Frank,' he offered. 'You two get back to work. There's probably some simple sort of explanation.'

Almost in spite of himself, Edouard wanted to get to the bottom of this. He gave his camera to Tony to leave on the veranda of the cottage where they had had tea, and ambled towards one of the smaller ones where the sound of hammering could be heard.

Theresa had followed behind him. 'Can I just listen on the veranda?' she pleaded.

Edouard shrugged. 'Why not? If you're very quiet.'

She rewarded him with a smile, and opened the door so that he could enter.

He located Frank in the back kitchen, repairing a shelf. Maybella was sweeping in one of the bedrooms. They could hear her singing to herself.

'Nice canoe you have there, Frank,' he began. 'Have you had it long?'

'A year or two.' Frank was very busy measuring.

'Got it new, did you?'

'Nearly new.' Frank amended, looking up briefly.

'Where'd you get it, Frank?' Edouard's tone was light. 'A bargain, was it?'

'I was lucky.' Frank put his measure down. He looked uneasy. Maybella had stopped singing, and the cabin was very quiet. 'It didn't cost me anything.'

'How was that?' Edouard felt that he managed to sound interested, in no way accusing. 'Found it, did you?'

'Yes.' Frank stood awkwardly on one foot.

'It was red, and you painted it black. Why was that?' The quiet questions went on.

Frank looked mulish, determined to give nothing away. It was Maybella, standing in the doorway, who broke the tension.

'Tell him, lad,' she urged. 'You haven't done anything wrong. You found it. She said you could keep it.'

'She made me promise never to tell anyone,' Frank protested. 'She said she'd take it away from me if I ever did.'

'Well, I didn't make any promise like that.' Maybella leaned against the doorway. 'Frank's like my own boy.' She spoke direct to Edouard. 'I never had any of my own, and Charlene and Frank have been like son and daughter to me. Frank wouldn't do anything wrong. When he found the canoe, he went right to Miss Falconer—Miss Marguerite, that is. Charlene was her maid, and knew she was sweet on Mr Russell.' Maybella paused for breath, and Edouard noticed that Theresa was standing behind her.

Edouard was surprised. Of course Marguerite had known Charles Russell. Did Maybella realise what she was saying?

'What do you mean?' he probed. 'Sweet on him.'

'Just what I said. Everybody knew it. They were going to get married—but she said that wasn't so, afterwards. That she'd never meant to marry him, but she did. That's why Frank went to her and asked if he could keep the canoe. He only found it two years after. It was hidden in some bushes.'

'Cached,' Frank corrected. 'People cache canoes so they can come back to them. But he wasn't going to come back. Not two years later—not now, either. That's what Miss Falconer said, when I talked to her. She looked so sad when she said it that I thought she was going to cry. She said I could keep it, if I painted it some other colour. So I did. I painted it black.'

'Someone should have the pleasure of it—them were her very words,' Maybella added. 'I've always remembered them from when Frank told me. He can keep the canoe, can't he?' She looked towards Theresa.

Edouard noted that the girl didn't hesitate. 'Of course he can. It's yours, Frank. You found it.'

'I'll show you where I found it, if you like,' Frank offered. 'It's kind of you to let me keep it.' He stammered his thanks. 'You might want it yourself.'

Edouard cut across Theresa's protests. 'Where did you find it, Frank? Far from here?'

'No, not far. I could take you there now. It's just through the woods a piece. We can walk there in ten or fifteen minutes.'

Edouard nodded. Perhaps a look at the spot might offer some clues.

They made quite a little procession as Frank, his hammer still in his hand, led the way out of the cottage, down to the beach and then along a little path among the tress. Single file, Edouard followed Frank, Theresa behind him, and Tony trailed in the rear, looking not quite sure if he would be turned back.

'Of course the cottages weren't here then,' Frank explained, as they went deep into the woods. 'It was all trees there, too.'

This might very well be the end of Theresa's search, Edouard reflected as they continued along the trail. He glanced back quickly at the girl. She was frowning, and he could see she was breathing quickly. Yes, she knew it might; they might find something conclusive here.

Frank stopped suddenly. 'It was just around here. There was a big pine tree and then some bushes.' He darted to one side of the path. 'Just wait here for a minute till I find the tree I'm looking for.'

Obediently they all halted, drawing together. In spite of the heat, Theresa shivered, and started violently when Frank reappeared behind her.

'I've found the tree.'

Once again he led the way, not forward this time, but away from the path and the shore. The immensity of woods and sky frightened Theresa. How could such an expanse of emptiness and similarity furnish any clues to her father?

Frank came to a halt, and gestured towards a thick patch of ferns and bracken. They all came to look.

'It was cached there. I wouldn't have found it, except my dog chased a squirrel and I went after him.'

Theresa could see no marks of any kind. If a canoe had lain there once, protected from human eye and the ravages of the weather, there was not a single trace of it now.

'Why would anyone leave it there?' she appealed to Frank.

'I don't know. He must have meant to come back for it.'

'But where would he go from here?' Theresa persisted.

'For a swim, perhaps—maybe hunting a deer or a fox.'

'My father didn't like hunting,' Tony broke in. 'I can remember that. He loved to fish, but not to hunt. He said he hadn't been bred to it. I never understood what bred had to do with it.'

The others looked at him.

'Not b-r-e-a-d,' Edouard spelled it out. 'But b-r-e-d.'

'He meant he hadn't grown up with hunting.' Theresa said gently, as Tony looked at her questioningly. She felt a sudden sympathy for this father who hadn't been bred to hunting.

They stood quietly contemplating the puzzle.

'Perhaps he was attacked by a bear or a wild-cat,' suggested Frank.

'Why hide the canoe, then?' Edouard looked round and back at him. 'If it was foul play, who would hide the canoe?'

No one answered. The fir trees stood silent sentinels, dark green timeless witnesses of what had happened here.

'Isn't there a railway-cutting around here?' Edouard asked. 'Somewhere where the train stops sometimes?' He looked to Frank. 'It seems to me I've heard Big Bob speak of meeting his friend from Renfrew here, and taking him to some hunting lodge on the other side of the river.'

'I think it does,' Frank agreed. 'It's not a regular stop, but Mr Falconer's friend is a railway official.'

'What does it mean?' Tony looked to Edouard for an explanation. 'If the train stopped, and someone got off and attacked him . . .' His words faltered to a halt.

'Or he got on the train?' Theresa found that the words uttered themselves. 'Where would he go?'

'Away,' Tony supplied bitterly. 'That's what they all said. He went away.'

'Why?' Theresa asked. 'Why should he go away?'

Tony bit his lip. 'He left his canoe. Do you suppose he meant to come back, Theresa?'

Thus appealed to, Theresa didn't know how to reply. 'Perhaps he couldn't.'

'He could do anything he wanted!' Tony kicked against a patch of dirt, and dislodged a stone which rolled a few feet from him. He picked it up and threw it into the trees. 'It doesn't matter. I don't care what he did. Theresa's going to take care of me now, and I'm going to take care of her. Let's go back to work, Frank.'

Frank looked at Edouard, and at his nod, he and the boy went back the way they had come.

Theresa wasn't prepared to leave yet. She faced Edouard. 'What was it Frank said about Miss Maddie looking sad?'

'So sad he thought she was going to cry.'

'No, not that part,' she said. 'He's not going to come back: that was what she said. How could she have known, I wonder? Suppose there was an accident, and she saw him drown? Frank doesn't think he's ever going to turn up again—not now, not ever. Perhaps they all know, and they just don't want to tell me that he's dead.' She swallowed hard.

'If he is dead,' said Edouard softly, 'you'll have to face it.'

Theresa turned from him. She wasn't going to cry, not in front of Edouard, who wanted her to face the unfaceable. She ran through the trees, turning away from him, not noticing where she was going, not caring.

He followed her. She heard him crashing through the undergrowth, calling to her to come back, and she was glad she had worn sandals with low heels. On and on she ran until all sounds of pursuit had faded. Then, breathless, panting and more than a little frightened of the solitude, she leaned against a gnarled tree trunk and let go. Great sobs shook her.

Her father was dead. They all knew it. How could she have been so stupid all along not to have realised it? They just didn't want to tell her. Even now, no one would tell her the full story. They were hiding something. She wept for her lost father and for herself. She'd never know him now. In this immensity of forest and river he had perished.

Edouard came up so silently behind her that the first thing she heard was his voice, and she jumped in alarm.

'You foolish girl!' he chided. 'What were you thinking of to run through the woods? You might never have found your way back.' He turned her round to face him. His voice was full of anger, but he held out his arms to her and she came into them.

She cried her heart out, locked in the circle of his embrace, and he rocked her gently as one might a child. Her tears hiccuped to a stop. 'He's dead, isn't he? Why didn't Marguerite tell me in the first place? She wouldn't have given his canoe to Frank if she'd thought he was alive.'

'You're jumping to conclusions there.' Edouard spoke softly, his arm still round her. 'Anyone might accept the fact of a permanent disappearance after two years' absence.'

Theresa moved a little away from him. 'If I asked her,' she began. 'She might . . .'

'She might think you held her responsible. It would be pointing a finger of suspicion at her—the kind of suspicion that grows and grows in a small community.'

'Ye-es. But,' she was thinking, 'if I say nothing at all, I may never know.'

Edouard took her hand. 'Think of it from her point of view. If she was considering marriage with Charles Russell, and he disappeared before the wedding, how must she have felt? She survived the jilting. How monstrous to be accused of what—murder? witnessing an accident? Even knowing why he left? No, best leave it alone.'

Theresa looked up at his set face. Yes, there was compassion in what he said, and even a rough kind of justice, she supposed. But he thought of the situation from Marguerite's side, not from hers. That hurt.

'Isn't there such a thing as truth?'

'The truth will emerge in its own good time,' he declared. 'If it's truth you want, I think you can begin to see it. You have begun to see it. A few minutes ago, you said your father was dead. Why are you fighting now to deny it?'

Theresa sighed and freed her hand. 'There's so much unexplained, so much unfinished.'

'That's the way life often is.' Edouard looked down at his shoulder, and she noticed that his shirt was wet from her tears.

She touched the damp spot. 'I'm sorry about that.'

'Let's sit down a minute,' he suggested, 'and I'll tell you a story.' He moved a few steps to a large rock, dappled by sunshine and shade, and seated himself. 'It will soon dry here.'

Theresa, a little unwilling to listen, sat in the shade. 'If he's dead,' she said, almost to herself, 'I should be sorry, and mourn for him. I was crying for myself before. How do you grieve for someone you've never known?'

'It's strange that you should ask that question,' he said very softly. 'When my mother died, that's exactly what I asked myself.'

'But you knew your mother. She took care of you when you came back wounded, and when you were little.'

'Yes, she did,' he admitted. 'But the picture she presented to me was that of a strong, unemotional woman—a woman who'd given up living and feeling when her husband died. I was seven when that happened. I can't remember her ever kissing me or touching me after that. She became a sort of general, who issued orders to both Ellen and me. Perhaps she was a little kinder with Ellen. She didn't give her so much trouble.'

Theresa sat very still, her eyes on Edouard's. She sensed that it was very hard for him to talk of his mother.

'When I refused to be a banker, and found myself a job in a hotel kitchen instead, she set her lips and said I'd soon learn sense with good hard work to help me. I paid the board money she demanded, though Ellen often helped me out there, and I found other jobs. She was right about the hard work in that kitchen. When I became a reporter, she gave me a wintry smile and remarked that she hoped I'd stick to it this time. I did, of course. It was the very job for me—the one I hadn't known I wanted. When I went to war, she nodded, and said every man must do his duty. When I came back wounded, she called me a war hero and got Tom McGregor, Ellen's husband and now installed as proprietor of his father's newspaper, to run a feature article on me. I didn't want a feature article. I wanted a job. I didn't know she knew that.' Edouard stopped abruptly.

The silence stretched between them.

Theresa put her hand on his knee. 'And then you got better and found a job.' She didn't know why he was telling her all this, but she wanted him to go on.

He smiled. 'That was her doing, too. I didn't know it then. I found out only when I read her diary after her death. It was all recorded there—the struggle she had with herself to ask a favour of Tom McGregor, the even harder fight she made against her pride to approach the family who'd rejected her when she married my father. Well, she struck lucky there—lucky for me. Her sister's boy, Jim Shaw, owned the *Clarion* and came to the rescue. The rest you know. He paid for my cure and left me his paper.' He put his hand on Theresa's. 'When I read my mother's diary, I cried for her and for all those bleak wasted years. It was plain that she had loved me and Ellen, and had never let us know. She had never been able to let us know.'

Theresa felt a lump in her throat. Whether it was for Edouard or for his tortured mother, she could not have said. She raised his hand to her lips and kissed it.

Edouard looked down at her, his expression unreadable. 'I didn't tell you that to gain your sympathy. I've never told it to another soul. I just thought it might help you to understand that life can be complicated, that people act from the strangest of motives in ways which are incomprehensible. Your father probably loved you and Tony in his own way, however odd that way may seem to you. Grieve for him, if you think you must, but leave Marguerite alone.'

If he had stopped before he uttered that last instruction, Theresa would have been in total sympathy with him. As it was, she dropped his hand and rose to her feet.

'Thank you,' she said stiffly. 'I won't make any accusations—if that's what you mean. I don't think I would have, anyway. I've only ever wanted to know the truth, however awful that might be. At least, you had the satisfaction of finding that.'

'Yes, eventually,' he agreed, rising and shaking a few leaves from himself. 'I waited a long time.'

'Yes, I know that's what you think I should do. Well, then, I shall.' She found he was very close beside her, watching her.

'But it isn't what you want to do.'

'No, it isn't what I want to do.'

Theresa turned away from him. When he was as close to her as this, all she wanted was to go back into the circle of his arms, even though he thought first of Marguerite.

'I must go back to work. Sal will wonder where I've got to.'

'I'll have a word with her,' offered Edouard, and led the way back.

CHAPTER TWELVE

PERHAPS IT was just as well for Theresa that the next ten days were filled with work. The cottages were put in shining order, the bookings sorted out and the summer visitors began to arrive. She and Tony drove Sal's green beast up and down the road so often that she knew every inch of it. Tony made friends with some of the summer children, and swam and lazed on the beach with them at least part of the day.

Simon took them to the pictures one evening. But, for the most part, Theresa was glad to fall into bed at night, exhausted, without any thought of the future or the past.

There was an article in the *Clarion*, with one of the photos Edouard had taken by the canoe, and he left some proofs at Sal's office for them. Tony was thrilled with them. Theresa tried to find the time to go in and thank him, but didn't manage it. She wrote him a note instead.

Sidney sent an invitation to a party on Friday at the roller-skating rink, and Theresa almost decided not to go, until Tony and Simon talked her into changing her mind. She had no idea who else would be there, nor was she sure what to wear. Neither she nor Tony had been skating before. She finally decided on a full navy skirt with her pink blouse. Tony wore his shorts and a clean cotton shirt. He was very excited.

They all met at the rink, and Sidney greeted Theresa with a welcoming smile. 'So glad you could come; and how nice to meet Tony. I don't suppose he remembers me.'

Tony shook his head at that, looking puzzled. 'I'm Sidney Falconer. You were only a very small boy when you were here last.' She didn't wait for any more, but added, 'There's no need to buy tickets. It's arranged with Edouard, and you're all coming back with me to the house for refreshments afterwards.'

Rosie appeared with Edouard, and they went in, chattering happily, and were given skates. Theresa was surprised to see that Sidney offered to help Tony, but he declined politely and attached himself firmly to Rosie.

Simon took immediate charge of Theresa and proved to be a very patient, encouraging teacher. That left Sidney and Edouard, who skated off together in perfect harmony.

Theresa at first was too busy thinking of her feet and balance to notice how anyone else was getting on. The gliding motion was quite unsettling, she found, but Simon supported her, smiling.

'Trust me,' he instructed. 'And take bigger steps. I'll hold you up. Take a look at Sidney.'

She looked. Sidney and Edouard were so at home on their skates that it looked more like dancing than skating.

'I'll never do that,' she protested, but she began to try.

The rink, merely a barn-like room with no partitions and a smooth wood floor, was a rough sort of building that had once been a warehouse. What windows there were were small and high up in the wall, and the place seemed to echo the rumble of the steel skate-wheels and the laughter and shrieks of the skaters.

Simon talked to Theresa in a relaxed way, and she felt very safe with him. She might master this sport after all.

'We're having an Open Day at the plant in two weeks' time. I'd like you and Sal and Tony to come. It's to show everyone what the reinforced cardboard boxes are like. My father's bringing all sorts of people up from Toronto, and all the businessmen of Creswal are coming with their wives and sons and daughters. We plan to make it a real occasion. We'll be sending out proper invitations, of course, but I wanted you to know in plenty of time.'

'That's very sweet of you,' exclaimed Theresa, making a sudden grab for him as her feet nearly went from under her. It wasn't as though her engagement book was full, she reflected.

When, shortly afterwards, Edouard claimed her as a partner, she hesitated. 'Promise you won't try anything fancy,' she begged him, uncertain.

'As if I would!' He held out his arm to her. 'You may cling to me. I'm like solid rock.'

Theresa did cling to him. She found him a lighter, more accomplished, skater than Simon, but inclined to introduce an extra step in a long glide. It wasn't, she felt, that he was trying to show off, but rather that he couldn't help himself, as he was so used to his skates. She envied him that.

'Don't try so hard,' he told her. 'Think of something else.'

Theresa tried to do as he said, but skating with Edouard was altogether more unpredictable and exciting somehow than with Simon. True, he didn't allow her to fall, but several times she felt on the brink of it. He held her close to him, much closer than Simon had done, and that was unsettling enough, because whenever she was touching him, her legs seemed to lose their strength.

'I had a letter from Patti Bronski,' she confided, breathless and trying to follow his instructions.

'Oh yes, the reporter in Ottawa.' His arm now round her waist.

'She apologised for not warning me about the write-up, but she wasn't sure that it was going to be printed. She says Maisie and Charlie from the orphanage have found homes—isn't that good news? I wrote back right away and enclosed a note for Charlie telling him how pleased I was. I asked her to forward it to him. I liked him very much.'

'That's the first time you've told me anything about the orphanage children,' Edouard observed. 'Getting to trust me at last, are you?'

Theresa knew she coloured up at that. 'It's not exactly that I don't trust you. I'm just afraid I'll see it in your paper.'

He laughed, and held her closer.

'You did a nice write-up of Tony finding the canoe,' she commented.

'Straight reporting—no accusations made, no names named—just Tony coming home and finding his father's canoe. And an appeal to anyone who might have seen it on the river on the right date five years ago.'

No names named—that brought Theresa up short. Except for that, and the immediate thoughts of Marguerite that it raised, she might have told Edouard about the letter that she'd had that week as well from Mr Roscoe, to thank her for Tony's birth certificate and reporting that the bank's laywers had set things in motion.

The moment was lost. Tony called to them, as he skated past between Simon and Rosie. Then a smiling Sidney skated up to them and offered to take Theresa off Edouard's hands, as his manager wanted to see him. She had forgotten that the rink belonged to him. Of course he had to go.

Sidney was solicitude itself with Theresa. 'You're doing very well, but don't worry. I'll see you come to no harm.'

Thus assured, she matched her steps to Sidney's. For several minutes, all went well.

'When did Simon meet Rosalinda?' Sidney demanded abruptly. She had been holding Theresa's arm, and now she detached herself and held her loosely by the hand only. 'I suppose you introduced them?'

Theresa didn't really feel safe, held so casually, but she wasn't going to ask Sidney for assistance she didn't mean to give her. 'She interviewed him for the paper.' she replied.

Sidney held her hand more tightly, and skated just a little faster. 'I saw them canoeing the other evening —and in my canoe, too.' She looked at Theresa.

No doubt to see how she was taking it, Theresa told herself, as she answered calmly, 'I think they've been out a few times in the canoe.'

'Have you . . . been out in it?' Again Sidney increased her pace.

'Not yet.'

'Cut you out, has she?'

'And you!' Theresa snapped, knowing that she was courting trouble, and no longer caring.

Sidney pulled at her so sharply that she managed to save herself only by clutching the other girl about the waist with her free hand.

They stood poised, impetus halted, eye to eye.

'I don't know what you mean,' Sidney growled. 'I could have Simon running after me again if I just crooked my finger.'

'Could you?' Theresa smiled sweetly. 'I notice that he hasn't skated with you yet.' She linked her arm firmly through Sidney's and hung on as they began to gather speed again.

'I'll soon remedy that,' Sidney announced, and she smiled at Simon as he skated by. 'But before I do, there's something I want to say to you.'

They negotiated a corner, Theresa keeping her balance only by the strength of her grip on Sidney. She said nothing, saving her breath and her attention for skating.

'Leave Aunt Maddie alone,' Sidney ordered. 'Stop spreading rumours about her . . .' Another corner was manoeuvred, with Theresa gasping. Had there been any way of keeping her feet—and any semblance of dignity—she would have let go, and even pushed Sidney away from her.

As it was, she held tighter, frightened and fighting for control. 'What rumours?' she asked through clenched teeth.

'You know what rumours! It's all over town that there was something between her and your father, that she gave his canoe away, that she had something to do with his disappearance. Nobody asked you to come here and upset everybody—or to bring that by-blow of his here. Why are you upsetting everybody? We Falconers don't like it.' Sidney let her arm grow limp, and gave Theresa a sudden shove towards the outside wall of the rink.

Theresa landed against it with some considerable force, winded and jarred. It was only by great good luck and the quick action of a fellow skater, a very tall burly young man, that she escaped a nasty fall.

They all surrounded her then, Sidney crying, 'Why did you let go?'

Theresa said nothing. She was too shocked. That had been quite deliberate.

Simon and Rosie declared that she mustn't let one little spill deter her from continuing when she was doing so well, and one on either side of her they pulled her away, the burly young man taking Tony in tow.

A disgruntled Sidney was left standing, alone.

'I saw it,' declared Rosie. 'She pushed you! Were you arguing?'

'I think you must be mistaken, Rosalinda,' Simon interrupted. 'No one would do that.'

'She would,' Theresa spoke up then. 'In fact, she did. She told me to stop spreading rumours about her aunt and my father. I haven't said anything about them—but I've thought it. Then she let go and pushed me.'

Rosie smiled. 'I know it's not funny, but why would she do that unless her aunt had something to hide?'

Simon grunted, 'That's not fair, is it? It shows a certain niceness in her character that she's fond of her auntie and values her good name.'

'Yes,' Rosie agreed drily. 'And not so fond of Theresa.'

'She was upset. She didn't mean it.' Simon tried to calm them.

'Isn't that just like a man?' Rosie said. 'You find it impossible to believe that a pretty girl would show any malice. I'll bet Eddie believes it when I tell him.'

'Even if it's true,' Simon pointed out stiffly, 'it's between Sidney and Theresa—and she might be mistaken.'

'Please, Rosie,' begged Theresa. 'Don't tell Edouard.

He's a friend of the Falconers, and he mightn't believe it either. Anyway, what good would it do? I wasn't hurt, and the unpleasantness would spoil everyone's evening. Remember, we're going on there afterwards.'

Rosie took a little more convincing, but eventually she agreed not to tell Edouard, and the three of them went on skating together, Theresa gaining more and more confidence.

By the time the rink closed at 9.30, she had regained her equilibrium and was pleased with the progress she had made. As they piled into Edouard's car, Tony was so enthusiastic about his evening and his new skating friend that she was able to take pleasure, too, in his enjoyment and forgot, almost, the incident with Sidney. In fact, the other girl was so sweet to them all that she found herself doubting it had ever happened. She even insisted on having Tony on her knee for the short trip.

At the Falconers' house, elegant refreshments were laid out in the lounge, and they all ate heartily. Tony, indeed, ate so much that Theresa began to wonder where he was putting it, and Rosie asked him if he had a hollow leg.

In the midst of the general merriment that Tony's puzzlement caused, Marguerite Falconer entered the room and began to greet them. Tony sat down beside Theresa, forgetting that he had been about to help himself to a cake.

Marguerite spoke to him. 'So you've come back, Antony. What a big boy you are now.'

She was smiling—a smile which didn't extend to her eyes, and Theresa could feel that Tony was trembling.

'Have you forgotten her, too?' asked Sidney, as he made no reply. 'The way you forgot me?'

'I haven't forgotten her.' Tony's voice came out as a squeak. 'She's just the same.'

Theresa bit her lip. Tony was frightened. She knew that. She was a little afraid herself, but what she feared was that Tony might add to that bald statement.

Marguerite's laugh was a throaty tinkle. 'It's five

years, isn't it? Am I to take that as a compliment?'

Tony made no reply, but put his hand in his sister's.

'I think he's rather tired,' said Theresa. 'It's been a long day for him, and he hasn't learned how to make a pretty compliment.'

'You'll have to teach him some social polish, Theresa.' Marguerite's tone was soft, almost indulgent. 'Boys need good manners drilled into them from an early age—they have to learn to stand up when a lady comes into the room—not sit down like he did. But then, of course, he's been deprived.'

The way she said 'deprived', thought Theresa furiously, sounded as though she meant deformed, ruined beyond all hope. This was the woman whose feelings Edouard was considering. She shot a look at him, but he was helping Marguerite to a cup of coffee.

Tony huddled beside Theresa, shaking his head to offers of more to eat, but he managed a smile as Big Bob entered the room and even stood up to greet him.

Big Bob swung him off his feet in a great hug of welcome, then stood back to look at him. 'I'd know you anywhere, son! You used to ride on my shoulders, but I'm afraid you've got too big for that.'

'I can remember.' Tony was excited. 'I sometimes held on to your hair, and you said it would all fall out. It hasn't, has it?'

Big Bob ruffled Tony's hair with a gentle hand as he shook his head. 'Not finished eating, have you? You must have a cake.' He pressed one on him, and the boy accepted it with every indication of pleasure.

But Theresa noticed that he was careful to put himself as far as possible from Marguerite, who had claimed Edouard's chair while he perched on the arm, smiling down at her.

Big Bob greeted the others and sat beside Theresa. 'Is the lad behaving himself?' he asked her.

'Of course I am,' said Tony. 'You can ask Sal if I'm not a good worker.'

Big Bob winked at Theresa. 'He looks to me as though

he'd make a good baseball player. Got a bat and ball, has he?'

Theresa looked at him blankly. She knew they played baseball in Canada, and Tony had mentioned that Charlie was a great player, but she'd been too busy to think of anything like that. She shook her head.

'We might do something about that. Every boy loves baseball.'

'I have a Meccano set,' Tony confided. 'A friend of Theresa's gave it to me in Ottawa—a Mr Roscoe—and he gave her a great big box of chocolates. I think it was because he liked her so much.'

Big Bob began to laugh, and Theresa didn't mind that at all. What she did mind was the attention of the whole room now directed at her. Tony had a piping voice, but it was certainly loud and clear.

'Well,' said Sidney. 'Fancy that!'

'Who is this beau of yours?' Marguerite demanded, waving a languid hand in Theresa's direction.

'He's not a beau,' she protested. 'Just a friend; a business acquaintance, I suppose you'd call him. He was very kind to me and to Tony. He said we should have something to mark the occasion of finding each other. I couldn't refuse. It would have been ungrateful.'

Simon frowned at her. 'A business acquaintance, you say. How old a man is he?'

'In his thirties—as old as Edouard, anyway.' Theresa knew her cheeks were pink. 'Why, does it matter?'

Marguerite's laugh trilled out. 'If an old man gives a girl a present, it's accepted as a fatherly gesture. If a young one does, that's a different matter, don't you think, Theresa? It usually means he wants something.'

'He didn't want anything.' Her denial was sharp. She was annoyed with Tony for landing her with this catechism.

But Tony wasn't finished. 'Does he want something from me, too?'

Simon answered him. 'I shouldn't think so. That's entirely different.'

'Why? Why is it different?' Tony ignored the burst of laughter that followed Simon's declaration. 'Do you mean he might want to marry Theresa?'

'Who mentioned marriage?' asked Sidney with a charming smile. 'You'll have to explain a few things to your brother, Theresa.'

Tony looked expectantly at Theresa.

'Not now.' She shook her head.

He looked unsure. 'Have I said something wrong? Mr Roscoe might want to marry you. He probably likes pretty girls.'

Once again laughter went round the room, and it was Edouard who came to Theresa's rescue. 'All men like pretty girls. And why shouldn't this Mr Roscoe give Theresa a box of chocolates? Where's the harm in that? After all, she said he was as old as I, so that makes him quite respectable.'

Theresa shot him a grateful glance. It brought the discussion to a close, but she couldn't help asking herself, from the dryness of his voice, if he thought she considered him too old. Too old for what? What was the matter with her tonight, that she couldn't seem to please anyone?

Edouard drove them home, dropping off Simon and Rosie on the way. Tony had slumped against Theresa in the front seat, asleep with the motion of the car. When the car stopped in front of the boarding-house, he held up his hand.

'Before you waken him, tell me one thing.' He spoke quietly. 'What are your plans?'

'What plans? I haven't made any plans.'

'Whatever you may mean to do about marriage, you have the boy to think of.'

'I don't mean to do anything about it,' Theresa snapped.

'Just waiting to be asked, you mean?'

'I don't know what you're talking about. No one's going to ask me.'

'Why not? It would be a pity if a girl like you didn't

find someone in the marriage mart.'

Theresa bridled. 'Well, I haven't found anyone yet. I'll let you know if I do.'

Edouard frowned. 'There's no need to be angry. You can't stay on in the boarding-house. It'll be too expensive for you, and certainly no way to bring up a boy. He needs a place to stretch his legs.'

'And play baseball,' she suggested. 'I don't know why men think that's so important.'

'Don't be ridiculous, Theresa! You must know I'm talking sense. Ask Sal what she has on the books. A little place with some grass would do.'

'Very well, I'll talk to Sal,' Theresa agreed, with a sigh. She was tired, and didn't want to think about the future.

'See that you do,' was his parting shot, as she managed to waken Tony sufficiently to get him up the path to the house. 'Our readers will want to know how the two of you are getting on.'

The sound of screaming woke Theresa—or half woke her. It was the crying which made her sit up in bed. Who was it? She tried to locate it.

Tony! It must be Tony! She slipped out of the covers and snatched up her robe. She flew out on the landing and into his room next door.

'Sh-h!' She sat on the bed and cradled him in her arms. 'It's probably a nightmare after all that food. What is it? A bad dream?'

Tony clung to her, half asleep, whispering. He had not closed the curtains at the window, and the moon high in the sky and with some of its brilliance gone gave Theresa enough light to see that he had curled himself into a ball. She tried to distinguish what he was saying.

Gradually she began to make sense of it. 'Don't go. Don't leave me,' was the recurring refrain.

She rubbed his back, and felt some of the tenseness leave it.

'Don't go hunting,' he pleaded. 'You've never liked

hunting. Something'll happen to you. I know it will.' His words were clearer now.

'I'm not going hunting,' Theresa whispered back, not sure if he were awake or not.

'Why did you say you were, if you're not?' Tony stiffened against her. 'Why are you going in the canoe? Are you going to meet her? She doesn't need you.'

'Who's she?' Theresa shook him slightly. 'What are you talking about?'

'You know who I'm talking about.' Tony squirmed out of Theresa's hold and burrowed to the other side of the bed. 'I don't like her. She doesn't like me. She's not going to be my mother. She said so . . .' He was trembling.

Theresa sat bolt upright. This had nothing to do with her and the present. This was buried in the past. It was his father Antony was talking to. Had the finding of the canoe triggered off this trip down memory's guilt? This poor tortured boy had some sort of knowledge deep in him, tearing him apart.

She reached out to him, soothing him with her voice and hands. 'Poor Tony, poor little boy. I'm here to stay.'

She heard him sigh. 'That's what you always say —always said. But you went with her just the same. You went in the canoe, the red canoe—with her.' He was crying softly now.

Theresa thought he was awake, but he lay quiet in her arms, not rubbing his eyes though the tears were flowing. She wiped them away. 'I know you went in the canoe other times with her at night. She told me so —Marguerite told me so. And she laughed. That was after I showed her the book. It was a funny laugh. Maybe she didn't like you, either. She said she was going to get even. Why should she want to do that? . . .' He was quiet for several minutes, and Theresa pulled a cover from the floor and wrapped it round both of them.

'I bit her then,' Tony's voice was very faint. 'She slapped me—Maddie slapped me. She said there wasn't any reason to be nice to me now—She'd never be my mother. I never told you before. I was afraid to tell you about her, because I knew you wanted her.'

Theresa could feel the heat of Tony's body with the blanket round them, and she shifted to a more comfortable position, dislodging the pillow which lay beside her. Tony's album was exposed in the soft moonlight. Was this the book he had shown to Marguerite Falconer?

Tony began to whisper again. 'You said she was delicious; but she didn't taste delicious when I bit her. You wouldn't have liked me doing that—Did she tell you?' Tony giggled. It was an eerie sound in the quiet room after what had gone before. His eyes opened wide. 'Theresa? What did I say, Theresa? Why are you here?'

'You had a dream. You called out.'

'That's all right, then. You can stay, if you like, till I'm properly asleep.' He relaxed completely against her and slid down into the bed.

Theresa was left sitting on the bedside, looking at the cover of the album. Tony had provided her with a glimpse of life with Charles Russell that she hadn't bargained for. Her father had been a passionate man, tied to a little boy who couldn't know or understand his needs, but only sense them. Well, who was she to judge him, this dead father of hers? She had discovered in Edouard's arms that she had passions she'd never suspected, needs that had never been explored. And what of Marguerite? Without even consciously making the decision, her hand reached out for the album she had promised she wouldn't look at without Tony's permission. Marguerite had looked. Theresa must know what she had seen there. She began to turn the pages.

There were bridges, pages of bridges. Some of them were with Charles Russell standing beside them, some were there on their own, poised in giant threads against the sky, reflected in the water. Quietly she turned one page after another, careful not to disturb the boy. People hadn't seemed to figure largely in her father's life. There was the occasional man leaning against a stanchion or before something that might have been a mine entrance, or, in one case, an enormous mountain of coal.

Tony stirred, and she sat perfectly still, a little cold, now that he had captured most of the blanket. She sighed and blew another leaf of the book over.

There it was—the picture Miss Maddie must have seen. It showed a little girl standing in front of a large building. She held the book up to get the maximum light on it. The moon had faded to a pale faint copy of itself, but the sky had begun to turn pearl and misty grey. She could see clearly enough who the child was, and where the picture had been taken. It was in front of the Liver Building, and the little girl was herself. As though to emphasise the fact, written under it in white ink was the caption, 'My Tessa'. No wonder Marguerite had remembered what Theresa had looked like at five. It was here in black and white.

What was it Tony had said that Marguerite had done? She had declared she would never be Tony's mother, and that she would get even with him.

Theresa began to tremble. Charles Russell must have proposed marriage to Marguerite, and then that picture had told her that he was still married, for she had known the story of the father who had been declared dead. Why hadn't Marguerite guessed at it in the first instance, when Charles Russell had arrived in Creswal?

The book slid from Theresa's fingers and landed on the floor with a soft thud. She held her breath, but Tony didn't waken. She bent down and carefully replaced it under his pillow. Then she rose and left the room.

Once back in her own bed, she huddled under the covers, shivering in the mild night, trying to get warm again. She didn't want to think about Marguerite and her threat to get even. She knew with absolute certainty that Miss Falconer would never have entered into a bigamous marriage. Yet Tony's mother must have done so. But she might not have known. It was that knowledge that had turned Marguerite to revenge. What had that revenge been?

Shuddering, Theresa wished she'd never opened the book. What was she to do? She couldn't tell Edouard. Marguerite was his friend. It would be too cruel to set a childish nightmare as proof against a woman he might love. Indeed there was no evidence that she had taken any sort of action, beyond slapping Tony for biting her. People said all sorts of things when they were hurt and angry. She couldn't even confront Marguerite with it. If she had a guilty secret, there was no reason why she should break down and confess it, especially not to Charles Russell's daughter. But she had known that he would not return. Or had she only guessed at it? Theresa eventually fell asleep to dreams of being pursued by a witch-like woman who shook her till she moaned and screamed.

She woke to morning, and Tony shaking her. 'What's the matter, Theresa? Aren't you getting up today?'

She blinked her eyes and looked at the sun streaming in where Tony had disarranged the curtains. Had she dreamed it all? He showed no signs of his nocturnal horrors, but was smiling and chattering. 'I'm used to getting up early. You don't want to be late getting to work, but I want to ask you a question.'

She groaned. 'Ask away!' She raised herself on an elbow.

'I've been thinking . . .' Tony paused. 'My dad was married to your mother, and you said the other day that your mother only died four years ago. How could Dad be married to two ladies at the same time?'

'Well, it's a long story.' Theresa longed to pull the cover over her head and not try to explain.

'It's early yet,' he assured her. 'You have time to tell me. It's twenty minutes before breakfast'll be ready.'

'Your dad married my mother.' Theresa hoped she could find the right words so that Tony wouldn't think badly of his father. 'Then he went missing—and was declared dead. My mother got married again, and so did your dad.'

'To different people,' Tony nodded. 'Yes, I see. But if he was dead, did he come alive again?'

Theresa felt sure the ground was slipping away from her. 'I think perhaps he just went missing, and people supposed he was dead.'

'Like now? Frank thinks he's dead. Do you?'

'Yes, ever since I was at the place where the canoe was hidden. The forest is so big, so quiet.' She put her hand on Tony's. 'Do you think he's dead?'

He didn't answer her directly. Neither did he meet her eyes. 'Perhaps he just wants people to think so. Has he gone missing again?' He turned to her. 'Is it the same as before? Is that what he does so that his children will find each other? Do you suppose there's any more of us?'

She shook her head. There might well have been more of them if Marguerite had gone ahead and married her father. She shivered at the idea. There just wasn't any way she could like the woman.

Tony, too, was silent, but he looked as though he wanted to say something else. 'Theresa,' he began, and then stopped.

'What is it?' she asked gently.

'It's something I want to ask you—but it's a bad word. I don't know how else to say it. Promise you won't be cross with me? I don't want you to be cross.'

'I promise.' Theresa felt sorry for the lad. 'What is this word?'

'Bastard.' Tony drew in his breath and shrank away a little on the bench. 'It's what they said Charlie was at the orphanage. His father wasn't properly married to his mother—neither was mine, Theresa. Is that what I am, too?'

'Not to me,' Theresa denied it hotly. 'You're my brother. I won't have you calling yourself that.'

'No, I won't call myself that, if you don't like it.' Tony gave her a sudden warm smile. 'But am I, Theresa? I have to know.'

She sighed, and pulled him down beside her on the bed. Truth was truth, and she could understand that that was what he sought, but everything in her objected to admitting it.

'It doesn't say so on your birth certificate,' she assured him. 'I'd let it go at that.'

'All right. Or I could ask my dad about it . . . If he comes back.'

'Yes, if . . .' Theresa paused. 'But we may never find him. How do you feel about that?'

'I used to feel bad about it, but I don't any more. Not now you've come to have me for your boy. I'd rather have you for a sister than anyone.'

'That's the way I feel, too!' Theresa had a lump in her throat as she hugged him.

She didn't know what lay ahead for either of them, but whatever it was, they'd face it together. In a few short weeks she'd grown very fond of this brother of hers. They'd manage somehow. It was time to get up, and it was time to find somewhere else to live. As usual, Edouard was right.

'Scoot!' she exclaimed. 'I'm going to get dressed.'

Tony scooted.

CHAPTER THIRTEEN

IT WAS Friday of the following week when Rosie arrived back from lunch with the announcement that Theresa and Tony were moving into a little house.

'It's a small bungalow on the Appledores' property,' she said to Edouard.

'Ah yes,' he said, trying to pretend that he had known about it all along. 'The United Empire Loyalist Lady. I expect Sal had a hand in it.'

'She must have,' Rosie agreed, throwing her hat on her desk and perching near him. 'The Appledores don't usually rent that small place to anyone except family. Sal must have been very persuasive.'

Edouard shrugged. Theresa might have told him herself.

'I'm surprised you didn't know before,' she went on. 'You didn't, did you?'

'No, I didn't.'

'I expect she's been busy.' Rosie smiled at him. 'Simon thought we might give her a hand tomorrow with the moving in.' She swung a neat leg along the desk, and studied it. 'You could come along, if you like.'

'I could,' he agreed, 'if I didn't have to go to Renfrew to see an official about roads. I don't know what you're trying to do with that leg, but I suggest you try whatever it is on Simon, not on me. I expect he's a good deal more susceptible than I am.'

Rosie grinned at him, and put her foot on the floor. She stood up. 'I can see you don't want me talking to you. You are an old grouch these days.' She walked over to her own desk and hung up her hat. 'Have you and Theresa had another difference about something?'

'What makes you think that?' he demanded. 'And if I

had, would it matter? She does jump to conclusions about people.'

'What people?'

Edouard didn't reply.

Rosie sat in her own chair. 'Marguerite Falconer, for example? I wondered about her the other night. Young Tony seemed frightened to death by her. I thought it was strange. Did you notice?'

'Yes.'

'He liked Big Bob—you could see that.'

'Yes.' Again Edouard answered with a monosyllable. He wished Rosie would stop pointing out the obvious. It only confirmed what Theresa had thought about Marguerite. Perhaps she did know something about the missing Charles Russell. Certainly the boy had reacted very strongly. It might have been only jealousy and dislike. Once you began to imagine things, the doubts grew.

'My mother says that Marguerite Falconer meant to marry Theresa's father, and something went wrong. Marguerite was very upset when he disappeared just before the wedding.'

'You've never mentioned this before.' Edouard was uneasy.

'My mother never said anything before.'

'Did she say anything else?' He was too much the newspaperman not to be curious.

'She thought the wedding date was still fixed, but afterwards they said it had been cancelled before he disappeared. It was a long time ago, and people's memories aren't always to be relied on. You know that. I can't recall much about it. I was just a kid.'

'Yes,' Edouard repeated again. If a man disappeared, the girl he was engaged to might very well want to forget the whole episode. He sighed. Theresa's face came into his mind, and her words about wanting the truth. He had known from that very first day that the calm of his life in Creswal was going to be disturbed. The Falconers were his friends. And Theresa? She hadn't been around all

week, and if he was honest with himself, he missed her.
It wasn't that he was interested in her, of course, but he
wanted to know how she and Tony were getting on, and
if the boy had said anything about his father. He just
might know something that would unravel the mystery.
Perhaps he would go along and see them in the little
house. It would be a friendly gesture.

Theresa had found the move easier than she had expected. Sal had lent the car, and Simon and Rosie had
helped. Mrs Appledore had left fresh bread and butter,
and there was milk as well in the ice-box. Tony had been
thrilled with the ice-box.

'Do you know?' he said to Theresa. 'A man with great
big tongs delivers ice. They take it from the river in the
winter and store it in an ice-house.'

She wasn't quite sure if this was so, but Rosie and
Tony both assured her that it was, and offered to show
her the place.

By late afternoon, clothes had been hung in cup-
boards, groceries stored in the larder, as Theresa called
it—the pantry, Tony declared it—and they sat down to
bread and tea with Sal, Rosie and Simon and, unexpectedly, Sidney. She had arrived with a big fruit cake
and a tin of home-made cookies at Aunt Marguerite's
command.

When the visitors had left, a still excited Tony led
Theresa through the little house, touching everything,
admiring everything. Both bedrooms were inspected,
and the beds tested for comfort. Tony sat in every chair
in the lounge, and enumerated all the food in the pantry,
and the dishes above the sink.

'It's all ours, Theresa,' he told her, smiling. 'We'll live
here for ever.' Then he went for a walk outside, taking
her round the small garden in the front.

It was hard for Theresa to believe that this happy
outgoing lad was the same shy boy she had taken from
the orphanage a few weeks ago. He had grown an inch,
his cheeks had filled out, his complexion was healthy. He

had completely lost the institutional look of grey uniformity. It pleased her enormously to see the progress he had made.

They sat on the small veranda until Tony began to yawn. When he went to bed, Theresa went inside and began a letter to the twins. A light rap at the kitchen door surprised, but didn't startle her. It was a day for dropping in.

It was Edouard who entered, with a hamper on his arm. 'What are you doing sitting in the dark? Where are the lamps?'

'In the larder—the pantry, I mean. I hadn't noticed the dusk creeping in.' Theresa rubbed her eyes. 'Is it so late?'

'It's hardly more than eight-thirty.' Edouard lit a lamp and set it on the kitchen table beside the hamper. 'I meant to get here earlier, but got held up. I'm starving. Have you eaten?'

'A long time ago I had bread and honey and tea.' She yawned. 'I don't know where the time went to.'

He opened the hamper, and Theresa put out plates and forks and knives.

When he pulled out a cooked chicken, she realised she was hungry. A container of salad followed, and a bottle of wine. 'That's home-made dandelion, and very good. My housekeeper will be disappointed if you don't have something nice to say about it.' He poured two glasses.

He sat down opposite Theresa, after seating her at the plain wood table with a flourish. 'To the new house and the folks in it!' he toasted gravely, raising his glass.

She was delighted with the ceremony. Edouard had the knack of pleasing her. He was charming. He appeared to have forgotten that they had parted in unfriendly fashion a week ago.

'To visitors!' Theresa raised her glass in turn.

Edouard laughed as he cut thin slices of chicken with a large carving-knife. 'Very nice. Do you know, now that I'm used to it, I'm beginning to like your new hair-style. It's so curly. It makes you look younger than ever.'

Theresa took a long sip of wine, and then another. Why did he always keep harping on her being so young? She longed to prove that she wasn't the child he seemed to think her. She helped herself to salad, and finished her first glass of wine. When Edouard hesitated to pour her another, she assured him that she was used to drinking wine, and that it was delicious.

'Stronger than you think, perhaps,' he suggested, but he poured her a second glass and helped her to a drumstick and some white meat. 'How did the move go?'

'Very well.' Theresa spoke with her mouth full. 'I didn't know I was so hungry.' He didn't make her feel uncomfortable about eating so quickly, but gave her an understanding smile.

They sat facing each other, enjoying heaped platefuls. The companionable silence that fell on them while they ate seemed quite natural to her. When she picked up a chicken-bone to give it her undivided attention, he did the same.

She poured more wine for both of them. It was strange, but she seemed to be getting through the wine faster than he was. Perhaps he wasn't as thirsty. She giggled. 'I never thought to have my first meal here with you at this hour of night.' There was something rather exciting about doing just that. The light from the paraffin lamp was soft, and flickering gently, with a pleasant little breeze finding its way through the screen door.

Edouard topped up her glass again, and drew out a cherry pie and a container of whipped cream from the opened hamper. 'Can I tempt you?'

'It looks lovely.'

He cut a piece for each of them, while Theresa fetched small plates.

As she returned from the shelves, she brushed against him, and he caught her lightly by the waist to steady her.

She began to sing, 'Can she bake a cherry pie, Billy Boy, Billy Boy?', and he joined in in a pleasant tenor voice.

She pulled him to his feet. 'I've never danced with you—and I love to dance!'

To the accompaniment of their own humming, he waltzed her round the room. Their steps matched well, and Theresa gave herself up to the dance and to being held in Edouard's arms. Flushed with the exertion of a vigorous waltz and the effect of the wine, she made no protest when he gravely escorted her back to the table and served the cherry pie with a flourish, and at her insistence, a further measure of wine.

'Is Madame satisfied with the entertainment and the service?' He bowed over her.

'Very satisfied,' she assured him, taking her first bite of pie. 'This is delicious. Won't you join me?'

'I was hoping Madame would suggest that.' He sat down at the table again and took up his fork.

Theresa sat back contentedly when she had finished. 'It's been a funny day. Everyone's come to see me, and now you're here.' She smiled.

'There's something very wicked about a midnight feast *à deux*.' Edouard pushed back his chair, dessert gone, wine-glass in his hand. He looked at her over its rim.

To her, there was suddenly something a little disturbing in the flash of his blue eyes. Perhaps it was wicked to be here at this time of night with such a man as Edouard . . . A little unsteadily, she rose to her feet and began to clear the table, moving swiftly from it to the sink. He put the remains of the chicken and the salad into the ice-box, and the cherry pie into the larder. Then he came over to her.

'The things are nicely stacked. Leave them till the morning.'

He was standing so close to Theresa that she could see his eyes were sparkling with amusement. 'As soon as a woman settles into a house, she becomes a housewife,' he teased.

As always when he was near her, she was unnerved. It was better to keep busy. 'I am not a housewife!' She lifted a plate, not knowing what she intended to do with it.

He took it from her and laid it down. He put his arm about her waist, so that she faced him.

'Is this what you want out of life?' he asked gently, 'To take care of Tony, as you would have taken care of his father?'

Theresa couldn't escape from him or his questions. She was trapped with the quickened beat of her heart, her breath in her throat. 'I don't know,' she whispered.

Edouard pulled her closer. His lips fastened on hers in a slow exploring kiss full of sweetness and promise. He had never kissed her like this before, as though he liked her, and was pleased by her. 'Theresa,' he murmured, 'the name suits you—gentle, steady, kind.' His lips tickled her ear.

For a long moment Theresa clung to him, more aroused than she had ever been. Her head was spinning just a little, her legs felt weak. It must be the effect of the wine.

'What about Theresa?' he asked, his voice soft. 'Isn't she entitled to some life of her own?'

She sighed, and closed her eyes. If life held moments like this, it was just what she wanted.

'Some excitement, some reality?' he went on softly. 'Not just more service for you—this time to a half-brother instead of two half-sisters. Don't you long to go wild?'

Theresa tried to draw away, but she was held fast. In spite of herself, in spite of her reluctance to reveal her secret thoughts, she heard herself say, 'Do you suppose I don't feel trapped sometimes? Some nights before I go to sleep . . .' She stopped in confusion. 'You don't want to hear about that.'

'Yes, tell me.'

There was something so comforting, so accepting in his voice, that she stopped fighting to get away and went on in a whisper. 'Before I go to sleep, I think I'm lying on a moonlight beach with the waves lapping the shore and a man coming towards . . .' Why was she telling this to Edouard, of all people? Was it the wine loosening her tongue? She hadn't been able to stop herself. She shivered, and let her cheek rest against his shoulder. 'I think it must be the warm Canadian nights,' she finished primly. 'In England I used to fall asleep right away.'

Edouard laughed, and kissed her again. 'There's nothing to be ashamed of in admitting you're human. So am I.' He held her away from him. 'I can see you're a comfortable girl, the sort of girl to make a man very content. You're not quite what I thought you at first, and you're growing up fast—too fast for me. I know it's time to go home.' Holding her hand now, he walked towards the screen door.

Theresa didn't want him to go. At the screen door, she managed to slide into his arms again. It was a long, lingering kiss, and she clung to him, arms tightly round his neck. She sensed that he was somehow reluctant now. Why did he want to go away?

He put her away from him with a sigh. 'If you kiss me like that, I shall never go home. There's a devil in you tonight!'

'No. The night we came back from the fair, you said I didn't know how it was between men and women. You kissed me then—you said it was the first lesson. I'm ready for the second.' She didn't understand herself, she forgot what the consequences might be, or simply didn't think of them.

'You didn't much like the first one,' he drawled. 'Besides, that isn't my role in life—to initiate young girls.' He looked down at her, no expression in his eyes. 'Is that how you think of me? As part of your education?'

'What else?' Theresa shrugged. Why was he making such a fuss about nothing? He'd been willing enough to kiss her before. 'I expect every girl needs an older man so that she will have some experience.' She didn't know what made her add that.

'Experience to stand her in good stead for the rest of her life—is that what you mean?'

In her tired, fuddled state, she was only vaguely aware of his question. Couldn't Edouard see how simple the situation was? The words just got in the way. She wanted him. As she placed his right hand on her breast, she wanted to rouse him to passion—not oratory.

'You're afraid of me,' she challenged, as she heard him draw a sharp breath. Because the words sounded slurred in her own ears, she made a question of them. 'Why are you afraid of me?'

'I'm afraid of myself.' Edouard disentangled himself. 'I'm afraid it's the wine talking. You're not used to it.'

'I have wine every Christmas,' she assured him with tipsy dignity, and tried to reclaim him.

'I should have guessed! I shouldn't have let you have so much.'

Theresa swayed on her feet. It was all becoming too much for her. She could have cried because it had all gone wrong. She was just a nuisance to him.

'Are you all right?' he asked sharply, putting his hand on her arm.

'I'm not sure,' Theresa admitted. 'Why is the room going round?'

He made a sound, half sympathy, half impatience. 'You want to get to bed and sleep it off.' In the dim light, he looked at her. 'Can you manage?'

'Of course I can.' She got the words out with difficulty, and stumbled as she tried to take a few steps away.

'Which is your room?' asked Edouard, holding her upright.

'Over there,' She gestured vaguely towards the big living-room.

He steered her in the direction indicated, bumping into a chair in the process.

'Damn,' he exclaimed. 'I can't see.'

'Sh-h,' whispered Theresa. 'You'll wake Tony! I can't see either, but I know my bedroom's there.' She pointed to a half-open door. 'If only there wasn't something wrong with my legs, I'd be perfectly all right.'

'It's not your legs, but your head, that needs attention

—and mine, for allowing this to happen.' He lifted her and carried her into the room, depositing her none too gently on the bed. 'I'm glad there's no one here to see this,' he muttered under his breath.

'No one here to see,' Theresa repeated. 'Nothing to worry about. I shan't tell anyone Edouard put me to bed.'

'See that you don't. Are you all right?' he asked once again. 'Can you loosen your dress?'

'No.' She was petulant now. 'Why should I?'

'Because you won't be very comfortable sleeping in it,' he snapped, his fingers fumbling with the buttons on it.

Without any help from her, Edouard managed to remove the dress and one of her petticoats and her shoes and stockings. Then he rolled her to one side of the bed and freed a blanket to cover her.

For a moment, he stood looking down at her. She looked a child with that short hair and her eyes closed, a half-smile on her face. It was lighter here in the bedroom. There must be a moon partly obscured by the shadow of the house.

Theresa opened her eyes. 'Good night, Edouard,' she said, her voice a warm slur. 'I like being put to bed by you. You must come again.'

He swore under his breath. What had he been thinking of to allow this to happen? He had fooled himself into the belief that Theresa was a child, too young for life, too young for him. Somehow she had become a woman —a desirable woman. It would have been very easy for him to have returned her kisses with even more fire than she had shown. He had surprised himself with the intensity of his longing for her. No, it wasn't just any woman whom he wanted. It was Theresa. Why had he been so blind not to have seen it before? And he had risked her reputation in coming here so late at night. If anyone had seen him arriving—if anyone saw him leaving—for her sake, he must be sure that no one did.

He went back to the kitchen, collected the hamper

and blew out the light before he let himself very quietly and stealthily out of the back door. Fortunately his car was parked out in the road, some fair distance away.

Like a shadow, a silent silhouette in the dark, he reached it and drove away. He hoped Theresa would remember nothing of the latter part of the evening.

'Whatever's wrong with you?' Sal asked Theresa in some exasperation. 'Every time I talk to you, you jump or else you stare into space. What's on your mind?'

'What should be on my mind?' Theresa knew she was stammering. 'Did you say something?'

'Yes,' Sal replied. 'Where is that wretched man?'

Theresa gave her a blank stare. 'What wretched man?'

'Edouard, of course! You haven't been listening.'

Edouard, Theresa sighed. Every hour, every day, she didn't see him was like a reprieve. She didn't want to see him or hear of him; she was too ashamed to face him. What would she say? It had been Saturday when they had moved into the little house, and now it was Thursday, and she hadn't seen him at all.

Since Sal was looking at her so strangely, she felt she must make some effort to give her her attention. 'What did you want him for?'

'Just to let him know the office will be closed tomorrow afternoon while we go to this Open Day at the paper mill. Still, I suppose he'll be there. I have one or two little improvements to talk over with him. Maybe I'll pop in to the *Clarion* tonight. By the way, what are you wearing tomorrow?'

'I don't know. Tony's been talking about it all week. Will people be very dressed up?' Theresa tore her mind from thoughts of facing Edouard. Perhaps, after all, it would be easier in a crowd.

'I have a new blue dress,' Sal announced smiling, 'and a big hat. You'll want to look your best. Everyone will be there. I understand the hotel will be full tonight. A lot of guests are arriving from Toronto. Some will stay till Sunday.'

'How do you know that?' Theresa was beginning to be interested, in spite of herself.

'People tell me things.' Sal assumed an innocent expression. 'I don't go round with my head in the clouds. Simon's father has arrived already,' she went on. 'I expect you'll be meeting him. He's very pleasant and friendly. You've nothing to worry about there,' she added kindly.

'Nothing to worry about?' Theresa looked at her blankly. Whatever did she mean?

Sal laughed. 'You give every indication of a girl in love. If it isn't Simon, who is it?'

A girl in love. Of course she wasn't in love! She denied it hotly. She just didn't know how to face Edouard after the exhibition she'd made of herself. That was all. But she couldn't tell Sal about it, or anyone. She went hot and cold at the remembrance that he had put her to bed and that she had asked him to come again. If only she could forget the whole wretched episode. And, yet, her blood still stirred as she recalled the way he had kissed her, and the way she had responded to those kisses. No wonder she had seen nothing of him this week. She sighed.

Sal shrugged. 'I suppose you'll tell me what it is you're dreaming about in your own good time. I'll still be here.'

Theresa shook her head. She was never going to tell anyone about Saturday night.

The following afternoon, the office closed after lunch, and Theresa and Tony rushed home to change for the Open Day celebration. Tony wore his new suit, the trousers already a little shorter on him; Theresa put on her black and white outfit with a new little concoction of a white hat with a veil that Sal had talked her into buying the previous day.

Sal called for them in the car, and Tony was quick to tell her that blue suited her and he'd never seen anything like her hat with a bird on it. He sat beside her, admiring it, which pleased her enormously. Neither of them appeared to notice Theresa's silence. If only she didn't have to meet Edouard.

Both Simon and his father met them at the entrance to the mill building, and Mr Radcliffe insisted on taking Theresa under his wing.

'We shall have our picture taken by the reporter who's come all the way from Toronto.' He signalled to a man who had been standing to one side, armed with a camera.

Theresa demurred, but her protests were swept aside. 'Mother would never forgive me if I went home without a picture of Simon's friend.' He took her arm. 'She wasn't able to be here today.'

Mr Radcliffe beamed at her, and Theresa smiled back. It wasn't that she minded being considered a friend of Simon's, but she had no means of indicating to this affable gentleman that she wasn't the special friend he seemed to think her.

It was, of course, as they were posing that Edouard Moreau appeared on the scene.

'The local newspaperman,' Mr Radcliffe murmured. 'Very competent, I'm sure, but not in the same league as the Toronto fellows.'

Theresa was sure this had been intended for her ears only, but as her eye caught Edouard's she was aware that he must have heard, for he swung away. Either that, or he resented Theresa being photographed by another paper. She wanted to go after him, but how could she? Simon's father was insisting on showing her round to see the whole process of making reinforced cardboard boxes.

The tour proved to be most interesting, and Mr Radcliffe very knowledgeable. Theresa knew there were more important people there than herself, and was half relieved when he was called to attend to more exalted visitors and she was left by the buffet table and instructed to help herself. The food was beautifully arranged with plates of dainty sandwiches, bite-sized hors d'oeuvres and small cakes, as well as generous pitchers of lemonade. She looked round for a companion with whom to share this largesse.

Edouard came from behind her. 'Lemonade?' he enquired. 'Or do you fancy something stronger? I imagine the punch-bowl for the men contains a little fire-water.'

'Lemonade,' stammered Theresa, remembering their last encounter vividly. 'Lemonade will be fine.'

He poured a glass for her. 'Given up drinking, have you?' he asked affably. 'Very wise.' He captured a plate of sandwiches, and she was propelled to the far corner of the room, his camera slung over his shoulder. She nearly choked on her lemonade. She had no desire to face Edouard here.

'Had any more midnight visitors?' he asked conversationally, as he offered the sandwiches.

She shook her head.

'Take one,' he urged. 'You need to keep up your strength. The Chairman of the Board will surely be back, and he's an older man.'

'What's that supposed to mean?'

'I had the distinct impression the other night that you welcomed older men.' Edouard bit into a sandwich. 'Is it the father or the son you're interested in? Best make up your mind.'

Theresa coloured up hotly, her cheeks burning. 'I had too much to drink the other night.'

'And had to be put to bed,' he said, very softly, as he took another sandwich. '*In vino veritas*, they say. Who would imagine the warm-blooded girl who lurks behind that prim facade you present to the world—if only they knew!'

Edouard was smiling. Theresa didn't know whether he was teasing or serious. A terrible thought struck her. Her hand flew to her mouth. 'You don't mean—oh you can't mean . . .' She hesitated. 'You're not going to tell your readers?' she whispered.

Was it her imagination, or did he recoil from her? His

expression was so cold that she shivered. She put out her hand, but didn't quite dare to touch him.

'Is that what you think I would do? It didn't worry you the other night. You begged me to stay.'

Theresa licked dry lips. This was a different Edouard, an Edouard who appeared to hate her. She shook her head. 'I don't know.' The words were forced from her.

His expression became even grimmer, and she bitterly regretted saying anything. Of course Edouard wouldn't. In her heart she knew that. But . . . if he did . . .

'And how would it look to my readers?' he drawled. 'What would they think of me, bringing drink to a young girl, putting her to bed? No, you may rest assured that I'll say nothing and write nothing about the whole episode.'

For a moment, she felt a surge of relief, and began to smile. The smile was wiped off her face as he continued.

'What, after all, is there to report?' He shrugged. 'You issued an invitation. I declined to accept it. Perhaps, if you make it again, cold sober, my answer might be different. There wouldn't be much pleasure for me with a girl who was totally inert—or in one who was just playing at being grown up. I had the distinct impression that any other man would have done just as well.'

Theresa bit her lip in wounded pride and vexation. She had not been playing at being grown up. She had wanted Edouard to go on kissing her. He was the one who had supplied the words after she had said she was ready for the second lesson. She talked too much when she was nervous. Now she was speechless, seething, wanting to deny what he had implied.

'Sex isn't a game for experimenting with,' he pointed out. 'Wait till you love someone and he loves you.' He half turned from her. 'I don't know why I bother trying to explain. I suppose I don't like to see a youngster acting so foolishly.'

A youngster! At last Theresa found her tongue. He had hurt her. She retaliated.

'You're hateful, loathsome!' She managed to keep her voice low, but it was full of anger. 'You think you know everything about me. Just because you're older than I am, you have no right to judge me, to call me foolish.' She stopped for breath, and to find the right words to tell him that she wouldn't have allowed any other man to kiss her or stay with her, that she had thought she wanted only him. Well, now she didn't want him at all, never would . . .

Before she could put him to rights, they were interrupted by the arrival of Sal and Marguerite. At any other time, Theresa might have wondered at this unlikely combination. She had never seen them together before.

Sal put her arm through Edouard's. 'I've been looking everywhere for you. Theresa's had you to herself for long enough, and you don't look too happy together, anyway. Whatever have you been saying to her?' She shook a finger at him. 'I won't have her upset. There's something we must talk about.' She led him away. He was carrying his camera. She picked up the plate of sandwiches. 'Men are always hungry, aren't they?'

Neither Marguerite nor Theresa answered that question.

'Of course, they're old friends,' Marguerite smiled faintly. 'Intimate friends, one might say, but I would have thought they could have waited for a less public spot to say whatever needed saying between them.'

She was in a lacy dress in a deep shade of turquoise, which set off her colouring admirably. She was beautiful, smart and at ease, her thick reddish-gold hair gleaming.

'Intimate friends?' Theresa repeated, wondering how much of her previous conversation Sal and Marguerite had heard. 'I didn't think they were friends at all—just business associates.'

'That's what they want people to think.' Marguerite smiled. 'Sal's a very attractive woman, and she's been married. I always think a woman who's survived that has a decided attraction for a certain type of man, particularly when there's no danger of any little complications. Sal will never marry again, of course.'

Theresa was torn between defending Sal out of loyalty to her and absolving Edouard of any blame, but suddenly it all began to fall into place. It wasn't Marguerite who mattered to him. He must be able to see through her. It was Sal. Why hadn't she seen it before? Sal was his partner in the summer cottages. It was Sal who had hired her at Edouard's instigation. She remembered that Simon had said that he seemed to favour both Sidney and Marguerite. No man who was serious about either would act like that.

And where did she fit into his harem? Quite obviously, she didn't. Hadn't he told her so, twice? It would be different from now on. She was armed, and warned against his charm. He was a man who couldn't help attracting women—like her own father, in fact. Why hadn't she realised it sooner? And what was it that the hotel proprietor had said in Ottawa—that Sal couldn't have any more babies. That was what Marguerite meant by no little complications. Sal was a modern women, a self-sufficient woman who had endured one bad marriage. She might not want to marry again. Theresa shuddered. Did they laugh about her?'

'Something the matter, dear?' enquired Marguerite. 'You've gone so pale. Does the heat bother you?' She fanned herself with a thin piece of cardboard. 'I must tell Simon what a good fan this makes. You're not used to Canadian summers.'

'It's nothing,' she replied, wanting to get away and hide. 'A little fresh air might help. Have you seen Tony? I wouldn't want him to miss me.' She looked around for her half-brother.

'Oh, you've nothing to worry about there! He's quite taken to the social life. The last time I saw him he was talking to that Toronto reporter. They seemed to be getting along like old friends. I wonder what they could have in common. Still, Tony was always inclined to be a bit of a blabbermouth—don't you find him so?'

To anyone else, Theresa might have replied that Tony sometimes let his tongue run away with him, but she wouldn't admit it to Marguerite. She knew her temper was rising. Why should she curb her tongue as Edouard had asked?

'Was it Tony who told you about the album, or did you ask him about it?' she found herself enquiring. She didn't have to be bound to keep quiet for ever.

She was rewarded by a sharply indrawn breath, but Marguerite recovered quickly. 'Whatever do you mean? What album?'

'The one with my picture in it, the picture you recognised because you'd seen me at five, the picture which told you he was married already—still married to my mother.'

Theresa saw Marguerite's fists clench, but she didn't allow her facial expression to change. She was still smiling. 'Why should it matter to me whether your father was married or not?'

'You meant to marry him, until that fact emerged.' She longed to shake Marguerite and force the truth out of her. Belatedly she realised that she had chosen the wrong place for such a confrontation.

'I to marry a married man?' Marguerite laughed at her. 'I knew he was married from the first. I wrote to your mother. She re—' She stopped abruptly.

'She replied that my father was dead. Was that what you were going to say? At least I now know who sent the clipping.'

'What if I did? It wasn't fair of him to pretend to be single. Your mother said that her first husband was dead. Your father denied he was that man. He said he came from Montreal, and had Tony to prove it. I believed him, until I saw the picture of you. Then I knew he'd been lying. But I never had a row with him over it, if that's what you're thinking. He disappeared before I had time to say any of the things I wanted to say. He disappeared, and everyone looked at me. I didn't raise my hand against him. I'm not responsible.' Marguerite was shaking. 'I didn't kill him, if that's what you think.'

Theresa was forced against every instinct to believe her, to admit to herself that Edouard had been right about her. She even felt a certain sympathy for her, could half understand why he had asked her to take no action. Oh yes, he would be angry when he found out. Let him be angry! He didn't care about her feelings. She put her hand on the other woman's arm, and would have apologised.

Marguerite shook herself free. 'If I were you, I'd drop the whole thing now, before you do any more harm. Before your precious half-brother is labelled what he is—a bastard! Why not leave now?' She gave her a long glance of distaste and hatred, and then turned on her heel and left.

A trembling Theresa was left to her own churning thoughts. She had let her tongue run away with her twice in a row and had quarrelled with two different people. What was the matter with her?

She was joined by Rosie in a white cotton dress with navy spots. 'I've just had my picture taken by that reporter with Simon's dad. It's a great afternoon, isn't it—and the food is delightful. Have you had one of those little cakes? They're yummy.' She adjusted her jade green hat. 'Simon poured me some of that gentlemen's punch. Would you like some?'

Theresa shuddered. 'I don't drink.'

'All right,' Rosie replied. 'No need to tell everyone.' She helped herself to some nuts. 'What a crowd; everybody is here! I've had a scrumptious time. A pity we're not invited to the dinner tonight, but it's for men only. Simon's dad is going home tomorrow. He says it'll all be different next time when he brings his wife. Sal's promised me a lift home. You and Tony too, but there's no need to go yet.'

It was some time later that Edouard saw them leave. Sal was in a state, he reflected, and he could hardly blame her. What a time for things to come to a head.

The afternoon had been something of a fiasco as far as he was concerned. He had resented the presence of the Toronto reporter. A rags to riches story—a pulp to boxes tale—he had told himself savagely, didn't need that kind of coverage. The Toronto man had known it, too. He hadn't liked the way Mr Radcliffe had kept summoning him to take more pictures with pretty girls, first Theresa, then Sidney and Rosie. The expression on his face had said it all.

Edouard frowned. That reporter's face; surely he knew it? It suddenly came to him. Alex Miller—but he'd been a crime reporter. What a come-down! He'd been quite good in his own way.

This was a puzzle. Why would Tom McGregor—and it was his paper, they'd all mentioned it by name—send a crime reporter to cover this cardboard story? There was something very wrong here. McGregor must be trying to find some further cover on the missing father scene. He'd already scored once with the Ottawa scoop. Why had he sent someone to sniff around here? To settle old scores with himself—that had to be the answer. Forewarned was forearmed. He'd keep an eye on Alex Miller. Sound him out, perhaps. He was bound to be at this dinner tonight.

Edouard smiled to himself and collected up his paraphernalia. At any rate, Alex Miller wasn't going to get to Theresa. He'd see to that . . .

CHAPTER FOURTEEN

SIMON CALLED on Theresa on Tuesday evening. He was full of news about the cardboard boxes and their astonishing success.

'Orders have been pouring in ever since the write-up in the Toronto paper.' He showed Theresa a copy of the newspaper. 'My father's absolutely delighted with the whole thing. He stayed over the weekend, and, you'll never guess, he's bought me a brand-new canoe! We went fishing in it on Saturday. The old man's a great fisherman.'

Theresa told him that was splendid. She was glad he'd had a good time with his father. Her weekend had not been so pleasant. She'd been turning over her situation in her mind and trying to find some way out of it. She could leave Creswal and go somewhere else. She longed to do it, but there was Tony, and he had settled so well here. He looked on this place as home. Besides, she had a job which she liked, a job created for her by Sal and Edouard. That was what chafed. No, she couldn't leave. She was trapped for the moment. She'd have to show them that whatever arrangement Sal and Edouard had, it didn't matter to her. She sighed.

'Where's Tony?' Simon looked about, as though expecting him to materialise out of the walls.

'Up at the big house.' Theresa came back to the present. 'Mrs Appledore has a grandson, Timmy, visiting for a few weeks. He's just about Tony's age, and they've taken to each other. Mr Appledore's teaching them to play cards. He won't be back for an hour or two.'

'Grand!' Simon exclaimed. 'Then you can come and see the canoe. Leave a note for Tony; we won't be long.'

Feeling like a child let out of school, she did as he

suggested, and they stole out of the little house like a pair of conspirators.

It wasn't far to the beach, and the canoe was waiting. Brand-new, as Simon had said—bright red with a silver trim.

'It's beautiful.' Theresa's hand rested on it reverently.

'It goes like a bird.' Simon lifted it from the sand, and together they carried it to the water and floated it.

'You had better take off your shoes and socks,' he advised. 'You'll have to step into it from the water.'

Theresa complied. This was a totally new experience for her. The canoe bobbed on the water, and the end of it that she entered rather gingerly threatened to scrape the sand on the bottom. She sat down on a rather narrow laced seat.

Simon pushed the canoe into deeper water, and climbed in. As he did so, Theresa wondered why the whole thing didn't tip right over, and she squealed in fright.

'Stay calm,' he chided. 'That's the whole secret of it. Don't make any sudden moves.' He paddled away from shore.

At first, scarcely daring to breathe, Theresa shut her eyes.

'It's perfectly all right,' Simon laughed. 'Canoes were in use on this river before the white man ever came. The Indians invented them. You'd be surprised at the speed they can go, even against the current and down through the rapids.'

Gradually, as they moved out into the centre of the river and Simon's paddle assumed a rhythm of its own, Theresa's fears were allayed. It was certainly much faster than a row-boat and seemed much less work.

'Some day, I'll teach you to paddle,' Simon promised. 'But not tonight. You need to get used to it first.'

She was sitting facing him at the other end of the boat. It was very pleasant to be swept along, the silver water suddenly assuming the bright hues of the setting sun.

As they left Creswal behind, the banks of the river

were lined with trees, now darker green, almost black in the changing light. There were only a few houses nestled far back among them. It was a quiet landscape, and their progress was silent, too: only the faint chuckle of the water under the bow and the soft drip of the paddle.

Peace began to enter into Theresa's soul. 'Beyond Paradise', Edouard had called this strip of sand and forest they were now passing. Edouard—it always came back to Edouard. She sighed.

'I thought you'd like it,' Simon said. 'But you're looking tired. I think you're doing too much. You're not used to hot days and a ten-year-old brother. My father said he admired you immensely for taking Tony on. A nice family feeling it showed. He was very impressed with you, Theresa.'

'I thought he was very nice.' She was pleased with the compliment.

'Next time he comes, he promised to bring Mother. You'll take to her. Everyone does.'

'Yes,' Theresa agreed, wondering why he was telling her about his parents.

'I was surprised to see that Toronto reporter out in a boat on Sunday. Is he staying somewhere in the neighbourhood? I know he isn't at the hotel.'

'He's with friends in one of the summer cottages. It seems they invited him to stay on for a holiday. I didn't know anything about it. Sal mentioned it yesterday morning. Then Edouard came round in the afternoon when I was bringing a new family in, and insisted that I meet him, but I don't know why. Alex Miller is his name. He didn't seem very interested in me. I told him I thought my father was dead.'

'You've given up searching for him any more, have you?' Simon's paddle took a slower arc.

Theresa dabbled her fingers in the water. It no longer seemed to matter very much. She had accepted that she would never see her father; it had just been a fantasy. Tony was real.

'But you're going to stay on here? I hope you are.'

She smiled at Simon, glad that someone wanted her. 'Yes, I'm staying. For the summer, anyway.' It was strange, she thought idly. She had dreaded facing Sal yesterday morning, had imagined she wouldn't be able to do it, yet Sal had been just the same astringent Sal. She didn't look triumphant or even particularly happy. In fact there were dark circles under her eyes, and a frown that might have been exhaustion might have been melancholy. It was only when she looked at Tony that her expression lightened. Theresa had found herself a little sad, looking at the two of them, that Sal couldn't have children of her own. She couldn't understand herself—first she was sorry for Marguerite and now for Sal. Men had a lot to answer for.

In this reflective mood, she felt very grateful to Simon. He was always kind to her, took her out of herself, made her feel comfortable. He was a true friend.

'You are good to me, Simon! I don't know what I'd do without you.'

'You don't have to do without me,' he replied practically. 'I enjoy being with you.' He turned the canoe for home. 'Another evening, we'll bring a picnic and our bathing costumes, perhaps. These summer evenings are perfect on the river.'

They arrived back at the little house at the same time as Tony did, and they all had a cup of tea and some fruit. For the first time since Friday, Theresa felt that life in Creswal might not be so bad after all. Simon was so comfortable to be with. When he kissed her good night, she responded with more enthusiasm than she had hitherto shown him.

'Steady on, Theresa!' he exclaimed. 'You are alone here, and I won't take advantage of you. It wouldn't be gentlemanly of me, and I respect you too much for that. But I'm pleased to see that you seem to be getting over that infatuation you had for Eddie Moreau . . . You're more like your real self tonight.' He kissed her on the forehead in farewell.

Theresa watched him leave, standing by the screen door in the kitchen. Getting over her infatuation for Edouard Moreau—she sincerely hoped she was. She contrasted Simon's impeccable behaviour with Edouard's of the other night, and sighed. Simon was a dear. She was very fond of him, she told herself. And she hated Edouard Moreau, who didn't know how to treat a girl properly and had no regard at all for her feelings. He was probably having an affair with Sal, and it was a long-standing one, if Marguerite was to be believed. Yes, it was certainly time to stop thinking about him. Simon was right. She had been infatuated with the man. Now her eyes were open, her mind clear. She could see him for what he was—a womaniser and a cheat. She would show him that he had absolutely no effect on her any more. She was free of him. She didn't even need his help, now that she had accepted that her father was dead. She went to bed with an untroubled mind. Tony was her concern—Tony, and perhaps Simon. She smiled to herself as she drifted off to sleep.

This state of euphoria lasted a few days—until Saturday, in fact. It was hot and muggy, a frustrating day with rain threatening. Everyone's temper seemed at breaking-point.

One family arrived early, only to find the others still in possession of the summer cottage. They had to wait, and didn't like it. Even when the others had gone, Maybella and Ruby had to rush round tidying and cleaning as the new ones moved in. Their baby cried, their older children squabbled, their dog chased a neighbour's cat. Pandemonium reigned.

Sal snapped at Theresa when the car refused to start for the trip to the station. Fortunately, Frank cranked it, and Theresa drove off, glad to be away from the mêlée. While she was installing this fresh lot of cottage-dwellers, Tony climbed a tree and got stuck there, afraid to come down. He had to be rescued by Frank and Harry, summoned from unloading, and they needed to go for a longer ladder. She was relieved when, late in the afternoon, Sal declared it was time to go home.

The trip back to town was accomplished in silence, with the sky darkening ominously, and a very subdued and repentant Tony in the back seat.

Sal left them at the path to Appledores', and Timmy, the visiting grandson, was waiting there for Tony. He came with them to their little house.

Theresa changed into an old cotton frock, faded and rather short. Discarding her stockings and girdle, she went barefoot round the kitchen, deciding they had just about enough food to last the weekend.

The boys meanwhile spread the Meccano set round the living-room, arguing whether to build a fort or a bridge. Timmy said it must be a bridge, and started work. Tony, as reluctant host, began to build a fort with the logs in the box by the fire.

Thunder rumbled above the little house, and lightning flashed in the most frightening way. It wasn't long before the heavens opened and a leak developed near the front door. Timmy put a bucket there, while Theresa and Tony flew round closing the windows on the side of the house where the rain was coming in. After that, the boys settled to playing amicably, if a little noisily, and Theresa sat in the kitchen shelling peas and watching the storm through the still open screen door.

When the meal was ready, it had become so dark that she lit one of the coal-oil lamps and placed it on the kitchen table. Timmy was invited to stay, and accepted readily. Fortunately, though it was a simple meal of cold ham, peas and salad, there was enough for the three of them, as there was plenty of bread and butter and fruit cake as well. The boys helped with the dishes, and when the rain lessened a little, both of them went off to the big house.

Peace at last, thought Theresa. She made herself a large cup of tea, and sat feet up in the living-room without bothering to look at its state of chaos, let alone tidy it. There were screws and bolts and pieces of metal on the floor, mixed with several discarded logs of wood.

The bucket, emptied by Tony before he left, still stood by the door.

He had opened the windows, too, and a breeze now came through them. The rain had halted, at least for the time being. She had brought the lamp through from the kitchen. For the first time all day, she was cool and comfortable. In the flickering light she was quite content to enjoy doing nothing.

Her calm was challenged suddenly by a determined knocking on the front door. She padded across to open it, thinking it must be Tony, and was considerably disconcerted to find Edouard Moreau and Big Bob Falconer on the threshold.

'May we come in?' asked Edouard. His tone was distinctly unfriendly.

Big Bob said nothing, but even in the dim light she was conscious of the scowl on his face.

Theresa stood on one bare foot and then the other as she opened the door wide. She knew her dress was old and short, her hair dishevelled.

'Won't you sit down?' she murmured politely, as they entered.

Big Bob knocked over the bucket and tripped on some discarded screws. 'Sit down?' he echoed. 'I nearly fell down! Can't you light another lamp?'

Theresa ran to the kitchen for the big Aladdin lamp, and managed to light it without setting fire to the mantle. Then she carried it in and set it on a sturdy table near Big Bob. He and Edouard were sitting side by side on the settee. She almost giggled to see them there, but controlled her mirth and sat facing them in the rocking-chair, trying to tuck her feet out of sight.

'What's wrong?' There was a quaver in her voice, when neither of them said anything. 'Has something happened to Tony?'

'Something will happen to Tony if I lay my hands on him.' Bib Bob spoke angrily. 'Where is he?'

'At the big house. What's wrong?'

Big Bob took a newspaper from his pocket and thrust

it at her. 'Read this,' he urged.

She spread it out. It was a Toronto paper, and before her was an article entitled, 'Missing Father—English Daughter says her Father Dead—Canadian Son that his Dad went to meet Woman and never returned'.

She read it through, both men watching her. She looked up then, clutching the paper, unable to believe it. Whoever had written it was blatantly accusing Marguerite Falconer of murder. He was very careful not to mention her name, and referred to her only as Charles Russell's fiancée, but anyone who knew anything about the people involved must recognise the portrait he painted.

'This is terrible!' she exclaimed.

'Trial by innuendo.' Edouard spoke for the first time since entering. 'The worst kind of yellow journalism. Just what Tom McGregor seems to be going in for these days! Did you put Tony up to this?'

'Tony?' Theresa gasped. 'How could I?'

'Perhaps you suggested it to Alex Miller yourself,' Edouard's voice was ice. 'Or did you just send Tony along to him to give him the story?'

Theresa looked at Edouard in utter disbelief. 'Why do you accuse me of it? The only time I ever talked to Mr Miller, you introduced me. You were there when I told him my father was dead; it was you and Frank who convinced me that he was. As far as I know, the only time Tony talked to him was on the Open Day at the paper mill.' She looked from one to the other, burning with anger. 'How could you suppose I'd lend myself to that?' She threw the paper at Edouard. 'If that's what you think of me, you can get out now!' She rose to her feet, shaking with indignation. 'Besides,' she added for good measure, 'Marguerite told me that she didn't kill him, and I believed her. Why should I do this to her, even though I felt she wasn't telling me everything she knew?'

It would have been hard to say which man was more dumbfounded.

'You asked Marguerite if she'd killed him?' Big Bob's mouth hung open. 'How dared you?'

There was a gleam in Edouard's eyes as he surveyed her. It might have been admiration. It might have been amusement. 'I would have liked to have overheard that conversation. Sit down, girl. Bare feet don't really lend themselves to high drama. How did you put it to her? Just a straight question?'

Theresa sat down abruptly. It was difficult to maintain any dignity with all eyes on her feet. 'If you mean did I ask her if she'd murdered my father, no, it wasn't quite like that. But we understood each other. I'm sure she didn't pull the trigger, throw the knife or supply him with poison. She said she hadn't.'

'The poison, the knife . . .' Big Bob spluttered. 'How was your father killed?'

Theresa shrugged. 'I don't know. I don't think Marguerite does, either. But she knows something. I'm almost sure of that.'

'That's a dangerous statement.' There was a steely edge to Big Bob's voice.

'Is it?' Theresa considered for a moment. 'I would have thought Mr Miller's article was far more dangerous, and damaging. He says he has a witness—a farmer who was on his veranda, grieving because his wife had died that day—that's how he remembers the date.'

'And what does this farmer say after all?' Big Bob demanded angrily. He answered his own question. 'He says he saw a red canoe with Charles Russell in it. He knew him, and he waved. Half an hour later there was another canoe going up-river in the same direction with a woman in it, but he couldn't make out who she was because she had some sort of covering on her head and he couldn't see the colour of her hair. The woman came back, according to him, an hour or so later, just as it was beginning to go dark. But Charles Russell didn't—not then, not later—and there was brilliant moonlight all night.'

'Why didn't he come forward before?' asked Theresa, rocking gently. 'It's a long time afterwards.'

She looked to Big Bob, but it was Edouard who answered. 'There was the funeral, and then he went to his daughter in Hull for a few weeks. By the time he came back, no one was talking about the disappearance of one man. A number of soldiers from this area had been killed in France. That was the topic of conversation.'

'I'll tell you one thing, young lady,' Big Bob broke in. 'I intend to hire a detective to find out about your father's past life. If he was murdered, there must be a reason.'

Far from feeling threatened by this new development, Theresa was puzzled. 'What you're likely to discover is that he was still married when Marguerite accepted his offer. And surely you know that already.'

Big Bob looked at her blankly. 'Was he?'

Theresa frowned at him. 'She must have told you.'

'You don't know that she knew.' Edouard corrected her coldly.

'Yes, I do. She saw the album. She as good as admitted it.'

Edouard put his hand to his head. 'You had better start at the beginning.'

So she did. She told them about Tony's nightmare, and her subsequent confrontation with Marguerite at the Open Day. But she didn't mention anything about Sal and Edouard.

'Why haven't I heard anything of this before?' said Edouard.

Big Bob sat as though stunned. 'I never knew. She never said a word. It was a terrible time for her when Charles Russell disappeared. The invitations had gone out for the wedding. She was in such a state that the doctor thought she might have a complete breakdown. When she recovered months later, she was utterly frozen—Didn't want to talk about him at all. Naturally I respected her wishes. If what you're saying in true . . .

But there's only your word for it.'

Theresa blinked. 'You can talk to her now, surely.'

'No, I can't. I sent her away. I wasn't going to have her subjected to this all over again. I've given out that Sidney is going to a summer school to study art. She's been begging to go for ages, and Marguerite is accompanying her. They've gone to the States. They won't be able to reach her there.'

He didn't specify who 'they' were, but Theresa supposed he meant the newspapers—or the police. 'That was quick!' she exclaimed.

'I don't believe in wasting time,' Big Bob responded. 'I'm used to making decisions.'

Edouard had risen to his feet and was standing over Theresa. 'Why didn't you tell me? Did you think I wouldn't have been interested?'

She quailed under the fierce look he directed at her. 'No, it wasn't that. I couldn't tell you about a lad's nightmare and expect you to attach too much importance to it. After the Open Day, I didn't want to speak to you.'

'Fallen out of favour, had I?'

Theresa nodded, not trusting herself to answer that gibe. 'Anyway, what could you have done?'

'At least been in your confidence. Do you suppose I've brought the story this far without wanting to know the truth about your father's disappearance, whoever was involved?'

Big Bob was ignored in this cross-fire, but he watched both of them.

'Is truth that important to you?' sneered Theresa. 'I remember that the first day I came to the *Clarion*, you said I might upset people here, and you didn't want that . . .'

Edouard regarded her thoughtfully. 'I knew you were trouble from the word go.'

'Exactly!' Her temper was taking over. What made him think he had the right to come here and question her? 'I knew Marguerite was your friend. I saved you the embarrassment of raising the question with her.'

'How kind of you. Did you think I'd lack the courage?'

'How should I know? Would you have asked her?'

'Yes, if only for her own sake,' was the daunting reply. 'Anyone should have the right of rebuttal, of defending her reputation.'

Theresa bit her lip. It wasn't her feelings he was concerned with, it was Marguerite's—only Marguerite's. He might have pointed out that if Marguerite had been a murderer, Theresa might well have been next on her list—a thought which had occurred to the English girl in the intervening days.

'It's no use you two going on like fishwives.' Big Bob was calmer than either of them. 'The damage's done. Where do we go from here?'

'That depends.' Edouard turned to face him. 'I think we should talk about that somewhere other than here.'

'I take your meaning.' Big Bob rose to his feet with a sidelong glance at Theresa. 'Perhaps get a lawyer's opinion? Is this Toronto reporter still in the neighbourhood?'

'Is he?' Edouard asked Theresa.

'I don't know. The family he's been staying with are still at the cottage, and I didn't drive him to the station. I only saw him that once with you.'

'Very well,' he said. 'Keep your shirt on—and your socks,' he added, with a glance at her feet. 'We won't bother you any more. I'll ask Sal.'

'We'll let ourselves out.' Big Bob motioned to her to stay where she was.

But Theresa bounded to her feet and opened the door for them. She saw that it was raining again quite hard, but she was too ruffled to invite them to stay till it had slackened off a little.

'Good night, gentlemen!' she called after them as they stepped into the downpour.

She closed the door and leaned against it. Why should she feel so mean and wretched? she asked herself. She didn't care about Edouard. It didn't matter what he thought of her. He was probably going off to see Sal now. That was the last thing he'd said, that he'd ask Sal.

She went back to her chair and sat staring into space. Perhaps she should seriously consider leaving Creswal. She didn't see how she could stay. Sunk in misery, she rocked to and fro.

A resounding knock on the front door shook her from her reverie. Once again, Edouard and Big Bob stood there. This time they held a young lad between them. He was dripping wet, his hair plastered to his head.

'He says he's looking for you,' Edouard said. 'Do you know him?'

Theresa had opened the door wide, so that they could all shelter from the rain on the threshold. She looked at the boy. Clad only in patchy trousers and a grey shirt and thick boots, he was shivering with cold, and stood pale and frightened between the two men.

'Charlie!' she exclaimed. 'It is Charlie from the orphanage, Tony's friend.' She held out her hands to him. 'Whatever are you doing here? Come in, you're soaking. You'll catch your death of cold.'

Charlie took her hand and clung to it. 'You wrote me a letter. You said you were my friend.'

'Of course I am.' Theresa pulled him forward to the light. 'Oh, Charlie, wherever have you been? I'll get something to wrap you in, and we'll get you out of those sodden things.'

Charlie gave her the ghost of a smile. 'I didn't mean to drip over everything.' He was standing in a pool of water.

'He needs a fire,' said Big Bob, 'and a hot drink. Have you any brandy in the house?'

Theresa, back with a towel, said, 'No.'

Edouard had said nothing, but he had gathered some of the logs strewn round the room and had a fire started. 'Come over here, Charlie,' he instructed, and undid his shirt, since the boy seemed too numb and dumb to do it for himself.

Big Bob followed them over. It was he who exclaimed

as the shirt was snatched off. 'Good God, lad! Who's done this to you?' He spun him round to show Edouard. 'I know what a beating looks like. Take a look!'

Theresa, too, craned to see. Charlie's back was a mass of weals and bruises, with some angry-looking scabs. Her hand flew to her mouth.

'Oh, Charlie,' she whispered, and wrapped the towel round his thin shoulders. 'Was it the farmer who took you from the orphanage who did this?'

'Yes.' The boy nodded, looking only at Theresa. 'He said he'd break me. He would have, except for your letter.' His face was stony. 'He wouldn't let me have your letter, but I stole it from his desk. It wasn't stealing. It was mine, but he beat me with his belt-buckle that time.' Charlie shivered, as Edouard pulled his trousers away to expose more scars.

Theresa enfolded him in a blanket, and sat rubbing his hair with him on her lap in the rocking-chair Big Bob had pulled forward.

'How did you get away from him?' she asked.

'I ran away in the night and got to the railway station. I crawled into a box-car and went to sleep. When I woke up, I didn't know where I was. It wasn't Ottawa, just some town. I got off because I thought they'd find me. They look in the box-cars, you know. I hung around the station all day, and I met a tramp. He told me the right trains to jump to get here. I've walked some of the way.'

'How long ago was this?' Theresa was appalled.

Charlie frowned, trying to remember. 'I don't know . . . Four or five nights ago, I think.'

'You've asked the wrong question,' Edouard interrupted. 'How long since you've eaten, Charlie?'

'A long time. Micky the tramp gave me some bread, and I've had some apples since, and some milk.'

Theresa noticed that he didn't say where the apples and milk had come from, and she didn't ask.

'I should have thought of food right away,' she said. 'I'll get you something.' She tried to move Charlie from her lap, but he held on to her.

'You won't let them send me back, will you? I can stay. Promise me I don't have to go back to him?'

Theresa could feel Charlie trembling, and she held him for a moment. 'You can stay. You'll never go back there. I swear it.'

Charlie half released her. 'Who are these men?' he whispered, looking at Edouard and Big Bob. 'Will they make you send me back?'

'No, they won't.'

'They're big men.' Charlie wasn't convinced. 'You're not married to either of them, are you?'

'No.' Theresa swallowed hard. 'They're just friends.'

Edouard heard her reply, and gave her a sardonic glance. 'Just friends—I'm Edouard Moreau, news-paperman, and he's Bob Falconer, mill owner. We've been calling on your hostess.' He bowed to Theresa. 'Get the boy something to eat.'

Theresa slid from the chair and went to the kitchen. What was best for a starving boy? In the larder, she realised with a sinking heart that there wasn't much there. How had she forgotten to put in that order?

She picked up a bowl with the last three eggs, and got out the frying-pan and lit the gas. It came on with a little plop. Thank heaven she'd mastered its use. At home they'd had a big coal range—and a cook.

In a short time, she returned to the living-room with a steaming cup of sweet milky tea for Charlie, as well as a plateful of scrambled eggs and a pile of bread and butter. She also brought a pot of tea and cups for the men, and some cake. If she only had a small cup herself, there'd be just about enough milk. Mrs Appledore might spare her some in the morning.

While Charlie ate till he could eat no more, and the men watched him gulping tea and finishing the last of the cake, Theresa racked her brains about how she was going to manage meals for three the next day. It was Sunday, and everything would be closed.

Charlie fell fast asleep in his chair, and Big Bob put

another log on the fire, then sat on a wooden stool, staring into the flames.

Edouard cleared the dishes on to a tray and brought it, laden, to the kitchen. Theresa followed him after a few minutes, since he did not return.

'I'll do the dishes in the morning,' she began to say to him, only to find him peering into the ice-box.

He turned to face her, shutting the door with a bang. 'What are you going to do about him?'

It was so quiet that she could hear the steady drum of the rain on the roof of the little house. 'Keep him, I suppose. I can't send him back.'

'You can't keep him, either.'

'What else can I do? He came to me.'

'Oh, Theresa!' Edouard took hold of her hands. 'You won't be able to manage two boys. What will you live on? There's precious little food in the house, as it is.'

She coloured. What right had he to look in her ice-box? He'd probably been in the pantry, too. 'I forgot to order anything.'

'I'll get my housekeeper to send you something in the morning.'

'I don't need charity!' She snatched her hands away. She didn't need him standing dangerously close to her either, upsetting her by his seeming concern.

'It's not charity.'

'What else would you call it?'

'Try—being neighbourly or helping you out. Some-one's going to have to. It's Sunday tomorrow, and you'll have two starving boys on your hands. What are you going to give them?'

Theresa didn't know. 'Next week I'll be more or-ganised.' She looked down at her feet. No wonder he thought her incompetent. She was half dressed, the living-room had been strewn with pieces of wood and Meccano, and there was not enough food for any of them.

'How can you be? You'll be working every day, and

you won't be able to trail two boys around with you. Sal can't put up with that.'

There it was again—Sal's name on his lips. She turned away from him. 'I'll manage somehow.'

'You'll have to get some help in the house—a woman to come in in the mornings, to tidy up and get a hot meal ready, to keep an eye on the boys. Can you afford it?'

'I don't know.' Theresa hadn't thought that far ahead. All she knew was that Charlie had come to her, depended on her, and had no one else who cared a scrap for him. 'I can't turn him away.'

'And you can't keep him.'

'I can, and I will.'

'They won't let you. The authorities will take him away.'

'I won't tell them he's here.'

'Someone else will.'

'You mean that you will.'

'That's unfair!'

They stood glaring at each other.

'Quarrelling again?' Big Bob was framed in the doorway, his shadow behind him. 'I never saw such a pair.'

'We're not a pair,' snapped Theresa.

'Thank heaven for that,' Edouard added. He appealed to Big Bob. 'You try talking some sense to her! I can't.'

'It's late. It's not the time for reasonable decisions. Leave it till tomorrow. Sleep on it. Theresa, do you want Charlie carried to a bed?'

She turned to him gratefully. 'Yes, please. There are bunk beds in Tony's room. If you'll put Charlie in the bottom one, I'll get another blanket and a pillow. Tony always uses the upper.'

Theresa carried the lamp into the bedroom, and Big Bob the sleeping boy.

'I suppose you'll want Tony from the big house?' Edouard followed them. 'We'll stop there on the way out, and I'll see he gets here. I'll tell him about Charlie, shall I?'

Theresa agreed, and once again bade the men good night. She went back to her rocking-chair by the fire to wait for Tony.

What was she going to do?

CHAPTER FIFTEEN

ON SUNDAY morning, Theresa woke to the sounds of the boys' chattering. Then she heard scurryings, and presently a cup of tea was brought to her by Tony, with Charlie behind him with a plate of muffins.

'They were in a basket by the back door with milk and some other things. Why were they there, Theresa?' asked Tony.

At her invitation, they both sat down on the bed. Charlie was wearing one of Tony's cotton shirts which was too small for him, and he had the blanket clutched round his middle.

'His things are still wet,' Tony explained, 'and I said you wouldn't want him to wear them anyway. They're old and torn.'

Theresa offered the boys the muffin plate. She didn't want to make any statements yet.

But Tony had no reservations about putting things on a recognised basis. 'He'll need some clothes if he's going to stay with us. Is he going to stay?'

Charlie hadn't said a word yet. Now he raised his eyes from his muffin to Theresa's face.

Theresa frowned. 'Blabbermouth', Marguerite had called Tony. She'd named him aptly. Theresa wanted to say No. Last night she'd denied everything that Edouard had said, but this morning she knew he was right. And yet, Charlie had come to her, trusting her, not having anyone else to turn to. She looked at him and was torn. He was pale and thin, but there was a light in his blue eyes that hadn't been there last night. His hair, dry now, was red and standing up in tufts all over his head. He wasn't handsome, or compact like Tony, but all bones and angles. Perhaps, when he filled out and began to adjust to his size, he wouldn't look so awkward. He looked as vulnerable, though, as he had that Friday afternoon in the orphanage when she had told him that Tony was the one she'd come to see. Even then, there had been something in Charlie that had cried out to her. She couldn't deny him again.

She struggled against it, biting her lip so hard that she tasted the salt of blood. His eyes didn't plead with her, but they looked at her intently. In their clear gaze, she knew she had no choice. 'He's staying,' she said. 'When I get up, we'll see about something for him to wear.'

It was a promise she found hard to fulfil. Tony's clothes were too small for him, hers too feminine. She settled temporarily by offering him a towel in exchange for the blanket, while they unpacked the basket of food which had arrived on the doorstep. It contained a large meat loaf as well as cold chicken and ham, a big apple pie, eggs, butter and rolls.

'Why did Edouard send it to us?' Tony wanted to know. 'Don't we have enough money to buy food?'

Once again, Theresa had to admit that she had forgotten the order. She added that it was very kind of Edouard to help her out.

'Will he help Charlie out by sending some clothes?'

Theresa began to wish he would. But it was Mrs Appledore from the big house who saved the day. She arrived with blue overalls, a blue checked shirt and a pair of moccasins. 'They're not new,' she apologised. 'Edouard said he was a big boy for his age, and I thought they might do for the present.'

Charlie was more than pleased with them. He couldn't believe anyone would give him anything. 'Will we have to pay for them?' he asked Theresa in a whisper.

Mrs Appledore laughed. 'If that doesn't beat all! I don't want any pay. They're a gift.' She hugged Charlie. 'I had a little brother once—I hope someone helped him.'

It was astonishing how many people brought or sent gifts for Charlie that day. There was a pail of ice-cream and a big chocolate cake from Big Bob. Sal sent a note asking Theresa to bring Charlie in the next day when she reported for work, because she wanted to buy him some clothes. Rosie brought socks and underwear that her brother had outgrown, and a red sweater. It clashed ferociously with Charlie's hair, but he loved it from the moment his hand fell on it. It was so soft that he would have worn it even in the heat of the day.

Simon came to give Theresa good advice. 'Two boys is too many,' he told her kindly. 'You can't afford it.'

She listened and said nothing. He only repeated what Edouard had said, and she knew it was true.

Edouard arrived in the late morning, his camera slung over his shoulder, with a man whom he introduced as the local doctor, an oldish man with a kind face.

'Dr Black's come to see Charlie,' he announced, and he took Theresa aside—outside, in fact, before she could voice any objections. 'I know a mulish woman when I tangle with one. I could see you'd made up your mind last night. If you must do it, I'm going to see it's done properly.'

'The doctor's a good idea,' she was forced to admit. 'But why the camera? I don't want Charlie's back exhibited to your readers, if that's what you're thinking of.'

'Would I do such a thing?' His glance was bland.

'You might, if you thought it would sell papers.'

'I have no intention of using it in the paper,' he said stiffly. 'How can I convince you that I'm not the ogre you think me?'

She looked away from him, down at her clasped hands. 'I don't think that, most of the time.'

There was silence between them for a while.

Theresa broke it. 'Thank you for the food. I don't know what we would have done without it today—and for telling people. They've been coming all morning.'

'That's all right. It might be a good idea just to take Charlie along to Sal's office in the morning. You'll be working in town this week, and two boys will be too distracting.'

There it was again, Theresa thought. Sal's name. And Edouard went on twisting the knife deeper.

'Sal's found you a young woman to help in the house. Her name's Gwendolyn. She has a small baby, and her husband's not working because he has a broken leg. Sal will ask her to come tomorrow to talk to you about hours and pay.'

Theresa felt that everything was being arranged for her by other people, and too quickly. 'I'll have to think about it.'

Edouard's blue eyes questioned her. 'Changing your mind? It's not too late to back out.'

She shook her head. She would have liked to tell him she could manage on her own, that she didn't need him and Sal to organise her, but who else would offer her such practical help?

'How much is she likely to charge?'

'Standard rates, Sal said, fifty cents a day, three dollars a week. That's for half-days, of course, say ten o'clock to three, and her lunch here.'

'Yes.' Theresa was mentally calculating how she could afford it.

'With two boys to feed,' Edouard went on, 'you'll probably have to break into your capital. Is that what's bothering you?'

Theresa frowned, not wanting to admit that it worried her. He had a disconcerting habit of putting his finger on the problem.

'I'll do it,' she said. 'Does this Gwendolyn like boys?'

'She's used to them. She comes from a large family. Sal's sure she's just the person for you. That's settled, then. Gwendolyn will deal with the boys and the housework. Now, let's talk about the real issues.' He took her by the arm. 'We want to be out of earshot of the house.' He led her to a part of the garden where flowers were growing, well away from where they had been standing, where there was a small bench. He remained on his feet, looking down at her.

'What real issues?'

'The boy, of course, and what you'll have to do to keep him. Ever heard of the Barnardo children?' Edouard asked.

Theresa was mystified. 'Everyone knows about Dr Barnardo in England—I'm not starting a home for boys!'

'I'm not talking about England. I'm talking about Canada. Dr Barnardo has sent thousands of orphans to this country to work on farms. They've had a hard time. Orphan is a word that arouses emotions here—and shame, too, in some cases.'

'I don't understand.'

'No, you wouldn't. I'll explain. Too many of these orphans were exploited—are still being exploited, beaten, turned into slaves, considered some sort of lower order of creature. It's nothing Canadians can be proud of.'

'What's that got to do with Charlie?'

'Everything—nothing. I'm just trying to tell you that orphans don't have rights—not rights that are recognised. They have to be fought for. Just how serious are you about Charlie? Are you willing to fight for him? Because you may have to.' His face was grim.

Theresa shrank back a little on the seat, the beauty of the flowers forgotten. 'How do you mean, fight for him?'

'Perhaps file an action against the farmer who had him. Go to court and give evidence. If it comes to that, it will take both time and money.'

She was shocked into silence. Her eyes followed a bee hovering over a yellow pansy.

'You heard what I said?' Edouard prompted.

Theresa swung her gaze back to him. 'Yes, I heard. But surely you can't be serious? I only want to give Charlie a home. If I write to the orphanage and say he's staying with me, won't that be enough?'

He laughed, a harsh sound in the morning sunshine. 'I doubt very much that it will be so simple. Ask Mrs Appledore, if you don't believe me.'

'Mrs Appledore?'

'She was one of the British orphans, separated from her little brother, and sent to a farm in this area. She was one of the lucky ones; she found a home with a good family and married an older man, a widower. He tried for years to trace her brother without success, as had the family she lived with before. They were willing to give him a home. Someone else had him—good or bad, kind or cruel—she never knew. They wouldn't even tell where he was.'

Theresa was stunned. 'But—But Charlie's a Canadian!'

'It won't make much difference. Officialdom takes no note of nationality. I asked you before . . .' Edouard was standing directly over her, his shadow blotting out her vision. 'Are you willing to fight for him?'

'Yes,' Theresa answered, shivering a little as she looked into his hard eyes. What he had said had strengthened her resolution. Charlie had no one else. She couldn't desert him.

'Then you'll need my help. I'm going to take a picture of Charlie in those old clothes of his, and I'm going to take a picture of his back for evidence, not for the paper.'

'Very well. I don't like it, but if you think it's necessary . . .'

'I do. By the way, that Toronto newspaperman is still here at the cottage. Sal's seen him.'

There it was again—Sal's name on his lips. 'Couldn't you tell him he's not welcome?' Theresa didn't want to let it upset her.

'I'd like to,' Edouard smiled bleakly. 'But it wouldn't be clever. At least, this way, I know where he is.'

'You think he's going to make more trouble, don't you?'

'Yes.'

'But why?'

'In a way it has nothing to do with you. It's between me and the paper's owner, Tom McGregor. I don't suppose he would have sent a man up here just on your story, but once he had one on another assignment he couldn't resist making good use of him, if only to get back at me. You'd better warn Tony about giving more interviews.'

'I shall.' Theresa sighed.

Edouard smiled, and sat down beside her. 'Why have you taken on all this responsibility at a time when you should be enjoying yourself?'

She shrugged, wondering why his attitude to her had suddenly softened. She couldn't explain to herself just how it had all happened. 'One thing led to another.'

'Most girls wouldn't have let it. Why are you different?'

'Am I?'

'I think so.'

Theresa flushed with pleasure. His voice was so gentle, so sincere. Why should it matter to her what he thought? She reminded herself that there was nothing personal in it—He was tied up with Sal. Still, it was pleasant.

'My mother was a great manager,' he continued. 'I learned a few things from her. Would you like me to go over your accounts with you?' He put his hand on hers.

She felt it there, comforting, warm. It brought her up with a jerk. 'No, I wouldn't,' she snapped. 'I kept the household accounts at home.' She wasn't going to let herself become dependent again on Edouard, only to be rejected again.

'There's no need to take my head off,' he said mildly. 'I have no intention of publishing your budget!'

'I should hope not!' Theresa knew he was only teasing, but she didn't leave it there. 'In any case, you're not going to get the chance to.'

'Why are you so prickly today?' His hand had moved to her knee.

She removed it, alarmed by his closeness and by the fact that she wanted his hand where it was. 'I'm not prickly.'

Edouard shrugged, and looked at his hand. 'Have it your way.'

'And another thing.' Theresa glared at him, forcing herself to be angry. 'Why are you always touching me? I don't like it.' That was a direct lie, and she knew it.

'I thought you did.' He moved to the far corner of the bench.

'I don't want you to do it again.' Theresa's lips were stiff, her hands locked together in her lap. She couldn't bear the thought of him touching her and then going home to Sal. Home? She questioned herself sharply, wondering whose home they used—his or hers?

'You can depend on it, I won't,' he assured her, getting to his feet. 'I'll take myself somewhere else, somewhere I'm more welcome.' He stood for a moment looking down at her, and she had the distinct impression that if she'd relented then and said she didn't mean it, that she was sorry, he would have stayed.

She clamped her lips together. Let him go, let him go back to Sal! Let him know there was one girl who didn't fall for his charm.

He turned and went towards the little house. She watched his disappearing back with fury—a fury that evaporated as soon as he was no longer there. If only she really mattered to him! Tears rose to her eyes, but she fought them. A man like that who flitted from woman to woman didn't deserve her tears. By the time she followed him into the house to hear the doctor's verdict on Charlie, she had herself under control.

'No bones broken,' he told her. 'I'll give you some salve for that back. Put him in a hot bath and give him a good soaking before you apply it. If it doesn't look much improved in a few days, bring him to me.'

The doctor departed, then Edouard took the pictures he wanted and called out the most perfunctory of goodbyes as he left.

Theresa could hear the boys chatting away while she put water on the stove to heat. She and Charlie carried the pots of hot water into the bathroom, and he, protesting, stripped and got in. She washed the angry weals and scabs as gently and thoroughly as she could. Charlie winced, and only once cried out. Theresa apologised, ashamed somehow to be inflicting more pain on this skinny little lad.

Charlie smiled at her. 'The doctor said he was a beast. Tony said you'd never hit him since he came to stay with you. Will you never hit me either?'

'I don't believe in beating little children. It seems wrong to me.'

'They used a strap in the orphanage.' Charlie washed his feet industriously, and submitted to Theresa washing his hair. 'That wasn't so bad, except if they did it too often.'

'And did they do it too often?' Theresa could never have imagined herself holding such a conversation with any child.

'Not with Tony,' Charlie admitted. 'He kept out of trouble, but I wasn't so lucky. They said I was quarrelsome, and blamed it on my red hair. Is there . . . Is there something bad about red hair?' He seemed so puzzled that Theresa hastened to assure him that she liked red hair.

Charlie wasn't convinced. 'But red-headed people have vile tempers—that's what they all said.' He frowned.

'Why are you telling me this?' she asked.. 'Are you trying to warn me that you aren't a very good boy?'

He seemed unable to look at her. He hugged his knees. 'Maybe,' he mumbled.

'I don't think you're a bad boy. I liked you the first time I saw you. I said to myself, I'm glad Tony has Charlie to take care of him. He wouldn't have known how to fight for himself.'

'He didn't. I had to teach him. He doesn't like fighting. He likes talking. I wish I could talk like him, or like Eddie—He said I could call him Eddie.'

'Yes, Eddie can talk,' Theresa agreed. 'But every-body can't be the same. I think you're too hard on yourself. A bad boy wouldn't have bothered with Tony, except to bully him. What other terrible things did you do?' She wasn't sure if this was the right way to deal with Charlie, but at least it was establishing some sort of link between them. It seemed sad to her that the boy should feel himself so much to blame.

'I answered them back. I said No when I should have said Yes, sir. They didn't like me much. Whenever anything went wrong, they asked where I was.'

'And where were you?' Theresa wasn't sure she wanted to hear.

'Sometimes I was there, sometimes I wasn't—it didn't seem to make any difference. So I thought I might as well be in trouble as not. I'd get blamed for it anyway.'

'Well, you won't be blamed for anything you don't do here,' Theresa promised. 'If something's not your fault, you'll only have to say so. I'll listen to you.'

'Will you really?'

'I promise.'

Charlie's smile was brilliant. He pulled out the plug, and rose from the bath with Theresa handing him a towel. 'No one's ever listened to me before.'

When he was dry, Theresa put the salve on his back and he dressed in his new overalls and shirt. With his hair washed and shining and slicked down, he began to look like any boy—not like the abandoned waif of last night.

After lunch, Big Bob called and offered to take them for a sail in his boat. It was an experience for all of them. Theresa had never sailed before, and neither had the boys. Charlie took to it quite naturally and earned Mr Falconer's praise, but Tony was much more cautious, and looked a little frightened when the boat swung into the wind as the sails filled from a different direction. However, seated close beside Theresa, he regained his courage and was soon pointing out that Simon and Rosie were canoeing on the far side of the river.

'We're going faster than they are,' he announced with

satisfaction. 'Won't they be surprised to see us?'

Charlie wasn't interested in any effect they might have on others. He was lost in sheer enjoyment. 'Gee whiz, Mr Falconer! It's like being a bird or a fish. How long does it take to be a sailor like you?'

'Years.' Big Bob was matter of fact. 'First, you need a boat.' But he let Charlie steer for a while.

Watching man and boy, Theresa felt a certain sympathy for Big Bob. He must have wanted a son desperately, and he and Charlie had quickly established themselves as friends. They seemed to understand each other.

As the boat skimmed along the river and they waved to the two in the canoe, Theresa guessed that Big Bob must be missing his daughter and his sister, and feeling a little lost without them. 'Come back to supper with us?' she invited, and he nodded a quick acceptance.

The four of them had a hilarious and informative meal, for Big Bob told them stories of working as a lumberjack. His tales ranged from the tricks the men played on each other and on newcomers, and the boys laughed at axes that flew off handles and trees that fell in the wrong direction. He shouted, 'Timber!' in such a loud voice that Theresa thought they must hear him at the big house. She listened enthralled as he described how a log-jam was straightened out.

'There's a trick to walking over the logs all caught together in the river. One false step, and the logger is under yards and yards of trees all trying to float down on the current. But the clever one goes right to the trouble, to the master log, and with one or two pushes of his iron spike unblocks the whole shebang. Then he runs back as it all begins to move. It's a pleasure to watch, and exciting to do it.'

'Could you do it?' Tony was big-eyed.

'Of course he could,' Charlie declared. 'He just said it was exciting.'

'I'll take you to watch it sometime,' Big Bob offered. 'It's only done in the spring when the river's running high and strong. It's cheaper and quicker than trucking them out.'

When the boys had gone to bed, Charlie especially looking on the point of exhaustion, Big Bob and Theresa sat in the living-room with the big Aladdin lamp casting a glow over them.

'I envy you those boys,' he declared. 'I always wanted a son—that's not to say Sidney's been a disappointment to me—but a son would have followed me into the timber mill.'

'You could marry again?'

'I could.' He seemed to brood on that for a moment. 'I should have done it before this. I've left it too late.'

Theresa smiled at him, hoping he didn't think she was putting herself forward. Still, he was a very attractive man, handsome and active. She changed the subject.

'Did you grow up here in Creswal?'

'No, but in the area around—twenty, thirty miles from here—up near the new dam. My father was a lumberjack, a rough man, especially when he'd been drinking.' He sighed. 'You wouldn't want to know about that.'

But, always curious, she asked, 'Is that how you knew Charlie hadn't been in an accident but had been beaten?'

'Yeah, you hit the nail on the head there. I saw him, and I knew it. My pa was a violent man towards me —and to ma. Never to Marguerite, I don't know why.' He sighed again.

'It still bothers you?'

'Now and then,' Big Bob admitted. 'Young Charlie brought it all back. I could see he felt it was all somehow his fault, just the way I used to feel—lacking in some way. But the lack wasn't in me any more than it is in poor Charlie. Some men are born mean and cruel. They have to take it out on someone smaller and weaker.' He smiled suddenly. 'Don't let them take that boy away from you! You'll make something of him.'

Theresa smiled back. At last here was someone who thought she was doing the right thing in keeping Charlie.

She warmed to him, recognising a friend, even an ally, in Big Bob. She could begin to understand better the curious conversation she had had with Charlie when he tried to tell her he was bad. She told Big Bob about it, and he nodded. 'That's it exactly.' He knew how it was.

'When he finds his feet, you'll find him more of a handful than your Tony,' Big Bob went on. 'But he needs affection and kindness desperately now, and I think you'll supply him with that, Miss Theresa. You have a big heart.'

He put his hand on hers and she allowed it to remain there. It was very pleasant to have a man who complimented her and applauded her actions—not like Edouard, who found fault with everything she did.

By the time Big Bob took his leave, they were on very friendly terms, and Theresa knew he'd be back to see her and the boys again. She was pleased, for the boys needed a man to take an interest in them.

In the morning, before Theresa set off for work, Gwendolyn Davis arrived to see her. She liked her at once. The girl was large and pleasant, with her hair in a neat bun at the back of her head and attired in a blue cotton dress that was a little long to Theresa's eyes, but suited her fair colouring. She smiled at the boys, and said Sal had mentioned that Theresa was bringing Charlie in with her this morning. She was willing to start at once, and had brought her apron with her. If Theresa would tell her where to begin . . .

Theresa did, feeling confident that she would suit them admirably. Tony looked disappointed that he was to remain behind, but when Gwendolyn said he would be a big help to her, he brightened considerably.

Theresa and Charlie set off for the office in the town. Once there, Sal and Charlie surveyed each other warily, and he looked quite crestfallen when she said that Theresa must go and see Eddie at the *Clarion* office while she escorted Charlie to the shops.

Theresa was well aware that she had disappointed

both boys this morning, and was in no mood for another encounter with Edouard. In some trepidation, she mounted the stairs to the newspaper office. She had not parted from Edouard yesterday on the best of terms, and didn't like being summoned by him at the beginning of the working day. When she opened the door at the top, he was standing with his back at her at the wall phone beside his desk. Rosie was not present.

He finished his call with a curt 'Thank you', and acknowledged Theresa's arrival with a quick nod in the direction of a chair. He sat down himself, and without any sort of greeting, announced, 'I'll need your signature.' He picked up some papers that were lying on his desk.

'What are they?'

'A letter to the orphanage admitting that you have Charlie, and a statement for beginning legal action against the farmer responsible for his well-being—just in case we need it—and to prove you're serious.'

'Does this mean a court case?' Theresa was upset. 'I thought you weren't going to do anything till we heard what the farmer was likely to do.'

'That'll be too late, I'm afraid. It has to be done now.' Edouard's expression was grim. 'You need to show intent.'

Theresa took a deep breath. 'How—How much will it cost?' She bit her lip. 'If it should come to court, I mean.'

'You don't need to worry about that. It's going to be taken care of.'

'By whom?'

'An anonymous donor—someone who takes an interest in orphans.'

Theresa digested this. 'It's very kind of him—or her—but why anonymously?'

'He doesn't want his good works to be known.'

'He? It's a man, then?'

'I haven't said that. I only call this person "he" because it's easier that way.'

'I'd like to thank him.' Theresa followed his lead in referring to 'him'.

'I'll convey your thanks.'

'Yes, please.' Theresa clasped her hands together. She was almost sure it wasn't Edouard who was the donor; he would have said so. Who, then? Big Bob? The Appledores? Someone she didn't know at all? 'Does this mean, if the case goes to court, this donor will continue to pay? Where would the case be heard?'

'Ottawa, probably.' He shrugged. 'He seems prepared to go as far as necessary.'

'You sound as though you don't approve.' Theresa caught some reservation in his tone.

'I'm not sure that I do.'

'Why not?'

'What if you change your mind half-way through?'

'I don't intend to change my mind.'

His eyebrows rose. 'How can you be so damn sure of yourself?'

Theresa flushed. She wouldn't use this language. 'I have doubts, just like anyone else.'

'Doubts about yourself, or about the boy?'

'Charlie's a good lad.'

'A rough lad,' Edouard corrected. 'He needs a man.'

She was beginning to be angry at this cross-questioning. 'It's all very well to say that. Men have let him down pretty dramatically so far—starting with the father who didn't bother to give him the benefit of his name, and ending with this farmer who abused him physically.'

'Obidiah Snelgrove—that's his name. I've been on the phone to a contact. Obidiah is a great Bible man —Spare the rod and spoil the child. A lot of people agree with him.'

Edouard pushed the documents across the desk towards her. 'Read them through and sign them.'

'Now?'

'Yes, now.'

Theresa did as she was told. The complaint against

Obidiah Snelgrove seemed quite straightforward. She frowned over the letter to the orphanage. 'Why don't I ask for Charlie to be my ward, or at least suggest that the whole thing might be permanent?'

'That's not the advice at this point. Do you think you know better than the legal mind?'

'No.' She met his gaze. 'I didn't know you'd consulted a lawyer. I just wondered why.' This donor must be rich!

'I'll tell you why.' Edouard sat back. 'It's because you're a woman, and women aren't allowed to adopt male children.'

She was considerably taken back. 'There was no problem about Tony!'

'You didn't try to adopt him. You just took him; with consent if you like, but there's a blood tie there.'

'Are you saying that I'll never be able to offer Charlie more than a short holiday?' Theresa was indignant.

'Not necessarily a short holiday,' Edouard pointed out. 'It's surprising how long a holiday can become. Out of sight, out of mind is a fine adage. But you won't ever be able to make things properly legal unless you can find some man to take both of you on—and Tony as well, because I don't suppose you'll abandon him. He'll be a brave man, won't he?' He gave her a mocking smile.

'A generous one,' she amended. 'But I think it's nonsense.' She was breathing hard at the injustice of it. 'If he's only on holiday with me, that means that whoever has charge of him could give him out to someone else who might mistreat him in the same sort of way. That's appalling.'

'I agree, but that's the way it is.'

'It's not fair. Can't it be changed?'

Edouard threw his hands in the air in a gesture that was completely Gallic. 'It hasn't happened yet; and with a bit of luck it won't. But you can understand why we have to ensure that Charlie doesn't go back to Mr Snelgrove.'

'Yes,' Theresa said grimly, and signed both documents with a flourish. 'Is that all?'

'No, it isn't.' He added his own signature. 'I'll witness it.'

Theresa waited. 'Can I go now?'

'No. I have something to say. I'm not sure how to tell you that you must be careful—very careful.'

'Careful?' She looked at him in astonishment. 'What do you mean?'

'Do you belong to a church?'

'I haven't joined one, if that's what you mean.'

'Do it now.'

'Why? Any particular one?' She was tired of his orders. There was an edge to her voice as she asked, 'Do you belong to one?'

'In name only.' He gave her a bleak smile.

'Then why tell me to become a church-goer? That's what you mean, isn't it?'

'It's different for you. You must be seen to lead a blameless life.'

'It's hypocritical to go to church for that reason. I gave up going after the war—everyone did. I don't suppose you go yourself.'

'Not often.' Edouard sighed. 'It doesn't matter to me what you believe, but it will to the people who preside in courts, who run orphanages.'

Theresa gave him an angry nod. 'Very well. I understand. I'll do it, and take the boys with me. What churches are there here?'

'Methodist, Presbyterian, Anglican, even an RC chapel. Ask Sal about them, or Mrs Appledore. They'll be able to advise you.'

'Yes,' she agreed without enthusiasm. She was beginning to feel tied down. 'Is there anything else?'

'Just another word of warning.' Edouard looked uncomfortable. 'It would be a shame if you established this solid reputation of a church-goer on a Sunday morning and spoiled it on a Sunday afternoon by going sailing with a well known free-thinker.'

Theresa nearly exploded at that. 'I suppose you mean Mr Falconer! It was very kind of him to take us sailing. I won't be told who's a suitable companion for me or for the boys.'

They glared at each other over the top of the desk.

'I'm not telling you he's unsuitable. He is a friend of mine! I'm just telling you it might be wiser not to go sailing on a Sunday afternoon, if you want to keep young Charlie.'

'All right, you've told me.' Theresa's eyes dropped first as it sank in that he might be right.

'And you'll think about it, at least?'

'I'll think about it.' She rose to her feet. Suddenly, life had become much more complicated, more hemmed in.

'I don't make the rules,' Edouard said gently. 'You mustn't forget that you're living in a small town.'

'No, you don't make them,' Theresa agreed bitterly. 'But you can't tell me you don't enjoy passing on the edicts.'

'I take it, then, that you're going to be a sensible girl.' Edouard grinned at her.

She stuck out her tongue at him.

Instead of being angry, he began to laugh. 'I don't blame you. We must be friends again if you're acting like that.'

Theresa didn't bother to reply. Let him think of her as a friend, if he wanted. That wasn't the way she thought of him. She turned away from the desk and walked to the door.

'Good-bye, Theresa,' he called after her. 'I'll let you know of any developments.'

She didn't turn back but stamped down the stairs, taking out her indignation on every step. Hateful, bossy, and laughing at her—that was Edouard Moreau.

CHAPTER SIXTEEN

THERE MUST be something wrong with Tony; Theresa was sure of it. All through the week that followed her visit to the *Clarion* office, he was quiet, almost surly. Charlie, on the other hand, when he wasn't eating or sleeping, went around with a broad grin on his face and kept asking her if she liked his new clothes.

He had returned from the shopping expedition with high praise for Sal and new brown shorts, a beige short-sleeved shirt and brown sandals. She had also purchased for him a pair of brown tweed knee-breeches and long brown socks, boots, and a warm woollen windbreaker jacket in a deep chocolate. It was lined in red and there was a peaked cap to match.

Theresa had been in two minds about Sal's gift. In fact she still was, for Sal was very irritable these days. She couldn't but applaud her generosity, but it made her uncomfortable that Sal had spent so much.

'Nonsense,' she said, when Theresa protested that she hadn't expected Charlie to be so fully equipped. 'He needed clothes, didn't he?'

It would have mattered less, were it not for a look of unhappiness in Sal's eyes. Theresa couldn't understand it, and asked herself if she was imagining it. She was sure she wasn't imagining Tony's malaise. Was he sickening for something?

On Friday night, Charlie went to bed early, and Theresa decided it was time to find out. Tony was busy putting together a jigsaw puzzle that Timmy had brought to the house.

Theresa watched him frowning over it in concentration. 'Is something bothering you?' she asked, coming closer.

'No, what would bother me?' Tony asked in return,

his mouth down at the corners.

'I don't know.' She put a piece of sky in the top end of the puzzle, and took it out because it didn't fit properly. 'I just wondered.' She sat down opposite him. 'You don't seem very cheerful.'

Tony looked up at her, and then away. 'Didn't Sal ask you where I was this week, and why I didn't come to work?'

'No.' Theresa didn't want to hurt Tony's feelings, but she began to see where the trouble was. 'We agreed that I wouldn't bring either of you boys with me unless I was going to the summer cottages. It's not that she doesn't like you any more. It's just that two boys are too many in a small office.'

'But Charlie went on Monday morning to the office, and on Wednesday afternoon to see the summer places.' Tony's lip trembled.

'I took him to the cottages because he hadn't seen them, and on Monday he came with me only so that she could buy him the clothes.' She blamed herself now for not realising that Tony might be jealous.

'He stayed all morning,' the boy protested. 'I haven't seen Sal all week.'

'He had to stay after the shopping.' Theresa felt she had to explain. 'He doesn't know his way about in Creswal, and we were busy. I brought him back here at lunch-time, and you'd been playing with Timmy all morning.'

'Charlie slept all afternoon.' Tony picked up a piece of the puzzle and fingered it. 'Why does he sleep so much? He never used to. I had to put the groceries away all by myself on Tuesday and today.'

'Yes, that was good of you. It saved me doing it.'

At that, Tony almost smiled. 'There were a lot of groceries. Do we really eat all that? It came to seven dollars for the week.'

'It is a lot of money, but I didn't want to go short again. I expect we'll eat it all.'

'Is Charlie going to stay with us all the time?' Tony

carefully didn't look at her, but gave his whole attention to fitting an odd-shaped piece in the centre.

'If they'll let us keep him. I thought you'd be pleased.'

Tony looked up. He was scowling. 'I am pleased.'

'You don't look it,' Theresa hazarded.

'Charlie's my friend.' He paused. 'I'm glad he's not with that horrible Obidiah.'

She took a deep breath. It would be better to give the subject a thorough airing. 'But you'd rather he wasn't here; is that it?' she asked softly.

'Not exactly.' He inserted a piece successfully, and picked up another.

'What, then?' She put her hand on the remaining bits. 'Let's talk about it.'

Tony looked at her properly. 'I don't like to talk about it.'

'Why not? You talk about everything. Tell me.'

Still Tony hesitated.

Theresa didn't want to put words in his mouth, but she could guess at the reasons. 'You are my brother, you know.'

'Maybe you'll like him better than me.' Tony brought out the words at last.

'Of course I won't. You're special—my first boy. You'll always be special to me.' She put her hand on his.

'Are the twins special to you too, even though you've left them behind in England?'

'Of course.' Theresa smiled. 'Now it's no good asking me if I like them better than you. It's just different, the way I feel about them. I can love more than one person. Can't you?'

Tony looked at her. 'I guess so. You mean like you and Sal and Eddie—and Charlie,' he added, almost as an afterthought.

'Yes.'

'Yes, but . . .'

'But what?' she probed.

'But . . . everybody likes Charlie best. They've all brought him presents. Big Bob gave him ice-cream and cake, and Sal never gave me a lovely peaked cap.' He pushed the puzzle away from him so that some of the pieces fell to the floor. 'It was just the same at the orphanage. Everybody liked Charlie best.'

'Everybody?' Theresa was puzzled. 'He told me he was always in trouble.'

'Oh that! You don't count that! The ones in charge had it in for him. But all the boys liked Charlie, especially the little ones—and the girls, too. Maisie liked him best of all. She told me so.'

'Why was that, I wonder?' She spoke aloud. A different side of Charlie was being revealed.

'Because he stood up for them. He's braver than I am. He didn't mind being hit as much as I did.'

Theresa's heart went out to Tony. He was admitting his true feelings, even being loyal and fair to his friend in spite of his natural jealousy.

'It's very brave of you to tell me how you feel.'

'Is it?' Tony was surprised. 'You just seemed to get it out of me. I didn't mean to tell anyone.'

'Nobody likes being hit,' she assured him. 'I wouldn't.' She was glad her stepfather had been such a kind man.

He gave a sudden gurgle of laughter. 'Nobody'd hit you! You're big. Besides, I wouldn't let them.'

Theresa joined in the laughter. 'There you are. It's the frightened person who's really brave.'

'Do you think so?' He looked almost pleased. 'Does everybody know that? Does Eddie?'

'I should think so. Why don't you ask him about it? He was wounded in the war.'

'I don't mind asking Eddie.' Tony brightened considerably. 'He likes me. I don't think he likes Charlie much.'

'What makes you say that?'

'I can tell. He's mad at you for keeping him. Timmy said so. He heard his gran and grampa talking. She's not really his gran. She's his step-gran.'

'Yes.'

'Will Charlie be a step to me? Like you're my half-sister, will he be my stepbrother?'

'No, there isn't really any relationship.'

'He'll just be a boy who lives here with us.'

'I suppose you could say that. We'll take care of him. I'll need your help to do that.'

'You mean you wouldn't keep him if I said No?'

'I'd have to think very seriously about it, and see if you wouldn't change your mind.' Theresa looked at him questioningly. 'Don't you want him?'

'He can stay,' Tony declared. 'He hasn't got any place else to go. He can have half my Meccano,' he added very gravely, 'if he'll let me wear his cap sometimes.'

Theresa kept her face straight with difficulty. 'That sounds a fair division.'

But Tony wasn't finished. 'Why did Sal buy him all those clothes? Don't we have enough money?'

'We're not rich, but we won't go hungry.' She ruffled Tony's hair. 'It's time for bed, my lad.' For the first time, she started to think of the gold shares in her father's bank. Now that she felt sure that he was dead, perhaps she should write to Mr Roscoe again. She could tell him about Charlie. No, maybe not—he might think her as foolish as everyone else did. But she could contact him. An advance of some kind would be comforting, or even a word that things were proceeding.

'I could get a job,' Tony suggested. 'Sal would say I was a good worker.'

Theresa gave him a quick hug. 'You don't need to get a job. Anyway you'll be going to school in September.'

'Next year, then, I'll be old enough.'

'We'll see. I'd like both you and Charlie to get a good education first.'

'That's what Big Bob said when I asked him for a job. He's going to think about it next year, too.' Tony yawned.

'There's no need to worry about money in the mean-time,' Theresa assured him. 'We'll manage. Now off to bed with you.'

This time the boy went, and she was left in the sitting-room to wonder just how long her money would last with three of them to feed and clothe.

She reflected, too, that she had told Tony she could love more than one person at once. The boys could share her love and attention, but she couldn't share Edouard with Sal. It was no use thinking like this, she told herself. Moping around wouldn't do.

Absently she bent to pick up the puzzle-pieces that had been swept to the floor. Simon, coming to the back door, looked in and found her on her knees.

'Whatever are you doing?' he demanded, peering through the screen panels. 'Can I come in?'

Theresa got to her feet to open the door. 'Lovely to see you!'

He followed her into the living-room and spread out a newspaper. 'I think you ought to see this.'

She could see it was the same Toronto paper as she had seen only last week, but this was the previous day's edition.

The headline on the exposed page leaped up at her: 'Was Charles Russell a Bigamist?'

It was a question Theresa had been forced a long time ago to ask herself, and she'd had to accept that he must have been.

Theresa sighed, and read on. The article mentioned that she now had another boy from the orphanage staying with her as well as her half-brother. It also quoted the dates of Charles Russell's two marriages and the date of death of Theresa's mother. It went on to suggest that his Creswal fiancée might have found out his duplicity and given him his *congé*; whereupon, overcome with remorse, he might have resorted to some desperate action. What the action might have been was not stated, only implied—had he bolted or killed himself?

She smiled grimly. The paper was being very careful not to draw conclusions that were too pointed. Perhaps Big Bob had threatened to sue. She put the paper down.

'You don't seem surprised.' Simon sank into a chair.

'No, I knew the dates. I just hoped that nobody else was going to hear about them. It was unrealistic of me, I suppose.'

'Did Moreau know?'

'Yes.'

'He didn't say anything about it in the *Clarion* yesterday. In fact, all he said was that Charlie was here on a holiday. You two are hand in glove, aren't you?'

'I wouldn't say that.'

'I guess you know he's away for the weekend.' Simon pursued the subject. 'He's gone to Toronto, Rosie says.'

'I didn't know.' Theresa felt somehow abandoned. She wouldn't be able to ask him any questions. 'What's he doing there?'

'She said he's gone to buy a newspaper. I think she must have been joking. He probably didn't want her to know.'

'Where did you get this copy?' Theresa asked, handing it back to him and sitting in the rocking-chair facing him.

'My father sent it. He said to tell you he was sorry about bringing the reporter here in the first place.'

'It's happened.' She shrugged. 'Still, it's good of him to think of me.'

'I'm not sure that he was thinking of you—not altogether.'

'What do you mean?'

'He liked you a lot.' Simon took out a handkerchief and wiped his forehead. 'So did I.'

Theresa caught the finality of that small statement. 'Did?' She asked a direct question. 'Don't you like me any more?'

'Of course I like you,' he protested. 'But I don't like to see your name in the papers.' Simon was picking his words carefully. 'No man would like to see a girl's name in such an article.' He indicated the newspaper. 'Not a girl he had any regard for at all.'

She understood quite well that Simon had taken

fright. A girl whose father might have killed himself wasn't a girl he would consider for a wife. An imp of mischief entered into her.

'I see,' she observed. 'Was Sidney any luckier than I? Last week her aunt's name was very considerately not mentioned in this very same paper, and the implication there was murder. Is having a possible murderer in the family more socially acceptable than having a possible suicide?'

'I don't know what you mean!' He was almost spluttering. Again he wiped his forehead. 'No one could possibly believe Maddie would kill anyone. You don't believe it yourself,' he accused.

'No, I don't!' Theresa retorted. 'I'd expect proof. But you're quite willing to believe that my father killed himself—on innuendo alone.' She paused to take a breath and control her voice. 'I can quite see I'm no longer suitable for you. Well, you're not suitable for me, either. I prefer a real man.'

'You mean Big Bob, I suppose,' he said waspishly. 'You're certainly getting yourself talked about there. He's old enough to be your father, and has always wanted a son. I guess a ready-made family of two boys and a young wife might just suit him.'

'You've said enough!' She couldn't control the flood of colour which rose to her face.

'I'm sorry.' He had the grace to apologise. 'But I just can't see why you're so ready to welcome Mr Falconer. Everyone knows Sal's been hanging out for him for years.'

'Sal?' Theresa was astonished. 'You're mistaken!'

'No, I'm not. Ask anyone.'

'You must be wrong. I thought it was Edouard.'

'Him again—do you never stop thinking of him?' There was an edge to Simon's voice. 'Not the way I've heard it. She's never even liked Eddie, let alone wanted him. They're business partners because they think alike about money. She's the only woman round here who's never set her cap at him. Why don't you ask her?'

'I couldn't.'

'She might have some interesting things to tell you about Big Bob. At all events, you'd be wise not to see too much of him. People will gossip.' Simon got up from the chair. 'I'm only telling you for your own good. I wouldn't want to stop being friends with you, you know.'

Theresa was seething. Why did everyone think they had the right to advise her about how to act and whom to see? She might have told Simon to mind his own business, and that she didn't need a friend like him, but she bit her tongue and kept the angry words in check. He had, after all, only said much the same things as Edouard had said to her, but in a different way. And he had told her that Sal and Eddie weren't interested in each other, and never had been. Had Marguerite lied? Yes—The answer came immediately from deep inside her consciousness. Marguerite had wanted to torment her, to make her suffer—to hold on to Edouard for herself. She had been gullible enough to fall for the story.

She bade Simon good-bye with a firm handshake and kind regards to his father.

On Saturday, Theresa took Tony and Charlie for a picnic swim, and on Sunday to church, accompanied by Mrs Appledore and Timmy.

If the congregation had read the Toronto paper, they seemingly didn't allow it to influence them. After the service, several of them came up and spoke to her with their families around them. The minister, too, was friendly and welcomed her and the boys to his flock. So pleasant were they all that Theresa was a little ashamed of her own churlishness when Edouard had mentioned joining a church. She could see that it would be good for the boys to meet other children and become part of the community. It was in a satisfied mood that she returned to the little house, and singing to herself, began to prepare lunch. She shooed the boys out into the garden to play.

She could not have said when she began to be aware

that two other boys had joined them. Her first inkling
that something was wrong was when she heard Tony's
voice raised in anger—'I am not a bastard. Bastard
yourself!'—and as she rushed out of the door, she saw
Tony being pummelled on the ground by a lad much
bigger than himself, and Charlie ferociously attacking
the other.

Screaming, 'Stop, stop!' she picked up the broom
lying on the path. What she would have done with it, she
was left to guess, for Big Bob appeared around the
corner of the house and parted Charlie from his oppo-
nent, who had a cut lip. He grabbed him in one hand and
Tony's attacker in the other.

'Well then, what's this all about?' he demanded,
holding up the squirming pair by the back of their
jackets.

Theresa could see the attackers plainly now. She
guessed they were a little older than Tony and Charlie
—perhaps eleven or twelve, and recognised them as
coming from families they had met at church. They
looked thoroughly frightened as Big Bob shook them.

'They called me a bastard!' Tony was quivering with
rage or indignation or hurt, Theresa wasn't sure which.
'And Charlie, too.'

'Is this true?' Big Bob shook his prisoners again.

'Yes,' they admitted in chorus. 'But they are
bastards.'

Theresa drew in her breath and stretched her arms
protectively around her boys, the broom falling to the
grass.

'What do you mean by bastard?' Another shake
produced a different answer from each of the name
callers.

'Dunno,' the smaller of the two admitted wretchedly.
'Please put me down.'

Big Bob set him on his feet. He made no move to
leave, but tried to wipe the blood from his cut lip with the
back of his hand.

The bigger boy wasn't so easily defeated. 'You know

what bastard means! It means their mothers and fathers weren't married.'

Big Bob raised his single captive so that their eyes were on a level. 'That's a word that dirties the mouth, and you keep on saying it. We'll have to see what we can do about cleaning you up.' He tucked the youngster under his arm. Arms and legs flailing madly, the boy was carried from garden to kitchen. The others trooped in behind.

'What are you going to do to him?' asked the smaller, freed, lad in a quavering voice.

'Wait and see,' accompanied by a fierce scowl, was the answer he was given, as Big Bob went towards the sink and picked up the bar of laundry soap that lay there in a small dish. Without another word, he broke off a piece with one hand and shoved it into his captive's mouth.

'That's right, chew on it for a while.' He kept the boy's lips pressed together until his eyes begged for mercy. Only then did he allow him to spit out soap and lather into the sink. Spluttering and making heaving noises, the lad was in no mood for further quarrelling.

Big Bob released his grip, blocking the exit with his big body. 'Who are you?' he asked the other lad.

'I'm Jim Ferguson and he's George Miller.' The smaller one couldn't get the names out fast enough.

Big Bob nodded. 'Ferguson, Miller—I shouldn't be surprised if both your fathers don't work for me. Do you know who I am?'

'You're Mr Falconer from the timber mill.'

'Right. I didn't ask your fathers whether they were bastards or not when I hired them. I don't judge a man by something he can't help. I judge him by what he is and by how he acts, and by that rule you two are louts, bullies, trouble-makers, mean bastards. I wouldn't have either of you working for me—and I'm the biggest employer in this town! Keep that in mind, my fine young bastards.'

The boys visibly quailed. The smaller one's lip quivered. 'You won't tell my dad, will you?'

The bigger one, mouth now rinsed, said nothing.

'I'll think about it. It depends on you.'

'We didn't mean . . .' the boy called George began.

Big Bob stopped him with a glance. 'I know what you meant. You meant to have a bit of fun at two smaller boys' expense. You can go back and tell your pals that Charlie and Tony here are under my protection, and if I hear of any name-calling, I'll give the callers the same sort of medicine I've given you. Is that understood?'

'Yes,' both Jim and George answered.

'Yes, what?' Big Bob prodded George.

'Yes, sir,' he muttered.

'Right. You can go now.' He stood aside to let George pass, and he ran out without a backward glance.

Jim made to follow, but Theresa stopped him. 'That lip's still bleeding. I'll bathe it for you.' She took him by the hand and led him to the sink, washing the blood away with her own handkerchief.

Tony, Charlie and Big Bob surveyed the scene with varying expressions of surprise.

Charlie recovered first. 'Perhaps I shouldn't have hit him so hard,' he observed, leaning forward for a better look.

'Perhaps you shouldn't,' Theresa agreed quietly.

'It was because they called Tony that—I've heard that word often enough. It always makes me mad.' Charlie looked at Theresa uneasily. 'You didn't like us fighting, did you?'

'No,' she admitted. 'But I picked up the broom to come to help you.' She had to give him an honest answer.

Big Bob laughed at her. 'Sometimes you have to fight.' He ruffled Tony's hair. 'Tony knows that.'

Tony flushed with pleasure and the subject of bastards was left alone.

'Run and fetch that salve of yours,' Theresa instructed Charlie. 'It will help this lip to heal.'

He was back in an instant, and it was Big Bob who smeared the cream on with a gentle hand.

'Are you going to shake and make it up?' he asked Jim. 'Charlie will.'

Charlie looked at Big Bob with a good deal of respect, and held out his hand to Jim.

Jim hesitated. 'You mean we should be friends?'

'Why not?' queried Big Bob. 'It takes a man to say he was wrong.'

Charlie and Jim shook hands solemnly.

'You nearly knocked me off my feet.' Charlie as victor was generous.

'Let's not fight again,' Jim had one eye on Big Bob. 'My mother'll kill me for getting blood on my Sunday shirt.'

'Theresa'll wash it out,' suggested Charlie, 'if you take it off now.'

So Theresa found herself sponging down the front of Jim's shirt, and by the time the sun had dried it, the three boys were playing ball together, and Jim's lip wasn't looking too bad.

'With boys, it's soon forgotten,' Big Bob observed. 'And better so. By the way, I came by to ask you and the boys for a sail this afternoon.'

'We'd be pleased to come.' In her gratitude, she threw caution to the winds. 'I'm so glad you were here. I couldn't have handled all that, or sent a message to all the boys of Creswal that they must leave Charlie and Tony alone or risk dire consequences.' She finished on a gurgle of laughter. 'You were magnificent.'

'I don't know about that!' he exclaimed. 'But we skirted the subject quite nicely, and you've won a friend in Jim. My way would only have earned two enemies.' He smiled at her. 'We make a good team, to my way of thinking. It's too soon for declarations, but think about it, Miss Theresa. It just might suit.' He didn't touch her, or say any more, but his eyes held hers.

Big Bob stayed for lunch, and the afternoon's sail was pure magic. It was a glorious day, the sun shining on the water, the wind just fresh enough to carry the boat along easily, and Big Bob and the boys in total harmony.

He beached the craft on a deserted strip of sand and they all went for a swim. His navy and white costume set off his fair colouring and golden brown skin. Theresa couldn't help noticing that he was a well-proportioned man with broad shoulders and a flat stomach. Neither boy could swim yet, but he showed them how, and held them while they tried.

Watching them, Theresa thought they might have been any family party enjoying themselves. It was so obviously what the boys truly wanted and needed—a fine man to stand behind them, to help them.

She sighed. If only . . . But Edouard didn't want her—he had said so. Whether he was involved with Sal or not, he had made it abundantly clear that she didn't figure in his future. Big Bob was a man she could respect—did respect, and like. With Marguerite and Sidney banished, he had shown himself very approachable and pleasant. He was a man to depend on; and with two boys, she must consider that. She sighed again, and swam out a little further.

Big Bob came up beside her, the boys safely in the shallows. His stroke was easy and confident. He floated beside her, treading water.

'River of Paradise, the Indians called it. I think they named it well. It has food and drink, sandy beaches, white water for excitement and trees along its banks to provide canoes. What more could anyone ask of a river?'

'What more, indeed?' Theresa murmured, and flashed him a smile. 'Race you to the shore!' She knew he would win, but he'd enjoy a moment of triumph. He was a man to relish success.

'Success,' Edouard mused to the sound of turning wheels on iron rails and the swaying motion of speed. 'What is success? If it's attaining a five-year ambition, then it's mine. I've just bought a Toronto daily, all signed for and delivered. It's just a small struggling one compared to McGregor's giant, but I'll soon change that.'

He sat back and closed his eyes, lulled by the glimpses of evening and dreary back streets through the train window. He should have been full of elation and triumph because he had accomplished what he'd striven for. Instead, he felt a curious flatness. Was another paper what he really wanted out of life? Did he want to return to city life with its noise and activity?

An image of the hidden river prospect that he had revealed to Theresa on her way to the dam, that first day in Creswal, flashed into his mind. Was it the thought of abandoning his River of Paradise that was depressing him so?

And yet, it wasn't the lovely picture of sun and shining water that stayed in his mind's eye. It was Theresa's face. Her green eyes questioned him, her short curls framing a face that wasn't beautiful, but somehow wouldn't go away.

Perhaps it was because of that sense of duty instilled in him from an early age, a trick of his mind, to keep that elusive vision there to remind him that he must break his journey in Ottawa to see what he could accomplish for Charlie Boyes.

The engine at the front of the train belched smoke in a sudden roar, but Edouard's eyes remained closed in the almost empty carriage.

He'd taken to Tony from the first, but he wasn't sure whether he'd ever like Charlie. Of course he was sorry for him. No boy should be treated as he had been, and he needed help to be rescued from his situation. A pity he looked so much like Tom McGregor—the same red-headed, aggressive Scottish type—but Tom had charm, the kind of charm that attracted women. Was that the basis of his own antipathy to Charlie Boyes? How unfair to lump an unrelated man and boy together just because a little English girl had turned stubborn and wouldn't give up the boy. It would have been simpler to return him to the orphanage with the evidence. With a rueful laugh at himself, he dismissed both boy and girl. They were taking up too much of his time, and his thoughts. He was very tired and just a little unhappy. Why must he always think of other people's troubles? He opened his eyes.

The train passed houses and fields and little towns. There must be something about travelling, particularly at this time of day's end, that made the psyche attach itself to the known—to people rather than places, as though to hold on to human reality. Take Sal, for instance.

Poor Sal! She had told him how she had mismanaged her life all along the way. Too young, she had married the wrong man, who had gone through her family's money—her pride and theirs—and then left for the war after he had caused the loss of her baby. She had finished with him. But he had not finished with her.

Terribly wounded in the war, he had spent six years dying in a military hospital outside Montreal, and only three months ago had been buried there. The guilty knowledge of his confinement had held her aloof from Edouard, for wasn't he the newspaperman who had campaigned for veterans' rights?

In those six long years, Sal had been to see her husband only once—for the funeral—and had denied his existence to everyone. Only Bob Falconer had been told of this, she had confided, and only because he had offered her marriage. She had been unable to contemplate divorce, and so had remained tied to a wreck of a man while she gave her favours to another. When she was at last free to marry, she had told Edouard quietly, Big Bob had wanted things to continue as they were. She had refused, and lost him altogether. It was cruelly hard on her. Big Bob had taken a new lease on life, and liberated now from all family ties with sister and daughter in the States, had Theresa and her boys in his sights.

Edouard devoutly hoped she had taken them all to church and not gone sailing again, courting trouble. If gossip spread, her chances of holding on to Charlie or even Tony would be very thin.

Public opinion was capricious. Creswal folk must have guessed at the relationship between Sal and Big Bob, but because they'd been discreet—and rich and important —they had never turned against them. But now, tongues would wag. People would side with Sal, and Theresa would be sure to suffer. She wouldn't be able to go on working for her, either; the situation would be intolerable.

The train began to slow as it climbed a gradient, and the smell of smoke and black cinders borne by the wind in a new direction made Edouard cough. He rose to shut the window.

The thought flashed into his mind as he moved. It needn't come to catastrophe. A plan occurred to him suddenly. Charlie was the log-jam—as Big Bob himself would express it—the master log. It was Charlie who had brought Big Bob Falconer to Theresa's house. If Charlie were no longer there . . .

Edouard began to smile. Yes, it could be done . . .

CHAPTER SEVENTEEN

IT WAS on Tuesday evening that Theresa looked up from her book and saw Edouard. She was alone in the garden, lying on a blanket spread on the grass in front of the little house, reading in the evening sunshine. The boys were up near the big house, playing bowls.

She hadn't seen him for some time, and was uncertain how to greet him because he was scowling at her. Her mouth smiled, but her heart sank. Surely he hadn't come to give her another lecture on sailing?

'May I join you?' he asked, and dropped down beside her, cross-legged.

For a moment they looked at each other, and Theresa thought that his blue eyes, usually so alive, looked tired. She noticed the laughter lines round them, but there was no laughter in them. 'I heard you were away,' she said, uncomfortable under his grave regard. 'Did you have a good trip?'

'So-so. I did what I set out to do. I also called in to talk to the clerk of the court in Ottawa. He's a man I've known for a long time.'

'Oh?' Theresa sat up with a quick motion of sliding her legs along the blanket, away from his immediate vicinity. They faced each other from opposite corners, like antagonists, she felt. 'Are you telling me something important?'

He answered that indirectly. 'The clerk is a man of great experience, and he says you're in a dangerous position at the moment. The orphanage hasn't actually given you permission to keep the boy yet, nor has it taken away permission from Mr Snelgrove to keep him. The best plan would be to send Charlie away . . .'

She didn't let him finish. 'I'm not sending Charlie away! You can get rid of that idea.'

Edouard didn't raise his voice, but his eyes blazed. 'Hear me out first. Charlie isn't safe with you. Just suppose our farmer wants Charlie back, and comes to get him.'

A cold chill of fear touched Theresa. 'I'd refuse him, too.'

'The Obidiahs of this world don't ask; they take,' he laughed. 'He's got right on his side, and the might of the press.'

'What do you mean?'

He folded his arms and looked at her. 'Just what I said.'

Sitting like that, he reminded Theresa of the statue of some inscrutable oriental god she had once seen in a museum.

'I don't understand. What press?'

'Our enterprising Toronto reporter has been to see Mr Snelgrove. I suppose he found out who had had Charlie from the orphanage records. In any case, he's interviewed him and told the world his findings. Obidiah claims that our Charlie is a difficult boy whom he has only tried to set on the path to righteousness. With the Lord's help he'd have been sure to succeed, except the boy was whisked away from him.'

'That's preposterous! People just don't realise what a monster he is.' Theresa was shaking.

'Is he? There are a lot of people who think exactly the same way. Children need beating.'

'Is that what you think?'

'No, it isn't, as a matter of fact, or I wouldn't be here with you trying to help. But I'm in a minority.'

Theresa felt a lifting of her heart at his words. He meant to go on helping her. 'What do we do now?'

'I'm not altogether sure.' Edouard frowned. 'The next thing McGregor will produce are character references for Snelgrove. He'll have scores of them. How many could you come up with?'

'I don't know. All the people who really know me are in England, but there's the doctor here, and his signed statement, and you have the picture of Charlie's back.'

'Snelgrove might well say that you hit Charlie. How could the doctor prove otherwise?'

'You and Big Bob were in from the beginning—You brought Charlie to me.'

He smiled for the first time. 'That's our trump card. We won't let Obidiah know about it. Not yet.'

'Then you think there's some hope for us?'

'There's always hope,' was the somewhat daunting reply.

'You're trying to frighten me!'

'I'm hope I'm succeeding. Tom McGregor's paper is already working up opinion against you. First he's labelled the English girl as a suicide's daughter. Now he's gone a step further.'

'How?'

'I've got today's paper. I'm afraid you'll have to see it.' Edouard unfolded his arms and took the Toronto paper from his pocket. 'I bought it in Ottawa today.'

Theresa took it from him. It was still creased open at the place he meant her to read. It was headed. 'English Girl Seduces Orphan'.

Horrified, she read it through. Under the lurid headline, she found her name and a reference to her father's supposed death. There followed the interview with Obidiah Snelgrove in which he claimed that Charlie Boyes was a wild, headstrong boy who needed a man's firm hand applied often to him, and he accused Theresa of seducing the lad. Her eyes must be deceiving her! She was filled with revulsion at the picture conjured up of her, and threw the paper down as though it were filthy. It lay on the blanket between them.

'It doesn't make for pleasant reading, does it?' he asked gently. 'But it will sell papers. I know it. So does Tom McGregor. There's nothing like a bit of titillation. Everyone likes to believe the worst.'

'Can't I do anything about it?' Theresa asked in a quivering voice. 'Make them retract?'

'Very difficult not to make matters worse.'

'Worse? How could they be worse?'

'I don't mean to let him get away with it,' Edouard assured her, 'but we need to be a little more subtle than he is. I have a plan of sorts.'

'Tell me.'

'First of all we find somewhere else for Charlie to stay. It's only for a short time.' He silenced the words on her lips. 'Next you move in with an older woman. That's Sal, and she's agreeable.'

'And Tony?'

'Tony stays with the Appledores. They're quite willing.'

'You've arranged it all!' Theresa exclaimed bitterly. 'I don't really have any say in it, do I?'

'If you're going to take that attitude, you may lose Tony as well as Charlie,' he replied stiffly.

She looked at his set face and gritted her teeth. There was nothing else she could do except fall in with his plans.

'I'm sorry,' she breathed. 'Who have you billeted Charlie on? Or am I not entitled to know?'

'It's not a matter of entitlement; but if you don't know, there's no way you'll be able to tell Obidiah Snelgrove. You won't be caught out in a lie. I am prepared to tell you that I have found a perfect place for him—with a family who train guard dogs. They have other qualifications, too, but you don't need to know about those. All you need to know is that he'll be absolutely safe from Obidiah.'

'Thank you,' said Theresa, fighting a battle with independence. 'I'm glad you've told me that. That is what's important to me, and to the lad.'

'Good!' Edouard reached out his hand to her, and then withdrew it swiftly. 'I forgot; you don't want to be touched.'

'No,' she replied, then she softened a little. 'We could shake hands on it, though.' She extended her hand. 'That is, if you want to?'

He took her hand in his. 'We'll make a good fight of it.'

Theresa let her hand stay where it was. Simon had said that Sal was not a rival, but she remembered that Edouard had refused her. Still, it was comforting to have him for an ally.

'Shall you tell Charlie, or shall I?' she asked. She had eyes only for Edouard, and had not noticed that the boys had finished their game. Tony and Timmy were rolling on the ground, and Charlie was standing by the blanket, looking down at both of them.

'Tell me what?' he demanded. 'Has something happened?' His eye fell on the newspaper, and he dropped to his knees before them on the blanket and picked up the article.

Theresa wanted to snatch it from him, but Edouard prevented her.

'"English Girl Seduces Orphan"—What does that mean, Theresa?' He was reading avidly. 'It's about you and me!' He looked up suddenly. 'What does it mean?'

She swallowed. She couldn't answer.

It was Edouard who replied. 'It means that Theresa charmed you away from Mr Snelgrove and persuaded you to come here. She enticed you to Creswal with some secret promise.' He put his hand on Charlie's shoulder. 'You mustn't believe everything you read in the papers.'

'How far is this farm from here?' Theresa exclaimed. 'A hundred miles—two hundred? How could I charm anyone from that distance?'

Charlie frowned at her. 'But you did, Theresa . . .' he began.

'Don't be ridiculous,' she snapped in the hardest tone she'd ever used to him.

The boy flushed almost as red as his hair. 'You did—You did! I never forgot you from that day in the orphanage. I wanted to be here with you and Tony, and when you wrote to me and said you were my friend and hoped I would be able to come here for a holiday—that you hadn't forgotten me—I knew I had to come! It was the only place I could come. You were the only one who liked me. You haven't changed your mind?'

'Oh, Charlie,' Theresa breathed. 'I do like you.' She gave him a hug. 'I'm glad you came.'

'Do you still have this letter?' Edouard asked, his eyes meeting Theresa's over the top of the boy's head.

Charlie nodded, and looked at him. 'It's hard to read, now. It got so wet the night I came, but I dried it out.'

'May I see it?'

'You won't take it away from me?'

'No, I promise.'

Charlie took a very tattered piece of notepaper from his pocket and handed it over.

Edouard smoothed it out.

'If you can't read any of the words, I know it by heart,' Charlie offered.

Dear Charlie,

I'm glad to hear you've found a home. I hope they're good people and kind to you. Perhaps they'll allow you to come for a week or two here. Let me know if you'd like to come, and I'll write to them. Tony sends his love and would like to see you again. I know you've always been his friend.

'It was signed "Theresa and Tony",' Charlie supplied, 'but that part's melted away with the rain.'

'Hardly the language of seduction,' Edouard commented, as he handed back the note.

Charlie looked from one to the other of them. 'I think it was the bit about them being good people and kind to me. It nearly made me cry—but somehow it made me think that perhaps there were good people somewhere, and Theresa would find them for me. I knew Mr Snelgrove would never let me come. He beat me because someone wrote to me. If I had stayed, he would have used a whip on me again just for reading my own letter.'

Theresa patted his knee. 'You did right to come. But now we're afraid he may come after you.'

Charlie shrank against her, and she could feel the tremor in his body. 'You won't let him, will you? Will you, Theresa?' He spoke to the girl, but his eyes were on Edouard.

Her heart ran cold at the way he mentioned whipping. 'No!' she cried out.

'I'm going to take you to a family,' Edouard said to the boy. 'A family with dogs and children. You'll be safe there, hidden.'

'Dogs?' Charlie's face lit up. 'I dreamed I'd have a dog one day.'

'Good! I'll take you there now. Get your things together.'

Charlie rose to his feet eagerly, then hesitated. 'Will Theresa be all right? Shouldn't I stay to look after her?'

'Theresa isn't going to stay here, either,' Edouard assured him quickly, 'nor Tony, but they'll be fine.'

'Is she going with you?' Charlie stood his ground, looking oddly mature.

'No, with Sal.'

'I'd rather she stayed with you . . . You could fight him, or Mr Falconer could!'

Edouard began to laugh. 'Don't worry. I shall watch out for Theresa. I'll see nothing terrible happens to her.'

'I'll go and get my things.'

'I'll help him.' Theresa, too, rose.

'While you're at it, get Tony's ready, and your own. Tony can be delivered to the Appledores as soon as he's ready, but I'll be back for you after I've left Charlie.'

Theresa nodded, and ran into the house. Charlie was stuffing his clothes into a brown paper bag.

'I'll fold them for you,' she offered. 'I wish you didn't have to go.' She took up his brown jacket.

Charlie stood beside her, his peaked cap in his hands. He thrust it at her. 'Keep this for Tony. He's always wanted it. I may not see him again.'

'Of course you'll see him again!' Theresa gave him a quick shake. 'You keep the cap. It will hide that mop of red hair, if anyone's looking for you.' She put the cap in the bag after the jacket.

'I haven't anything to give you,' Charlie hugged his parcel of belongings to him.

'You don't need to give me anything, except a kiss, and a promise to come back.'

'Would you really kiss me?' Charlie's cheeks were flushed, his eyes dark.

Theresa held him to her, bag and all, and kissed him soundly on the cheek. 'We'll all be together again.'

Charlie hugged her, dropping his possessions in the process so that they lay scattered on the floor. He clung to her for a moment, and then they both bent down to pick them up.

'Edouard will be waiting for me.' Charlie stood up, and ran from her.

Theresa knew that he was on the verge of tears but wouldn't want them to show. She rubbed her cheek where he had kissed her. It was the first sign of affection he had given her. Poor Charlie! She went to the door to wave good-bye, but he and Edouard were gone.

By the time she had called Tony, explained the situation to him, packed for both of them and escorted him to the big house, with Mrs Appledore's assurances that it would be no trouble at all and they'd keep an eye on things, Theresa felt drained.

She sat in the rocking-chair, waiting, her case beside her. It was there that Edouard found her on his return.

'Ready?' he asked, rocking the chair gently by the ball that rested on the top of the frame.

'It's worse than leaving home was,' she said in a subdued voice. 'Then it was exciting! I was going off to great adventures. Now I'm running away—and frightened. What if . . .' She found she couldn't go on.

'Don't,' Edouard instructed. 'Don't let yourself worry like that. Anyone would think your boys were going off to war—and I can tell you my mother was a good deal less emotional when I left, for that very reason.'

'Perhaps she hid it better.'

'Perhaps she did,' he agreed. 'She hid it, too, when I came back in a wheelchair. She didn't kiss me, as you did Charlie, on either going or coming back.'

There was so much pain in that simple statement of fact that Theresa instinctively reached out her hand to touch him.

'It didn't have to mean that she didn't love you. My mother was never very demonstrative.' It seemed to Theresa at that moment that he was as vulnerable as Charlie. That was ridiculous, she told herself, but he held the hand she reached out to him and pulled her gently to her feet. 'Wipe your tears. It's time to go.'

'I'm not crying,' she replied, facing him and very close. 'But I feel like it.'

Edouard smiled. 'I remember the last time you did. You have a gift for releasing your emotions.'

'So do I remember,' Theresa admitted ruefully. 'Your shirt got wet. I hate good-byes. That was a kind of farewell to my father.'

'Charlie was upset, too.' Edouard was still holding her hand. 'He's a boy of some feeling.'

'Does that surprise you?'

'Yes, I think it does. I liked him for wanting to be sure you'd be taken care of.'

'That's probably the first time you allowed yourself to see him as a person.'

'That's very perceptive of you.'

'You might grow to like him.'

'I might. I asked him if I might write him up in the paper, and do you know what he said?'

Theresa shook her head.

'He said he wished he could talk and write like I do, then he'd tell you what it meant to him to have been here these ten days. He had them numbered, and he remembered something from each day.'

'What sorts of things?'

'Just things that most people take for granted. Like —he had a bath on the first Sunday, and you put that ointment on his back, and then you all had home-made ice-cream for lunch.'

'Big Bob sent it—and a cake.'

'Yes, so he said. He seems to have a great admiration for him as well.' Edouard released Theresa's hand. 'Is this your case?' She nodded, and he picked it up. 'Shall we go, then?'

She had a last quick look round the room and followed him to the door. She locked it behind them.

After the wrench of departure, Theresa found the following day a bit flat. She missed the boys, and spoke to Tony on the phone, at Sal's suggestion. He was perfectly happy and full of news of things happening with Timmy and the Appledores. Quite obviously he wasn't moping, and she cheered up a little. They were busy enough at work to keep her mind occupied, but she couldn't help wishing there was news of Charlie.

In the evening, she and Sal went to the pictures, and then back in Sal's comfortable flat above the shop they drank cocoa, sitting out on the veranda high above the main street, under the stars.

'Do you know that Charlie wanted to leave Tony his cap as a good-bye present?' Theresa sipped her drink.

'Didn't he like it, then?' Sal sounded a little put out.

'That's just it. He loved it. It was very generous of him to want to give it to Tony, but I wouldn't let him.'

'Why not?' Sal put down her cup and lit a cigarette. 'I'm surprised you didn't get Tony one of his own, if he liked Charlie's so much.' She inhaled deeply.

'Children shouldn't have everything they want.'

'How prim you sound!' Sal blew delicate smoke-rings. 'Watch out you don't become one of those rigid women who always know best.'

'Do you think I might?' Theresa was perturbed at the notion.

'None of us knows what we'll become.' Sal sat back, looking up at the stars. 'I used to think—when I was a girl—that I'd grow up and marry and be happy and have children, just like anyone else. They'd grow up around me, always loving, always good.' She finished on a laugh. 'You can see how young I was. Well, it didn't happen.'

Theresa caught a note of despair beneath the laughter. 'Did you never think of marrying again?'

'Oh, yes, I thought of it.' The laugh was more bitter this time, and the smoke-rings bigger. 'There was a man here. It was like some elaborate dance or a children's game. When he wanted to marry, I couldn't. When I wanted to, he wouldn't.' Sal sighed, a lonely sound high above the deserted streets.

Theresa sensed that there was something here she didn't understand, but she hesitated to probe. She remained silent.

'Take what you can get from life, Theresa,' Sal went on. 'It may be all you'll have.'

Theresa knew she was out of her depth. She took another drink of cocoa, but a skin had formed on the top and she felt it on her lips and her tongue, and spat it out. 'Ugh! I hate skin,' she murmured.

'I don't know why I'm telling you,' Sal continued. 'You are taking what you can from life, aren't you?'

'Am I?'

'No, that's not fair,' Sal admitted, inhaling once again. 'You don't just take. You give—to your sisters, to those boys. That's what I couldn't do—give. I should have forgiven Mike and brought him home to die, but I couldn't bear the thought of his maimed body. Even after all he'd done, I suppose I still loved him.'

'But he died a long time ago,' Theresa objected. 'Why do you blame yourself now?'

'That's just it. He didn't.' Sal's voice was low. 'He died three months ago. I went to the funeral. He was in that military hospital ever since 1917, and I never saw him once.'

Theresa began to comprehend all at once. It was Big Bob who wouldn't marry Sal. What Simon had told her was true, but she was sure that Sal didn't know she knew about Big Bob. Nor was it really Big Bob whom Sal was talking about now.

'You're grieving for him,' Theresa said gently.

'Grieving for him?' Sal considered it. 'Yes, I suppose I am—for him and for myself. I told myself I couldn't divorce him, when what I meant was that I couldn't give him up. Neither had I the courage to bring him home.'

'Edouard's mother took him home.' Theresa mused aloud, trying to give Sal some comfort. 'It's strange, but he seemed to feel she did it only out of duty. Perhaps your Mike would have felt the same, and resented it and you.'

'Now that's an odd thing for you to say,' Sal observed. 'Fancy Eddie telling you that! I've known him for years, and he's never told me one tiny thing about his family. What made him tell you? Can it be that our Edouard has a chink in his armour?'

'His armour? Why does he have armour?'

'Why do any of us?' Sal shrugged. 'To keep us from the hurts of the world—our own and others. Your Charlie has it already, and he's only ten. He tries to pretend he's tough and rough. He's like the rest of us—jelly inside.'

Theresa began to giggle—She couldn't help it. She knew that what Sal had said made a good deal of sense, but the thought of Charlie all jelly inside was too much for her.

'You can laugh!' declared Sal, smiling herself. 'I think I'll change the way I live. I'm going to start living my own life, and stop waiting for some man to take charge. I think I'll follow your example and adopt a child. I can't have any of my own, but there's no reason why I can't take a little girl who needs a home and give her one. I can afford it.'

Theresa could see nothing against the idea, and told her about the children she had seen at the orphanage who were longing for homes. By the time they went to bed, the two of them were deep in plans and in full accord.

*　　*　　*

Thursday was *Clarion* day, and Theresa was busy at the summer cottages, so she didn't see the paper until late in the afternoon when she came into the office to report.

Sal handed her the paper. 'Have a look at page 3.'

Theresa sat on the edge of the counter and opened it as instructed. 'Ten Days that Changed a Life', it was headed, and was the story of Charlie's ten days with her. It was all listed there from his arrival, and the sorry state of it, to ice-cream for lunch the following day and the gifts of clothing he had received. The chores he had done for Theresa around the house were noted, from washing up to hoeing the garden. It was a catalogue of small, everyday, events such as any child might experience. Underneath it, in stark contrast, was exposed ten days with the farmer he had worked for. The beatings were listed, and even how many strokes and with what article. There was also a description of the jobs he had been expected to accomplish.

There were tears in Theresa's eyes as she looked up at Sal. 'He's made everybody see it just the way it was. I wonder how he got all that information out of Charlie. He only told me a little of it. I knew he had to milk the cows and clean the barn—and he'd never even seen a cow before, poor lad.'

'It's all there,' Sal agreed. 'Chopping wood, lighting fires, working in the fields—a fifteen- or sixteen-hour day for a boy of ten, and all of it work almost too heavy for a man.'

'And gruel twice a day to keep him going. He was beaten once for taking a raw egg and gulping it down!' Theresa shook with indignation. 'It's a wonder he had the energy to run away.'

'And the good luck to make it to Creswal and to you,' Sal added. 'You'd be surprised at the number of people who've been in today wanting to help Charlie. If that Obidiah Snelgrove turns up here, he'll get short shrift from folks.'

'Has Edouard been in?' asked Theresa.

'No, he phoned to say he had to go to Renfrew. He was glad to hear you weren't driving about on your own, but had Frank with you.'

'I'm not sure if all this protection for me isn't a waste of time,' Theresa sighed. 'I'm not complaining, but it makes me feel that I have to keep looking over my shoulder, and expecting I don't know what.'

'Bear with it,' said Sal. 'Eddie thinks it's necessary, and newspapermen are great believers in what they call hunches. I think he's run this article in that Toronto newspaper he's bought. It makes quite an interesting contrast to the seduction one our ex-resident reporter wrote on you. I very much fear Edouard is hankering after bigger fields and fresher pastures.'

'You mean he might leave Creswal?' Theresa didn't quite understand why that made her feel sad. If he stayed or went, it was all one to her, surely. She recalled that Rosie a long time ago had mentioned going with him to Toronto.

She put down the paper and went to sort out the bills for Sal. 'He didn't say anything about how Charlie was going on, did he?' she asked.

'He'll be fine,' Sal assured her. 'Eddie said he'd see him sometime over the weekend, and let you know. And Mrs Appledore has invited us both round for a meal on Saturday evening so that you can see Tony, and Rosie wants you to go swimming with her on Saturday afternoon.'

The weekend passed quite pleasantly. Saturday was very social; Sunday was restful, with church in the morning and a walk with Simon in the afternoon along the river bank. He had been invited back for tea at Sal's, and when he and Theresa arrived, Edouard and Big Bob were sitting side by side on the small green and white settee in her parlour.

They rose to their feet, and then Theresa found herself sitting beside Big Bob, with Edouard and Simon in soft chairs facing them. Sal presided at a small round table, serving tea and sandwiches. Conversation was awkward and sporadic, with the three males as ill at ease as Theresa and Sal.

Theresa wasn't sure who knew what about her arrangements, as she certainly hadn't taken Simon totally into her confidence, and hesitated to ask how Charlie was. Fortunately, Big Bob had no such inhibitions, and proceeded to tell her that Charlie had made friends with the dogs and the children, and had been promised a pup.

Theresa had visions of her family expanding yet again. 'How nice,' she murmured, 'But we'll have to see.'

'Every boy needs a dog,' Big Bob boomed. 'He looks a different boy already. I've never seen such a change in anyone as in that lad.' He patted Theresa's knee, and the other three looked on—Edouard with a raised eyebrow and Simon a little smile, while Sal dropped a plate and bent to retrieve it.

Theresa couldn't help feeling relieved when they all left. Sal appeared unwontedly quiet, and spent the evening with a book.

Monday was a dull grey morning, hot and humid. Sal and Theresa struggled with forward bookings all through it, trying to juggle families of the wrong size into cottages that should be vacant on the dates asked for. They gave up, and had a light lunch at twelve.

Immediately after, Sal phoned Edouard to report that everything was normal, and they went back to work.

'We could put cots on the veranda, maybe.'

'Or, if we put the Robinsons in that big cabin for one week, and then moved them.' Theresa, frowning, made the suggestion as she looked up at Sal.

She was facing the door, and drew in her breath sharply as a man came through. Dark-haired, dark-bearded, he was neither tall nor short, young nor old. He was dressed in a shiny black suit and carried a cane. He didn't fit Charlie's description of a large, threatening man. In fact there was nothing about him to suggest that he was any different from the ordinary men of Creswal, but Theresa knew this was Obidiah Snelgrove even before he spoke.

'Which one of you is Theresa Russell?' he demanded in a soft voice.

'I am,' Theresa said, glad that the counter separated them.

'I want the boy,' he said. 'My boy. Where is he? I know he's not at your house; I've been there.'

'He's safe,' said Theresa.

Sal picked up the phone and asked the operator to connect her to Edouard's number.

Obidiah Snelgrove paid no attention to her, but brought his cane down on the counter, so that the papers lying there fluttered and fell back.

'I'm ready to take him home.'

Theresa began to understand the fear this man had induced in Charlie. If she had been alone, if the counter hadn't been between them, she might not have been able to withstand his demands. There was something in his eyes, in the set of his face, that ordered obedience to his wishes.

'You may be ready to take him, I'm not ready to give him up.'

Obidiah took a paper from his jacket pocket. 'The law says he's mine. You have no choice. Here, read it for yourself.' He held the paper out to Theresa.

Like a rabbit mesmerised by a snake, she was forced to leave her chair and come on trembling legs to pick up the paper. Before she even had a chance to read it, his hand had captured her wrist.

'Where is he?' he repeated, increasing the pressure until she gasped in pain.

Now Theresa's temper began to rise. She slid her free hand beneath the counter to the catch that controlled the entrance flap, and released it. In a single reflex action she flipped the section of the counter up, and it narrowly missed Mr Snelgrove's jaw.

In his surprise he released her, and she managed to get

the board back in place again and locked. She picked up the paper.

It was some sort of order from the orphanage declaring that they had surrendered Charlie Boyes, orphan, to Obidiah Snelgrove, farmer. Theresa was strangely calm now. She tore the paper in two and then in two again, and let the pieces fall to the floor.

'That's what I think of your orders!'

Obidiah Snelgrove gave a roar of protest. 'I mean to have the boy. Whether you tear up paper or not, he's mine.' He brought the cane down on the counter again.

It was fortunate that Edouard arrived then, with Rosie's brother Peter. The printer pinioned Mr Snelgrove's arms, and Edouard took the cane from him.

'Is this fellow causing trouble?' Edouard asked.

'Yes,' cried Sal and Theresa in unison.

Theresa sat down suddenly on her desk. Her legs felt strange and rubbery. Had she really nearly knocked out this man and torn up that document? She looked at the paper on the floor. She must have done!

'He attacked her,' she heard Sal say. 'He grabbed her by the wrist. He might have broken it.'

'Call the police,' Edouard instructed.

'Yes, call the police,' Mr Snelgrove echoed. 'We'll see who's in the right about this.'

Sal picked up the phone and began to speak to the operator.

CHAPTER EIGHTEEN

THINGS HAPPENED so quickly after Obidiah's appearance on the scene that Theresa was never quite sure afterwards of their exact sequence.

She knew that someone took Mr Snelgrove out of the office, and that Edouard was beside her, holding her head down to her knees and then offering her a sip of medicinal brandy and then another, and telling her he wouldn't let her have too much this time. He examined her wrist, and deplored the bruise-mark already forming, but whether that was after the brandy or before it she couldn't recall. She distinctly remembered giving a statement to a policeman, and she knew that Sal had glued Mr Snelgrove's document together very painstakingly.

Sal had sent her upstairs and made her a cup of tea, and in spite of her protests had insisted she have the rest of the afternoon off.

Theresa sat on the veranda with her tea, and it was there that Edouard came to find her. She couldn't seem to get warm. He saw her shivering, and draped a blanket round her.

'It's all arranged,' he said, sitting in the other canvas chair beside her. 'One of the Orphanage Board members is going to be with us tomorrow, with a Children's Welfare Inspector from the Province, for an informal hearing.'

'And Mr Snelgrove?' she asked, still shivering.

'He's going to spend a night at Creswal's expense—In the local lock-up, since he wouldn't promise not to continue his search for Charlie till after tomorrow.'

'But how has it all been arranged so quickly?' asked Theresa, astounded, at last beginning to feel the warmth of a fitful sun.

Edouard looked pleased with himself. 'I went to see a couple of the Board of Governors last week in Ottawa after I'd been to Toronto, and they agreed that the sooner things were settled, the better.'

'Just like that? So easily?'

'Not quite,' he admitted. 'But they were quick to see the kind of publicity my new Toronto paper was capable of giving them after my article, "Ten Days in the Life of an Orphan". You might say that it moved them.' He shrugged. 'Now, then, we must organise a little for this hearing. First, we need a room where we won't be disturbed. Big Bob has volunteered his study, and he's offered the Board Member, Albert Green, a bed for either tonight or tomorrow night or both. Sal will book a room at the hotel for the Inspector when we're sure of his arrival time.'

Theresa was more than a little impressed. 'It is good of you,' she declared, 'and I'm very grateful. Do we—Do we stand a good chance of winning?'

'It's the best chance we'll ever have, and we must make the most of it. You'll be there, of course, and the Appledores and Charlie—Charlie must appear.' He silenced her protests. 'And Sal and the head of the family Charlie's staying with; Big Bob, of course; and, I think, the doctor.'

She naturally agreed and let him take care of it all, grateful for his energy and ability.

The next morning, they all assembled at the Falconers' house. Obidiah Snelgrove was escorted by a man in blue. Theresa and Sal arrived by car.

Theresa had nervously debated what to wear, and had decided it must be her black and white costume with the new white hat. She hoped that she would look old enough and sensible enough to offer a home to a second boy as well as to her brother. Inspecting her, Sal had said that the brown curls escaping from under her hat made her look younger than ever. So Theresa had tried to keep them inside, but they kept slipping out, despite her efforts. Sal wore blue, and it suited her.

They went in, and sat down as far away from Obidiah as possible. When Charlie arrived, he went directly to Theresa, and sat as close as he could to her, trying not to look at the farmer. His host of the week, Dave McCann, a big raw-boned, red-headed man, was introduced to Theresa, and sat on Charlie's far side. Edouard sat on Theresa's other side, with Sal and the Appledores. Big Bob settled himself next to Obidiah Snelgrove, dwarfing him by his size. The doctor was late, and stayed by the door.

Mr Green, the Board Member, and the Inspector, Mr Oswald, a quiet, little, fair, dried-up sort of man in his fifties, were in straight-backed chairs behind a large desk. Mr Green was white-haired, blue-eyed, ruddy-cheeked, a large, well-proportioned figure.

Mr Green began by telling the assembled company that it was a little irregular to hold such a hearing away from Ottawa, but very necessary in this case. He asked Edouard first and then Big Bob to describe how they had found Charlie, and in what sort of state he was. They told him in conversational tones, both mentioning their horror at his condition.

'He had been beaten unmercifully,' Big Bob declared, with a sidelong look at his neighbour.

' "For wicked and deceitful mouths are opened against me," ' Obidiah interrupted, as Big Bob finished. 'For the ungodly among you, that's Psalm 109.'

His audience stared at him. Surely he wasn't bringing the Bible to bear witness for him?

The Inspector, spoke up mildly. ' "Blessed is the man to whom the Lord imputes no iniquity", Psalm 32.'

The doctor coughed, and Edouard hid a smile as he caught Theresa's eye.

'Quite,' declared Mr Green with a frown, 'You'll have your chance to speak presently, Mr Snelgrove.' He called upon the doctor.

' "A cruel man hurts himself", Proverbs 11, verse 17,' the doctor began, with a direct glance at Obidiah. 'But in this case,' he turned back to Mr Green, 'I wouldn't mind being let loose with this cruel fellow. I examined Charlie Boyes on Sunday morning and was appalled at what I found.' He went on to describe Charlie's condition, and passed the picture Edouard had taken to Mr Green and the Inspector. 'Besides the whippings and canings and strikings, the child had been starved of food and was in a filthy condition. His clothes had to be burned.'

'"Do you have children?",' Mr Snelgrove demanded, as the picture was being examined. '"Discipline them", Ecclesiasticus 7, verse 23.'

They all looked at him in revulsion.

Again Mr Oswald spoke up. 'I see you read your Bible, Mr Snelgrove. I wonder you passed over, without noticing, Ecclesiasticus 7, verse 20. "Do not abuse a servant who performs his work faithfully." Did Charlie Boyes not accomplish all the tasks you set him?'

'No, he did not. He had to be shown the error of his ways.'

'Perhaps you'd care to tell us what tasks you set him, and how he failed,' Mr Green interposed smoothly.

Obidiah glared at them all, and began to speak. 'He was only expected to do the jobs any farmer does—no more, no less. Light the kitchen fire at five, chop some wood, milk the cows and drive them to the fields, clean the barn, fetch water from the well, feed swill to the pigs and muck out the sties, hoe in the fields, scrub the dairy down . . .'

'His day began at five,' Mr Green interrupted. 'At what time did it end?'

'Why, after dark; the same as mine.'

'At this time of year, dark falls between nine and ten, would you say?' the Inspector's voice was still calm, still quiet.

'That's right,' Obidiah agreed.

'So between ten at night and five in the morning, he was allowed to sleep—in a proper bed, I suppose? With sheets and a blanket?'

'No, in the barn, in the hay. I wouldn't have trash like him—a bastard—in the house. Say what you like about orphans'—he fixed them all with his staring eyes—'they're vermin.'

Theresa felt Charlie shrinking beside her, and she held his hand.

'I know what the Bible says,' Obidiah went on. '"Children of adulterers will not come to maturity", Wisdom of Solomon 3, verse 16. "Even if they live long, they will be held of no account", verse 17.' His voice held such a ring of conviction and sincerity that Theresa winced.

A shock seemed to have stunned his hearers. The man had condemned himself out of his own mouth.

'That's enough, Mr Snelgrove.' Mr Green spoke into the silence. 'I have no hesitation in removing Charlie Boyes entirely from your care. Nor will you ever be given charge of any other orphanage child.' He picked up the document before him on the desk.

Theresa could see it was the one that Sal had carefully pieced together the day before.

Mr Green looked at it in distaste, and then tore it into small pieces. 'I would strongly advise you to return home when you are released, remembering that "The Lord works vindication and justice for all who are oppressed", Psalm 103.'

'Is that strumpet to have him, then?' Obidiah rose to his feet, and pointed to Theresa. 'I saw that he went to church and Sunday school.'

'That needn't concern you,' he was told by Mr Green, who signalled to Mr Falconer to remove Obidiah from the room.

As the door opened, Theresa saw that the policeman was waiting outside.

Then Mr Green asked Charlie questions about living with Theresa, and if he wanted to stay with her.

'Yes, for ever, if she'll have me,' was his fervent answer to that. He looked nonplussed when everyone laughed—even the little Inspector, but it was kind laughter, and Theresa began to hope she would be allowed to keep Charlie.

Mr Green consulted some notes he had, and said they spoke of Charlie as a wild, headstrong boy who needed a firm hand. He asked Sal and the Appledores and Dave McCann how they would describe Charlie, and a different picture of him emerged as an ordinary ten-year-old boy of strong will but generous impulses.

Last, Mr Green asked Theresa why she wanted to take him, and she replied that it was simply because he had come to her, and that she loved him.

The Inspector blew his nose.

Big Bob exclaimed, 'Hurrah! He'll make a grand lad, and when he's a little older, he can have a job with me if he wants one.'

Mr Green noted that down, and announced that he had no objections at all to Charlie remaining with Theresa for an indefinite holiday.

Theresa burst into tears, so great was her relief. Charlie threw his arms round her, and told her about the puppy Dave McCann had for him. Then they were all kissing her and hugging her, and wishing her and Charlie well.

Big Bob's housekeeper had prepared a buffet lunch, and they all trooped into the dining-room to eat it.

Charlie kept thanking Edouard. Theresa heard the boy telling him that he might not work for Big Bob after all; he thought a newspaper must be the best place in the world to work. She saw Sal having a long earnest discussion with Mr Green, and then a shorter one with the Inspector.

It was Big Bob who waited on Theresa and made sure that she had enough to eat. Then he tucked his arm in hers, and brought her over to Mr Green.

She thanked him, but was somewhat chagrined when Big Bob added that of course it was only a temporary arrangement, as Theresa wouldn't remain single for long.

Mr Green smiled, and said that in his view that would

be all to the good. He shook her warmly by the hand, taking her protests that marriage wasn't on her horizon as maidenly reluctance.

'Naturally, my dear, you don't want to say anything now.' He smiled at her in a fatherly fashion. 'But it would be very suitable; a pleasant solution to your difficulties.' He looked towards Big Bob, now engaged in conversation with Dave McCann. 'Mr Falconer is a fine man—and a generous one.'

Theresa bit her lip, realising that the subject was better left alone, and Mr Green began to ask her about England, and where she had lived, and if she found many differences in life in Canada.

It was a very sociable luncheon party, with everyone mixing. Theresa was content to let several conversations wash over her. She heard Big Bob promising to take Charlie sailing again, and later Sal telling him about the skating rink, and what a first-rate skater Eddie was.

'I shall be sorry to lose Charlie,' Dave McCann told the Inspector. 'The dogs took to him directly. There's some as are frightened of the creatures, and they sense that right away.'

It was Edouard who brought Theresa back to a sense of reality. 'When this shindig's over, we'll go and pick up Charlie's things from the McCanns'. Tony might like to come with us to see the dogs, and to feel that he belongs as well.'

'It's very thoughtful of you to include him. How did you know that Tony was feeling a little jealous of Charlie before all this?'

'I have eyes,' he answered, 'and I use them. I saw Bob Falconer doing you a favour with Mr Green, too. That won't do you any harm.'

She felt the colour sweeping into her face at his words, and had no control over it. 'I tried to tell him . . .' she murmured, hoping no one else was listening.

'But he didn't want to believe you.' Edouard smiled. 'Just as well, I think. It will go down better with the other

Board Members if he's able to tell them about your prospects.'

Theresa was annoyed. Edouard might not think her pretty or desirable, but Bob Falconer did. She knew that. 'Big Bob treats me like a lady. Not as you do. He doesn't order me about, or try to put me down.'

'That's because he wants something from you,' he retorted. 'Ask yourself if the drawing card is your fatal charm—or Charlie for a son?'

She felt as though she had suddenly been deluged with a pail of cold water. 'That's plain talking!' She looked at Edouard speculatively. 'Why shouldn't it be my charm? Just because it's never been fatal with you . . .' She didn't finish. She wasn't allowed to.

'Girls who play with fire end up with burnt fingers,' was his swift return, but whether he referred to Big Bob or himself wasn't quite clear to Theresa.

By this time the others were beginning to say their goodbyes and to leave. Edouard extricated Charlie from Sal and the Appledores, took Theresa by the arm, and led the pair of them to his car.

They collected an excited Tony on the way, and drove out to the house where Charlie had sheltered for a week. It was a mile or so out of town in the opposite direction to the dam, well set back from the road. A dog ran to greet them, and immediately quietened down when Charlie spoke to it.

When Theresa met the assembled McCann family —Dave and his wife Nora and seven little ones—she began to smile and then to giggle. She had never seen so many red heads in one room in all her life. Some were fiery red, some deeper, but all were red, and Charlie fitted in among them like another carbon copy.

'I'm sorry for laughing,' she apologised to Nora. 'Edouard never told me. Charlie couldn't have been better hidden anywhere, could he?'

The laughter was infectious, and they all joined in, even the smallest one.

'It was the second line of defence,' said Edouard. 'Just in case things went very wrong.'

'You have a very devious mind!' Theresa whispered to him.

He only smiled at that. 'I'm a great schemer.'

The promised puppy was brought in and displayed to Theresa and to Tony—a furry bundle of black and tan. 'It's not old enough yet to leave its mother.' Charlie handed it to Tony, and it licked his finger. 'But in a month or two we can take it home, if Theresa lets us.'

Faced with two imploring sets of eyes, Theresa capitulated. Today she would agree to anything. It wasn't a time to hold back. They left the McCanns' the best of friends, promising they'd be back, and Edouard drove Theresa and the boys home.

It was good to be home. The boys ran through the little house and collapsed on the bottom bunk bed with Charlie's bundle of clothes. Theresa could hear them chattering as she faced Edouard in the living-room.

As she began to thank him once again with a very full heart for all he'd done, he put a finger to her lips. 'There is something you can do for me,' he said.

'Tell me.'

'Do you remember when you went to the women's club meeting with Rosie?'

'And met Mrs Appledore? Yes, I do.' Theresa couldn't imagine what was coming next.

'If you remember, they were planning a dance. It's two weeks this Saturday, and I'd like you to come with me to it.' He sounded almost diffident about asking her.

'I'd be delighted!' She couldn't believe her ears. Was Edouard actually wanting to take her to a dance? 'Is it very formal?'

'Oh yes, the Charity Ball is a big occasion. You'll need a long dress.'

'I have one.'

'That's grand, then. It's a date. Now I must get back to work.' Without another word, he left her.

Theresa sank down in the rocking-chair. Edouard had

asked her to a dance; 'a big occasion', he had called it. Probably he had been going to take Marguerite, she warned herself. But she's away in the States, and won't be back for it. She argued that she didn't care if she was second choice. He'd asked her, and that was enough.

Strangely enough perhaps, it was enough. In the two weeks that followed, Theresa hugged to herself the knowledge that Edouard was taking her to a dance, and the contentment of that spread into her daily life.

The boys had settled back into their ordinary routine and were really helpful round the house. They got on well with Gwen, and went swimming often with Timmy and their new friend Jimmy. Work was busy but interesting. Sal, too, seemed much better satisfied with life. When the news came out that Charlie was staying on with Theresa, many people of the town congratulated her, and she began to feel she had made a place for herself, and for the boys, in the community. Edouard reported that Obidiah Snelgrove had been released and put on a train back to his farm. The man had been threatened with dire penalties should he ever set foot in Creswal again or try to interfere with Charlie or with her.

Big Bob took her and the boys sailing again, and made no mention of future plans. They all went skating with Edouard, Simon and Rosie one evening, and Charlie and Bob Falconer surprised everyone by skating very well indeed. It was a happy time. Theresa wanted it to go on for ever.

Then suddenly it was the Saturday of the Charity Ball. Theresa had a letter in the morning from Mr Roscoe in Ottawa, reporting that there was to be a hearing in the next two weeks about her father's money, and he felt very optimistic indeed about the outcome. He knew she would be pleased to hear the good news, particularly now that she had two boys to support. He applauded her courage, added that it had won her the early action, and wished her good luck.

Theresa felt that the good luck was already hers. Sal had declared an early finish to the morning, and advised her to have a rest. She was going to—and she added with a smile that Big Bob Falconer was taking her to the Ball. It had been arranged a long time ago, and he had not changed his mind.

After an early meal for the boys, Theresa had a long luxurious bath and got dressed. She had brought with her from Liverpool, at the twins' insistence, a pink chiffon evening frock. She had claimed she'd never have the opportunity to wear it and that it wasn't her style, but the twins had won the day, and now she was grateful that they had.

The dress swirled about her, panels of softest chiffon floating out in shades from palest peach to deep cyclamen and the same shades were mingled in cunning pleats in the long clinging bodice. It brought out the apricot tones of her skin and the brown sheen of her hair. Her hair was a little longer now than it had been when first cut, and curled about her face to give her an elfin look that went well with the dress. Her shoes and bag matched its predominant pink. When she looked in the mirror, she knew she looked her best, her green eyes sparkling back at her.

'Oh-h!' exclaimed the boys in unison. 'You look lovely! Edouard will like you even better than usual.'

This was an opinion which was reinforced when he arrived, for he stood back and called her 'an English rose' in tones that could only be called reverent. Then, while the boys looked on, he kissed her on both cheeks so delicately, so gently, that she felt as fragile and as beautiful as a piece of porcelain. Gwen had come to mind the boys for the evening, and she added her compliments to his.

Theresa and Edouard went up to the big house, and Mrs Appledore welcomed them with a tangy punch.

'Non-alcoholic!' Edouard assured Theresa, with a teasing smile.

Mrs Appledore, in soft turquoise blue, admired

Theresa's finery, and told her what a handsome couple they made.

'You'll meet all sorts of people tonight,' Mr Appledore told her, as they all climbed into Edouard's car. 'And they'll all look as grand as we do, or nearly so! It's our big social event in Creswal—when the ladies take us out and we open our wallets for all the charities.'

It was a magical evening. The ballroom of the hotel was decked out in pink and white, with big bunches of flowers everywhere, and a band playing the kind of music Theresa loved. She began to sway to it. Edouard made sure that her programme was full. He claimed two dances for himself, and so did Big Bob and Simon. She danced with Mr Appledore, and many other men whom she scarcely knew, and she loved it all. She waved to Rosie and Sal, and almost felt sorry for Marguerite and Sidney who were missing this marvellous time.

Everyone had a smile for Theresa, and a welcoming word. The refreshments at eleven were mouth-watering, and she sat at a round table with Edouard and the Appledores, and many of their friends came and talked to them. She felt as though she belonged.

At midnight, Mr Appledore announced the target figures for the various charities of this year. There were five in all, and each had managed to exceed last year's high level. There was a great deal of cheering and back-slapping among the men, as they stood around listening.

'This year,' he went on, 'we've all got together and raised a special fund for a special citizen who's impressed us all. It's a little lady who's taken on the care of her half-brother, when she could easily have left him where he was. And, not content with that, she's taken on another orphan lad!'

Edouard pushed Theresa forward, although she tried to hang back. Clapping started, and she found herself propelled forward by the parting of the crowd before her so that she stood with Mr Appledore.

'We've raised a thousand dollars!' He beamed at her.

'It will help you and the boys to have a secure future here with us.'

'Oh no!' she gasped, thinking of the mining stock in the Ottawa bank, and Mr Roscoe's hopeful letter of that very morning. 'No, I couldn't . . . You shouldn't!' She was overcome.

'Of course we should, and you can and must accept,' Mr Appledore was expansive, mistaking her reluctance for natural modesty. 'We want you to have it.'

Theresa felt like a hunted animal. She looked wildly about her. They were all laughing and clapping, encouraging her.

Again she said No, and added, 'You don't understand.' Why hadn't she told anyone about the possibility of the bank money? Nothing had prepared her for this, and she burst into tears, her explanations barely coherent.

Far from listening to her protests, Mr Appledore put his arm round her and thanked the crowd on her behalf. His wife came forward and hugged her, and the clapping began again. The people had taken her to their hearts, and they only loved her the more for being so overcome, so unassuming. She smiled at them through her tears. Then Edouard was beside her.

'Take me home, Edouard?' she begged.

'We'll all go home,' said Mrs Appledore. 'And both of you shall come to our place and have a drink.'

Edouard drove them, and very shortly they were installed in the large lounge of the big house, with cups of tea or coffee. Every time Theresa tried to say something, Mrs Appledore forestalled her by exclaiming, 'Finish your tea first, dear! You've had quite a shock.'

'Now, then,' said Edouard, when the hot sweet liquid had done its work and a little colour had come back into her cheeks. 'What is it that's bothering you?' His tone was so kind that she nearly cried again.

'It's the money,' she declared. 'It was very kind of everyone—very generous—but I can't take it. I should have told you about Mr Roscoe and the bank. I meant to tell you before, but it seemed to impossible. I never really believed that it could be mine and Tony's. Mr Roscoe said I shouldn't count on it.'

She spoke to Edouard, but they all looked at her.

'What money?' he asked. 'What bank? You had better start at the beginning.'

So Theresa did. As she told the story of the mining stock her father had left in the bank in Ottawa, and of the petition the bank were making on her behalf in the courts, she could see that Edouard was drawing back.

'Why haven't I heard about this before?' was his only comment.

Mrs Appleford, on the other hand, was enthusiastic. 'That's good news, dear! Wonderful news. I'm so happy for you.'

Mr Appledore, too, was congratulatory. 'With a pair of boys to support, it's splendid. This Mr Roscoe was well advised to warn you not to expect anything. Mining stock has great ups and downs. Even with an early hearing, it's not sure you'll get the money. Besides the possibility of a fall in the market, the courts may decide not to sell till the seven-year period is up—or may not find in your favour. I suppose he told you to keep quiet about it?'

Theresa shook her head. 'No, I don't think he did. It was my decision. I didn't believe it, you see—I still don't, altogether. It seems like a fairy-tale.'

'With good rewarded and evil punished!' he pointed out with a beaming smile. 'I'm very pleased for you, my dear.'

'I can quite see why you burst into tears when the cheque was given to you at the Ball,' his wife reassured her. 'You want to give it back. Is that it, dear?'

Theresa nodded.

'I don't think she should.' He was frowning. 'After all, she isn't sure she'll ever have the money from Ottawa. Certainly we can inform the committee of the possibility —they'll be as thrilled as we are.'

'I think I should give it back.' Theresa was embarrassed by the whole episode.

'At least sleep on it,' suggested Mr Appledore. 'You
don't want to be too hasty. Don't you agree, Edouard?'

'She must do as she thinks best,' was his repressive
answer.

She knew Edouard was angry by the sound of his voice
as much as by his words, but she was comforted by the
Appledores' pleasure in her good fortune. They thought
no less of her for keeping it to herself—rather more, for
being so prudent.

When Theresa looked at Edouard uncertainly, he
only said that it was getting late and they'd all be the
brighter tomorrow for a good night's rest. He thanked
his host and hostess, and asked her if she was ready to
leave.

Good-byes said, he declared that of course he was
taking Theresa back to the little house, and driving her
baby-sitter home. They set off on the short distance to
the cottage.

The moon was shining, the stars bright in the curtain
of the sky, the evening mild and peaceful. Theresa heard
an owl cry, and the croak of a frog somewhere ahead on
the path. The leaves rustled gently on the trees above
them. It was a night for romance, for soft promises, for
kissing.

Theresa sighed. Edouard said nothing, but she felt
that he was holding his anger in check. He walked beside
her, but they might have been two strangers for the
distance between them. She stumbled, and he righted
her, and would have gone on.

'Please, Edouard,' she whispered, her hand on his
arm. 'Why are you so cross with me?'

He looked at her, distaste in his eyes. 'If you have to
ask that, you're a good deal stupider than I credited
you.'

She looked up at him. She could have walked on then,
but she took a deep breath, and asked, 'Is it because I
didn't trust you enough to tell you?'

'Exactly! Did I ever give you any reason not to trust me? Even when you threw yourself at me, did I take advantage of you? No, fool that I was, I looked into those clear eyes of yours and walked away leaving you untouched. Well, I've finished acting the gentleman.' His hands closed hard on her shoulders and he drew her to him. 'I'm as much a man as any other.' His arms encircled her waist, forcing her close to him.

'Please don't,' she begged him. 'It was as Mr Appledore said—a sort of fairy-tale, that money . . .' He slackened his hold just a little, she thought, and she tried to press this slight advantage by keeping talking. 'Mr Roscoe wrote in his letter today that it was because of the boys—first Tony and then Charlie. He doesn't think they'll refuse now.'

Far from placating him, this seemed to inflame him the more. 'So that's how it was! First you took your half-brother, and when that wasn't enough to make them move, you fought for Charlie. Did this Mr Roscoe advise your course of action, or did you plan it all yourself?'

Theresa cried out in pain. 'If that's what you think of me, I was right not to trust you. Think what you like—I don't care.' She knew she couldn't break the hold his arms had round her, but she stamped on his foot.

She heard him gasp, and exclaim, 'Damn you' under his breath, but he didn't let her go.

Instead, his mouth found hers, and in a hard, bruising kiss that hurt her lips he forced a flame awake in her—a flame part-anger, part-desire, but wholly demanding. When his hand cupped her breast she welcomed it, yearning for him.

With a sound that might have been a groan, he pushed her away. 'Perhaps Obidiah wasn't so far wrong! You beguile a man into thinking you're everything he wants. Perhaps you did seduce Charlie—but not me, you English witch.' He stood back from her on the path, blocking the way. 'Straighten your dress, smooth your hair and take that frightened look from your face—I've changed my mind. We wouldn't want Gwen to see you were anything but a sweet innocent returning from a dance, would we?'

With shaking hands, Theresa did her best to comply, and followed him along the path. She must have succeeded tolerably well, for the half-asleep Gwen only smiled and said she was sure they'd had a good time, as they looked so happy. Theresa thanked her, and managed to reply that it had been a great occasion.

Gwen left with Edouard, chatting easily.

Theresa leaned against the door as she closed it behind them, and the tears began.

He despised her. He'd made that plain. Well, she loathed him. She'd never forgive him for the way he'd acted tonight. She didn't want to see him ever again. He'd made her acknowledge to him, and to herself, that her body wanted him, and then he'd pushed her aside. She couldn't forgive him for that. She wept tears of despair and shame.

CHAPTER NINETEEN

THE WEEK that followed the dance was the worst that
Theresa had ever endured. She told herself to forget
Edouard, that he wasn't worth even thinking about; but
always that seemed to be exactly what she was doing.
Why did he believe the worst of her whenever there was
a choice? Why had the lovely evening finished so dis-
astrously?

She drifted through the days, pale and listless. Even
the boys noticed, and Charlie took to bringing her a cup
of tea first thing in the morning and begging her to eat.
By Friday, Sal asked if she felt well. 'I would have
thought you'd be on top of the world, with all your
worries behind you. Instead, you look as though you're
heading straight for a decline. Try some raw liver.'

Theresa shuddered and looked away.

'There's only one other person in town who looks as
bad, and that's Edouard. It's taken him a different way.
He's snapping at everyone. Rosie says he's made up his
mind to go to Toronto and leave us. The decision doesn't
seem to be giving him much pleasure,' Sal went on.
'Have you two had a tiff?'

Theresa only shook her head. 'A tiff?' To describe
what had happened between her and Edouard as a tiff
was almost laughable. A pity she couldn't quite bring
herself to laughter—nor could she explain to Sal—it
hurt too much.

'What you need, my girl, is a change,' Sal decided.
'Tomorrow we'll take the boys to the summer cottages in
the morning, and when we've finished with the visitors,
we'll have a picnic and a swim. I warn you, I'll get to the
bottom of this trouble of yours!'

There was no resisting Sal in this mood. Theresa
agreed, and brought the boys with her the following

morning. They were very excited, and that cheered her a little.

It was an easy change-over at the cottages, since there were only two new families to settle, and by mid-morning Charlie and Frank were out in Frank's canoe, fishing, while Tony and Sal collected wood for a small fire on the beach to cook their lunch. They had left Theresa sitting on a rock staring at the river.

Dazzled by the glare of the sun on the water, she looked up at a slight sound to find Edouard beside her. She half rose, not wanting anything to do with him. 'We have nothing more to say to each other,' she told him.

'You're wrong. We have,' was his terse reply. 'Sit down and listen. I'm no more anxious than you to be here, but something's happened.'

She sank down. 'What's happened? And don't stand hovering over me! I hate people who do that,' she added pettishly.

He dropped to his knees on the sand, and picked up a handful. He let it slide away from him. 'I've had a phone call. You don't look well.'

'So people keep telling me, but I'm perfectly all right.' She half rose again. 'Was that what you came to say?'

'Hold your tongue,' said Edouard mildly, picking up more sand, 'and sit still. My phone call was very surprising.'

'Oh?' Theresa was polite, nothing more.

'A Mrs Charles called me from Southern Ontario—a place called Niagara-on-the-Lake.'

'Yes?'

'She claims to be married to your father.' He let the sand trickle through his fingers.

'My father? Married?' She frowned. 'Everyone knows my father is dead! Why else did Marguerite have to go away, and the town raise money for me? Because they knew it'—she answered her own question—'and felt sorry for me.'

'Stop that, Theresa,' he commanded. 'No one has any need to feel sorry for you.'

'Why have you bothered to come and tell me this nonsense? I don't believe it.'

'If you'd stop being so superior, I might tell you.'

Theresa drew in her breath. How dared he!

'Listen to me,' he went on. 'Your father is alive, and has two little girls.'

'Another family?'

'Another family,' he agreed.

'And you believe her?'

'Yes, I think I do. She wants you to bring Tony, and come and visit them. It all hangs together. It seems that her father was canoeing on the river and was joined by your father. They rode the white water together and there was an upset—an accident. Charles was hit on the head and suffered a kind of memory lapse. For some reason his name got changed round, and he's been known as Russell Charles ever since.'

'Has he found his memory now?' Theresa couldn't bring herself to believe any of this.

'No, he hasn't. That's why she wants Tony there. She thinks it may help.'

'To jog his memory? How far is this Niagara-on-the-Lake?'

'Three or four hundred miles. We could travel overnight on the train.'

'We?'

'I'd come with you. I'm not going to miss the end of the story.'

'Is that all it is to you—a story?'

'What else?' Edouard shrugged.

Theresa was so wounded by this that her hands shook, and she clasped them together so that he wouldn't notice. 'What if it doesn't work? It's a lot to ask of Tony.' Why had this man the power to hurt her still?

'You'll have to explain it to him. He's old enough to understand.'

She frowned, undecided. 'Why didn't Mrs Charles get in touch before?'

'She wanted to. It seems that she read the article your

friend Patti wrote, and didn't want to believe that her husband had a son and a daughter—by other women.'

'Now she's reconciled to that?'

'She's ready to accept it, and to accept both of you, after my article about Charlie in the Toronto paper. She likes the sound of you now, and hopes that you can make her husband a complete man.'

Theresa nodded at that. Unlike Edouard, this woman liked her! What if it were true? The unknown Mrs Charles became a little more real to her. She was putting her husband's interests first. That was another point in her favour.

'He has green eyes,' he said softly. 'Just like yours. So has one of the little girls. She says she looks like the picture of you in the paper.'

'You had a long conversation with her.' Theresa felt somehow aggrieved. 'What colour are her eyes? I suppose you know that too.'

'Blue.' Edouard smiled for the first time. 'She's a blue-eyed blonde. Very pretty, I imagine. Your father has a taste for good-looking women.'

She gave him no answering smile. 'What if it's just a hoax?'

'That's the chance you have to take. I talked to her for quite a long time, and I think she's genuine. Isn't it worth going to see?'

'How much is the rail fare?'

'About fifteen dollars, I think. I don't know whether Tony can go half-fare on a sleeper. The paper will advance the money, if you're short.'

'I'll go to the bank,' Theresa said stiffly.

'I doubt if there'll be time. You can give me a cheque, if you feel like that. I took the liberty of asking Gwen to pack a few things for you and Tony—I've brought the bag with me.'

'You were pretty sure I'd fall in with your plans,' she complained.

'I hoped you would,' he replied blandly. 'Besides, I

didn't want anyone to know about it—I want a scoop for my papers.'

'Now who's being secretive?' she demanded bitterly. 'We can go on our own, you know . . . I think I'd rather.'

'No. You have no choice; I'm going with you. Oh, not to hold your hand. I suppose we can manage to get along for a short time, can't we?'

Theresa didn't answer that directly. 'I'll have to ask Sal if I can have a few days off—if it should happen to be true.'

'I'll ask her,' he offered. 'Then we'll all have some lunch—we'll need it. We've a long trip ahead of us.'

'What about Charlie?'

'It would only complicate matters to bring him. If Sal would keep him, that would be the best solution, since she'll have to know anyway. But I don't think we'll tell either boy just yet. You can concoct some story for Charlie for the moment, and Sal will explain it to him later. As for Tony, we'll tell him alone. There's no use preparing him too far in advance. It might upset him; and besides, there's Frank.'

'Very well. I suppose I could say that Tony and I were going on a little holiday—and I'll take Charlie later on—that I'd like to get to know them each separately. He might be quite pleased. He does rather feel Charlie's had all the excitement.'

So Edouard walked over the beach to Sal, and sent Tony running back to Theresa.

'Edouard said you wanted me,' the boy said. 'I didn't know he was coming on our picnic?'

'Neither did I,' Theresa admitted. 'How would you like to go on a little holiday with me and Edouard?'

'And Charlie?'

'No, just you and me.'

He considered it. 'It'd be all right, I guess. When shall we go?'

'This afternoon, after we've had our lunch.'

'I won't be able to go out in the boat with Frank, then, for my turn. Does it have to be today?'

'Yes, it does.'

There must have been such finality in her tone that Tony looked at her, and agreed very quietly.

He was very quiet, too, as he ate his lunch. Charlie, on the other hand, said he'd be pleased to stay with Sal, and anyway Big Bob was taking him sailing on Sunday. He assured Theresa he didn't mind; and that she needed a holiday.

The train was on time, and they boarded it in silence. Theresa had told herself over and over again that Edouard believed the man they were going to see was her father, but she didn't feel it could be true. She wouldn't even allow herself to hope; and as for Tony, she couldn't understand why he wasn't pleased to be going on a holiday. That's what she'd told him it was after Edouard's instructions on secrecy, but she'd felt, somehow, that it was wrong.

Now a very subdued Tony sat beside Theresa on the plush seat, while Edouard stowed their luggage on the rack above.

'We change at Ottawa,' he informed them.

Tony's face crumpled at that. 'You're not going to do it!' He scrambled to his feet and began to run down the passage between the rows of seats as the train got under way. 'You're not taking me back to the orphanage!'

Edouard raced after him and pulled him back.

Tony struggled to be free, kicking and hitting. 'I won't! You can't make me. Mr Appledore will have me as his boy. He's often said he would. It's because you've got Charlie now, isn't it?'

Theresa tried to put her arm about him and talk to him, but he threw it off. 'So much for saying nothing,' she exclaimed in anger to Edouard, as the boy kept up his struggle.

The other passengers had turned round in their seats at the commotion and were listening avidly.

'Sit down,' said Edouard, putting the boy forcibly on the seat beside himself, and holding him there. 'Nobody's getting rid of you! But if you keep on acting like this, they may be tempted to. We're taking you to see your father.'

'My father?' Tony sat motionless, quiet at least. 'I haven't got a father any more.' He turned to Theresa. 'I don't have to go, do I?'

'I thought you'd want to.'

'I don't think I do. He doesn't want me any more, or he wouldn't have left me. I thought you liked having me for your boy, Theresa.'

'I do.' She put her hand on his knee, and her eyes met Edouard's over his head.

'Well, then, we won't bother with him.' He smiled in satisfaction.

'It's not as easy as that,' Edouard broke in. 'Theresa's come all the way from England to find him. She wants to see him.'

'She can go on her own, then, or you can take her. You don't need me.'

'That's where you're wrong. Theresa's never seen him. You're the only one who knows what he looks like. We need you to tell us if this man is really your father.'

Tony considered this for a moment. 'Can't he tell you himself?' He looked at Theresa. 'You haven't ever seen him, have you? I suppose you do need me, just to be sure. A father that runs away might say anything. He might say you're not his daughter.' He nodded. 'Very well, I'll go with you. But I'll just say Yes he is or No he isn't, and then I'll go away. Promise you'll take me back, Theresa?'

'I promise.' She wanted to explain to him that their father had lost his memory, but even as she began to open her mouth to speak the words, Edouard shook his head at her.

'*Tais-toi*,' he said.

Theresa had enough French to know that he was telling her to hold her tongue. She wasn't sure whether he was right or not, but perhaps it would be easier on the lad to say nothing more now. He seemed content enough with her promise. She reached across and hugged him.

It was a long trip. In Ottawa they had a meal, and caught the sleeper to Toronto. On Sunday morning at Toronto, they changed trains again.

At Niagara-on-the-Lake they alighted, and were met by a blonde woman with a little girl. The child was so much like Theresa herself that she knew immediately that this was Mrs Charles, and that 'Mr Charles' must be the missing father of her search. Looking at her again, all her doubts were swept away.

Edouard shook her arm. 'Theresa, this is Olga Charles.'

She took her eyes from the little girl. The mother was six foot tall, and handsome as an Amazon. Her skin was golden tan, her eyes sea-blue, and her pale gold hair was braided in a thick coil round her head. Theresa could see that she was nervous and not at all sure of herself as she held out her hand to her.

It seemed incredible to her that this beautiful woman, who couldn't be more than ten years her senior, might be her stepmother—was her stepmother. She was certain of it. She ignored the outstretched hand, and put her arms round Olga, and a laughing Olga lifted her off her feet.

'We shall get along fine! I need not have worried,' Olga declared. 'Come, I have brought the horse and buggy. They're waiting for you.' She led the way across the station yard.

Olga had not hugged Tony but had shaken hands with him, sensing, perhaps, some hostility. The little girl, Anna, had no such reservations. She clung to his hand and insisted on sitting on his knee, while her mother took charge of the driving, Edouard beside her.

Theresa sat facing the two children under the fringed top of the swaying open buggy. She breathed in the pure air, and let her eyes rest on the lush green of the countryside. This was more like England, like home. There were neat farms and orchards, a field of peas, a field of onions, and trees along the roads; even grass and horses and cows. This was a land of promise, a soft place, comfortable and prosperous. Creswal had been much harsher, much less settled. There man and nature had wrestled with each other; here man and nature might be at peace.

She smiled at Tony and he grinned back at her, not at all put out by Anna's advances to him.

'I wouldn't mind having Anna for my sister,' he admitted. 'In the orphanage, the lucky ones had sisters. They had someone to hug. They didn't want them around all the time, but it must have been nice to know they were there.'

Theresa hadn't slept very well on the train. Now it was enough to relax, and to let things happen as they would. Olga was in charge, and she and Edouard were chattering away as though they'd known each other all their lives.

When the horses turned and went up a long drive edged with apple trees, she looked towards the approaching farmhouse with interest. It was of grey wood with a white trim, and low and sprawling. There was a large barn behind it, and some other building to one side. It all looked well kept.

The man standing on the veranda steps came forward to the horse's head, as the buggy came to a halt. This must be Charles Russell. Why, he was small—much smaller than she'd imagined!

Theresa rose from her seat to look at him. Yes! Yes, it was the man in the newspaper clipping that she had carried with her for so long—a little older, perhaps —and he had a moustache and some grey in his hair. She knew him in some deep corner of her being. This was her father. She had no doubts. Whatever he had done, wherever he had been, there was a kind of recognition . . .

'Where have you been, Olga?' he asked. 'Not at church this long? I was worried.' His voice was low and deep, and had more than a touch of a Canadian accent. 'Who are these people?' He smiled at Tony.

The boy shrank back. 'That's him, Theresa. That moustache doesn't fool me!'

'That's him, Tessa,' little Anna repeated. 'That's my daddy.' She threw herself into his arms. Theresa wanted to do the same.

'Tessa, Tessa!' Mr Charles set the child upon her feet, and looked at Theresa. 'I knew a green-eyed Tessa once.' He put a hand to his forehead as though to wipe a thought away.

'Tessa Russell,' said Olga softly. 'She has green eyes, just like Anna—and like you.'

Mr Charles began to shake. The tremor started in the hand he held out to Theresa. 'Come down, Tessa Russell, and let me see you.'

She put her hand in his and alighted.

They looked deep into each other's eyes. His hand still gripped hers. She held it tight to still the shiver that now extended up his arm.

'I had a daughter, Tessa,' he whispered, 'a long, long time ago. I had to leave her—there was nothing else to do.'

Theresa was overcome. Tears welled up in her eyes. She couldn't understand how it was that she had triggered his memory. 'I am that daughter,' she murmured, swallowing the lump in her throat.

He kissed her. 'Little Tessa, all grown up and beautiful.' He was swaying on his feet now, and Olga was crying. She held on to Edouard, and wouldn't let him move to help the other man.

'Leave her be,' Theresa heard her say.

Theresa led her father to the veranda steps. He sat down, and she sat beside him, holding his hand.

'You had a son, too,' she whispered to him. 'Antony.'

He looked at her vaguely. 'Tony!' He shouted the name. 'Oh God, where's Tony? Did I leave him, too?' He tried to get up.

Tony leapt out of the buggy. 'I'm here, Dad! Dad, why did you go?' He stood before his father, scowling.

'I'd never leave Tony,' Mr Charles assured him. 'Tony

was my only son—just a little lad—a good little lad. No father would ever leave him.'

'Well, you did! You left me, and they put me in an orphanage, and I hate you.'

'I don't understand,' Mr Charles turned to Theresa. 'Tony never spoke like that to me! Besides, he was small. He's not my Antony.'

'Yes, he is,' said Theresa, not knowing whether she was sorrier for the father or the son. 'I went to the orphanage and got him out. He's missed you.'

'No, I haven't.' Tony denied it hotly. 'I like Theresa better. I'm her boy, now.'

'Theresa's boy?' Mr Charles put his head in his hands. 'No, that can't be! Tessa's not old enough to have a big boy like you.' He took his hands away, and shook his head. 'You're Violetta's son.' He tried to touch Tony, but the boy stepped back.

'We can go now, Theresa. Can't we?' he implored her, coming to sit beside her on the step and away from his father.

Theresa looked helplessly from one to the other.

Olga, brushing away tears with the back of her hand, came to Tony and said, 'I hope you'll stay just a little longer. You must be tired, and I'll soon have lunch ready.'

He looked up at her. 'All right, I'll stay till then.'

Olga smiled, and Anna took Tony by the hand. 'You're a naughty boy to shout, Tony,' she exclaimed, 'but I think I like you just the same. I'll show you something, if you promise to be quiet.' She led him up the veranda steps.

Mr Charles, upset, confused, was helped by Olga and Theresa to get to his feet. He allowed them to take him inside the house. Edouard followed after them, as a man came from the barn to put the horse and cart away.

Theresa saw that Olga and Edouard were well able to help her father to his bedroom, and went out on to the veranda again. She could hear Tony and Anna talking, and she went to join them. She couldn't have said how she felt about her father, or what she thought; that would come later. But she was too excited to stay still.

There was a wicker cradle in the shade of the gallery, and the two children were before it. Anna gave it a little push, and it swung slightly. The blonde, blue-eyed baby lying there gave a gurgle of delight and kicked her feet into the air.

'That's Tilda,' Anna announced proudly, 'I expect she's hungry. She's always eating.'

If Tilda was hungry, she gave no sign of it, but laughed up at them all and caught Theresa's finger.

They all laughed back, and Tony took the baby's other hand. 'Is she my sister, too?'

Theresa nodded. 'And mine, I suppose.' Strangely, that moved her more than finding their common father.

Edouard came up behind them. 'Perfect!' he declared. 'All Charles Russell's children—or all we know about so far . . .' he amended, for Theresa's ears only.

She couldn't help laughing ruefully at that. 'Will he tell us the whole story when he wakes up, do you think?'

'Perhaps not all at once. But as it comes back to him, he'll want to talk about it.'

'Yes,' said Theresa. 'It's been locked away in him for all these years.' She frowned. 'He'll need some luck to convince Tony of his intentions.'

Olga came to them then, and agreed with Edouard that it would make a splendid picture if the children posed together. She placed the baby Tilda in Theresa's arms, and kept the little group smiling while Edouard set up his camera.

After the first photo, he wanted one of Olga and Theresa and Tony, and one of Theresa and Anna together. Then Anna demanded one of herself and her new brother, and Tony consented without a murmur. 'Just so long as you don't take me with that man.'

'Your father, you mean.' Edouard only smiled. 'I'll take you together only if you ask me. I must have one of Theresa with him, of course. She's the one who went looking for her father.'

'And gave up hope of finding him,' Theresa added. 'I wouldn't have succeeded without you, Edouard. I want you to know that I'm grateful to you—and Tony might be one day.' She still didn't feel altogether easy with him, but her innate politeness wouldn't allow her not to acknowledge the help he had given all along.

'Edouard is the real hero of this story,' Olga said. 'He must have believed in you from the first.'

'Not entirely,' he admitted to her, with a sidelong look at Theresa, now with the baby in her lap. 'But she wouldn't go away. She wouldn't take No for an answer. It's those green eyes of hers. Anna's are the same; just like your husband's.'

'I must thank you, too,' declared Olga. 'You've no idea how pleased I am for Russ. I can't think of him as "Charles", but I suppose I must. He'll be a complete man now. When I saw that first article in the Ottawa paper, I began to wonder about Russ, but I didn't have the courage to come forward. I waited, half hoping that I was wrong. Then when the Toronto paper came out with the story of Theresa seducing an orphan, I told myself I had been wise to wait. She was not the kind of daughter Russ would want. But someone showed me the piece you wrote about Charlie's ten days, and I knew I must match this English girl's generosity and prepare myself to share Russ with her. She is a fine girl, is she not?'

Theresa looked up at that, and smiled at her step-mother. She liked her more for admitting her doubts and her jealousy. She waited for Edouard's reply.

His answer was not direct. 'Charlie loves her. He told the hearing he wanted to stay with her for ever. There must be something about her.'

It wasn't the reply Theresa hoped to hear, but it was better than she might have expected after the previous Saturday night.

'Tony loves her, too.' Olga gave Edouard a speculative glance. 'What have you done with Charlie, while you're here?'

'He's with a friend,' Theresa said. 'The woman I work for.'

'He must come to us later, for a visit at least,' she insisted. 'But it was wise to leave him behind today.'

Olga began to prepare lunch, and Theresa helped her. Tony and Anna set the table, and Edouard was relegated to spooning mush into Tilda. She loved it, and wouldn't let him leave her. Every time he tried to move away, she cried, and then smiled when he came back.

That made Olga laugh. 'Are you a married man?' she asked him.

When he said he wasn't, she laughed harder, and advised Theresa that he was good husband material.

Theresa blushed, and hated herself. She pretended to be very busy with boiling vegetables, and hoped fervently that the steam concealed her confusion. Edouard said nothing.

When lunch was nearly ready, Olga woke Charles Russell and they all gathered at the table, Tilda in a high chair next to Edouard.

Olga had Tony on one side of her and Anna on the other, at her end of the table. Theresa sat beside her father at the other end, with Edouard opposite her.

Olga said Grace, and they all helped themselves from steaming platters and tureens. There was home-made soup, and lamb with roast potatoes, and carrots and peas and gravy. Ice-cream with maple syrup followed, with thick cream, and coffee. The children were allowed to get down from the table, the baby was settled for a nap, and the dishes were cleared away.

'Now, then,' Olga instructed a much stronger looking Russ. 'You must start at the beginning and tell how you left Theresa in England and came here to start two other families.'

Charles Russell laughed. 'It's the strangest thing, but I remember everything now. I think it was the sight of Theresa and Anna together in the buggy that did it. They are very alike. It's wonderful to know who I am, to look back on my life.' He looked at Olga. 'Nobody's life is perfect, and heaven knows I've made mistakes—bad ones—but I shall tell it all.'

'No more mysteries,' agreed Olga, 'I've had enough of those. I know who you are, but I want to know what made you that way.' She smiled so confidingly at her husband that Theresa envied her that trust.

'I was twenty-two when I married for the first time,' Charles told his listeners. Even Tony and Anna playing on the floor were quiet and came closer.

'I was working in Birmingham, as junior engineer on a bridge. Myrtle was nineteen and worked in a shop. She was an orphan, as I was. When that job finished, I found a better one in Leeds, and we moved to a little rented house, for Theresa was on the way. We were happy, though money was always tight; tighter, of course, when the baby arrived.' He raised his glass to Theresa. 'My Tessa was a lovely baby, and I might have stayed there all my days, except that the following year I had what I considered a grand piece of luck. Through an old friend, I was offered a job in a gold mine in Peru at twice the salary I was earning. We talked about it, and I was keen to go—both for the experience and for the money. So keen, that Myrtle gave way. The company arranged for a percentage to be paid to her so that she'd have security.

'On a dull, rainy, English summer day, I kissed Myrtle and Tessa good-bye, and sailed for Peru. Tessa wasn't two yet. The voyage was pleasant; the job all I had hoped for; and I began to save a little, even from my portion of my pay. I missed my wife and baby, but I was carried away with the adventure of it all.' He paused for breath, and Olga took Anna on her lap.

'Everything was set fair,' he went on. 'Letters passed back and forth between Myrtle and myself, and the year I had bargained on was drawing to a close. I could go home much richer. Fate makes fools of us all!' He shrugged. 'There was an accident at the mine—a bad accident. The supports caved in, and lives were lost.' His face was bleak. 'I was one of the lucky ones—I lived. But

I had two broken legs, concussion and a fractured skull. I didn't know anything about it for a considerable time, and finally found myself in a hospital in Lima with no idea of what had happened or why I was there. To cap it all, I developed pneumonia. It was three or four months later that I heard the story. The owners of the mine had disappeared. I had no money. What I had saved had gone on hospital expenses, and no letters came from Myrtle. I wrote to her, and received no reply. I was desperate, but I had no way of getting back to England. I had no one to turn to, but jobs were plentiful, though my health wasn't good. No employer paid me the kind of money I'd been earning at the mine. Fortunately by now, I had a good command of Spanish. But each time I had a little saved, it disappeared in medicines and doctors. It took me over a year to get my passage money and enough over to search for my wife in England.'

'But you never came,' Theresa interrupted him.

'Oh, yes, I came,' he said. 'I spent eleven months in searching for you both, and was forced before that to find employment. Finally I tracked you down in Liverpool, to discover that I had been legally declared dead, and that Myrtle had married again and was the mother of twin girls.'

When he sighed, his listeners followed suit, caught up in this desperate turn of fortune.

'At first, I cursed her and called her fickle. I was determined that she should leave him and come back to me; then I softened a little towards her, thinking of the hardships she must have endured. I thought perhaps I'd see how things were between them, and how my Tessa was. I dressed like a workman, and took to hanging round the district where they lived, and one Sunday afternoon I saw them all out together. Tessa was holding her stepfather's hand, and laughing up at him as though she was his real daughter, and Myrtle, who was pushing the twins, turned to him with such a look of love on her face that I almost wept from loneliness. They were the family. I was the outsider.'

Theresa put her hand on her father's, her eyes wet with unshed tears. 'He was always kind and good to me.'

'Yes,' Charles nodded. 'I saw it then. That was when I decided to go away. But first I must have a picture of my little girl. I made a friend of the housemaid, and one day when she took you out, I got my photo. That was all I had of you.'

'It's the one in the album, isn't it?' Tony asked, his anger forgotten in his interest. 'The one Marguerite saw.' He was leaning against Theresa.

'Who's Marguerite?' asked Olga, her arms round Anna. 'Tony's mother?'

'No. Tony's mother was Violetta Ortenzi, a little Italian girl, a darling. I married her in Montreal after I left England to start a new life in Canada.'

'But you were still married, surely?' It was Edouard who asked the question.

'I didn't see it that way,' Charles tried to explain. 'That Mr Russell was dead—a court had said so. I was a different man. Charles Russell was alone in the world. He wanted a wife.'

Olga nodded as though she understood. 'Every man does.'

'In my mind,' he went on, 'I felt justified. Divorce was unthinkable—there were the twins, after all, and that other father. No one would be harmed, for the simple reason that no one would know. And no one did know. At any rate, Violetta and I were blessed with a son, and I had a good job and a good life. Tony was the son any man would be proud of. I forgot that other child in England. This one was mine. I was well pleased.'

Tony drew closer to his father. 'What happened to Violetta?'

'She died of the flu.' Charles stretched out a hand to his son's shoulder. 'Do you remember her at all?'

Tony frowned. 'There was a lady who danced and sang . . .'

'That was Violetta,' Charles agreed. 'Her family wanted to keep you, but I wasn't going to give up this child. I kept you. It wasn't easy, but it was my choice.'

'You really wanted me?' Theresa had to strain to hear that whisper, but Charles heard it too.

'I always wanted you. Never doubt that.'

Olga blew her nose, and went to get him some lemonade.

'But you left me in Creswal,' Tony protested. 'That was your choice, too.' There was only hurt in his voice; no anger now.

'That's where Marguerite comes into it,' declared Olga. 'I know it in my bones.'

Charles looked away from his wife's glance. 'Yes, this is where Marguerite comes into it. She was a woman in Creswal, the sister of a very important man there who owned the local timber mill and a great deal else.'

'A very beautiful woman,' Edouard pointed out, and Theresa felt like kicking him.

'Yes, a beautiful woman. We got on well together. I asked her to marry me, and she accepted.'

'And then?' Olga prompted. 'Remember I want all the story. Don't think to spare my feelings.' The words were harsh, but the tone of her voice was not.

Theresa leaned forward and her eyes met Edouard's. She couldn't read their expression.

'A few weeks before the wedding was due to take place, she came to me and asked if we might go away together for a few days to her brother's hunting lodge —just the two of us. It was, I suppose, an unusual request from a lady who was of a certain position in the town, but I thought perhaps she was unsure of me and unsure of her relationship with Tony, and needed to know that I would consider her feelings. So I agreed.' He paused, and sipped his lemonade.

Theresa stole another look at Edouard. He didn't look any different: his expression was still bland and unreadable.

'Besides, she was a beautiful woman,' Olga said, no rancour in her tone.

'Handsome is as handsome does,' was the sombre

comment. 'Naturally, she didn't wish anyone else to know about it, so we agreed to go each in our separate canoes to a meeting place. I had to bring only myself and some blankets. She promised to bring the food. We met as planned on a little beach, where we cached my canoe and went on together in hers. She said that she was tired of paddling, and most of the supplies were in her canoe anyway, which was a large one. So I moved myself and my belongings to her boat after we had hidden mine—I don't suppose anyone has found it yet.'

'Oh, yes, it's been found,' Edouard told him. 'And Marguerite said that the lad who found it could keep it.'

Charles nodded. 'That was fair, I suppose. She must have known by then that I wasn't coming back.'

'I saw it!' Tony broke in. 'Frank had painted it black, but I knew by the mark I'd put in it.'

'T for Tony—I remember.' He smiled at his son. 'To get back to the story. It was sensible for both of us to paddle, for the current was fairly strong and it was beginning to be dusk. We both put our backs into it, since the hunting cabin was on the other side of the river and still a few miles away. When we got to the beach beyond which it lay, we secured Marguerite's canoe and carried the supplies to the cabin.' He paused again.

'We couldn't take everything in one go, so we came back for the blankets and coal-oil for the lamps. That's when we had an almighty row, standing on that beach with no one around for miles, and a thin sickle of moon appearing in the sky as dark descended . . .'

He went on grimly, 'I had the blankets in my arms, when she told me she had seen that picture of Tessa in my album and knew who she was, and that I was still married to Myrtle—at least in name. She reviled me for lying to her in the first place, for I had denied that I had ever been married to anyone but Tony's mother when she had questioned me about my name when I arrived in Creswal. She had said she knew a family called Russell in England—the man had worked in South America somewhere, and had died tragically. I'd laughed, and said I wasn't dead, and she'd accepted that. Now she knew differently. I dropped the blankets when she told me.' He took another sip.

'She refused to marry me bigamously and demanded that I obtain a divorce from my English wife. She assured me that if it was handled quietly enough, there would be no need for any hint of scandal to reach Creswal. She gave no thought to the effect of scandal on the English family. It only meant postponing the wedding for a while.'

'Did you feel she was right?' asked Olga, as Anna leaned against her and closed her eyes.

Charles shrugged. 'I don't know.' He frowned. 'No, I don't think so. I considered myself free to marry, and I didn't want to hurt Myrtle or Tessa, who had been caught in a trap not of their own making. I couldn't see my way clear to do what she wanted. I told her so.' He stopped.

'And then?' Olga prompted.

'Then she began to cry and said I didn't love her. I walked towards her, meaning to take her in my arms, to make her see how it was, and she ran from me to the canoe. She pushed it away into the river and called back that I could think it over, that she was leaving. I was furious, hurt, angry—I don't know which. I called after her that I was marooned on the wrong side of the river and might never come back. She shouted that I was very clever at finding my way out of things, and had food for nearly a week if I was careful.'

Theresa sighed. She could see the furious man left on the shore, and Marguerite in a towering rage at last even with him—as she had told Tony.

Charles sat with his head in his hands.

Olga rocked her sleeping daughter. Her expression was withdrawn. Did it hurt her, Theresa wondered, to know that he had loved another woman? That made three before her.

Olga sighed, too. She rose with the sleeping child.

'She must have her nap in peace. I shall put her down.'
She went into the house.

Theresa looked at Edouard. 'Perhaps she meant to go
back after a few days.'

'Perhaps she did go back. Maybe that's what she
didn't tell you,' he suggested. 'Would you like a stronger
drink?' he asked Charles, and poured him a small
measure from a flask from his pocket.

He stirred and took it from him. 'Memories are very
painful. They were banished from my mind for some
time. Now they've come back to haunt me. I have to face
them now. I couldn't then. My mind ran away from
them.' He sighed.

Tony stirred by Theresa's side. 'I'm glad you didn't
marry Marguerite. I never liked her.'

His father smiled at him. 'You never told me that
before.'

'I was little. You wouldn't have listened.'

'I expect you're right, son. I was determined that I was
right. Now, I'm not so sure.'

Theresa stretched out her hand to her father. 'It's
different now. My mother is dead, and you're married to
Olga. When she comes back, you must go on with the
rest of the story.'

'I shall,' he promised.

CHAPTER TWENTY

IT WAS evening before Charles continued. Edouard had taken pictures of him with Theresa. Tony had made no more mention of going back to Creswal immediately, and had consented to be included in a group photo with his father, provided Theresa stood with them.

Theresa was impatient to hear the rest of the saga, but Olga made excuses to postpone it—Russ was exhausted; she was busy; Edouard and Theresa should see the orchards. It seemed to Theresa that Olga as well as Charles must have time to come to terms with his past life.

Olga insisted that there was no hurry; that of course Edouard must stay the night. It was unthinkable that he should go back so soon. And Theresa was welcome for as long as she cared to remain.

So Theresa and Edouard walked in the orchard together, and he pointed out the cherry trees, the plum trees and the apple trees in the August sunshine. He didn't let her forget that he had come for a story. He asked how she had felt: if there had been that spark of recognition between her and her father that she had been so sure of originally.

'Just at first there was,' she admitted. 'When I stood up in the buggy and saw him, and when he recognised me—I knew he was my father. That was all that mattered. I had searched for him and I had found him.'

Edouard leaned against an apple tree heavy with fruit, and Theresa sat down on a stump. 'And now?' he asked, his eyebrows lifted.

'I don't know—I'm not sure I like him.'

'Not quite so heroic as you thought?'

'Not that, exactly.' She tried to pin it down. 'I could

almost feel sorry for Marguerite wanting so desperately
to be respectable.'

'It's that tidy mind of yours.' Edouard examined an
apple that hung low down on the branch. 'This will be
good for eating in another month.' He smiled. 'Your
father is a man of action. You're rather like him, in fact.
Once you get hold of an idea, you don't let go, either. I
shouldn't waste too much sympathy on Marguerite, if I
were you. She was getting her own back for Charles's
deceit, and it backfired on her.'

'I wouldn't have expected you to say that.'

'You think you know me, do you?'

'Does anyone ever know anyone else?' she countered.
'I imagine Olga is asking herself how well she knows the
man she married—that is, if they are married legally.'

He nodded. 'You're learning. Legally or not, they're
promised to each other. That's all that matters.'

'I don't think Olga'll let him go.'

Edouard laughed. 'You're right. Tony will stay with
them, of course.'

'Will he? He doesn't seem very eager at the moment.'

'He'll stay.' Edouard came closer to where she sat.
'And you? Now that you've found your heart's desire,
do you intend to remain?'

'My heart's desire,' Theresa thought bitterly. 'My
father is not my heart's desire—that's you,' she wanted
to cry out. 'My heart has fastened on you. No other will
do for me.' She shook her head. 'There's Charlie—he's
my responsibility. My father has his own life.'

'You don't have to keep Charlie. You could find
someone else to take him on—perhaps to adopt
him . . .'

Again Theresa shook her head. 'Too many people
have let him down. I can't pass him on as no longer
wanted.'

'Are you thinking of Charlie—or yourself?' he asked
gently. 'He might be better with a family.'

Theresa looked up at him indignantly. His face was in
shadow, and she couldn't read his expression.

'Why do you always make me doubt myself?'

'I don't know.' Edouard drew back a little. 'Perhaps it just seems to me that you rush in with your emotions, and then when they've landed you somewhere, you begin to think about what you've done.'

She knew that he spoke the truth, or something very close to it. It wakened her from the sense of flatness, of anticlimax, that she had begun to experience since she had discovered her father. Her emotions spoke out. 'It's better than being like you, with all emotions battened down and reason in command!' She found she was breathing hard.

'*Touché!*' Edouard exclaimed, laughing. 'I shall not quarrel with you again.'

'Ever?'

'I can't promise that,' was his bland response. 'But try to understand your father. You really are very like him.'

He held out his hand to help her up, and she took it, thinking that perhaps he was right. At any rate, she felt a little comforted. She mustn't judge her father, but accept him as he was. They went back to the house.

Tony had spent the afternoon with Charles. What passed between them Theresa never knew, but it was plain that they had come to an understanding and Tony was addressing him as 'Dad'. She was pleased to see that. So was Olga, for she remarked on it.

After the evening meal and putting all the children to bed, the four adults gathered on the veranda to talk again. Olga said comfortably that she knew what had happened next, and she was sorry that Edouard and Theresa had had to wait to hear it.

Charles picked up the thread where he had left off. 'I had food and shelter; the hunting cabin to myself; time to think, as Marguerite had meant. In the eyes of the world, I was forced to acknowledge that she was right. I was married. Yet how could I bring disgrace and ostracism to that English family? It was an impossible situation. The only honourable solution, I supposed, would be to return to Creswal, but then Marguerite would suffer, and I would be forced to give up my job and move away. So I decided that the first step must be to leave the cabin and somehow get across the river. I would need to find some other hunters with a boat, or start building some sort of raft. I sat by the river and began to plan. When a lone canoeist appeared, I was overjoyed. I waved to him, and called out that I needed help, and he came in to land.'

'My father,' Olga supplied. 'He had gone to find some peace among the stillness of the lakes and trees. He had just had word that my brother had died in France—it was 1917, after all.'

'It was evening, and the canoeist came ashore and we ate and talked. For some reason, when I told him my name he misunderstood me, and thought I was Russell Charles. All my life people had been getting the order of my names mixed up, so I didn't correct him. In any case, he called me "Russ", and that suited me. We liked each other from the start, and he offered to take me with him further up river and we would ride the white water of the rapids together, since I knew the area and had no need to return immediately. It would do Marguerite good, I thought, to wonder where I was, if she did return.' He caught Edouard's eye. 'No, it wasn't a nice thought. I admit it. The idea of shooting the rapids appealed to me. It would release some of the anger that had built up in me. Olga's father seemed to share my need for head-strong action—I suppose he had his own ghosts to banish, so we agreed to go.' He paused for a moment.

'The following morning, though the weather was much wilder, we repacked his canoe to accommodate some of my possessions, and set off up river. It began to rain before we had gone much further, and that made it harder to see clearly, but we pressed on like men demented. We both shouted with exhilaration, everything else forgotten. There was only the rapids, the rain, and us in our frail canoe. I think we hit a rock, the canoe overturned, and we were in the rushing river.' He came to a halt with a graphic gesture of his hands.

'My father said you saved his life,' Olga was quick to put in.

'I suppose I might have,' Charles shrugged. 'I was a strong swimmer, and I knew the river fairly well. We managed finally to rescue the canoe as well as ourselves, but all our clobber was gone, and we were cold and wet. We found shelter of a sort among the trees by tearing branches down and pulling them together. We even managed to get a fire going eventually, and to catch a fish. It took the rest of the day. We spent a wretched night, and in the morning the wind was blowing even stronger. All around us trees were bending before it, and when the thunder and lightning started, we knew there'd be no moving till the storm was over. We tried to reinforce our shelter, but all we had was the knife I carried in my belt, and it was hard going. I remember hearing the crack of a falling tree, but I wasn't quick enough to escape it. I saw it fall, heading for me, yet I was powerless to move as I was so cold and wet. I believe from what Olga's father told me that I had only caught a glancing blow from it, but when I came to, I could remember nothing of who I was or how I'd come to where I was.' Charles sighed heavily.

'Perhaps I didn't want to remember; perhaps it was nature's way of releasing me from the worry of my situation. The only clear idea I had in my head was that I must get away, far away . . .'

Olga took up the story. 'That was what my father said. You kept repeating that you must get away. He didn't know what to do. He began to wonder if you were a deserter from the army camp. Even if you were, he decided to help you. You'd saved his life.'

'Did he think that?' Charles began to laugh. He turned to Edouard, 'You had better not put that in your paper!'

'I don't remember, even now, much of that trip up river to the railway stop, but we had the canoe, and I think we fished for food. I do recall climbing on the train—I had some money in my back trouser-pocket, and paid for both of us.'

'So my father brought you here, and you've been here ever since, learning to be a fruit farmer,' said Olga. 'I suppose I should be grateful to this Marguerite. Except for her and her strong values, we would never have met.' She turned to Edouard. 'Tell me. What happened to her. Has she married?'

'No,' he replied. 'I think she's carried the knowledge of her anger through the years. It's soured her life. Perhaps, now, she'll be able to forget her guilt and sense of loss.'

Olga frowned. 'I hope so. It was a cruel thing she did, but it shouldn't follow her for the rest of her life.'

'I hope you won't need to print in your paper that she left me at the hunting lodge, or even that she had asked me there,' Charles broke in. 'She would hate the gossip. I know I haven't the right to ask, but people will talk about it. After all, she couldn't have known how it would all turn out.'

'She should have thought.' Olga spoke firmly. 'She caused Russ and Tony a great deal of grief, and she did nothing for the boy. She put her own security before anyone else's. She showed no kindness.'

'She's suffered enough.' Theresa added her plea. 'She must have hated it when the papers hinted that she had somehow been responsible for Russ's death.' She had fallen into the way of calling her father 'Russ'—she couldn't manage Tony's easy 'Dad'.

'I think we can get around it,' Edouard conceded. 'It was understandable for her to be upset to find that the man she planned to marry wasn't free, and had lied to her.'

'Yes,' Olga agreed, speaking more softly now. 'She could have asked him how it was, and listened to his story, if she had truly loved him. She was the only one who knew about that little girl in England and that wife.'

'No,' said Russ. 'I had lied to her, and denied that story. She saw things in black and white.'

Olga's blue eyes were flashing.

Theresa could see that she was becoming angry. She thought it strange that Olga could have accepted the existence of other wives so calmly, and yet reject Marguerite because she considered that she hadn't loved Russ enough.

Olga spoke now only to her husband—the others might not have been there. 'She couldn't have loved you.'

'Not as you love me.' He smiled at her. 'Oh, I know how it is with you, and what you did when the minister here raised some objections to our marriage and told you you didn't know about my past.'

'You know?' queried Olga, blushing furiously. 'Who told you?'

'The minister.'

Theresa looked blankly from one to the other. 'Please, what did you do?'

Olga began to laugh. 'There's no reason why you shouldn't know. This is a day for confessions. I told the minister I would live with Russ anyway, wedding or not—so he gave way and married us, on the 10th of August 1918.'

Theresa drew in her breath sharply. 'My mother died at the end of July that year.' She took Olga's hand. 'You are truly married.'

'We've been married all along,' Olga told her comfortably. 'What is marriage, after all? Only a promise between two people—a trust between them.'

At these simple words, a lump rose in Theresa's throat. 'A trust between them', that's what it was. It was that lack of trust for which Edouard could not forgive her. She began to cry. Now she understood why Edouard had been so angry with her after the Charity Ball. She hadn't ever trusted him enough to tell him. There'd been many opportunities, but she'd ignored them, hugging her secret to her. She couldn't bear to look at him now.

Olga took her hand. 'There's nothing to cry about! This is the time to be happy. You've crossed an ocean, found a new place to live, befriended two boys—now is the time for happiness, for rejoicing. What's wrong?'

'Nothing,' sobbed Theresa.

It was Edouard who handed her a clean white handkerchief. 'Aren't you going to tell your father the good news?'

'What good news?' She raised swimming eyes to him.

'About the money. He'll want to know.'

'What money?' asked Russ. 'We have the farm, but we don't have much money.'

'We're comfortable,' declared Olga. 'That's enough.'

Theresa blew her nose. 'You're going to be a good deal more comfortable.' She turned to her father. 'Do you remember that you had some mining stock?' She gave Edouard back his handkerchief.

Russ frowned, 'Pretty worthless it was, too. I had high hope for it when I bought it. Don't tell me it's still in some bank?'

'In Ottawa. Mr Roscoe said it was worth in the region of two hundred thousand dollars.'

'Two hundred thousand dollars!' Russ repeated. 'You must be funning me.'

Olga looked at Theresa. 'It can't be true!'

'Oh, yes, it's true enough. We'll have to stop the hearing, which is due next week. Mr Roscoe thought, like everyone else, that you were dead.' She smiled at her father. 'He said Tony and I must be your heirs —unless anyone else came forward.'

Russ reached out and put his hand on Theresa's. 'You could have had all that money, and yet you came here today prepared to give it up—just to help me? I call that generosity!'

'No!' Theresa flushed with pleasure, and warmed to this man who was her father. He knew she wasn't after his money, and had never sought it. 'Tony needed a father. So did I, I think, or I wouldn't have come all this way to find one. I'm relieved that the money's yours. I never believed, in spite of Mr Roscoe's enthusiasm, that it was mine.'

Olga blew her nose. 'I'm ashamed of myself.'

'Whatever for?' asked Theresa.

'Because I thought so poorly of you from what I read in the paper, and I took so long to get in touch with you. You have a fine daughter, Russ. I shall be very pleased if ours turn out half as well.' Olga blew her nose again.

Theresa was quite overcome. Edouard thrust his handkerchief back at her, and she looked up at him.

'You never mentioned, the other night, just how much money was involved,' he said. 'I thought perhaps ten or twenty thousand. You are a strange girl!'

Theresa couldn't read his expression. 'You didn't ask how much it was.'

'Would you have told me, then?'

'Yes. In a way I wanted someone to ask me, but it seemed so ostentatious to come out with such a figure. Besides, it wasn't mine. I never felt it was, or even could be.'

Russ and Olga weren't listening to this by-play. They were sitting very close together.

Olga held out her hand to Theresa. 'I'm frightened of so much money. We'll have to think and plan what to do with it, but we're certain of one thing—both Russ and I. We want you to share in it. Will you live with us—and bring Charlie too? If it hadn't been for him, none of this would have happened, I suppose. We shall be a family.'

Theresa was very touched. She hugged Olga and her father, and both she and Olga cried. She was very tempted to accept. It would be splendid to have a family about her, people who cared for her—but it would mean leaving Creswal—and Edouard. Perhaps it would be just as well if he were going to Toronto.

'I don't know,' she replied. 'It is so very good of you.'

'A girl needs a family,' Olga pointed out. 'There are many nice young men in the neighbourhood. It will be my pleasure to introduce you to them—unless perhaps there is someone special . . .' She let the words hang in the air, as she looked at Edouard and then at her stepdaughter.

'There's no one.' Theresa shook her head.

Edouard said nothing.

'Well, you don't have to make up your mind tonight,' Russ said comfortably. 'Stay with us for a while, and see how you feel about us. But I don't want to lose my daughter just as I've found her. I want to get to know her.'

Theresa hugged her father.

'Why don't you start by calling me "Dad"?' he suggested.

'All right—Dad . . .' Theresa smiled. She liked the sound of it.

'We'll get out some wine,' said Olga, 'This is a celebration!'

Russ laughed. 'Indeed it is. It's home-made wine. Olga and I make it, but only enough for birthdays and Christmas and the like. You'll join us?' He included Edouard. 'We'll toast Theresa and her new life.'

'And yours too, Dad,' Theresa added. 'And I'll have as much wine as I like!' That was for Edouard's benefit.

Olga brought the wine and glasses and poured with a liberal hand. 'It's crab-apple wine from three years ago.'

'And very strong,' Russ declared.

'Just right for Theresa,' said Edouard, raising his glass to her.

For all her brave words about having as much wine as she wanted, Theresa treated it with respect, and sipped slowly. It was delicious as well as strong. She lost count of the number of toasts they drank, but she remembered that Edouard sat beside her and said she could stay as long as she liked. He would square it with Sal and Charlie.

On Monday morning, Theresa woke to streaming sunshine glowing through lacy curtains on to her feather bed.

Olga must have heard her stirring, for she appeared with a plate of ham and eggs, and fresh-baked bread, and a pot of tea.

'I've made a proper breakfast for you—the kind Russ likes. You shall stay in bed and eat it.'

She refused to listen to Theresa's protests that she was not an invalid to be waited on.

'You look pale and tired to me,' she was told very firmly. 'That nice Edouard Moreau said you needed someone to fuss over you and take care of you. We shall all do it for him.' She settled Theresa comfortably, with pillows behind her back. 'He wanted to stay himself, but of course he couldn't. He had to go to Toronto to get his copy to the paper. It will be in tonight's edition—your story. He's a good man, that Edouard.'

'He stayed last night, didn't he?' Theresa attacked her ham and eggs. 'Is he—Is he coming back tonight?'

'I think he told Russ that he was going on to Creswal then. Russ drove him very early this morning to town to catch the train.'

Theresa swallowed hard. That finished it, then. Edouard was back in Creswal, or would be soon. What had she expected? She finished her breakfast, and went to the kitchen to offer her help to Olga.

'No, I have a woman who works for me on a Monday, and we can easily manage between us. You sit on the veranda and rest. It's very warm today, and it will do you good.'

Thus dismissed, Theresa sat on the screened-in porch, and was joined by Anna and her dolls. They got along very well together.

'Tony's with my dad in the barn,' Anna said. 'Is he really and truly my brother, and going to stay with us?'

'Really and truly,' Theresa agreed. 'Will you be pleased to have him here?'

'Yes,' said her half-sister. 'I like him! Will you stay, too?'

'I don't know.' It was a question Theresa was still asking herself. She had a job in Creswal, and a place to live, and Charlie. Her common sense told her that Charlie would be better off with a family, but he would be well treated here, and so would she. She sighed, and went to stand at the veranda doorway, looking down the drive.

A small truck was approaching slowly up it.

'Who's that?' she asked Anna.

'I don't know.' The child jumped up to see. 'I'll ask Mama.'

The van pulled to a stop before the steps, and a man in cap and overalls emerged holding a sheaf of flowers, just as Olga came to the door.

'Flowers!' Olga exclaimed, wiping her hands on her pinafore. 'Who would send flowers to us? There must be some mistake.'

'Mrs Charles?' the delivery man asked. She nodded, and he held out the flowers to her. 'Wait a minute, there's another one.' He went back to the van and came back with an even bigger bunch.

Olga was still exclaiming. 'How kind—they're from Mr Moreau! Oh, he needn't have—but how nice!'

'Miss Theresa Russell live here?' the man enquired.

Olga signed for the flowers, and handed them to Theresa. She took them, disbelieving, as the man drove off. 'They can't be for me!'

'Of course they are!' Olga assured her. 'You heard the man say so. Look, there's a little card.'

Theresa tore open the attached envelope with trembling fingers, hardly able to take her eyes from the beauty of the flowers. A dozen pink roses with longer stems than she had ever seen, and a dozen white ones.

'Oh, let me see,' begged Anna, climbing onto the arm of a chair to get closer. Her mother grabbed her and held her up.

'They're from Edouard,' breathed Theresa. 'And look, the card says, "To an English rose".' She held it out to Olga.

'How nice of him. He must think a lot of you! Roses aren't cheap—and to have them delivered out here! He's not a married man, is he, Tessa? He said he wasn't.'

'No, he's not married.'

'He's a good friend?' The catechism went on.

'Yes, a good friend.'

'A special friend?' Olga didn't wait for an answer. 'I told Russ that he liked you.'

Theresa was still holding the roses in her arms, and the scent of them filled her nostrils. What a marvellous present. How splendid of Edouard to think of them. And how kind to send Olga flowers as well. Hers were carnations.

'I'll need a vase,' she said.

'What am I thinking of?' Olga exclaimed. 'Of course you will. So shall I. I haven't seen flowers like this since my wedding! What a lucky girl you are. Roses and ferns and baby's breath.' She fingered the lacy-white tiny blooms that accompanied the roses: forgetting her own bouquet in her pleasure in Theresa's.

'You do like him, don't you?'

'Yes.' Theresa couldn't deny it.

'I'll fetch a vase, and you shall arrange the roses to suit yourself. I shall go and show mine to Russ.'

She brought a large white container, and Theresa was still trying to display her roses to the best advantage when her father and Tony arrived back for lunch.

'I like this Edouard,' said her father, and kissed her. 'Only, perhaps, I shall not have my Tessa for very long.'

She blushed. With such a present, she could hope a little.

'Oh, I don't know,' said Tony. 'Mr Roscoe sent her chocolates and me a Meccano set. Do chocolates mean more than roses?'

They all laughed at that, and Olga wanted to know more about Mr Roscoe. She said that Russ must go and see him soon.

To Theresa, it was astonishing how they had all slipped into the ways of family. It was almost as though they had known each other for a long time. She ruffled Tony's hair, and Anna took his hand and demanded that he play with her. Olga hugged her, and said that the meal was ready. Afterwards, she fed the baby, and Theresa bathed little Tilda. It was a very pleasant day, and they were all happy and relaxed with each other. They waited up for the evening Toronto paper, and were very pleased with what Edouard had written. Tony cut out his picture.

On Tuesday, Theresa's father took her to Niagara Falls, just the two of them. Olga had declared that it would do them both good, and cheerfully waved them goodbye. She had packed them a lunch to eat by the Falls.

It wasn't a very long journey by train, but to Theresa it was a delight, a chance to get to know this father of hers whom she had searched for and found. He proved a pleasant companion and an interesting one. He told her about the area and about the farm, and confided that with the unexpected nest-egg he wanted to start producing wine and jam. 'Tomorrow I shall go to the bank,' he assured her. 'There is no hurry, after all this time. The soil here is marvellous, and the climate is good—warmer than anywhere else in Canada. I'm sure we can make good wines from the grapes we grow.'

'Do you never think to go back to engineering?' she asked him shyly.

'No, I've done with wandering and with moving. I have all my family about me now. That's the way I want it to stay.' He laughed at himself. 'Is this Edouard Moreau serious about you, then? See, already, the heavy-handed papa! You could meet someone here,' he suggested, and looked at her expectantly. Whatever he saw in her face made him add, 'Perhaps not—the heart makes its own choices. But I want you to know that you will always be welcome with us.' He clasped her hand. 'I'll say no more.'

He was as good as his word. He took her by the hand when they left the train, and brought her to the Falls, and listened to her expressions of astonishment at the grandeur of the sight. They ate their lunch—and a delicious one it was—on the *Maid of the Mist*, the boat that carried them under the Falls and their spray. He entertained her with stories of South America, and asked her about Creswal and her life there. He told her he would always be in her debt for restoring Tony to him, and that the lad would stay with him.

'It was a generous thing you did to take him on, and I can see that he loves you. And so do I.'

Theresa's eyes filled with tears at this tribute.

'Nay, lass, there's nought to grieve o'er in that!' He lapsed into broad Yorkshire, and made her giggle.

It was a happy day, a day Theresa would always remember, so close did she feel to this man she had never known about all through her childhood.

When they returned, Olga was delighted with them. 'Yes, I see you understand each other. But, Tessa, something more has come for you. Tony, will you show her?'

Smiling broadly, Tony brought her a parcel—the largest box of chocolates she had ever seen.

'To sweet Theresa,' said the card. 'From Edouard.'

She didn't know what to say, but no one else had lost the power of speech.

'It's a bigger box than Mr Roscoe gave you,' declared Tony.

'He's serious,' said her father, and sighed.

'He's wooing you,' Olga breathed. 'Did you have a quarrel?'

Theresa opened the box and they all had chocolates. Anna wanted to give Tilda one, but Olga said that perhaps better not. There was no sense in waking her.

In the morning, Tony and Anna set up vigil on the veranda. Olga wanted to know what they were doing there, watching the drive.

'We're waiting.'

'Waiting? What for?'

'The next present.'

'There won't be any more presents,' Theresa declared. But she was wrong. The pearls arrived just before noon. As she opened the box, they all stood round.

'Pretty beads,' said Anna. 'Lucky Tessa!'

'I liked the chocolates better,' declared Tony, and lost all interest.

'How romantic,' sighed Olga, 'to be showered with presents.'

'I can't keep them! But they're beautiful.' Theresa tried them on, and loved the feel of them against her skin.

'Why not?' asked Olga. 'Of course you can! He means to have you, Tessa.'

'Does he?'

'Yes. He loves you. He's telling you so.'

'He hasn't said the words.'

'He will.'

'Do you think so? When?'

Olga began to laugh. 'That's up to you.'

'Up to me? What do you mean?'

'He's there. You're here.'

'You mean—go to him? Oh, I couldn't.' She drew back at the very thought. What if he didn't love her, or want to marry her? He might just be apologising for the cruel things he'd said to her.

Olga said no more.

Theresa began to turn over the idea in her mind. If she should go . . . mind, only if she should . . . she could be there by Thursday morning. The story—her story and Russ's—would be in the *Clarion*. It would seem natural for her to be in Creswal and to share the triumph with Edouard. The presents he had sent her surely meant that they were friends again. Friendship was a fine thing, and it was better to have it than to have nothing. This wasn't the time to hold aloof. She began to pack.

Olga helped her, smiling. 'He's a good man, just right for you. You'll be happy with him.' She wiped away a tear. 'I wish you weren't going so far away.'

Theresa hugged her. 'I may be back sooner than you think.'

Olga shook her head and blew her nose. She put her hand to her chest. 'No, I feel it here. You'll patch up your differences, whatever they were. Don't be too proud to admit that you might have been wrong. Make him see he truly matters to you. He's a man who needs to be assured of that.' She hugged Theresa again. 'We'll miss you here.'

Theresa didn't think for a moment that it would be as easy as her stepmother imagined, but she set out with some hope, having kissed them all goodbye.

When it came to Tony's turn, he hung on to her. 'I'll miss you, Theresa, but I'm staying with my dad. You see how it is—he wants me.'

'He's wanted you all along!' She hugged him. 'He just didn't know it.'

'It's the same with you and Edouard, isn't it?' he asked. 'He wants you, now.'

'I hope so,' she murmured. 'Oh, I hope so,' but she said it under her breath, just to Tony.

He crossed his fingers solemnly, then hid them behind his back.

CHAPTER TWENTY-ONE

WHEN THERESA arrived back in Creswal, it was mid-morning. The sun was shining, but it was cooler than the day before. She had only a very small case with her, so she carried it from the station. The *Clarion* office wasn't very far.

'What am I going to say to Edouard,' she asked herself, as she strolled through the residential streets and then into Main Street. She had rehearsed a dozen openings. She could thank him for the presents. He would notice that one of the roses was tucked into the band of her hat, and another peeped through the buttonhole of her black and white costume. The pearls were clasped round her neck.

She bought a paper from a little shop, and there she was, and Tony and her father, looking up at her from the front page. It was strange to read about herself. She didn't suppose she'd ever get used to it, but she wouldn't be written about any more. That was the perfect opening! She would congratulate him on his article, and tell him how much pleasure it had given her family, and how grateful they all were to him.

She framed her opening words to herself as she climbed to the editorial office. This was where it had all begun. These were the steps she had mounted when her courage had been ebbing on that first day. It was ebbing now, too. Why had she let herself be convinced that Edouard wanted her? Only because she wanted to believe it.

She stood on the top step, facing the closed frosted door before her. Her breathing was shallow, and her heart beat fast. What of Charlie? she suddenly asked herself? Was she going to forget him, abandon him for her own selfish reasons?

No, the whole idea of coming back had been a mistake; she should have waited. She would have been safe with her family. For several minutes she hesitated, undecided, wavering. She almost turned to go down again. The sharp thought came to her that her father had run away—and kept on running.

She knocked gently on the door and opened it.

At the editorial desk sat a strange young man. She was so astonished that she was speechless. Was she in the wrong place? She looked about the large room. The black telephone still hung upon the wall, just out of reach of the person at the desk. The large black kewpie doll that she had won at the fair still stood in its short grass skirt and shiny beads, smirking down from her high shelf at all who entered. But now a black and white tie encircled her neck. It was very much like the scarf Theresa had worn on her first visit. She wasn't wearing it today. She looked towards the back desk. No Rosie.

The strange young man adjusted the glasses on the bridge of his nose, and looked up at her expectantly. 'Was there someone you wanted to see?'

'Yes, the editor,' Theresa gulped. 'Edouard Moreau. Where is he?'

'I'm the new editor. William Foxton. Is there something I can do for you?'

Theresa shook her head. She couldn't understand what had happened. She gazed at William Foxton, uncomprehending. She was tired from the long journey and was somehow imagining all this. She put a hand to her face.

'Come in and sit down. Tell me about it. Why, you're Theresa Russell, aren't you?' he went on, as she sank into the chair before his desk. 'The girl on today's front page—it's a heart-warming story. But what are you doing here? You're supposed to be with your family in Niagara-on-the-Lake!' He sounded almost accusing.

Theresa looked at him fully. Brown haired, brown suited, brown eyed, in his late twenties—there was nothing to hold the eye in his appearance except the dark eyebrows which looked as though they had been pinned on in a hurry over the curved frame of his dark-rimmed spectacles.

'I came back,' she said curtly, and then felt she had to add something. 'There's Charlie, you see . . .'

'Your father, you mean. Has something happened?' He leaned forward, his eyebrows shooting up.

Theresa shook her head. Why didn't this bad dream go away?

'There's nothing wrong with my father. Please, where are Rosie and Edouard?'

'Rosie is down at O'Reilly's Realty, minding the shop.' The young man smiled. 'We aren't busy, fortunately, on a Thursday. Mr Moreau is at home—in bed, I imagine. He was up till four getting out today's paper. He might be in later.'

'Why is Rosie at Sal's office? Is Sal ill?' Theresa at last realised that she was awake, not half asleep.

'She's gone on a trip, I believe.'

'What sort of trip?'

'To Ottawa, I think they said. Rosie seemed surprised.'

Theresa rose to her feet. 'Thank you. I'll go and see her.'

'You could phone her,' suggested William Foxton.

'No, I'll go and see her. I work for Sal. I should be there if Sal's away.' She was impatient to go. 'Thank you for your help,' she called back to him over her shoulder as she went to the door.

More than a little alarmed, she ran down the stairs, her case still clutched in her hand. She must go and free Rosie, and find out what was going on. She had not realised that she'd be putting other people out to such an extent by being away. She hurried up the street to O'Reilly's Realty, thoughts of Edouard submerged for the moment.

Rosie was sitting behind the counter doing a cross-word puzzle. She rose to her feet and flipped the counter up, and hugged Theresa. 'You're back! How good to see you! I'm so pleased it's turned out grand for you. But why have you come back so soon? Eddie said you'd be away all week.'

Theresa took off her hat and laid it on the counter. She had dropped her suitcase with the enthusiasm of Rosie's greeting. 'What's happened to Sal?'

'Sit down,' suggested Rosie, going back through the open flap and waving Theresa to a chair. 'I'll tell you all about it. You aren't the only one whose life is changing.' She waved an elegant hand again before Theresa's face.

Theresa focused on that left hand this time. There was a diamond ring on its third finger. 'You're engaged! It's Simon, isn't it?' She got up to hug the other girl.

'I though you'd never notice,' Rosie laughed. 'We got engaged on Saturday, and we're going to get married in two months' time and live in Toronto. Simon's father wants him to start a box factory there. Oh, Theresa, I'm so happy. Isn't it wonderful that we can be happy together? You've found your family, and Simon and I have found each other!' She beamed at her.

Theresa was truly delighted for her friend. She listened quietly to all her plans for a church wedding and a trousseau, and a recital of the gifts she had already received. Only then did she raise the subject of Sal again.

'Why has Sal gone to Ottawa?'

'You'll never guess! She's going to adopt a little girl, and she's gone to pick her out—from the same orphanage where you found Tony and Charlie. It seems that she spoke to someone at Charlie's hearing the other week, and he's helping her to do it quickly.'

Theresa began to smile. 'She said she would. I'm very glad for her.'

'You may not be so glad about the next part,' Rosie hesitated.

'Oh, why not?' She couldn't imagine what was coming next. She steeled herself to hear something she wouldn't want to hear—something about Edouard.

'Eddie and Big Bob Falconer had a row yesterday. I wasn't supposed to hear it.'

'What—What was it about?' Theresa's lips were trembling.

'About your Charlie. Big Bob wanted him, and Eddie told him he'd never have him. I don't know why, because they shut up when they found that I was there, and left the office together. I heard them still arguing when they went down the stairs, and Big Bob said he meant to have a son one way or another. What do you suppose he meant by that? And why should Eddie say he'd never have Charlie? Is your father going to have him?'

'He's offered to,' said Theresa slowly.

'Well, if he really wants him'—Rosie bit the end of the pencil she picked up—'he had better move fast, or maybe you should, because I hear Big Bob has gone to Ottawa as well.'

'To the orphanage, you mean?' Theresa couldn't believe this was happening. Why had Edouard antagonised Bob Falconer to such an extent? There he was, interfering in her affairs again! Her fury began to mount, and she forgot in her anger that she and Edouard were friends, that she had come to seek him out because she thought he just might love her. 'He can't do that!' she went on. 'They said I could have Charlie.'

'For a holiday,' Rosie amended gently.

'An extended holiday!' Theresa bit her lip. 'I thought that meant that I'd really keep him.'

Rosie put her hand on Theresa's. 'Maybe it's for the best. Big Bob could to a lot for Charlie. He'd have a secure future—probably inherit the mill . . .'

'He'd spoil him! Besides, what about Sidney and Marguerite? They'll be coming back now the gossip's all blown over, and how do you suppose they'll feel about an interloper like Charlie? They'd soon have him out. No, it's unthinkable.'

'I hadn't thought of that,' Rosie reflected. 'I rather felt that Big Bob meant to include you in his plans. Perhaps he still does. Simon thinks it would be a good match for you . . .' She let the words trail away. 'You don't?'

Theresa shook her head.

Rosie shrugged, and then smiled. 'A woman always has the right to say No.'

'He hasn't asked me. Not in so many words, but the answer would be No.' She was certain of that.

'So,' said Rosie. 'What now?'

'Sal had Charlie when I left.' Theresa was beginning to think again after the shocks of the morning. 'Where is he now?'

'At Eddie's. He picked him up from Sal's on Tuesday. He's been there ever since.'

'At Edouard's?' That made Theresa pause. 'What's happening with Edouard, anyway? Why is this William Foxton the editor?'

'Oh, you've met him?' Rosie laughed. 'He's the new editor—I expect he told you. He's very pleased about it. Eddie is going to be editor of that Toronto paper he bought, once William is trained in. Everything's changing, you see.'

'Yes, I see.' Theresa's heart sank—and her spirits. She had been away less than a week, and everything was certainly changing. It was all very difficult. If she stayed in Creswal, she'd be alone. Perhaps she mightn't even have Charlie.

She got up. It was time to go and find Edouard and have it out with him. She smiled grimly to herself. Charlie had come to her. She had promised to come back to him.

'I don't even know where Edouard lives,' Theresa said aloud. 'I've never been to his house. Is it far?'

'Not very,' Rosie smiled. 'I'll give you directions.'

'But I should stay here,' Theresa wavered. 'You're doing my job for me. He might come and see me here later.'

'Nonsense!' Rosie poured scorn on that idea. Eddie'd kill me if I let you take over when you've travelled all night and just got back. You can leave your case here. I'll find someone to take it to your place. There's no point in carrying it to Eddie's. You might frighten him into thinking you'd come to stay. Besides, think of what the neighbours would say! I'll draw you a map.'

That made Theresa laugh, because it reminded her of the first time Rosie had drawn her a map and Edouard had made a joke of it. For her, it always came back to him.

She followed Rosie's directions, and found the house quite easily. It was at the bottom of a tree-lined street, a small, white-painted clapboard house of two storeys, and a medium-sized garden. There were big daisies in the border, and marigolds and pansies all in bloom. It looked comfortable, if not particularly imposing. She went up the path and knocked at the door, still undecided about what to say.

No one answered. She didn't know what to do. Perhaps Edouard had a housekeeper who was busy somewhere at the back of the house. Perhaps he was still upstairs, sleeping. Theresa went down the front steps, round the side of the house, following the path.

She heard their voices before she saw them. Both Edouard and Charlie were there. But what in heaven's name were they doing?

Overcome by shyness, she stopped. Both of them were bent over a dog—a dog which Charlie was holding and Edouard was painting. He was daubing a white dog pink. Theresa couldn't believe her eyes.

'Stop it!' she cried, upset and alarmed both.

Charlie looked up and saw her, his face breaking into a delighted grin. 'Theresa,' he called out, and let go of the dog. He ran towards her.

Edouard reached out and grabbed him before she could open her arms to the boy.

The dog with a fearful howl ran under the veranda and cowered there. Yes, it really was a pink streak of fear.

'Your timing is perfect,' exclaimed Edouard. 'This young man of yours has been in the wars.'

Theresa could understand none of this. She looked from Charlie, held prisoner, to Edouard. She was tired.

She was hot—and she was angry. She was also conscious suddenly of a most objectionable smell.

'What is it?' she asked faintly.

'Skunk,' they answered in unison, both serious.

'Skunk?' Theresa echoed. 'Here, in your back yard?'

'Ah, no,' said Edouard. 'That's where Charlie comes into it. In the few days he's been here, he's made friends with all the dogs in the neighbourhood, and some of the ones from the other end of town, I'd swear. This one hiding from us now is a particular favourite. He belongs to the old lady next door and looks to Charlie as his saviour—or did until just now. It might just be the end of a beautiful friendship.'

'But you were painting him,' Theresa objected. She noticed for the first time that Edouard, who was usually dressed in a suit and a shirt with a starched collar, was wearing what could only be described as the most disreputable pair of old trousers and something that looked remarkably like an old pyjama-top.

'Anointing him,' he corrected, releasing Charlie with strict instructions not to touch Theresa. She could see that Charlie's things were almost the same colour as the dog. 'Anointing him with the juice of the tomato.' Edouard finished. 'A tried and tested remedy to kill the smell.'

'Just the same, I'm glad you're here,' said Charlie, standing on one foot. 'I didn't know that old lady's dog was silly enough to chase a skunk when we went in the woods over there.'

'He'll know better next time. So, I hope, will you! Now, off to the pump and we'll sluice you down.' Edouard put his hand on Charlie's shoulder. 'You'll have to excuse us.'

'Do I have to?' asked a reluctant boy. 'Won't tomato juice do just as well for me?'

'We might put some on your hair,' Edouard suggested. 'That's the only bit of fur on you.'

They both walked away from Theresa and she sank down on the back steps watching them.

Charlie was small, so he fitted pretty well under the mouth of the pump and didn't seem to mind at all, after the first shock of the cold water, the dousing he was getting.

'Now it's your turn,' Theresa heard him say to Edouard, as he emerged dripping.

Edouard took his hand from the handle and noticed that Theresa was watching. 'Go sit on the front veranda,' he called out to her, 'because there are two fellows here who are going to shed all their clothes and leave them out here. We may even burn them later.'

She rose to her feet. Charlie was already taking off his shirt. She didn't mind him being naked, but Edouard was another matter. Going round to the front again, she found herself a comfortable chair.

The little pink dog, after a few minutes, crept round the side of the house and sat under the steps. Waiting for Charlie, perhaps, Theresa mused. There was one new aspect about the whole episode: she had never seen Edouard and Charlie in such accord. She knew Charlie had been in some awe of him, but it had always seemed to her that Edouard had felt some antipathy towards the lad. It made her think.

Charlie came down first, in a pair of cotton trousers Theresa hadn't seen before, and his best shirt, his hair slicked to his head. A faint odour of skunk still clung to him. He hugged her and wanted to know all about her father and Tony.

'It's swell staying with Eddie,' he told her. 'He doesn't mean half he says, does he? He knows everything —where the best swimming-places are, and the trees to climb, and how to take the smell of skunk away. I thought he might be really mad when I got him up this morning, but he only grumbled a bit and made me squash the tomatoes and then hold Towser. He's going to tell Mrs Jenkins what happened before I bring the dog back. Towser looks really ashamed of himself. I don't think he wants to go home.'

Theresa had never heard Charlie volunteer so much

information. She had been afraid that his terrible experiences might make him draw into himself when she wasn't there. Perhaps she thought herself more important in his life than she really was. Edouard had said that she took too much on herself. She sighed.

'I'm going to the Appledores' this afternoon. Eddie said it was all right, even if it was your first afternoon home. It's Timmy's last day, and they're taking us out to see the dam and then for a bonfire on the beach after.'

'That'll be nice for you.' Theresa resented just a little Edouard's assumption of authority and the lad's ready acceptance of it.

'He's got a surprise for you,' Charlie went on. 'He said I mustn't tell you. We picked it out together.'

'Oh! Then I'll wait.'

'Eddie says girls like presents, and fellows get their pleasure from giving them. Do you like presents, Theresa?'

'Yes!'

'Eddie's usually right about things.' Charlie said it with some satisfaction. 'What sorts of presents? I've never seen you wearing those pearls before, or flowers —did your father give you those? You don't mind me asking, do you?'

'No,' she replied, one hand on her pearls, 'I don't mind. Not my father. Eddie gave me these; he sent them.'

Charlie whistled. 'Do you think he likes you—or does he just like giving presents? He gave me these trousers.'

Theresa was saved from commenting by the arrival of Edouard, looking considerably smarter than before. He was wearing a short-sleeved blue shirt, open at the neck, and checked trousers in a light material. He couldn't mean to go to the *Clarion* in them, she decided.

He brought her a cup of tea and a sandwich. 'It's my housekeeper's day off,' he explained. 'But it will do to be going on with while Charlie and I see to a few things.'

In no time at all, Towser had been despatched to his owner and Charlie to his outing. Theresa had eaten, and changed to a summer dress and her sandals which had appeared as if by magic, and then was whisked away in Edouard's car.

'Where are we going?' she asked, not really caring, because she was with Edouard, and he was smiling.

'To a place where we can be alone with no interruptions,' he said as they bowled along on the road which she knew led to the dam.

But they did not go as far as that. He stopped the car off the road at the place where he had taken her to see the river that first day she had come with him.

He picked up bundles and a basket from the back, and waved away Theresa's offer to help.

'Your bathing-costume is here too,' he announced. 'The powers of the telephone are great!'

Smiling, she followed him down the path to the beach. It was just as she had remembered it from that first time, the sun shining on the water, the trees nodding in the wind, and peace everywhere.

Edouard had dumped his burden on the fine sand. Now, as she turned to him, he opened his arms and she went into them . . .

This was what Theresa had been waiting for, yearning for with all her being. She clung to him, heart beating in delight, straining to be close to him. His kiss, his embrace were necessities to her.

'I love you,' he whispered against her ear. *'Je t'aime, chère Thérèse.* I don't know why it's taken me so long to admit it.'

'I love you, too,' she breathed.

'I know. I tried to stop you in the beginning, but I could see you'd set your heart on me—just as you did with Tony and Charlie. I should have known it was no good resisting!'

'Beast!' she exclaimed, but she kissed him as she said it.

This hot, heady excitement between them was all that she wanted, but she found that she had to breathe.

When she did, Edouard said softly, 'Remember when

I told you you must grow into a woman?' He traced a gentle finger down the line from her chin to her bosom. 'I didn't notice it happening, but I think you have.' His kisses followed the line his finger had traced a moment before.

Theresa felt fire stirring in her, that flame of longing which only he could raise. Her arms closed about him.

'Every time I saw you, you upset my orderly existence and made me think about my life and myself. How could I believe you were real, meeting everything head on, taking on a brother and then another boy? I don't think I ever really believed it was for the money—that was just hurt pride that you hadn't confided in me.'

Putting her fingers to his lips, she silenced him. 'I promise there'll be no more secrets between us.'

'My darling!' Edouard murmured, putting his arm round her waist and freeing himself a little. 'When we are married . . .'

'It's the first I've heard of marriage,' she teased him.

'Of course we're going to be married!' Edouard put his hand on the pearls which circled Theresa's throat. 'Why else are you wearing these? Why else have you come for me?'

She blushed a rosy pink, but couldn't contradict him.

'Did you think I wouldn't come for you?' he asked very gently. 'You'll have missed today's gift.'

'Today's gift?'

'A white velvet shawl.'

'Oh, Edouard,' Theresa breathed.

'And tomorrow's,' he continued. 'Framed pictures of you and your family. And the day after that I would have arrived to ask you to marry me.'

'Oh, Edouard,' she repeated.

He smiled at her, and shrugged. 'The Hippolytes of this world enjoy an extravagant gesture or two. Since I've been denied that satisfaction, I have something else.'

'Yes?'

Edouard took a small box from his pocket and gave it to her. 'Go ahead, open it. See if you like it.'

Theresa took a trembling breath and did as he instructed. Inside the box was a ring—an engagement ring—three diamonds set with pearls between, in gold. It was beautiful.

He slipped it on her finger, and they kissed again.

When he released her, Theresa was smiling. 'Is this the present Charlie chose with you? He wouldn't tell me what it was.'

'Ah yes, Charlie. The pearls were his idea—I would have settled for diamonds. Some folks say pearls are for tears . . .'

A kind of sad fear stirred in her. She had known all along they would come to Charlie. She sighed. The superstition meant nothing to her—she had never heard it before. It was the thought of Charlie.

Edouard spread the blanket on the sand, and she sank on to it, drawing him down.

'Tell me,' he said, not touching her but with his eyes holding hers. 'If it came to a straight choice between us, how would you choose—Edouard or Charlie?'

'Does it have to be a choice?'

'If it were,' he probed, not helping her at all, 'how would you choose?'

'Don't make me,' pleaded Theresa, eyes swimming.

Edouard waited.

'I don't think . . .' Theresa got the words out at last in a very low voice, and feeling she would never have such a hard decision to make, 'that I could ever give you up. You are the beat of my heart, the meaning of my life . . . I know my father will have Charlie as well as Tony, and perhaps I flatter myself in thinking I am the one he needs most . . .'

She was allowed to go no further. Edouard caught her hands in his. 'I'm deeply moved. I hoped you'd answer this way. There is another solution . . .'

'Big Bob, you mean?' She shook her head. 'He'd never get back with Sal then; besides, Rosie said . . .'

'You must get over this habit of listening to gossip,' he admonished with a grin. 'Big Bob has followed Sal to Ottawa, and the orphanage, and it's my guess they'll make up their differences and come back with a girl for her and a boy for him. And if they have any sense at all, they'll get married there and present his sister and daughter with accomplished facts.'

Theresa laughed at that. She couldn't help it. What he said was so right. 'And Charlie?' She bit her lip.

'Why, we shall have Charlie, of course. I shall just have to buy a big house when we move to Toronto, because I am marrying the sort of girl who takes in waifs and strays, and will no doubt continue to do so . . .'

Theresa's smile lit up her face. 'You're a kinder man than you pretend to be.' She kissed him tenderly. 'I thought, watching you this morning, that you had begun to like him.'

'I've liked him well enough all along,' he protested, 'I fought to free him from slavery.'

'I know you did, and that was even more commendable'—Theresa held his hand—'because you weren't sure about your feelings about him.'

Edouard smiled ruefully. 'No secrets between us, indeed! All right, I took against him—he looked too much like my brother-in-law for comfort—I know it wasn't the lad's fault—people don't feel with their minds. But now that Charlie's been around me this week, I've got used to him. He doesn't have that streak of cruelty that Tom McGregor always had—he's just a boy who needs a home and most of all a mother. He remembers his, you know.'

'Does he?' Theresa was astonished. 'He's never said anything to me about her. But then, you've charmed him. When he was talking to me before, every sentence began with "Eddie says" and "Eddie does".'

He laughed aloud. 'Jealous?'

Theresa laughed too. 'Piqued, I guess! No, I'm pleased he likes you.'

Edouard rose to his feet and pulled Theresa up.

'That's enough of Charlie. We're here to enjoy ourselves. Into your bathing costume, and we shall swim the river.' He tossed her her swimming-costume.

They swam together in the cool water, playing tig like children, lying kissing in the shallows, the sun warm above them. The afternoon was theirs. The River of Paradise welcomed them.

Afterwards, they collected branches and lit a fire and warmed themselves by it, Theresa kneeling to dry her hair.

Edouard had come prepared with steaks and wine, and potatoes for baking, and popcorn.

'In every Canadian there is a pioneer—a man who wants an open fire, the dark skies above him, the trees standing sentinel behind him.' Edouard was busy with the meal. 'Tell me, are you hungry?'

'Starving.' By the time the food was ready, Theresa found this was the absolute truth. She was famished, and it was delicious.

They sat talking, arms entwined about each other, in no hurry to leave as the first faint stars of evening peeped through the grey canopy of the sky, and the promise of a full red August moon began to weave her magic spell overhead so that the harsh lines of trees and hills merged darkly with the water. It was very quiet, with only the crackling of the fire and the gentle lapping of the river against the narrow beach. An owl hooted and flew over them, searching for some small moving creature against its hunger.

Theresa was conscious of a little breeze soughing in the top branches of the pines and spruce and maples, and now and then the sharp crack of a twig as some forest inhabitant scampered over it. The noises of the nightly hunt held no terror for her. Edouard was here.

Together they watched the moon turn from watery pink to shining red, lighting a path along the river, reflecting itself back along the sand, so that she felt they were bathed in glowing light, the only man and woman in the world, a world as ancient as time, as new as their declaration of love.

Theresa was held fast in Edouard's love, in Edouard's arms, a willing captive, wanting only the delight and ecstacy of shared pleasure—of belonging, of giving and receiving. This was bliss. Beyond Paradise, he had called this place. He had named it well.

'I've bought this land,' Edouard said. 'It's ours. We'll build on it and return in the summers. In a way both our roots are here.' He changed the subject abruptly. 'Will you like living in Toronto?'

'I'll like living wherever you live.' She threw some more wood on the fire. 'Why did you decide to move?'

'I've enjoyed being here, but it's time to move, I suppose. With a wife and family, I need to make my mark, to live again in a busy world.' He shrugged. 'With you beside me, how can I fail?'

Theresa put her arms round him. It was time to live, and love, to reach out to the future. She had found herself, her mate, her place in this new land.

The River of Paradise glinted in the moonlight. The fire burned with a red glow, a flame leaping up along the new wood. Theresa gave herself up to complete enjoyment as her lips opened under Edouard's.

This was Beyond Paradise, the place they would return to again and again to refresh themselves against the demands of the world. It was a state of mind, a sharing and a trust they would find here in the future as they found it now in the present.

That was the promise of Paradise . . .

And Beyond Paradise . . . Ah, that was yet to come.

The kiss of the sun for pardon,
The song of the bird for mirth,
one is nearer to god in a
                              garden,
than anywhere else on earth.